DEBORAH, JUDGE, PROPHETESS *and* SEER

Also by Carole M. Lunde

Stories From Martha's House
The Biblical Gathering Place for Friends and Strangers

You Are In The Bible
Metaphysical Interpretation For Your Life

The Divine Design
How To Spiritually Interpret Your Life

Special thanks to my friend and editor,
Linda Lea of San Jose, California

Cover Art "Deborah" by Gustave Dore'

DEBORAH, JUDGE, PROPHETESS *and* SEER

*The woman born to become God's
military leader*

CAROLE M. LUNDE

iUniverse, Inc.
Bloomington

Deborah, Judge, Prophetess and Seer
The woman born to become God's military leader

8|13

iUniverse books may be ordered through booksellers or by contacting:

iUniverse
1663 Liberty Drive
Bloomington, IN 47403
www.iuniverse.com
1-800-Authors (1-800-288-4677)

ISBN: 978-1-4759-9460-5 (sc)
ISBN: 978-1-4759-9461-2 (ebk)

Printed in the United States of America

iUniverse rev. date: 06/24/2013

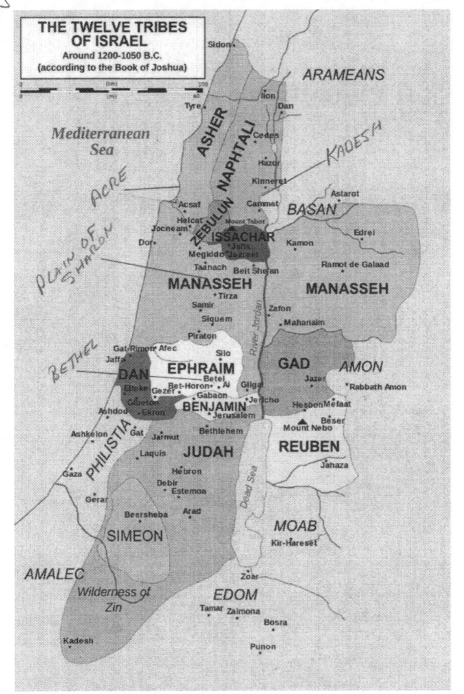

THE TWELVE TRIBES
OF ISRAEL
Around 1200-1050 B.C.
(according to the Book of Joshua)

CHAPTER 1

1 050 BC, in the era of Judges, was a fortunate year for Israel. Deborah was born in Kadesh-Napthali in the rolling hills near the Sea of Galilee. Her father was bitterly disappointed that his firstborn was a girl and turned away from her. He knew the elders at the city gate would not celebrate, but look at him with pity. How could he face them? He kept his eyes to the ground and went about his work in a sullen mood. His wife, Judith, tried to console him by reminding him she was still young, and there would be more children.

"But why could you not have a boy child for me the first time? Why am I being punished?" growled Amram.

Are you blaming me, Amram?" asked Judith in a very quiet voice. She knew most men would blame their wives. Would he?

"Is it you? Is it God? Who do I blame? Myself, of course! A man of daughters is a laughing stock in his village! What have I done to deserve this?"

"Amram, girls are born every day. Without them, who would have the babies to carry on God's chosen people? Please, Amram, hold your head high and proud, and do not turn away from us. There will be more children."

Over the ensuing weeks his mood slowly brightened, but he still did not look at his baby daughter. He refused to hold her and left it to Judith to name her. Judith stood her ground and refused to be put down by Amram's attempts to belittle them all.

"I will call her Deborah after the favorite nurse of Israel's great mother, Rebecca. She will be a helper to me, a busy bee, and a joy to both of us if you will let her." announced Judith.

Amram nodded and growled, "Deborah, a bee. What good is that?"

Judith stood nearly as tall as Amram and seemed to tower over him when she was angry. Her eyes became narrow and dark. She stared him down. "Some day, Amram, you will regret your words. She will be great and you will be ashamed of yourself, not because the elders look upon you with pity, but because you pity yourself. This is not like the man I married!"

Amram rocked back on his heels as if he had been struck. His face turned red. She thought he might strike her, but he did not. He turned and tramped out of the house into the olive grove.

Judith looked at the sweet face peeking out of her swaddling clothes. "You will be great, my daughter, greater than women are allowed to be. You will save Israel and raise all women to a higher place, even me. You will show them all."

The baby, Deborah, smiled, reached a tiny hand toward Judith's cheek, and kicked until the covering fell away from her curled up toes.

"Not yet, my daughter. But the time will come. I will pray to God that your destiny is great . . . great like Sarah, Rebecca, and Rachel. Great like Eve, mother of all living."

* * *

Young Deborah was sitting by her mother watching her feed her brother, Moshe, born four years ago. She was now twelve. Her wispy sun bleached blonde hair escaped her efforts to control it and fanned out like a halo. Her face was pale and the sun freckled her nose. She was lean and strong, and her demeanor serious. She always seemed lost in her own thoughts.

"Some day, Deborah, you will have babies of your own," said Judith trying to draw her out, "and you will know how to take care of them as I have shown you."

Deborah shuddered. After all this time she still remembered hearing her mother's screams in the night. Even covering her ears with her hands didn't shut out the sound. Her mother lay exhausted for days after Moshe was born and Deborah feared she would die like her Aunt Rachel. Aunt Rachel died after days of hard labor and the infant was dead as well. It was a terrible sight for a young girl to see. The keening and mourning went on as if it would never stop. Oh how Deborah wished the memory of it would leave her mind.

"How can anyone think of having babies when they cause so much pain? Aunt Rachel even died when her child was born! I do not ever want to have babies. I will not."

"Of course you will! We cannot stop birthing God's chosen ones. This is just the way life goes on, Deborah. Here, hold him while I get a clean tunic for him."

Reluctantly Deborah took her brother onto her lap. Under her breath she whispered, "I will never do this. I will never do this. I would die first and not wait until after all the pain like Aunt Rachel. No, I was born for something good, but not this." Moshe stiffened his body, sliding off her lap and began to cry.

Judith emerged from the door of the house shaking out a white scrap. "Here is a clean cloth. You change his tunic, Deborah, and bathe him just like I showed you."

Deborah closed her eyes and sat frozen. "I cannot do this," she whispered again.

Moshe began to cry and kicked at Deborah.

"Deborah, Deborah! What is wrong with you? Here, let me do it." Judith was becoming angry. "You are a very stubborn girl!"

"I am sorry, Mother. Really I am. I guess I am better suited to herd sheep. They do not need me to clean up after them."

"Suited to donkeys would be more like it! You are obstinate like them."

Deborah sighed, a little ashamed. She picked up the dirty tunic and took it the stream to wash it. She left it on a tree branch to dry in the hot sun. When she returned Moshe reached up for her. She took his hand and spoke softly to him. Judith returned to her baking with a secret smile on her lips.

*   *   *

Deborah's favorite place was the arbor by the village well. She could sit there and dream of what she might some day become. She felt sure she was destined for something special, but what could it be? Her elderly friend, the widow Hannah, who lived in the hills, told her that over and over. But she always said God is the one that knows and will reveal it when a person is ready to receive it.

This always made Deborah squirm. She wanted God to hurry! "Why wait? What is the matter with now? Perhaps it is because I am not smart enough, or wise enough, or I am stubborn like my mother said." These thoughts always left her exasperated.

Hannah was an elderly widow who had no children living. Her hair glowed light gray and her skin was like wrinkled parchment, dried from long exposure to the sun. When her husband died he no longer had any living brothers to marry her or take her in. But Hannah was content to live alone in the small stone two-room dwelling they had shared in the country. She loved the quiet of the hills, the gurgle of the stream at the foot of the hill, the sweet smell of morning, and the calls of the birds. Her life was full even though she was alone. It was full of God and the blessings of her age, which allowed her to be free and at peace.

*   *   *

Young girls of the village came to sit by the well in the afternoons with Deborah. They told her their problems and waited breathlessly for her advice. Sometimes a group of girls came and they spoke in low tones about everything, especially women, men, weddings, and sex. The sounds in the night from their parents' rooms and the activity of the animals in the fields piqued their curiosity and they speculated endlessly. Deborah listened patiently, not comfortable with their excitement about sex and children, but she reassured them their futures would be bright.

Mara, a shy village girl, came often and alone to sit with Deborah. She had a dark complexion and coal black hair. She was very tall and embarrassed about her height. She hunched her shoulders and kept her head down to seem shorter. It emphasized her height instead.

Deborah always tried to encourage her. "Mara, you should stand tall and not hunch over. You are beautiful like a goddess! Stand tall as you can!"

"But my mother said the young men will look past me because I am taller than they are. How will I ever find a husband if I tower over them and they turn away to look at some girl shorter than me?"

"If they turn away, it is because you keep yourself hidden and they think you do not like them. God made you tall for a very special purpose, Mara. Any man who passes you by because you are tall is a fool! Be proud of God's gifts to you. Ask him what you are to do with them."

Mara stood up and shook her hair as it fell over her shoulders. It had sparks of blue highlights everywhere. She squared her shoulders and laughed. "Like this?"

"Oh yes! Like that! If you could only see yourself the way I do. Promise me you will always stand like that and smile. You look wonderful!"

One of the boys of the village walked by them at that moment. He was pulling a struggling goat by a rope tied around its neck. He turned to look at Mara and smiled a bashful smile.

"See, I told you!" whispered Deborah.

"But he was leading a goat! Am I to attract only goat herders?"

"Mara, they are all men or will be. If he looked at you, so will others. They are all alike," laughed Deborah. "You will have your pick, I am sure." They both burst out in laughter until their sides hurt.

Young Barak came running to the well and breathlessly threw himself down beside Deborah. He was younger, not yet ten. He thought of Deborah as his best friend and confidant.

He looked up doubtfully at Mara. She took the hint saying, "I have to go home. My mother will be needing me."

"See you tomorrow, Mara?" inquired Deborah.

"Yes! I will come! Shalom!" Grinning impishly Mara walked away straight and tall, drew her scarf over her hair and waved over her shoulder to Barak and Deborah.

Barak studied his hands and bit his fingernails. "The older boys chased me away again. They said I am too small to play in their games. I think they are mean! I am as good as any of them."

Deborah smiled at him. "You are right. They are mean and stupid not to choose you. They are afraid you just might be better and make them look foolish."

"Do you think so? Really? How do you know?"

"Some day, Barak, you will be a great warrior. Your time will come to be the biggest and best one. You will see!" exclaimed Deborah attempting to reassure him. "You are growing so fast. Just think about your future and the way you want to be. And ignore their stupidity."

"I want to be a general! I will have a huge army to fight the enemies of Israel. My mother says I have too many foolish dreams, but you know I am not foolish. You know that do you not, Deborah?"

"You know I do not think your dreams are foolish, Barak. But keep them between you and God so no one will crush them."

"You mean not talk about them, even to you?"

"Well sometimes we can talk about them. But mostly talk to God about them. It is God who will show you the way. You are young yet. You have lots of time to grow up."

"I do not want to be young any more! I want to be older like my cousins and their friends. I want to be able to push them around like they push me all the time. I want to sit in the fields at night watching the sheep and thinking up battle plans. I need to be ready!"

"Barak, this is not the time for battle plans. They come from God when they are needed. If you talk to God, he will show you the right time."

"But what if God thinks I am too young and will never be big enough? What if he forgets to tell me? Or chooses someone else." His chin trembled at the thought of being left out even by God—especially by God.

"God is not like your cousins, Barak. God is the great Creator that created all things and knows everything. He will remember you and call upon you. Do not worry!"

Barak nodded doubtfully, slid off the bench and shuffled away, leaving Deborah to her own thoughts and dreams.

*   *   *

Three years passed all too quickly. Deborah kept busy helping her mother with household tasks and teaching her brother, Moshe, about the sheep. She tried to ignore the mention of a husband for her. She was fifteen now and her slim body was changing into a woman's. This meant she was of marriageable age. It was hard to forget about it because she could not help hearing her father and mother whispering in the next room. Marriage and men were definitely not on Deborah's mind. She knew they brought on babies just like the rams and the ewes, and the thought of it made her feel sick.

The girls in the village were very excited to be married and discussed it incessantly. They were full of questions, anticipation, and dreams of the rich merchants who came through the village on their way to the city. Even Mara shared their excitement and remembered to walk in a queenly manner. None of these things were of interest to Deborah, although she pretended and gave them her polite attention. There was almost no one she could talk to about how she felt, not Mara, not her mother, only God and Hannah.

Several times a week Deborah finished her tasks as quickly as possible so she could go to visit Hannah. Moshe wanted to tag along, but Deborah sternly told him he must stay with father and the sheep. He scowled at her and kicked at the stones as he turned away. He was growing so fast and becoming a pest. When she wanted to sit quietly by the stream and think, he wanted to come too and babble the whole time. She tried shooing him away but it didn't work. So she taught him to pile up stones to make a village, and select twigs to be people and soldiers. They selected the ones from the bushes that had forked ends for legs. Using dried grasses they tied dried leaves on for tunics and robes. He loved it and was soon absorbed in his building efforts. Once again Deborah had a little peace.

At Hannah's house she loved to work in the herb garden, cultivating and drying herbs for Hannah's store of medicines and remedies. And most of all she loved to talk to her about life and God. The wisdom Deborah handed down to those who came to her at the village well often came from Hannah's sharp wit and clear understanding.

"How can I avoid having to be married?" moaned Deborah. "It is so awful to be a girl, to be used for housework and having children. It terrifies me!"

Hannah smiled as she climbed onto a bench so she could hang the herbs that she took from her apron onto an already crowded beam. She smiled as she remembered having the same thoughts as a young girl.

"Yes, Deborah, I know what you are feeling. But as women this is our part in the human lot. I learned to keep my mind on God whatever I had to do in this world. I kept asking for strength. If I kept complaining about things, I was always unhappy. If I fought the way things are, I was always afraid. I did not wish to live my life unhappy and afraid."

"So, what did you do to keep your mind on God who seems so far away?"

Hannah hung the last plant from her apron and stepped down. She pushed the graying strands of hair from her face and sat on a bench near her stone oven. "Oh, I thought up little prayers about everything. I gave thanks for waking up early in the morning and for the cool air that still lingered. I gave thanks that there was good food to prepare and that I never went hungry. I asked God to show me the use of these herbs and how to prepare them, and he did. I thanked the herbs for their healing balm. I gave thanks for every little thing. I asked God about everything, every question I could think of. God has ways of answering we do not always see right away. That way you learn to understand more about what God can do and you learn to trust God."

"Do you still do that? Think up prayers, I mean?"

"Well, I have thought of so many over the years, they just seem to roll through my mind on their own now. If you want wisdom, Deborah, you must live in a world of prayer. It keeps your mind tuned to God where the wisdom comes from. You will learn to hear God's answers. What is bothering you?"

"My father has been talking to a rabbi, the father of a young man I do not even know, and I am sure plans for my marriage are being made without asking me. I do not know what to do. I can say I refuse him, but my parents would be so upset and wonder what is wrong with me. Maybe I would hurt his feelings, too. What can I do?"

"Pray and ask God what to do, and wait for an answer, Deborah."

"How will I know when the answer comes and what it will be? It may be too late! Will God speak to me in words or signs? What if I do not understand? What if I do not even like God's answer? I could be unhappy for the rest of my life!"

Deborah flopped down on the bench beside Hannah, put her elbows on her knees and her chin in the palms of her hands. Hannah patted her shoulder and went to make the special tea that Deborah liked the best.

"Trust, Deborah, Trust! If you are always doubting and troubling about everything, that is not trust. Trust brings calm confidence and the assurance that all will be well."

Deborah gratefully took the tea and sipped it slowly. "I guess I do not know how to trust. It sounds really frightening to me. It is like giving up."

"I suppose it does seem that way at first. Do you trust that your father will provide for your family? Do you trust that your mother loves you and teaches you what you need to know? Do you trust that the earth in my garden will grow the herbs if we plant them correctly? Do you trust that the sun will shine each day? There are so many ways in which you trust that you do not think about. You just know certain things will be there."

Deborah looked around Hannah's house thinking about how she had trusted Hannah through all her young years to be her confidant and advisor. She trusted Hannah to never reveal the secrets she shared with her. She trusted Hannah's toothless smile that lit up when she came to visit and help. Hannah was always there for her. "So that is trust," she thought.

"This is all natural," continued Hannah. "Now things are different. You are no longer a young girl. As women we suffer the sins of Adam and Eve. Women will bring forth children in pain. That is what is written."

"But Adam and Eve did not know they were sinning against God, did they? Why do we have to be the ones to pay for it? Why just the women? God does not sound very fair."

"We only know we are sinning when we bring pain to ourselves or others by what we say and how we act. Pain tells us we are on the wrong path."

"But Eve did not have pain until after they were put out of the garden, did she? How could she be on the wrong path if she did not know? How could God punish her for what she did not understand?"

"Deborah, this story tries to explain why we have such a hard life and why there is pain in the world. It is not told in order to blame Adam and Eve or God. It is told to relieve our day-to-day anxieties. Most people feel better if there is an explanation of some kind."

"So there was not really an Adam and Eve? Were they not real people?"

"No one knows. You see, Deborah, you are already thinking far beyond most people's ability! Rarely does anyone ask the questions you do. No one knows if Adam and Eve lived or where. The story gives us a place to start our thinking. They are real as a lesson that is very important, and we must discover within ourselves what that lesson means to each of us."

"Why do I think far beyond others?" Deborah was now waving her hands in the air in frustration. "These questions just come up on their own and make me worry!"

"These questions come up because God has some very special purpose for your life. It is a sign. Keep asking God what the story is telling you."

Deborah's womanly courses began painfully which heightened her anxieties about everything. She found it hard to recapture the trust she and Hannah had spoken of. Everything irritated her. She was angry that her body had betrayed her by suddenly launching her into the world of women. She didn't enjoy sitting by the well talking with other girls, and thought their questions were trivial and stupid. She even avoided Barak when she could, not wanting to snap at him. Life had suddenly become confusing. Who was she and what was she? She was an alien in a world where she did not fit!

A few months after her eighteenth birthday Deborah came back home one day and was greeted by her father. He was never home at this hour nor did he ever smile at her. He had a smile so broad on his weathered face that a shiver went down her spine and she held her breath. She knew what was coming.

"Deborah, I am glad you are here. Your mother and I have something important to tell you! The father of Ya'akov, and Ya'akov himself of course, has accepted you to be his son's bride! Are you not pleased?"

Deborah reached for the doorframe for support and tried to smile but the corners of her mouth only twitched.

"What is the matter with you Deborah? We finally found a man willing to take you, old as you are . . . and strange!"

"What do you mean, 'willing to take me?' Have I been of no value to you? I work hard and do everything you tell me to do, and now you just throw me away like a stillborn lamb? How many men have you approached that turned me down? What are you saying?"

Amram raised his hand to strike her but she quickly turned and entered the room where her mother sat beaming happily. "I will miss you, daughter. You have always been such a help to me. But now you must think of your own home and family. We are doing what all parents of daughters do, Deborah. We found you a good husband."

Once again Deborah tried to smile, but her mouth would not move. Finally she stammered, "Thank you, Mother. I have always tried to please you."

"Of course you please me, Deborah!" exclaimed Judith. "You have always pleased me from the day you were born. I know many things trouble you right now, but I will still be your mother, here to help you accustom yourself to your new life."

Deborah grabbed onto a thought from Hannah that gave her a moment of relief. "Will you give me a little time to ask God? I must know if this is right. I mean if Ya'akov is right for me or I for him."

Amram's face was turning red as he entered the room. "Of course this is right! God has already made it so! What is the matter with you, Deborah? What time? How much time does it take God to answer when God has already said yes?"

"Please, Amram, let me talk to her alone. There are things a woman must discuss with a woman," pleaded Judith.

"Well, talk to her all you want! It is settled! I have given my word!" Amram turned abruptly and left the room.

Deborah and her mother sat down together, stunned at Amram's vehemence. "He did not even ask me if I knew Ya'akov! I will not be forced into a marriage with a stranger! Why did he give his word without telling me?" wailed Deborah.

"Deborah, calm yourself. You wanted to pray and I suggest you do that now. Please do not anger your father further with careless words."

Deborah ran from the house toward the hills and Hannah. Hannah would know what to do. Judith stood by the door watching the disappearing figure of her daughter and shook her head sadly. "Why can she not confide in me as she does in Hannah? Am I not her mother? She is not like other girls, I know, and often I do not know how to help her."

Abruptly Amram came to her side and hissed, "So did she pray? Who does she think is in charge in this family?"

"Be patient, Amram. Deborah has always been different from the other girls of the village. She is more thoughtful and her council is always wise. She needs time to council with herself now."

"She will not make a fool of me in front of the elders of the village! I will not permit it!"

"She will not do any such thing! Men go into marriage without any changes in their lives. They just take a woman and get children on her. A woman must leave her own family and live with the family of her husband, a family of strangers. She has had changes in her body that are painful. Let her adjust to the thought of a new life."

"There is no reason for a woman to think! She should do as she is told."

Judith placed her hand on his shoulder, smiled at him and teased, "Did I *not* think in order to keep the household accounts while you were ill? Did I *not* think when I spoke out courageously against those who would take our sheep in payment? I made those merchants

14

flee for fear of the judgment of the elders! Amram, your daughter can think to benefit her family too. This is a good thing."

Amram looked at the back of his hands and nodded his head. "She frightens me at times. I often feel stupid around her." '

"Amram, she is your daughter, even though you barely acknowledged her because she was not a son. You feel frightened because you never talk to her even now. Just give her time to sort out her own feelings."

*   *   *

Hannah was taking fresh baked bread from her oven when Deborah burst through the door. "Hannah, help me! Help me pray! Help . . ."

Hannah spun around to see Deborah towering over her, wide-eyed and out of breath. "Now, child, sit down and tell me what has happened. I am sure I already know, but tell me everything from the beginning."

Hannah broke the loaf and handed half to Deborah while she breathlessly recounted the conversation with her mother and father. Tears were running down her face and her hands shook as she bit into the bread, half choking on sobs. "We need to pray, Hannah! Before it is too late!"

"I will pray with you in a moment when you are calm," said Hannah reassuringly. "We do not storm the gates of heaven with shouting and expect to hear the still small voice of God."

Deborah was still shaking but managed to quiet her sobs and eat a little more bread. Hannah handed her a cup of tea that would quiet her trembling and sat down beside her.

"Now my dear, tell me your worst fear. What frightens you the most?"

"I still have nightmares about my mother who is screaming in pain and I can do nothing to help her."

"So, you are afraid of being helpless?"

"Yes! Helpless to decide what my life will be! Helpless as my father forces a marriage on me!" Deborah began shaking again and tears flooded her eyes.

"This sounds more like rage than fear to me, rage that someone can inflict pain on you at will as if your feelings are unimportant."

"Oh Hannah, you are always reading my thoughts! I am angry at my body for changing. I am angry at my mother for putting up with so much without a complaint. I am angry at my father for being so bullheaded and demanding that I bow down instantly to his every command! I am angry at the girls in the village who follow along like dumb sheep!"

"Good! And are you angry at God also?"

"God! I never thought of it. But, yes! I suppose I am! How could God let such an unfair life be given to women? Why are just the men in charge?" Deborah dabbed her eyes and looked up balefully at Hannah. "Why did you say good?"

"How do you feel now?" chuckled Hannah. "See, your hands have stopped shaking and you have ceased to shout for the first time since you came through the door."

Deborah turned a bit red. "I am sorry, Hannah. I did not mean to shout at you."

"Oh, you were not shouting at me, my dear. You were shouting at yourself, at all the pent up anger and frustration within you. This is good. Now you can see what is really inside and be in control of yourself."

Taking a generous bite of the bread, Deborah swallowed hard and sighed. Mournfully she whispered, "What do I do now?"

"Let us pray and then you can tell me what you know about this young man and his family."

*   *   *

Deborah walked slowly down the stony path from Hannah's house toward home. She wasn't sure she wanted to go home and face her mother and father, but it had to be done. She was feeling a little more in charge of herself and the panic was slowly subsiding. A few field flowers caught her attention and she picked them to take to her mother. Somehow having a peace offering in hand gave her a little more confidence.

Judith met her at the door. "Your father has gone to the village council. I convinced him to proudly tell them he is consulting his daughter."

Deborah broke into a wide grin and threw herself into her mother's arms. "Thank you! Thank you! Look, I brought you some flowers." Companionably they sat down on a garden bench together.

"I know you are not happy about marriage. I am sure you know how devastating to our family it would be if you refused to marry at all. Tell me how I can help you."

Deborah looked confused. "What do you mean, how you can help me? I am supposed to be helping you . . . am I not? Who can help me when things are decided for me?"

"I can help you by telling you what happens between a husband and wife. I am sure you have heard things from the girls in the village but they may not be right."

"Yes, they all talk about the sounds they hear in the night from their parents' bed mats. And . . . and I have heard you and father as well.

17

I did not want you to know that. I do not want you to think I am listening in order to gossip with the girls."

"Deborah, I know you would not do that. The sounds you hear are about happiness and joy between two people. Sometimes it ends too quickly, and sometimes not quickly enough, but you keep thinking about the beautiful children it makes."

Deborah shuddered as she often did at the thought of the marriage bed and childbirth. "I do not think this is helping, Mother. Childbirth still terrifies and repels me. Forgive me but I do not want to talk about it any more just now."

Judith smiled thoughtfully. "Take a good look at me, Deborah. I am healthy, happy, and have a wonderful family. God has blessed me with a good and kind husband, and two beautiful children. When you have questions, you can ask me anything at all. I need hide nothing."

"But Aunt Rachel! She died! How is that a blessing?"

"People die of many things, Deborah. Life is not easy. We are not promised that everything will be the way we want it. We strive to accept the way things are, especially when we cannot change them." A little frustrated Judith turned to her chores.

There was nothing more Deborah could say. She wanted to lash out, run away, and scream at the sky. But instead she collapsed onto a bench in the garden and sat mute, exhausted, and spent. It felt as if her life were over almost before it began.

CHAPTER 2

Ya'akov sat quietly with his father in his father's study. He was a scholarly young man, thin, pale, and slightly nervous. He coughed softly and kept his eyes to the floor. As they awaited the arrival of Amram and Deborah, not a word was spoken between them. Rabbi Amri was always occupied with his scrolls and scriptures, and had little interest in talking about family matters.

Finally Ya'akov found his voice. "But Father, how can you ask a woman to take me as her husband when my health is so poor? I look like a ghost. She will hate me," he almost whispered.

"Your mother is right, Ya'akov. You need a wife to take care of you and your children. She will not hate you. You are a good and gentle man and an excellent scholar. The world needs more like you, my son."

A loud knock on the door lintel caused them both to jump. "Yes! Yes, come in," called out Rabbi Amri as he went to open the door. "Amram! Welcome. We are glad to see you, are we not, Ya'akov?"

Ya'akov stood up quickly and nodded. He looked embarrassed and uncertain about what to do next. He kept his hands clasped in front of him.

Deborah stayed well behind her father, feeling embarrassed as well and slightly ill. She remembered seeing Ya'akov at the synagogue and then only in passing. Would they be introduced? Would they be just thrown together without their consent? Would he hate her? Could she ever learn to be a wife to him or even to like him? Her head began to swim with doubts and again her stomach churned.

Abruptly Amram turned to Deborah pulling her forward by her arm and announced, "Well Deborah what do you think? Are you willing to have Ya'akov as your husband?" He held her arm tight and glared at her as though forbidding her to say anything but yes.

Deborah was so shocked she just stood there wide-eyed and unable to speak. Ya'akov blushed and started to turn his face away.

But Amri stepped closer addressing Amram, "Now, Amram! Let them get to know each other before we speak of them becoming husband and wife. Yes? Ya'akov has seen Deborah only at a distance as is proper. He has agreed that I should approach you about her and I have. I am pleased that you will consider our offer." Then he motioned to Ya'akov to follow him, and then Deborah. He ushered them out into the garden and bid them sit down on a bench under a tree. Then he returned to the house to speak further with Amram.

Deborah was feeling dizzy as she sat down. She did not look at Ya'akov because she felt so strange. A lurch in her midsection caused her to jump up and blurt out, "I am sorry, Ya'akov." She ran into a grove of olive trees where she lost her breakfast behind the trunk of a large ancient tree.

Ya'akov followed after her and gently lifted her from the place where she had fallen to her knees. "Are you all right now, Deborah? I am so sorry. This has been a most difficult time for both of us." He led her to a bench farther from the house and sat down with her once again.

"I am so embarrassed," whispered Deborah.

"There is no need. My breakfast sits like stones in my belly, too, and I wish I could do the same thing. But do not be concerned. I will not."

They looked at each other and burst out laughing. It seemed wise to both to walk to a small stream to splash cool water on their faces and refresh themselves. Sitting down on the grassy bank of the stream, shyly Deborah began to talk.

"I must tell you Ya'akov, I have never wanted marriage or to bear babies. The whole thing terrifies me. I feel God is calling me to something much different, but I do not know what it is. I wish I could study like you and all boys are allowed to do. Then maybe I would understand more."

"I have only studied the scrolls of the Torah and other writings. I have not been instructed in life as a man. I only know what I see of my parents, and they hardly speak of it or even look at each other when I ask. I would prefer just to continue studies and become a rabbi. But my father said that is only part of a man's work. I must be a whole man before God."

"Ya'akov? I would like it if you would be my friend, or at least not hate me. I think you are a nice person and I want to hear more about your thoughts."

"Oh, I would never hate you, Deborah. I do not know how to be a friend to a woman, but I would like to know. Men and women are not to be friends, unless they are married and even then maybe not. Brothers and sisters are not always friends. It is certainly a—a new idea! Can you tell me more about it?"

Deborah sat quietly picking at the grass and thought for a while before she began to speak. "Barak and I are friends," ventured Deborah. "But of course he is still very young. He asks me lots of questions and we talk about them."

"What sort of questions?" asked Ya'akov becoming very interested.

"Oh, questions about Israel, great generals, huge armies, and battles, the things many young boys dream of I suppose. Even my brother, Moshe, is beginning to play like a tiny soldier."

"I have always been interested only in learning about the sacred scriptures. What else have you thought about? I should like to meet with Barak and hear about his dreams of generals and battles."

"Please do not tell him what I told you. He will think I am giving his secrets away. I have already told him to keep them between himself and God until he is older."

"I will keep our conversation completely to myself, Deborah. And I will treasure it as our first introduction to each other. Perhaps we shall be able to speak again soon."

Deborah was feeling much easier now and the thought of meeting Ya'akov not so frightening. She preferred not to go beyond this conversation to thoughts of marriage, but perhaps Hannah was right. She did not need to be so afraid. Then she felt her stomach churn again.

Gratefully she heard her father's call to return home. She and Ya'akov bid each other farewell with assurances of pleasure in seeing each other again.

*　　*　　*

Deborah worked diligently in Hannah's garden, making more progress than ever before. The herb garden and the fruit trees were beautiful and a sweet fragrance was all around.

"Heavens child, you do not have to work yourself to the bone! Or is something else driving you? What is on your mind? Ya'akov?"

"Well, not Ya'akov himself but everything around us. He is gentle and nice. He is bright and interested in learning about many things. I feel good when I am with him until I think of marriage, and then I want to lose my breakfast again."

"Again?" Hannah's gray eyebrows shot up deepening the wrinkles already lining her forehead.

"Yes, again." Deborah recounted the whole scene for Hannah. Hannah began to laugh and laugh some more. She was shaking all over from laughter and could hardly stand up.

"Hannah, it was not funny! I was mortified!"

"I am sorry, my dear. I can only imagine how mortified you were. And still, what a great way to discover if the young man was caring or not! I know you did not plan it, but it could not have been a better indication of what life might be like with him. You always manage to do the best thing even if it feels like the worst thing imaginable, Deborah!"

"I always feel like a fool," she pouted.

"You are never a fool! You are bright and I am always delighted when you visit me. You lift my day. I hope you are always different and never just like everyone else. Hold your head up proudly, Deborah, no matter what happens. This is the only way you can really serve God. This is how God meant you to be!"

"Can I tell you a secret, Hannah? I mean a really deep secret so ridiculous I have to dream about it at night and do not dare talk about it in the daytime."

Hannah put down her herb basket and guided Deborah into the house. "What on earth are you talking about? Has something unspeakable happened? What is this terrible secret?"

"Nothing has happened. It is about Barak. He speaks to me about being a great general who leads a great army to defend Israel. I know most young boys daydream about that. But I dream about it too . . . at night."

"About Barak being a general?"

"No! About me! I am the general! I am leading the armies and Barak is at my side. I am judging and defending Israel. I keep telling God in my prayers that this would not be permitted of a woman, and I know nothing about battles and armies. But the dream still comes back again and again."

"And you have not told anyone of this, Deborah? Not even your parents?"

"Absolutely not! Especially not my parents! You are the only one I have told. You are the only one I could tell. I need to know what you think. I need to know if this is God telling me something. I do not understand at all. Help me, Hannah. Please. And tell no one, I beg you."

"So this is the cause of the turmoil you feel about everything a woman should be doing. Having a husband, a family, and always doing what your father or husband want. It is in such great conflict with your dream. Sit with me for a spell, child. I need to think more on this."

Deborah sat quietly, aware she was feeling as if she were suddenly expelled from a prison into an unfamiliar world. She was free and in danger at the same time. Thrilled and terrified. After a seemingly long time, she felt Hannah's hand on her knee.

"Go home, child, and say nothing to anyone. Do not be afraid of the dream or of living your life as a woman should. God brings about all things in the fullness of time. There is nothing you need do about this dream but wait upon the Lord. Will you do that?"

"I will say nothing. It will be between you, God, and me. I will wait, but I am not sure I will marry even if God wants me to!" Deborah hugged Hannah and swept out the door as if she were on her way to her first battle.

Hannah smiled benignly and whispered to herself, "And God will win!"

*   *   *

In the following months, cold weather came with rain and wind. Deborah and Ya'akov decided not to marry, at least not in the near future. Amram was perplexed and Judith was resigned. "Give them time, Amram. They cannot be forced into this."

"But what if they are seen talking together and others start talking about them? No one else will want her. I will be disgraced!"

"They are seen only in proper places. There is nothing for anyone to talk about."

"What proper places?" shouted Amram? "There are no proper places for unmarried people to meet. They must marry and then they can talk later! The elders are beginning to look at me as if I am crazy. I am sure they think I should control my daughter. Make her do what is right!"

"They meet in Rabbi Amri's study when he and Leah are present. Rabbi Amri delights in their conversations and is glad for Deborah's wisdom. They do nothing wrong."

"It is not right. Nothing is right anymore. Maybe I am going crazy!" Holding his head Amram left the house and went out into the fields to look for his sheep. Somehow gathering his sheep and counting them to be sure they were all there and safe made him feel sane again. The hot afternoon sun on his face and the breezes moving his robe were comforting.

*　　*　　*

As this winter wore on Deborah and Ya'akov met to study scripture less and less often. Ya'akov's health became very fragile and he stayed in his bed more and more. Deborah would inquire of his mother how he was, but she would just shake her head and tears would fill her eyes.

"No one thought Ya'akov would live at his birth," she told Deborah. "His heart was rapid and his breathing difficult. He has always had trouble breathing so he turned to his scrolls for entertainment instead of the games of the young boys," lamented Leah. "Now perhaps this time the winter will take him. I do not know. He is so young. Not yet to live as a man and have children."

Deborah hung her head. She felt it was her fault all this was happening. She could have married him and had his child, but she refused. Perhaps someone warm to sleep beside him would have made his winters easier. It should have been her, and yet she knew it simply could not be. She and Ya'akov agreed from the beginning to be friends. No one else would understand that except Hannah.

She looked in on Ya'akov from time to time. He would begin coughing violently in his sleep. Even Hannah's herbs did not stop his deterioration. Hannah's words rang in her mind. "Deborah, there was nothing you could do. Nothing at all. Stop torturing yourself." There was indeed nothing she could do now except leave Ya'akov to his encroaching death and his mother, Leah, to her sorrow. Deborah walked slowly home.

The funeral for Ya'akov was more difficult for Deborah than she imagined it would be. He was her bulwark against her fears. He stood between her and the impending doom of marriage. He was her open doorway to education that was closed to girls. Now he was gone and she felt naked, vulnerable, wretched, and alone. It pleased her parents that at least she appeared to grieve for him. Amram hoped that would bring other offers of marriage.

*   *   *

The summers came and went, and Barak was growing taller by the year. He stood nearly six feet tall at fifteen years old, which was amazing to everyone in the village. No one grew that tall except the Nephilim! They were the giants encountered by Joshua and his men as they scouted the land for Moses. But Nephilim were slow and stupid. Barak was energetic, quick, and intelligent.

Eagerly he sought the company of soldiers and questioned them endlessly about their prowess in battle. He would go into the hills with them and practice their drills. He handled weapons skillfully and often beat them in sparring contests. The older men considered him a young upstart and did not encourage him in any way. In fact they preferred not to notice him at all.

*   *   *

Deborah went to live with Rabbi Amri and Leah in order to continue her studies from the scrolls that so entranced Ya'akov. She pleaded with her mother and father to understand she just had to know more. She had to study and the only opportunity was in the home of Ya'akov's family.

Amram threatened to disown Deborah, but Judith gave her consent.

"How can you give your consent? It is not your place! You are a woman! You are her mother! You know this is not right!" shouted Amram.

Judith's eyes flashed in anger. Amram had never seen her really angry, especially with him. He seemed to shrink as she rose to confront him. "How can you even think of disowning your own daughter who has done nothing to merit such punishment? She has always been a blessing, not a disgrace! You could never see that, even at her birth. You turned your face away from her."

Presently she took his arm and guided him to a seat. "Yes, I am a woman and I am her mother," she said quietly and intensely. "I have always tried to tell you that she is different from other girls. I spoke to Hannah who believes Deborah has a special commission from God that she must follow. Moses was a prince of Egypt and left riches and power to follow God. Sarai obeyed the will of God and became known as Sarah, mother of a nation. Who are we to thwart the will of God, Amram? Who are you to defy the will of God by disowning her? Rabbi Amri and Leah are good people, well respected. They will bring no shame on us."

27

Once again Amram left the house grumbling and went out to gather his sheep. His life was changing around him and he had no control over it. How would he face the elders? What could he say if questioned about Deborah? Would he lose face in the village as a father and a man? It was all too much. Again the bleating of the sheep, their noses bumping against his leg as he walked among them, comforted him. But the answers would not come. There was only the bleak gray fog of fear and unending confusion in his mind.

Deborah continued to learn about herbs and the healing arts from Hannah. She could always find time to hike to Hannah's house and dig at the weeds in her garden. She was happier than she had ever been. The pain of Ya'akov's death lessened as time went on and the comfort of reading the scrolls he had read brought a sense of his presence when she needed it.

She seldom saw Barak now. He was busy with the army and his soldiering. He would wave to her when she went to the well if he happened to be passing by. She admired the man he was becoming and knew he was following his God-given pathway. Again the thought of her dream intervened and she could see herself riding beside him. What could it mean? How could it be?

*   *   *

Today Hannah had something on her mind. Deborah now made the tea and brought it to her because Hannah's hands trembled a bit more every year. "What is troubling you, Hannah? You have been very quiet and your eyes look far away. Are you ill?"

"No, child, I am not ill. I have been praying about something and it seems to take God a long time to answer."

"Praying about what? Please tell me."

Hannah took a long breath and a sip of the tea. "I have a cousin whose son is coming to visit me. His name is Lapidoth. I have not

28

seen him in many years but he was a strong, silent young boy, full of strange ideas. He has not married, but travels as a merchant. He wanted to know more about the world outside Ephraim. The message I received said his path is calling him here to see me. I keep asking God what that could be about, but I get no answer."

"When is he coming?" queried Deborah as perplexed as Hannah.

"Soon I think. I do not know where he is now or how far he must travel. Perhaps he is not too far away since a young boy brought the message early this morning. I have a feeling he is coming for you, Deborah."

Deborah almost choked on her tea. "Hannah, how could that be? Coming for me for what? Who knows about me other than people here in this village and a little beyond?"

Hannah was silent and Deborah could read her mind. "Marriage. Is that what you are thinking?"

"I keep telling God that is the wrong answer. That is probably why God is not speaking to me any more about it. God does not justify or argue. I should know that, but I know how you feel about marriage."

"I have been living with Rabbi Amri and Leah since Ya'akov died and I see every day how gentle and attentive they have become with each other since his death. I am sure that is why God gave Ya'akov to them as their son. He taught them gentleness. I have grown up a little in these last few years just as Barak has, and I am a little more inclined to consider things I have always feared."

"Things?"

"All right, marriage. I have thought about marriage. I know that sounds strange coming from me. The only marriage I saw as a young girl was my mother and father. Father blustered and mother ducked her head. Eventually he would listen to her, but it took a long time and lots of arguing. I certainly never want to live like that. Aunt Rachel died in childbirth and I just could not see any good in it all. Now maybe things will look different. Perhaps I can think of some good in it."

Hannah reached a gnarled hand to touch Deborah's cheek and smiled her now toothless grin. "It will be all right, girl. I know it will. You pray. God will answer you. He is probably tired of arguing with this stubborn old woman."

"Hannah you are not a stubborn old woman! You are my mentor and teacher and friend. My life would have been terrible without you. No one could understand me but you. If he comes here I will meet your cousin's son, Lapidoth, and we shall see what God has in mind."

An amazed Hannah looked up at Deborah and began to laugh uproariously. "Go home, Deborah! He will find you when he comes." Hannah continued to laugh and Deborah with her. She gathered the herbs Hannah gave her to take to Leah, and started for the village.

That night Deborah had the dream again. She was sitting in a large tent under a date palm tree. Kings, merchants, and all manner of foreigners came to seek her wisdom. The scene changed and she summoned Barak. When he came she told him of God's plan to vanquish Jabin of Canaan. Jabin had a cruel ally and general named Sisera who had great armies, nine hundred chariots of iron. Jabin had ruled over Israel for 20 years. Barak was astounded and declared he would only go if Deborah led the army. Then she woke up suddenly, soaked with perspiration.

"How can this be? How will this happen? What about Hannah's cousin who seeks me this very day?" she whispered.

She dressed and slipped down to the kitchen to join Leah at breakfast. She wanted to get her mind on something besides the dream that would not go away. She was happy to return to the scrolls and work diligently on understanding them. She wrote comments of her own that she kept to herself unless Rabbi Amri asked her about something she had written. When she read them to him, he always seemed pleased.

The days went by slowly and Deborah could not shake the turmoil she felt. She went to see her mother when Amram would be at the village gate with the elders. She would not tell her mother anything, but would just have simple woman-to-woman chats with her. Judith gave her a scarf she was making. She was always delighted when her daughter came to talk with her.

"Oh, my mother, how sad I cannot tell you of my thoughts, of Rabbi Amri and Leah, or of Lapidoth who has yet to appear," Deborah thought as she examined the beautiful scarf and hugged her mother.

A few weeks later Deborah was sitting in Leah's garden deep in meditation when the words came to her mind, "He spreads light abroad. He lights the lamps of the mind and teaches the unenlightened."

She raced into Rabbi Amri's study and jolted him out of one of his contemplative moods. "Forgive my intrusion, Rabbi. What is the Hebrew meaning of the name Lapidoth?"

Amri's eyebrows went up and he rubbed his beard. "So urgent, Deborah? Is anything wrong?"

"Please, Rabbi, do you know the meaning of this name?"

"Well it means 'spreads light, lights lamps of the mind.' Does this have some significance for you, Deborah?" He smiled one of his rare smiles and set aside his scrolls.

Haltingly Deborah said, "I am told by the seer, Hannah, that a man by that name seeks me."

"Indeed? And do you know who he is?"

"He is the son of her cousin. He is a merchant and is coming to visit her. She tells me he seeks me, perhaps my hand in marriage. Please know, dear Rabbi, I will always hold your son, Ya'akov, in my heart and I mean his memory no disrespect."

"Deborah, I have worried that you mourn Ya'akov too long. You must go on with your life. Your presence here has been such a blessing to Leah and me, and has helped us over our grief as much as can be. But it is not forever that you should stay here. We have known that too." He got up from him chair, smiled, and patted her hand. "Go. Ya'akov would understand."

Unexpectedly Deborah burst into tears and buried her face in his shoulder. Her sobbing went on as if it would never stop. "I am so sorry," she whispered.

"You have held your sorrow in too long," he said helping her mop her eyes. "Do not be sorry. It is good. Only good."

*   *   *

Judith was ailing and Deborah moved back into her family home to care for her. Amram solemnly welcomed her and said nothing further. Judith was comforted by her presence and began slowly to recover her strength. "I think you are pining for your children, Mother. I am at Rabbi Amri and Leah's, and Moshe is away with other shepherds tending your many flocks. Soon he will be a man and has vowed to join Barak in the army."

Judith smiled weakly at Deborah and said, "It is just the passage of time, my dear daughter. I will be fully recovered soon. It is so good to have you here again. I think of you every day and night. I pray for your safety."

Again a surge of guilt assailed Deborah. First she failed Ya'akov who needed her care and now her mother who needed her became ill. She whispered a prayer Hannah had taught her to say so long ago.

"What is it, my daughter? I did not hear you. What are you saying?"

Deborah told her about Hannah's prayers. "I am saying them for you that God will heal you and make you well."

Judith smiled as she closed her eyes. "I know this is true. I have always believed God is with me."

Hannah had not visited anyone for a long time, so Deborah was surprised to see her coming up the path to her home. "I thought it was time," said Hannah a little out of breath." I have been too much a hermit and feel at times I have stolen your daughter away, Judith. It is time for me to come to you myself and be of whatever assistance I can."

Hannah brought healing herbs, and began making the tea with them. The herbs helped immensely and soon Judith was all smiles.

"Hannah, I have always understood that Deborah needed you. I have known what a different and special child she is, and that she must find her own way. I am so grateful you have been in her life to help her. I am sorry to say sometimes what a daughter needs is beyond what her mother can comprehend."

The two embraced and walked slowly together into the garden. They spent the morning talking of many things, including the expectation of Lapidoth's arrival and what he might be like. Deborah brought them tea and dates, and left them alone. She would soon be out of their lives and they would need each other. She was awaiting the arrival of Lapidoth as well, eager and nervous to know what he would bring to her life.

Many weeks later in the afternoon the dust on the road was rising in the distance. Caravans were so few these days. They avoided the main roads that led past Sisera's territory.

As it came closer Deborah stood by the village well on tiptoes, her hand shading her eyes. She was sure it must be him. Who else could it be? A shiver went through her whole body and her mouth went dry. The moment she had been preparing for was about to unfold. She did not know what to do and a quiet voice within her said, "Wait. Wait and pray."

Wagons filled with goods passed by, then came a few camels with men from distant lands astride them. Behind them peasants walked herding sheep and children of all sizes ran through them shouting and laughing. Still Deborah waited and prayed. She tried to keep her eyes lowered and not stare, but it was hard. She whispered to herself, "Surely he must be in this caravan. But what if he is not?"

Feeling more foolish by the moment, Deborah got up to leave. She walked toward the gate of the grove of date palms and stopped. There was a man standing by a horse near the grove. "Are you Deborah?" he asked.

She opened her mouth to answer but her voice would not come. Again he asked, "Are you Deborah? I was told I might find you here. Are you not Hannah's friend?"

Finally, "Yes, I am Deborah, friend of Hannah." She could think of nothing more to say, even after all the scenarios she had rehearsed in her mind since Hannah told her about him. He was of medium height and dark with somber black eyes. His robes were dusty but expensive, and his face was creased by hours of squinting in the sun. His horse stamped impatiently and shook his mane.

"I am Lapidoth, cousin of Hannah. I have come to seek your hand if you will have me."

Stunned at the suddenness of his announcement, she could only point toward her house. "My father will be home now."

He bowed slightly and turned to go. She stood frozen not knowing what to do. Then she remembered the story of Rebecca and said, "May I draw water for your horse?"

He smiled broadly and so did she. She returned to the well and drew the water. He took the bucket from her and offered it to his horse. Then turning he said, "Will you accompany me to your father's house or should I find it alone?"

With a deep breath Deborah regained her poise, raised her chin, and moved step-by-step in his direction. The mysterious promise of her future loomed in the back of her mind struggling to make a connection with the reality of the man she now faced.

*   *   *

Barak worked hard and was at last being recognized as a good soldier. He had experienced being pushed around by his cousins, jostled by the fellow soldiers claiming their own positions of power in the army, and now, they finally accepted him. But he found this acceptance came at a price. They expected him to join them in their revelry, drunkenness, and rowdy treatment of the locals.

Barak could not bring himself to push others around the way he had been treated for so long. He could not look upon the locals as something to be made sport of. He hung back from their rough and tumble back slapping and drunken brawls. He could not take advantage of the girls even if they were loose women frequenting the inns and taverns for that purpose. He did his best to conceal his reluctance by not being at the head of the pack, but only seeming to be like them. Eventually he could trail off and disappear.

Occasionally he thought of Deborah. What would she advise him to do? Then he would remember she said God would lead him. He should stay true to himself and ask God for help. He tried to remember how she prayed. In the quiet of an oasis he would kneel down and ask God to help. Afraid of being ridiculed he would be quick so the other men would not see him. He didn't get immediate answers when he tried to pray, so he became frustrated as time went on and eventually gave up. Perhaps God would not speak to him because of his transgressions, or God was not really there.

Barak became hardened like the other soldiers and enjoyed their increasing acceptance of him. To stave off feelings of guilt Barak did his best to forget about God. The wine flowed freely in and out of his cup and he took more notice of the women in the inns they frequented. Life was exciting and full of adventure at every turn. The still small voice of guilt in the back of his mind became quiet as the overflowing wine and raucous laughter increased. Months went by in a whirlwind. The army grew in size and the activity in the army camp increased. Soon he forgot completely about prayer and God. The thrill of battle became his god.

CHAPTER 3

When Abinoam, Barak's father, heard of this he traveled from Kadesh-Napthali on a donkey to see his son. After much questioning of soldiers along the roads, he found Barak at an encampment. Barak's reputation had grown as a courageous and skilled fighter, so it was not difficult to find those who knew him. To Abinoam's chagrin they extolled his capacity for wine and his prowess with the women.

Barak was pleased and puzzled to see his father. He ran to embrace Abinoam. "Why have you come? Is mother not well?"

Abinoam returned his embrace and kissed him. "All is well my son, but I fear for you. Word has come that you denounce the Lord in the taverns and are cruel to the people. This is not the son who grew up in my house. Tell me it is not true."

Barak hung his head for the first time since he was a little boy caught chasing the sheep. "I am a soldier now, father. The life of a soldier is different. If I am to lead armies in great battles, I must have the respect of my men."

"Then it is true," cried his father. "You have blasphemed against the Lord our God and punishment will surely come to all of Israel! Jabin is already dragging our people off to his terrible prisons and he kills others outright in the streets and fields. Sisera threatens us at every turn. Can you not see if we disobey God, we will be punished? Can you not see that God is using Jabin to punish us for your sins?"

Barak was taken aback. "You think I am the cause of Israel's oppression! How can that be true when all the soldiers do as I do? How can God single me out from all the thousands and thousands to blame? Why? We are fighting *for* our God! Not against him!"

"My son, my son," said Abinoam urgently, "do not treat our people as if they are the enemy, too. You must not exploit our own people for any reason. Your army must not steal our flocks and rape our women."

"Do you expect me to turn a whole army around? I will be laughed out of my regiment. They would stone me, or worse. I would be the laughing stock of every soldier! Barak the soft! Barak the meek! Barak the coward!"

Abinoam laid his hand on Barak's arm, his eyes wide and pleading. "You cannot turn an army around by being like them. You must turn yourself around first. And then all who will serve under you will one day follow your example. I expect you to return to God and follow his commandments. Return, my son, before it is too late and we are all doomed forever."

Barak slowly pulled his arm away from his father's grip. "You are asking me to make myself look the fool before all the men. Am I not able to serve God by winning our wars? We must win wars! It is the only way!"

"God would rather have your faithfulness than a thousand triumphs in war," said his father. "There is no doubt we must fight when others threaten us, but to lose your soul before the battle even begins is utter defeat. Remember in your childhood when boys came to you with skinned knees and you attended to them, even though they attacked you the day before? You saw what was right and you did what was right in the sight of the Lord. What has changed? Are you less of a person now than you were then?"

Barak could not look into his father's eyes. He could not bear to see disappointment there. His mind was in turmoil and he said, "Father I know you have traveled far, but I must go."

As he walked away, Abinoam said, "Just think about what I have said, Barak, my son. The existence of Israel depends upon it."

Barak went back to his troops with a heavy heart. He had no answer for his father. He reached his tent and went in to pray. Words were difficult in coming and he began to ask questions of God. "How shall I heed my father's words? What do you want me to do to keep face with my troops and with you, Lord God? Give me answers clearly that I may know what to do!"

Barak fell asleep shortly after his dinner and his dreams were dark with battle and full of blood. There were no triumphs but only defeat. He awoke in the night wet with sweat and thrashed about for a lamp. Abel, his guard, heard him and came in to inquire, "Barak, Barak where are you? Are you all right?"

"Yes, I am all right," growled Barak. "Where is the lamp? I need a lamp!"

Abel lit a lamp and brought it to him. "Is there something wrong, my friend? It is not like you to awaken in the night. You were shouting in your sleep."

Barak held his throbbing head and looked around with bleary eyes. "Just a dream, Abel. Thank you for the lamp. Go back to your post."

Reluctantly Abel turned and left Barak's tent.

Barak sat gazing into the flame of the lamp wondering, "What am I to do? Already my guard thinks I am possessed. I must find Deborah. She will know the meaning of the dream. Not only will my men now think I am possessed, but will I confirm it by running off to inquire of a woman what I should do? I can leave in the night and tell them my father needs me."

*   *   *

Amram was quite puzzled at the sudden appearance of this man who was asking for Deborah's hand in marriage. At the same time he was pleased. He was sure Deborah had missed her one chance and no one would want her ever again. Perhaps God had granted him one more chance to save face in the council of the elders!

"I know this is quite sudden and you do not know me," began Lapidoth. "I am a cousin of Hannah, whom I have not seen for many years. I have been traveling and selling merchandise for my family. In my travels I try to bring a word of hope to those who have none. There are so many in our kingdom who are afraid to go out for fear of King Jabin's patrols. They are losing hope and I want to bring them the news that God has not forgotten them."

"A noble thing," said Amram in amazement. "Are you not afraid of Jabin's patrols? Might they not attack you as well and endanger my daughter?"

"Yes, I have some fear of them, but they know I sell excellent merchandise to those in the palaces and they do not wish to interfere with commerce in and around Jabin's court. What I do is risky, but I must help the common people who are simply trying to go on with their every day lives. When arrested they are used for sport at the whims of drunken soldiers. Someone must bring them knowledge and hope."

Deborah stood silently in the doorway. Amram was so taken with Lapidoth that he did not see her there. But Lapidoth knew she was there and beckoned her to come in. He smiled at her and said, "I had a dream in which I saw you and heard your name. When I wondered who you were, a vision of Hannah entered the dream and beckoned to me. I knew then I must come to Hannah for the answer."

Amram, in an attempt to regain his position as father of his house, cleared his throat and said, "You are a traveling man! What kind of life would that be for a wife? I mean what do you offer her?"

Judith came in from the market, arrived in the doorway, and stopped abruptly. She looked from Amram to Lapidoth and then to Deborah.

"Deborah, go out and speak with your mother while Lapidoth and I talk," blustered Amram trying to wave them back out the door.

"I would prefer they both be here while we talk, father Amram," said Lapidoth quietly. "I want everyone to know who I am and my intentions. Is there any more of your family I should seek?"

Amram again felt the loss of control in this stranger's presence. He tried to think of an answer to Lapidoth's question but none came to his mind.

"Only the family I have been living with, Rabbi Amri and Leah," interjected Deborah. "They are the family of Ya'akov, may he be blessed. He died three winters ago. He was my friend. He delighted in the scriptures and his father taught us both before Ya'akov died. I have continued my studies in their home. I came back here when my mother fell ill."

Amram flushed deep red and grumbled, "I cannot control my daughter. She does what she pleases. Maybe you can make her obey."

Judith was livid, "How can you speak of Deborah that way! She is not wild or disobedient. She has a calling from God which she and I respect, even if you do not! She does nothing to tarnish your precious reputation."

There was breathless silence. All eyes were cast down toward the floor.

Lapidoth eventually broke the silence. "Hannah has told me of your calling, Deborah, and I honor that you follow it. She told me of your wisdom, those who come to you for wise counsel, and your skills in the use of healing herbs. I wish to know more about these things, if you will tell me."

Amram was nearly apoplectic and Deborah was not sure she should speak and make things worse. But Lapidoth looked at her so expectantly, that she felt she must say something. "I will be happy to speak with you about these things, perhaps when you and my father are finished with the business of our betrothal."

"What if I would like to speak with you before a betrothal is finalized? Would that not be wiser since it will concern you as well as me?" Lapidoth was clearly in charge which pleased Deborah, though she was not quite sure why.

"Oh! Then perhaps we could go into the garden after the meal and I will tell you what I can. Surely you will stay and eat with us, Lapidoth?" There, she had said his name. It tasted sweet on her lips and she smiled.

"Of course you will stay, Lapidoth," chirped Judith. "I was just about to finish preparing the meal. You and Deborah can go to the garden now while I get it ready."

"Do you need my assistance, Mother?"

"Oh, no, dear. Amram will help me just like he used to do when we were first married."

Amram's eyebrows shot up high into his hairline. Judith motioned him to follow her and he obeyed. Deborah tried to hide her smile as Amram followed Judith. She had never seen her father led by her mother. She and Lapidoth walked into the garden, bright with the sun beating down, to a bench where they sat down a discrete distance apart.

"So tell me Deborah," began Lapidoth quietly, "tell me about your life, your calling, and your studies. Tell me about Ya'akov if you care to."

Deborah startled at the mention of Ya'akov. Hot tears began to fill her eyes unbidden.

"I am sorry, Deborah. Have I said something to upset you?" said Lapidoth in almost a whisper. "Hannah told me about him. She was afraid there would be gossip in the village and wanted me to know the truth. I hope you will not be afraid to talk to me. Perhaps I am too eager. This is too soon."

"You have said nothing wrong, Lapidoth. Sometimes the grief comes over me at the mention of him. It does not happen very often." Her words felt strained and jerky. She marveled at how much easier it was to tell Ya'akov her thoughts than this stranger. She could see that she needed time to organize her thinking and select more carefully what she should tell him and when. Surely she could never tell him about her dream of being the leader of the armies.

She began to speak of her childhood and her friends including Barak. Lapidoth seemed most interested in Barak. He frowned a little when she spoke of her fears about marriage and having children. As she continued, the old fears were once again creeping in and she felt a bit queasy. It was easy to think of marriage in a more mature way until now when she was face to face with the man she would marry.

In an attempt to quiet her jitters she hurried on to tell him of her studies, counseling villagers in the palm grove, and learning about healing herbs with Hannah. Was she saying too much? Were some things too precious to place under the scrutiny of a stranger and one who would eventually have control over her? Yes, a husband would have control over her! She stopped for a moment to catch her breath.

In the pause Lapidoth cleared his throat and asked, "But what is that calling your mother spoke of, Deborah?"

Slowly and uncertainly she began, "A calling is an urging that has no specific words to describe it. It seems I am being led to where I must go, and I do not always know what that will be or where. I only know it is from God. I am sorry. I know I must not be making much sense."

"You are doing fine, Deborah. Please do go on," he gently urged her.

"God places thoughts in my mind and words in my mouth for certain others to hear. I seem to know what to tell those who come to me for counsel. God sent me Ya'akov not for marriage, but to help me learn from the scriptures. He was my friend, or you might say my study . . . brother and his family became my family too."

Lapidoth was quiet and looking off into the distance. "Your life seems very full for a young woman. Will you make room for a husband? Must I compete with God for my rightful place in your life?"

There it was again, the hint of control she dreaded.

CHAPTER 4

"**I** am sure God already has you in mind. Why else would you dream my name and come to visit Hannah after such a long absence? She said she had not seen you for many years." Feeling a surge of courage, Deborah asked, "Why is it you are not already married?"

"I must think on your questions," said Lapidoth. "But I will answer your last question."

Deborah was still a little uncomfortable and felt perhaps she had pried, but she would have to know something about him. Wouldn't she? Surely God did not expect her to go into this blind!

"I am not married because I travel. I cannot give up these travels because it is our family business. For this reason I have been rejected as a suitor. 'This man will wake up in a different city every morning. How can this be good for my daughter and our family? How can this be a marriage?' So you see, until God called me to seek you through my cousin, Hannah, there was no chance of my being married."

Deborah thought for a few minutes before she spoke. "You will continue to travel and I will continue to study and counsel. What will be the purpose of our being together? How will we conduct a marriage? We will be expected to have children. Shall I have them and raise them alone? Where will our home be? Do you have other

45

family? What have you and my father spoken of? I am sorry, but more questions seem to keep rushing into my mind."

"We have both been following our paths completely on faith until those paths brought us here together. I can see we need a little time to work these things out between us," said Lapidoth. "We have only just met." He began to feel uncomfortable with the direction of their conversation. Should a woman be able to question him like this?

"So you do pray? Do you go to the synagogue? Do you know the scriptures?" continued Deborah hopeful that this might be a connection, but he smiled and did not answer.

Judith stood in the doorway waiting for Lapidoth and Deborah to look her way. But they did not, so she called to them that the meal was ready. Deborah hurried into the house to help Judith. She was sure Amram would be grateful and she needed to give her mind a rest. Too many anxieties and fears were whirling around in it.

Lapidoth delayed coming in, taking advantage of a few minutes while food was placed on the table, feeling a desperate need to think. He had no trouble overpowering Amram but Deborah was quite another thing. She was somehow formidable.

The meal began with the usual prayer and was otherwise silent. Deborah and Lapidoth were deep in thought. Amram presently began to speak of the village, the elders, the new well they were digging, and the soldiers of Jabin. He complained of the ever-rising taxes and the wolf that took a lamb from his flock. Judith smiled at Deborah. She would speak to her later in private.

*   *   *

Late one morning, Abinoam, father of Barak, came to the house of Amram and Judith seeking Deborah. His face was lined and worried and his step slow. Judith hurried to summon Deborah from her studies at the home of Amri and Leah. Judith had not been to their home and felt a little uneasy as she knocked on the door.

"Judith!" exclaimed Leah. "How good to see you. I hope all is well. Come in!"

"Yes, Leah, all is well. I have come for Deborah. Abinoam, father of Barak, has come asking for her. I hope nothing has happened to Barak."

"Mother! Has anything happened?" said a startled Deborah at seeing her mother here.

"I do not know. Abinoam has come seeking you. He is very troubled. Can you come with me now?"

"Yes, of course!" Deborah put her papyrus into a fold of her shawl and hurried out the door with Judith.

Deborah and Judith found Abinoam in the garden drinking the water Judith gave him.

"Ah, Deborah, friend of my son Barak. I need your counsel. I fear Barak no longer seeks the Lord. He has been drawn away by a soldier's life to indulge in all the ribaldry and sinful deeds of the army men. I went to him and spoke with him, but he turned away angrily and would speak with me no more. God will surely punish us even more than He already has! What will become of us? What will become of all Israel! Oh, my son, you will bring the wrath of God down on all of us!"

Deborah looked at her mother and at Abinoam. Then she said quietly, "Take me to him."

Judith wanted to object, but Deborah immediately went into the house to prepare to leave. Judith followed after her saying, "But what will Lapidoth think? How can you just leave like this, and go to an army camp? It is not proper for a young woman to do this!"

"Mother, you know I must do this. I cannot let anything stand in my way. Lapidoth will understand or he will not. If there is to be a marriage, this is how it will be for me. I cannot suddenly turn from my calling. I cannot be tied down, unable to respond where I am called."

"Yes, I know." Judith wrung her hands. "I just do not know what will happen next. I am never prepared for things to happen so suddenly. Especially when you just get up and go! I could never do that. Forgive me. Go with my blessing and prayers, my daughter."

"Thank you, Mother. I know this is not easy for you, and father will be completely upset. Explain as best you can to Lapidoth if he asks and I will talk to him when I return. He must understand or I cannot be his wife." Wife. There, she said it and the word felt very strange in her mouth.

Immediately, Abinoam and Deborah set off in the direction of the army encampment. Seeing how lame Abinoam was Amram gave them his donkey and cart. It was almost a day's brisk walk and this would be faster, so they could be assured to arrive by nightfall.

They stopped for water in the villages they passed through. Deborah's stern glance deterred anyone attempting to delay them. The plateau rose ahead of them where the encampment lay. The sun was setting behind the western hills.

Deborah and Abinoam walked quickly to the general's tent to inquire about Barak. There were looks of surprise from those in the tent, but one of them, recognizing Abinoam from his earlier visit, offered to find Barak and bring him.

"We will wait by our cart," said Deborah, not wishing to spend any more time in this soldier's tent. She covered her face with her shawl and walked out.

Abinoam stayed a moment longer to speak with one of the soldiers. "You have seen my son? Is he well?"

Waving his wine jug in the air the soldier answered, "Don't worry old man. He is the best of the best. No one would dare harm him. He can whip a whole cohort with one hand!"

Abinoam thanked the man and backed out of the tent. He hobbled back to the cart at the same time Barak approached.

"Father! Deborah! Why are you here? Has something happened at home?"

Deborah turned to him and planted her feet. "The trouble is not at home but here. Your father has told me of your life here, and how it has caused you to turn from God to wanton ways. I urgently need to speak with you."

Barak was shocked. Forgetting his plan to find Deborah he blustered, "I have not asked for your counsel, Deborah! I am not the child of the village any more. I have important work to do here and I am enjoying it. Life does not have to be grim!"

Deborah took a deep breath and spoke softly in reply. "Please do not be disrespectful, Barak. We have been friends all of our lives, and I would not come to you if it were not of the greatest importance."

Barak looked at the darkening sky. "I will take you to the inn near the village where you can spend the night, and I will come to you in the morning. Let us go now before the men think you are a wronged maiden come to claim me as father of your child."

"The father of your child! How could you say such a thing to me?" In the gathering darkness Deborah could feel her face burning with anger. She took the animal's halter after Abinoam was helped into the cart and they started for the village. They said nothing as they walked. At the inn Barak helped his father from the cart, paid for their stay, and abruptly left to return to camp.

Abinoam shot Deborah a worried look. "Is there any hope? Can you reason with him?"

"Tomorrow perhaps. Right now I could throw animal dung on him for that remark."

Abinoam shook his head sadly, patted her hand and said, "God will show you the way, dear daughter. The doubts are only mine and I will be patient with myself. His mother knows nothing of this and believes I am taking food to him."

Deborah began to wonder in the night why Barak's remark had stung her so. She felt rage at him for not being her friend, at Lapidoth for being a stranger, at Ya'akov for dying, at her father's stubbornness, and at God for leaving her in such confusion. She fell asleep praying for understanding.

Barak came to the inn the next morning as he promised. His demeanor was quiet and low key. "I am here to listen to what you have to say, Deborah. I am sorry for the things I said to you last evening. We have been friends too long for me to react that way."

Deborah now knew how God would want her to handle this moment and what to say. "Dear Barak, indeed we have been friends since childhood. You were a little younger, so you listened well then. Now you are a man and have a right to your own thoughts and decisions. I am here to reform our friendship as two adults rather than two children. Your father came to me to ask that I visit you and bring you his concerns, which he knew would be my concerns also."

Barak interjected, "Yes, my father wishes me to conduct myself as other than a soldier, which would shame me before my men. He accuses me of bringing God's wrath down on all of Israel. That is too big a burden for me to carry. The welfare of my men and our ability to defend Israel is enough on my shoulders."

Abinoam nodded in agreement. "This is indeed what I said to you, Barak, my son. I am much aggrieved that you have turned from the Lord. Please hear Deborah."

"I am not here to chastise you, Barak. I am here to begin a new part of God's plan that involves us both. Let us plan together how we will respond to the will of God as well as the needs of your army and our people. They are not separate things. Your army is made up of young men, many of whom have not been taught the commandments brought down from the mountain by our father, Moses. Those commandments are rules for becoming a civilized people, learning to live together, and to interact in commerce and trade. Through them we honor God. The will of God is that we live well and someday in peace. We are a people of herders, nomads who are establishing ourselves as a nation. Our tribes must come together as one nation. Then we will be strong, and those who would attack us, seeing our strength, might rather negotiate and trade peacefully with us."

Barak listened to Deborah with great interest. His defensiveness slowly evaporated. Abinoam had dozed off with a contented smile on his lips.

Deborah continued, "The commandment said we shall not kill. It means we shall not commit wanton murder. But it does understand that we must defend ourselves when enemies attack. You must explain the commandments to your soldiers in a way that causes them to agree and wish to abide by them."

Barak frowned. "That will not be easy. They like the way things are at the camp. They are away from home, out from under their father's rule at last. I must say I enjoy that freedom as well."

"When young men commit fornication and adultery, coveting the wives, daughters, and the property of others, they dissipate their own strength. Only a focus upon God will bring back this strength and even greater. An army cannot win without discipline, strength, and the sure knowledge that God is with them. Although they have left their homes and families to be in the army of Israel, to still honor their fathers and mothers is the tie back to Adam and Eve, and thus to God. If they break this tie, they are wandering lost without direction in their lives, and become weak. Then the army becomes weak. Can you understand this, Barak?"

"I can understand, Deborah. You have always been wise, even now you know about armies! But I do not know how to begin. Where do I start?"

"Surely you do not need to do this alone. With God we can work together. I still study the scriptures as I did with my dear Ya'akov. His father allows me to use his study and scrolls and he answers my questions. I know without God this would not be possible for a woman. We ourselves could not possibly defeat Sisera and Jabin. But with God all things are possible, Barak! I know it well!"

Barak and Deborah worked through the day to create a plan for teaching the soldiers what they must know about God's plan for their success. Deborah would supply the lessons for Barak to use. They would begin with military training coupled with the commandments. Barak would give them a scripture teaching with each kind of training and require them to understand and recite it before they could pass on to the next training. Deborah assured him the soldiers would begin to demand to know more and more about God, and would begin to teach each other.

"But Deborah how will you know what lessons fit with which training?"

"You will teach me about military training and battle field strategy so I can supply you with the proper scripture and explanation."

Barak looked at Deborah thoughtfully for several minutes. Deborah thought he might refuse, but he did not. Barak's enthusiasm was growing as they filled in the details. "Deborah, you will be the first woman to lead armies!"

"Privately, my commanders have despaired of teaching soldiers anything but fighting. This will be the answer that will restore their hope and strengthen them as well. I will tell them about you, Deborah, a prophet, judge, and seer, a Mother in Israel, one who keeps the heritage of Yahweh for His people."

Deborah's mouth dropped open at his words. She was seeing the dream coming true, the dreams she had at night that she hardly dared reveal to anyone but Hannah and Ya'akov. "So this is the first step of how it happens," she said to herself. "God has put the plans in my mind and the words in my mouth as he promised! And God, through Barak, will give me the military knowledge as well. Everything Hannah has told me is coming into place more easily than I could ever imagine."

CHAPTER 5

Amram and Judith were waiting anxiously as Deborah and Abinoam arrived home. "We were worried for your safety!" exclaimed Judith. "Did you see Barak? Is he well?"

"We are all right, Mother, I assure you. Yes, we met Barak and he is well, too."

Amram cleared his throat and grumbled, "What will you tell Lapidoth? It would serve you right if he left you! Then what will we do? You are not getting any younger, you know. Soon no one will marry you. We will lose out! I will be disgraced before the elders!"

"Father, please do not worry about Lapidoth and me. As you said a long time ago, 'God has made it right. What is there to think about?'"

Amram looked suddenly at Judith. "I should have known women talk! You told her I said that?"

"Yes, we talk," laughed Judith. "We must share what we know to keep life going. Men say nothing and expect everything to just happen out of the air."

Deborah admired how her mother could express such practical wisdom in the face of her father's blustering, and with such patience and kindness. It was as though she was seeing another face of God in her mother. Perhaps God shows up in different ways allowing each person to be an individual.

They helped Abinoam out of the cart. Amram took the donkey to the shelter and fed him. He pulled the cart around to the back of the shelter and inspected the wheels and harness for any damage. Judith led Abinoam into the house to a room where he could rest. "You will stay with us today and return home when you are rested.

"Does anyone know where Lapidoth might be?" Deborah asked cautiously, not wanting to stir up Amram's anger again.

Judith shook her head as she started for the kitchen. "Perhaps it is well that he was not here to witness this scene with your father. He might agree that you are surely getting too old!" Then she turned and smiled at Deborah and they broke into laughter together.

Deborah sat down in the garden to think about the plans she and Barak had layed out. She decided to go to Amri and Leah's the next day to look up scriptures in Amri's study. When she and Barak met again, she would be prepared to incorporate them into the army training.

She wandered into the village wondering about Lapidoth, and stopped at the well. The women were talking about Jabin's new decrees and a greater threat of Sisera's goons turning villages into rubble if they did not comply.

Lapidoth saw her and came to her side immediately. "Deborah, we are in much danger here. Word has come that Sisera's troops are not far away."

Deborah looked puzzled. "I was at Barak's encampment yesterday with Abinoam, Barak's father, and heard nothing about it. We saw no Canaanite soldiers on the roads."

"You were at Barak's camp? Alone?" Lapidoth's face was grim.

"Of course not. Abinoam, Barak's father, was with me. It was at his behest that we went to speak with Barak. It was a mission for God."

Lapidoth was lost for a reply to this seeming impropriety. He cleared his throat and took a more commanding approach. "The news came this morning. Barak's encampment is immediately moving farther into the hills to avoid attack. We must go to your father, arrange a wedding quickly, and go south to Ephraim to my family property between Bethel and Ramah where you will be safe."

Deborah scowled as she followed behind him to her home. "What do you mean I will be safe? Where will you be? Are you not going to be there with me?"

"Yes, for a while. I have business to take care of. You will stay with my family until we prepare our own place. I have much property there, many fields and vineyards. It is a good place, Deborah."

Suddenly the reality of having a husband order her life hit her hard. She stopped mid-stride and looked up at him. The last thing she wanted to do was rush through a wedding and dash away with someone she barely knew. She felt the old panic rising and the urge to flee. But she knew she could not. She felt trapped. She must think this through and pray.

Amram agreed immediately and Judith burst into tears. King Jabin had already decreed there are new gods to be worshipped and the Jews must comply. New taxes were levied on the poorest of villages and Sisera, Jabin's commander, had loosed his viciousness upon some of them already.

"I cannot go without you," wailed Deborah throwing her arms around Judith. "You and father must come with us! You are not safe either!"

Judith smoothed Deborah's hair and stroked her cheek. "We cannot go, Deborah. This is our home and we must dwell here. You must go with your husband. The Lord will be with us and with you," said Judith wiping her tears with her shawl.

Amram was nodding sadly in agreement. "I must go to the gate and confer with the elders." Muttering he shuffled out of the house toward the village gate.

While the plans were hurriedly made, Lapidoth and Deborah went to see Hannah. She received them happily and quietly. She was fascinated as Deborah told her and Lapidoth about the plans she and Barak had made. Lapidoth listened attentively, this being the first time Deborah told him what transpired at the camp.

He was shocked and tried not to show it because he was not completely at ease around Hannah. When they were married and alone he would command Deborah as his wife to stay out of the military business. Going quickly to Ephraim would prevent her from carrying out further meetings with Barak.

Deborah had that same thought in the form of a question, "How will Barak and I continue if I am far away in Bethel-Ramah and his encampment moves to God knows where? It seems so strange that we should just get started on God's work together and then be separated by a great distance."

"And a marriage," thought Lapidoth.

Hannah replied, "Has God not found a way wherever you and Barak are, Deborah? You were not sure how your dream would unfold, and yet it is doing just that. God is always working. God is the Great Creator who can do anything. Just look at the land and sky, the stars and moon, the waters and rivers! If the Creator can do all that, I am sure he can work this out."

Deborah began to laugh as she had not laughed in months. Everything seemed so serious and so huge, and now not so much. "Why do I keep forgetting this? I am quick to tell Barak and others the same things, and yet forget to tell myself."

Lapidoth did not laugh but did his best to smile. It seemed that God and Hannah were in collusion and he was somehow pushed aside.

How would he regain his rightful place as head of the marriage and household? Would he remain diminished before a powerful woman as his father had?

The wedding took place in the home of Amri and Leah. They had the larger place and Leah so wanted to be part of it. It would somehow ease her always-present grief for her son, Ya'akov. Many came to wish them well and offer gifts. There occurred the customary dancing and celebrating, although a little abbreviated.

Soon after the celebration and departure of the guests, they returned to Deborah's home to finish loading supplies for the journey. They packed into the night and now it was barely dawn. Lapidoth stayed in the home of Amri and Leah, and Deborah spent what was left of one last night in her childhood home.

Amram came to help Deborah with bundles of goods, gave her a quick hug and wished her well.

Young Moshe came in from the fields to see them off. "Do not worry, Deborah! In a few months I will join Barak and we will defend our land," he announced. "We will defeat Sisera and then you can safely come back home."

Deborah could hardly believe her eyes. This shepherd boy, this young brother with whom she spent so little time, would be a young man before she knew it. She wondered what he would be like the next time she saw him. Would it be months or years? It was a sobering thought. And her parents! What if something should happen to them and she could not be here to help them!

She threw her arms around Moshe and hugged him tightly. "Take care of our mother and father, Moshe. And take care of yourself. Have you spoken to Barak yet?"

"Not yet," replied Moshe a little downcast. Then he brightened. "But I will and he will accept me. I know he will!"

Deborah hugged her mother again. It was all so sudden. All had happened in such a short time and it was hard to take in.

Hannah came down the path waving a bag of herbal supplies and shouting, "You will need these, Deborah! Do not forget what you have learned. I pray I will see you again, but if I do not, remember me in your heart."

Deborah ran to meet Hannah. They fell into each other's arms. "Go now, child," Hannah whispered. "This is right. God is with you and you are always in my prayers."

Lapidoth brought mules hitched to a wagon to carry the supplies. He tied his horse to the back of the wagon and helped Deborah onto the wagon seat.

There were tearful goodbyes as Deborah and Lapidoth climbed into the wagon for the journey to Bethel-Ramah, the tribe of Ephraim, in the northernmost part of Judah.

Nodding his last respects to them all, Lapidoth climbed onto the seat beside Deborah. With a smack of the reins on the mule's rumps the wagon lurched forward and they began their journey south.

Deborah suddenly felt bereft and empty as her beloved home disappeared from view behind them. From time to time she glanced at Lapidoth but he kept his eyes intently on the road. She assumed he was watching for any robbers or other dangers. Unease gripped her midsection. Why did she now not feel safe with him? What was changed? He did not even look like the same man who shared her wedding.

She wanted to pull the scriptures out of her bundle of belongings and look at them for reassurance, but she did not want Lapidoth to know she had them with her. Not yet, anyway. She had been so free and now suddenly, she was alone, distrustful, and very unsure of herself. He had spoken of helping the poor, but somehow it seemed very disconnected from what little she knew of him.

A jolt of the wagon brought her back to the moment. "What has happened?"

"Just a boulder in the road. I should have seen it and avoided it." He got out of the wagon to inspect the wheels. "No damage that I can see."

As they continued he went back to being silent again. Deborah tried again to break the silence. "Shall we speak of our families so that I may get to know something of the family I am going to live with?"

"I really need to watch the road, Deborah. Later on perhaps."

Certainly this was not the Lapidoth who had made such a fine impression when they first met! Now he did not wish to speak with her or hear her. It seemed as though she was no longer welcome to interact except at his convenience. As the hours went by she tried to concentrate on Hannah, going back over all the conversations between them she could remember. She forced herself to recall their earliest ones and the words they had spoken. Tired as she was, it was the only thing that gave her comfort in this alien situation.

Thoughts of Ya'akov kept surfacing, his gentleness, his interest in her every thought. Ya'akov would never treat her like this, and tears welled up in her eyes. She pulled her hood closer to her face to hide them.

At each stop Lapidoth busied himself with care for the animals, accommodations, and conversations with people along the way about the dangers of attack. Deborah would turn in early and sleep separately from him. She did not know when he retired or when he arose to start the day. Soon she no longer thought about it nor did she care. Gloom was rushing in on her mind and thoughts of the future carried no hope. She found herself longing for Barak and the battle. She prayed for this strange interlude in her progress toward God's plan to end soon. She dreamed at night that brigands carried her off and deposited her in Barak's camp just in time to confront Sisera. Disappointment arrived with the morning light.

She decided to chase the gloom by once again engaging Lapidoth in conversation at breakfast. He smiled briefly, answered her questions with short responses, and hurried off to get the animals and wagon ready to continue.

"Perhaps this is not the time," she thought. "He has much responsibility and maybe it worries him. I am being a silly child. When we arrive at his home in Bethel-Ramah, it will all surely change and we will be the way we were when we met."

As the wagon bumped along, Deborah found it difficult to maintain those brighter thoughts. They only brought up contrasting doubts. How many times did she stop her mother from talking about marriage and sex? How much was left unsaid? But she did not want to hear about those things then and she had not changed her mind. She still did not truly want marriage the way she saw it at home. How could she have talked herself into this after her years of renouncing it and being sure it was not her destiny? How?!

CHAPTER 6

Barak became captain of the troops. He had little time to think about what he and Deborah planned. In fact, most of the time he forgot about their plans completely. He was busy preparing his troops to break camp and retreat further south. They planned to move by night, west toward the Plain of Sharon, and back east into the mountains to avoid being observed. He would tell his men the time was not yet right to confront Sisera's chariots and his hoards of soldiers. But in reality the thought of going up against Sisera's chariots with his still untrained troops and lack of weapons was frightening.

He sent scouts to find a place south of the Jezreel Valley deep in the hills. Finally his scouts brought information about ideal campsites far away from King Jabin in Hazor and Sisera who dwelt in Harosheth of the Gentiles.

Abel was still Barak's most trusted aide. "Captain, the search party has returned with good news. There are many places, well hidden, with water and places to store food. I have chosen the largest one, which I believe is the best. It will accommodate everything"

"So they return with good news and not like Joshua's men who returned with tales of giants! We are ready to move and will begin at sunset."

Horrified, Abel almost shouted, "But Captain, it is Shabbat! We must wait a day!"

"That is just what Sisera would expect us to do," scoffed Barak, "wait while he plots our capture! No Abel, we will move tonight when everyone else is looking forward to the day of rest. We will be gone before anyone will notice our movements."

"But, but the Lord," . . . whispered Abel.

Barak clapped a hand on Abel's shoulder and laughed. "The Lord is more interested in our success and the freedom of Israel. We go at sunset." Barak was thankful that most of the soldiers did not really care much about Jewish rituals and would not question him. His main concern was the danger of moving at night. It would be slow going to avoid accidents and loss of men, animals, and what little equipment they had.

The soldiers moved out into the darkness in small groups keeping torches small and low. They put feedbags on their few horses to keep them from calling to each other. They would split up, each group under a capable guide. They would take several different routes and regroup on the Plain of Sharon near the Great Sea.

The night sky was overcast and starless. The going was indeed slow, each soldier picking his way carefully for himself and the animals he tended. The flocks of sheep wanted to stop and sleep, but were prodded along and kept from the cliffs. The bellwether, a large castrated male sheep with a bell on his collar, was secured to a wagon so he would not stray. The sheep would follow the sound of the bell and keep moving with the troops.

It was near dawn when the last of the encampment was broken down and carried into the hills on pack animals and soldiers backs. Progress was slow and arduous. It would be weeks before they neared the new encampment. The hair prickled on the back of Barak's neck whenever he thought that Sisera's men might have spies and be pursuing them at this vulnerable time. His scouts patrolled from the front to the back of the caravans of soldiers, animals, and equipment to be sure they were not followed.

It was dawn when Abel took several soldiers and galloped to the back of the caravan. There was dust in the air back down the trail. "It cannot be ours," said Abel. "Our dust settled long ago." He signaled his soldiers bringing up the rear to ride off the trail into the trees and wait. They hid and peered over the rocks to see Sisera's soldiers going in the opposite direction. "They never saw us!" whispered Abel. "God must have averted their eyes to keep us safe." Quietly they rode back to Barak's side to tell him the news.

"No, God did not avert their eyes, Abel. They were not looking for us. They were doing something else."

"But what could that be? How could they miss our fresh trail of animals and soldiers? It must be God has forgiven us for moving on Shabbat!"

"You can believe whatever you want to believe, Abel. Be sure each camp is cleaned up after we move on. Leave no clues behind."

Each morning before dawn the soldiers and aides finished the task of setting up the temporary shelters and tore them down as evening approached. They packed everything and brought up the rear of the caravan.

It was especially cold in the mountains and the soldiers hovered over small campfires to keep warm. They whispered to each other, eager to be down on the warmer Plain of Sharon. They dreamed of the fresh food from the orchards and the sea. Most of them did not know how different the great sea was from the small Sea of Galilee they experienced. Galilee was just a large lake and the Great Sea was massive.

They began to travel in the daylight now that they were farther south. Days were hard and the nights found them all exhausted as they slowly moved closer to their destination. The farther Barak was from Sisera the better he liked it. In the night his mind would again suddenly shift to Deborah and the plans they made. How far away and unreal it all seemed now. He had pangs of guilt when he thought of his father, Abinoam. He felt helpless and torn at having to leave his family behind and unprotected. He prayed as best he could that his father and all he knew and loved would be safe. His childhood dreams of fighting for Israel hung on a thread. How could this army, small and barely trained be victorious against the chariots of Sisera? Was Deborah right? Could it happen only by the hand of God?

Echoing Barak's fears was Abel's prayer, "Oh God, we will need help. Send us help! Barak, how will we know when it is time? How can we do this without help? Who will come to our aid besides God?"

"I do not know. Somehow God will be with us I am told. But I do not know anything about God. Deborah was teaching me but now we are going to be far away from each other."

"Some of the men went to a village south of here to scout and heard of a woman named Deborah and her husband Lapidoth. They were traveling south. Could it be your friend, Deborah? Do you know if she married?"

Shock registered on Barak's face. "I did not know! How could that happen? No one sent word! Surely she would send someone . . ."

"Perhaps they are fleeing Sisera the same as we are, Barak. If that is true, things would be done in haste. No time for plans and great gatherings for a wedding."

"But I did not even know she had a suitor! Her friend Ya'akov sleeps with our fathers. Where would another suitor come from so quickly? She did not want marriage. How could this be?" Barak sat down and put his head in his hands. "Everything is suddenly very confusing. I thought our plans were solid and reasonable, and now? Where has she gone? Is everything ruined?"

*　　*　　*

Deborah and Lapidoth traveled from village to village and accommodations were easily available. "I know this is not what we would have planned, Deborah. I expected it to be different. I know it was hard for you to leave your family and my cousin Hannah behind."

"Tell me more of what you did expect, Lapidoth? What did you envision would happen after finding me? Did you ever think about getting to know the woman you would marry?"

"I am not certain what I expected. What does it mean to get to know someone? You have told me about your past and your call from God. What else is there?"

"We could tell each other our life stories, about our families, our childhoods, whatever comes to mind," suggested Deborah. She was hoping the anxiety that knotted her chest and nearly choked off her breathing would be eased.

The road south was hot and dusty. Lapidoth spoke mostly about the road ahead and what they could expect. "It is strange to see no other travelers. This road to Jericho is always bustling with merchants, animals being taken to market. Now we seem to be the only ones today."

Deborah nodded as he spoke, but nothing of their lives was shared. She was thinking, "He does not want to share with me. Am I to be just another of those wives who do their chores, have the babies, and nothing more? Is he perhaps hiding something from me?" Deborah's anxieties flared up again. She was in a cart with a stranger going to who knows where!

They veered off the road to Jericho and took a smaller one to the west. If Sisera were coming south he would surely take the main roads. One evening they crested a hill and saw a village down below them.

"That would be Tirzah, Deborah. We will stop at an inn there for the night."

"Do you know anyone in Tirzah?"

"No. Bethel-Ramah is over the hills to the west. I have not come this way before. I always travel near the coast of the Great Sea."

"Is that not the territory of the Philistines?"

"Yes."

"Are you friendly with them?"

"No. Not friendly. I just do business with them. They tolerate me."

"But why risk your life among them?"

Ignoring her question he craned his neck forward. "We are almost to Tirzah. I will take the horse and ride ahead to secure a room at an inn. Just keep the mules from straying off the road until you get there."

Deborah stared at the mules and back at Lapidoth. She could not believe her ears. He was going to leave her here on the road alone with all their worldly goods. He dropped the reins into her hands and jumped down. He saddled the horse and rode off without another word.

As the dust settled from Lapidoth's departure, Deborah sat for a few moments wondering what kind of man he really was and what she had gotten herself into by agreeing to marry someone she did not know. But it was on the strength of Hannah's wisdom that never failed her that she went ahead. She remembered Ya'akov's attentiveness and special regard for her. Ya'akov. Tears sprang to her eyes at the thought of him and their life before he died. She was so comfortable and content. Now where was she?

Gathering her courage Deborah snapped the reigns and the mules slowly moved forward. The road twisted and turned down the long grade to Tirzah. She was not as adept as Lapidoth at guiding the wheels around rocks and gullies. A wheel caught on a rock and nearly tipped the wagon. She pulled the reigns hard to stop the team and got out to examine the situation. The rock was too large and wedged into the ground. It could not be moved. She shaded her eyes and strained to see if perhaps Lapidoth was coming back. No, of course he was not. She had to do this alone.

She went to the heads of the mules and pushed on their noses to get them to back up. They brayed loudly and took one unwilling step back after another until the wagon lurched back down off the rock. She kept pushing them until the wheel was well clear, pulled their heads to the side so they would turn the wagon. It worked. They just narrowly cleared the rock when she pulled them forward again. Back on the hard wagon seat, she clucked to them and snapped the reins.

It was nearly dark when she came close to Tirzah, hoping desperately that Lapidoth had not run into any trouble. Why did he not come back for her? The question burned in her mind. She saw the stable at the edge of town and turned the animals toward it. As she approached, Lapidoth was just leading his horse out to the paddock. Then he saw Deborah and waved.

"The nerve," thought Deborah becoming angrier by the moment. "What took you so long?" she nearly shouted. She could not keep the irritation out of her voice.

"I went to two inns before I could get rooms. It took three mugs of beer before I could convince the second innkeeper to rent us rooms."

As he came closer she could smell the drink on his breath and he was a little too jovial. Disgusted she climbed down out of the cart avoiding his hand extended to help her.

"Deborah! What is the matter?"

"I got in and out of the cart by myself with no help. I dislodged the wheel of the cart from the rocks with no help. And I drove this team never having done it before . . . with no help! I did not expect you would desert me on the road, leaving me unprotected. That is what is the matter!" Now Deborah was shouting. "What kind of husband are you?"

Lapidoth said nothing more. He took the animals into the livery, pushed the wagon into the shelter and paid the stable man handsomely to watch over their belongings. Silently they walked together to the inn. Lapidoth took long strides but Deborah kept up. "I will not walk behind you, ever," she said just loud enough for him to hear.

He slowed up and turned to her. "The wife walks behind her husband to show respect."

"The same respect you showed me by leaving me on the road? I will walk beside you, but not behind you. Believe me, behind you is the last place you will want me to be if you continue to mistreat me!"

Angrily Lapidoth reached forward and swung the door open. He showed her to a table in a far corner of the inn. They washed the dust from their throats with watered wine and gratefully received the bread and cheese brought by a very young girl.

"You first, Deborah. You must tell me everything from the beginning."

Deborah nearly choked. It sounded like a command. Summoning a calm voice she said, "I have already told you about Barak and me as children. He had childhood dreams of leading the armies of Israel and defeating out enemies. I also had dreams only mine came in my sleep.

"What was your dream?"

Deborah raised her chin and looked at him out of the corner of her eye. "You may think me crazy, but I dreamed that I was head of the military. I was directing the armies."

Lapidoth sucked in his breath in surprise. Then he started to laugh. "Is this a joke? A man's army would not follow a woman!"

"I do not know how it could be, Lapidoth! I have no control over what I dream in my sleep. That is God's domain. I have told Hannah because I knew only she would understand. My family would not. And now my husband thinks it is a joke."

"Did you tell Ya'akov?"

Deborah stiffened at his insensitivity to bring up Ya'akov. "No. It was not important to us. Why do you want to know if I told Ya'akov?"

"I do not know. Perhaps I am still a bit jealous of your friendship with him." Hoping to assuage her anger he tried to sound more conciliatory. "I want to be your friend as well as your husband, but I do not know how. Tell me more about that."

"Ya'akov and I agreed to study together. We did not demand anything of each other. We were equals that way. I could trust him. Can you understand that?"

He ignored the question. "Surely you can trust me, Deborah. I am your husband and the head of our household, or will be when we acquire servants."

"I am not sure you have earned my trust or my friendship. I am with you only because of Hannah. She trusted her visions and knew you would come. I trusted her. She has trusted you."

He sat back and was pensive. "I hope you will give me your trust. A woman owes her husband that."

"Trust is not owed, Lapidoth. It is earned. Today was not a good start."

Squirming a little under her directness he changed the subject. "And children, Deborah?"

"I never wanted children and that has not changed. I am sorry I did not tell you that before we married. I know it is assumed that people who marry will have them or suffer the shame of barrenness. Children were never in my dreams at night so I assumed it was not in God's plan for me."

"I do not know what to say. It is strange for a woman not to want to bear children."

"Unusual, but not strange. Many women have died giving birth, but they had no choice. They would not shame their families by remaining barren. So they died! Do you want children, Lapidoth?"

He paused, his brows furrowed. "I do not know. I never thought it was a choice. I will need time to think on it. Tell me about your studies. It is unusual for a woman to study scriptures. Surely you cannot continue now that you are married. How could that fit into our lives?"

Deborah became more agitated at his attitude. Again she forced her voice to have a calm but strong tone. "I have studied for several years and learned much. You heard me tell Hannah about my conversation with Barak. I believe I can guide him in the ways of God. It is all part of God's plan for me."

Deborah decided she would not tell Lapidoth that she had many notes on pieces of parchment hidden in her belongings among her woman's rags. She now knew she was not able to trust him and her notes were essential to carrying out her plans with Barak. Should Lapidoth force her to destroy them, all would be lost.

Shifting her mind quickly, Deborah continued, "Tell me about your family, Lapidoth. Who will we be meeting when we arrive in Bethel-Ramah? What are they like?"

Lapidoth sat up straighter and leaned his elbows on the table. "I have not been there for a year. My travels take me to far away cities and I return home when I am close by again. My Mother demands to have control over me and the direction of my life. My father will be disapproving because I did not marry someone from Ephraim and settle down to raise a family and work in my fields with my kin. They will regale you with questions. It would be best not to tell them about your calling and studies. Just talk about your family. Except for my mother they are a simple folk, steeped in tradition."

"How is it that your mother is so different? What plans did she have for your life beyond the usual ones that a mother keeps in her heart?"

"You will see for yourself when we arrive there. I do not care to speak further about her."

At the foreboding in his voice Deborah slipped into a gloomy mood. "I will say nothing."

"My mother is Miriam. My sister is Tamar and her husband is Joab. They have two sons. I cannot remember their names. Tamar has a sharp tongue, and she and Joab shout rather than speak to each other. The sons scatter into the hills to herd sheep rather than become the target of their frustration."

Lapidoth stopped and thought a minute. "There are several cousins, some of whom are elders in the village of Bethel. One is a merchant whose wife spins and weaves cloth for sale. One cousin is a woman who refuses to marry and we fear she plays the harlot. The others pretend she does not exist to avoid the shame. She lives in the hills and comes home when she pleases. Her name is Rahab."

"You said you had much land. Is this true? How large?"

"Yes. My father has given me many large fields cultivated by Joab. I am happy to allow my family to live on the property and work the land, even though it is rightfully mine. Joab was injured by a fall from some rocks and works as well as he can. He is in enough pain without his wife's constant complaining."

Deborah began to wonder if this was a place or a family she would care to live anywhere near. She determined to pray about it until she received a clear answer. Only God would know what is in store for her and how she could cope with them all.

It was getting late and they went up to their rooms at the back of the inn. Deborah and Lapidoth slept separately again, not sharing one bed. Deborah was grateful not to be rushed into intimacy with someone who was still a stranger to her. Lapidoth seemed not to care and made no sexual demands. It was obvious their relationship would be different in many ways. It was already strained. Their differences had deep roots, not apparent when they met. She was still puzzled about how this marriage was to be part of God's plan for her.

Early morning brought news of Sisera's army camping close to the village where Deborah and Lapidoth were staying. The inn was full of soldiers shouting and overturning furniture. Homes were being ransacked and women dragged into the streets. Children were running everywhere in terror.

There was a single knock on their door and they froze hardly breathing. "It is I, the innkeeper," whispered a man as he entered their room. "Come with me quickly!"

Deborah and Lapidoth grabbed their belongings and followed the man. They went through a door across the hall and down a back staircase past the first floor and on down into a narrow wine cellar passage way.

"Follow this passage until you come out in a wadi. Follow the wadi down and then stay close to the foothills until you reach the Jordan River. It is a considerable distance, but the only safe way. Hurry!"

There were other hotel guests ahead of them and behind them. Deborah almost stumbled over the feet of an old woman who had tripped and fallen, blinded by the light as she came out of the dark tunnel. Deborah stopped. Lapidoth almost stumbled into her.

"Where are you hurt?" asked Deborah. "Let me help you."

"It is only my ankle. You must go on! Get away! I cannot walk."

Deborah wrapped the woman's ankle tightly in a length of cloth. Lapidoth impatiently scooped her up off the ground and carried her down the wadi. "It is twelve miles to the Jordan River," said Lapidoth. "I will go with you to the river, and then double back through the hills to Tirzah to retrieve our animals and wagon if they are still there. Keep traveling south along the river. Stay out of sight as much as possible. I will catch up with you."

Deborah was startled. "You could be killed! Are those things so important?"

"We deserve to have everything, Deborah, and not let Sisera's thugs scare us into accepting theft. Maybe there will be others I can help escape."

This imperious side of Lapidoth loomed larger the more she got to know him. He was leaving her alone again and this time with strangers. She lifted her chin in defiance and marched forward toward the Jordan.

Everyone who came through the passage made it to the banks of the Jordan. They organized themselves into groups; those who would scout ahead, those who would bring up the rear, and those who would help the physically less able travelers.

Lapidoth started north up the river to avoid anyone who might have pursued them from Tirzah. He waded through swampy areas, climbed grassy hills and rocky cliffs. He hid in the caves until evening and proceeded into Tirzah by a goat path through some orchards. No one seemed to be about. Household goods were scattered in the streets, pottery smashed, but no people.

He went to the stables to find his wagon and animals, especially his horse. They were still there where he stabled them and a soldier in a ragged uniform was on guard. The soldier was seated on a pile of wood swigging wine or ale from a flask. Lapidoth was sure the soldier had been there for some time and someone might come to relieve him. He slipped around the stable and found a hole in the wall. He climbed through quietly. He could hear the snores of the soldier close in front of him by the door. Lapidoth picked up a hay rake and hit him on the back of the head. The soldier slumped forward and dropped the flask. Lapidoth pulled him into the stable and hid him behind some feed sacks.

The horse and mules were stamping nervously now and Lapidoth harnessed them as quickly as he could in the dark barn, pulled the wagon forward and backed them into the traces. He led them far to the other side of the orchards near the caves where he had spent some time watching for movement. When he detected none he stole back into the town to look for the inhabitants.

Going from place to place, the houses were ravaged and empty. It was close to nightfall and he was about to leave when three children crept out from hiding. "Come with me," whispered Lapidoth, "and be very quiet." He took them to the caves and hid them there. "Is anyone else alive?"

They shook their heads, their eyes wide with fear. He couldn't afford to wait much longer. He wrapped the children in the robes from the chest in the wagon, tucked them in snugly among some bundles and sacks of feed, and led the animals back over goat paths and wooded areas toward the Jordan River. The way was difficult and Lapidoth had to pry the wheels out of ruts time and again.

Large stones loomed up in the dark unexpectedly on the sides of the path blocking the wagon and another route had to be found. He thought of what Deborah had said about the wagon being hung up on a rock coming the last few miles to Tirzah. Guilt assailed him for a moment. But at last he reached the valley and the grassy areas, which made the going easier. The sky was now dimly lit overhead.

When morning light shown over the banks of the Jordan and the children rolled out of the robes and peered over the feed sacks. Lapidoth introduced himself and lifted them down from the wagon bed. There were two boys and a girl, Dismas, Zuhar, and Ruth. They were from the same family and their ages were probably 5, 8, and 9, Dismas being the youngest and Ruth the eldest. Lapidoth feared for their parents. Most likely they were killed in the raid. He invited the children to splash in the cool waters of the Jordan and to eat some bread and cheese before they continued on. Lapidoth was thankful the raiders had left his wagon contents intact.

He led the animals and wagon across to the other side of the river at a shallow ford, loaded up the children, and proceeded south toward Jericho on the east side of the river. He planned to cross back over when he was sure Tirzah was far enough behind. Perhaps Deborah would be in Jericho by now or he would hear news of her and the others from someone. He began to second-guess himself as he walked along. Questions loomed up in his mind. Should he have left Deborah? What if she did not make it to Jericho? What if there were bandits along the way?

Jericho came into sight in the very late afternoon. Lapidoth crossed back over the river. The children were delighted to help push the wagon through the muddy water and up on to the bank. He looked back up the river thinking he might spot Deborah. But she must surely be in Jericho by now, so he drove the wagon down the road into Jericho. He turned the team into a narrow difficult alley to the house of an acquaintance. He would inquire there.

CHAPTER 7

N ehemiah came out of his house to greet Lapidoth, kissing him on both cheeks. "What brings you here, my friend? It has been a long time! Come in and rest yourself! And who are these children?"

Lapidoth motioned three wide-eyed children to follow him. He stepped into Nehemiah's beautiful house, gratefully accepting the invitation. He told Nehemiah about the raid in Tirzah and how they barely escaped. He introduced the children as survivors of the raid. Immediately and mercifully the three were taken to the kitchen to be fed and cared for by Nehemiah's housekeeper, Dinah.

"Have you heard anything of my wife, Deborah, and a small band of people who also escaped and traveled separately from me?"

"Your wife?" Nehemiah's brows furrowed. "How did you get separated?"

"It was my own foolishness. Can you help me?"

Sensing Lapidoth's discomfort he did not pursue the question. "I have not heard, but I will send a servant to inquire. Servants have swift and secret lines of communication. If they arrived we will know within the hour. I pray they are safe!"

For the first time, Lapidoth was not at all sure of himself. He was accustomed to being alone, traveling alone, and not being questioned about his decisions. The terrifying certainty flooded into his mind that in the eyes of his friend and surely others, he should not have left Deborah. Now his hands began to shake and his mouth went dry. He had abandoned his wife without servants or family around her. She was alone with strangers and it was his fault. It was his responsibility to keep her safe.

Nehemiah poured them both some wine and sat down to await the servant. "You are married, Lapidoth? I never thought you would marry! All the young girls pined after you, and you never even looked at them!" laughed Nehemiah.

"I was not a good choice for any girl of the village since I was absent for months at a time. One night I had a dream. Her name was in the dream and instructions that I must visit my cousin Hannah in Kadesh-Napthali. Deborah is a young friend of my cousin Hannah. She is educated in the scriptures, herbs and healing. She was a counselor to many in her village. It was as though she expected me! Deborah, I mean. Yes and Hannah too. Nothing could ever be hidden from Hannah."

True to Nehemiah's prediction the servant, Agur, was back in a short time. "Master, we have heard nothing of these people. Nothing of a woman named Deborah. I am sorry. Shall I try again farther north on the river?"

"We shall all go!" announced Nehemiah. "Agur! Gather the men servants, saddle horses, and mules. Come Lapidoth, we will ride north and find her!"

Lapidoth was still in shock. He felt sick with shame and terror at the same time, two new emotions for him. He was responsible for any harm that might come to her. He had left her alone and in danger. He wondered what Nehemiah was thinking.

Mounted and on their way, they hastened out of Jericho to the north along the trade route that followed the Jordan River. The road before the rule of Jabin was very busy. Now it was deserted. Lapidoth's heart sank. Had Sisera's men followed them this far after all?

They rode swiftly to the north half way to Tirzah and started back south. Evening was darkening overhead and still no sign of Deborah or the others. Lapidoth managed to banish the terrifying images that came to his mind so he could think clearly.

"Nehemiah, there is a road to Ai not far from here. Deborah knew my people's village to be in that direction. Perhaps they did not risk coming to a strange city such as Jericho, and thought it safer to take the road to the west. In the haste of escaping the raid I did not think to give her your name or tell her to come to Jericho and ask for you in the marketplace. How stupid of me!"

"Lapidoth, you are not stupid! You were barely escaping with your lives! What man, unless he is an army general accustomed to battle decisions, thinks of everything at a time like that? We will take the road to Ai. It is a good suggestion. We will not get to the city before dark. We will have to camp for the night. But we will go as far as we can."

"What exactly did you tell her?" asked Nehemiah.

"I told her to head south. I would go back to Tirzah for our belongings and anyone who might have survived the raid, and I would catch up with her. So she may even think I am dead. She may think Sisera's men caught me when I went back to Tirzah and killed me. She is alone not knowing if her husband is dead or live."

"What was so important that you went back?" asked Nehemiah.

Lapidoth drew a deep breath and prepared a face-saving lie so Nehemiah would be satisfied enough to cease his questioning. "Deborah had something in her possession that was extremely important to her. So important she did not trust me to know what it was. I saw her stow some papyrus away in her bundle.

Each time I was about to ask her about it she changed the subject abruptly. She has many mysteries about her, and I must wait until she trusts me completely to learn what they are. So, I went back to find her possessions if possible. It seemed like a case of life and death to her."

He was ashamed to lie about her. Most likely Deborah had taken everything important with her, but he decided not to share that with Nehemiah. He could not bring himself to say that his horse, wagon, and mules were the reason he risked his life. It sounded so paltry and ridiculous. Nehemiah would certainly think he should value his wife above these things and rightly disapprove!

"How strange," mused Nehemiah. "The secrets women carry are usually not on papyrus, but in their hearts."

"Deborah is not the usual woman. She believes she has a high calling from God and it takes her places other women do not go. I have pledged to honor that calling wherever it takes us."

"You have pledged?"

"Yes, Hannah insisted. And one does not refuse or go back on a pledge to Hannah!"

"How will you know it is true?"

"Because I saw Deborah in a dream, heard her name, saw her as my wife, and was instructed to visit Hannah. It seems I am part of whatever it is. I could not refuse." Again a lie to save his honor.

Night was indeed falling and the servants began to set up a camp near some trees. They were in the hills now and the cold night air chilled them quickly.

* * *

The others from the inn had continued on toward Jericho or to other places beyond the Jordan. Deborah chose to turn toward Bethel-Ramah where she was sure Lapidoth would catch up to her on the road. The climb from the river into the higher elevations was difficult. Sometimes the road became as narrow as a goat path and threatened at times to disappear altogether.

When there was no sign of Lapidoth, she left the road to find shelter for the night. She stumbled upon a small hut that was almost hidden by brush. Cautiously she made a way in pushing away the branches and watching for animals that might have taken up residence there. Relieved there were none, she crept in. She wrapped herself in all the clothing in her bag against the night chill, and dosed fitfully, watching for the morning light.

Dreams came in the night of her riding a horse leading army troops, Deborah and Barak arguing over battle plans, and the enemy coming at a dead run toward them. She woke up with a jolt when she heard voices. It was finally dawn. Someone was calling her name!

Slowly she got up and dragged her bundle as she crawled out of the hut. The dazzling white sky of morning stung her eyes until she could hardly see. She scrambled over the brush and rocks toward the road. The calling was getting fainter. They were not coming toward her, but had passed her and were going away. She got to the road and looked everywhere, but could see no one. She shouted Lapidoth's name repeatedly, but no answering call came back.

"Did I dream it?" she thought. "I hardly slept and yet there were armies and battles, and then someone calling my name."

As the morning wore on Deborah trudged in the direction of the sun as it moved from the east westward. She climbed to the top of a pass and looked down. In the distance she could see a line that looked like another road. "That is the road I thought I had taken. No wonder this one looks more and more a goat path. It is a goat path!" She turned around and around trying to get her bearings.

"How could I have been so foolish? When the others went south and east, I simply took the first turn to the west. It was not the road at all. "Lapidoth where are you? Where am I?"

Deborah sat down on a large rock, the wind blowing through her hair. "Pray. I must pray! Hannah would tell me that. Oh, Hannah, how far away you seem now. Are you safe? Is my family safe? Has Sisera passed by our village without harming it? Oh, God, I pray it is so." She closed her eyes and prayed with all her heart that God would be with her and all she loved.

"Are you lost, woman?"

Deborah opened her eyes with a start and turned to see an elderly shepherd standing before her.

"I am Othniel of Bethel," he said. "I am driving my flocks down from the heights for the winter. May I help you?"

"I am going to Bethel-Ramah, to the people of my husband, Lapidoth. I thought I was on the right road, but now I see I am not. I believe I am still going in the right direction. I was just praying to God to keep my family safe."

"You are indeed going in the right direction. You have simply taken the shepherd's path, which is much harder, but you are safe from soldiers here. How do you come to be traveling alone? Why is your husband not with you?"

The question took Deborah by surprise. It had not occurred to her that anyone would question why her husband was not with her. Now she was embarrassed. She recounted the attack at Tirzah and how they escaped. "Lapidoth sent me on south along the Jordan River. He went back to Tirzah to see if anyone had survived and to get our wagon and animals if the marauders had not taken them. He promised he would catch up with me on the road."

The shepherd pulled his long gray beard. "That was a dangerous thing to do to, go back. How can you know if he is dead or alive?"

Deborah's eyes widened. She had not thought that Lapidoth might actually be killed. "I cannot know! Perhaps I really am alone!" she whispered.

"I-I thought I heard him call my name this morning, but it may have been a dream. I really do not know," she said barely breathing. "I rushed toward the sound, but it faded Perhaps it was not there at all, but just the wind in the rocks."

"Is your name Deborah?"

"Yes, I am Deborah."

"You were not dreaming. I heard it too. But it was many hours ago and sounded far away. He must have been on the main road."

Relieved, Deborah exhaled and dropped her face into her hands.

"You are welcome to travel with me as my young son and I drive our sheep home. It will take longer but you will not be alone. Bethel is not so far away. We should be there by evening. Come with us."

"I should hurry!" replied a worried Deborah. "I should catch up with my husband." The word husband was so new to her that it sounded strange to her ears. Her husband. She was married. How odd it felt to think those words.

"If I may suggest it, you would be safer with us. If you are attacked, you may not get there at all. Soldiers and thieves are everywhere. Please, let us help you."

For the first time Deborah's eyes focused on the kindly face of Othniel. She could see the concern in his eyes and realized it would be foolish to go on alone. After all, she had prayed and God had sent help. Here was his answer. "Yes, I will go with you. Where are your flocks and your young son?"

"They are just behind us. I was traveling ahead to be sure we could get through. Sometimes the large stones tumble into the path during storms." Turning he pointed at an opening in the rocks where a few sheep were appearing and bleating loudly. They kept coming until Deborah thought all the sheep in the world must be there. Soon a young freckle faced boy with sun-bleached hair appeared in the midst of them urging them on.

"This is my son, Joshua. Does he not look like Joshua leading the people to the Promised Land?" said Othniel with a half toothless grin. "He is my only son and the treasure of my heart."

Deborah smiled. She remembered when Barak was his age, and Moshe. "I can see he is a fine boy," affirmed Deborah. The three of them followed the sheep down toward the valley and Bethel.

"Can you tell me anything of Lapidoth's family? Do you know them?"

"I know only Joab, a hard working man. He suffered an injury many years ago, and oversees the fields. He has been kindly toward me when I passed his way."

Deborah felt a little more hopeful at hearing these words. Perhaps there was one in the family of Lapidoth that was not completely frightening.

"Are the land and the town of Bethel prosperous? Are they good places to live?"

"Ah yes. Ephraim is a good tribe. We are far enough from the Philistines that they leave us alone. There are far more prosperous cities for them to raid near the coast of the Great Sea."

"Have you seen the Great Sea?"

"Oh indeed I have. When I was a very young man, we fought the sea peoples and beat them back into the waters. It was a magnificent sight! The waves were crashing upon the shore and coming closer to us with each one. But then we dared not linger for fear others might be coming. So we quickly retreated into the hills and home."

"Did you have battle plans? Was your army trained?"

"Army? Battle plans? We were young fools. We grabbed our crude weapons and ran as fast as we could after them! We had no leader. We shouted mightily and they dropped their weapons and ran! They were very young too. Now that I think about it, they were probably a hunting party gathering food and not prepared for battle. And we were foolish enough to take after them, not really knowing who they were. There could have been a huge army behind them to greet us! And I would not be here to talk to you, or enjoy my son and our sheep."

Deborah was a little disappointed. She thought it was her first chance to hear about war and battles, and it was only a chase. But she did think about the foolishness of charging forward without knowing what was ahead. Surely God will keep her and Barak safe from that folly.

Barak. Where was he now? She had gone away with Lapidoth without a thought of Barak or of sending him a message. She was so concerned with his turning back to God that she had not thought about her upcoming marriage at all when she last spoke with him.

Then came the marriage ceremony and it was all done in such haste. She had not had time to think of anything except getting to know Lapidoth and fleeing Sisera.

"Are you ill?" inquired the Othniel. Deborah did not realize she had suddenly turned pale and faltered in her step. "Have you eaten?"

"No, I brought no food with me." She told him briefly of their quick marriage and flight from Sisera. "I have just begun to think back over it all. It is a shock."

He handed her a bag of dates which she gratefully accepted. She had not realized how hungry she was.

"Perhaps it is better to think of now and look to the future. We can do nothing about the past. It can only disturb our happiness," mused Othniel.

Deborah was a little surprised at the wisdom of this old shepherd.

He continued, "Shepherds often tend the sheep near the end of their lives by choice. They have seen much of life and prefer the quiet times on the hillsides and by the streams. God is so much closer there and temptations to join the sins of man's wars and strife seem to fade."

Yes, how much Deborah missed those times with Hannah and the quiet hills around her home. And then the quiet times in Rabbi Amri's study with Ya'akov and the scriptures. Hannah told her she could always take prayer and scripture with her, but not the quiet hills and the peaceful study. How hard it will be to remember those places within her in the midst of battle! Yes, God must be there too! She and Barak could not do it alone.

The day was cool and the sun was warm. Breezes played around their robes and hair. Othniel walked briskly along tapping his shepherd's crook with every other step. Something in Deborah wanted this peaceful moment to go on forever. Facing Lapidoth's family would surely be an unwelcome trial and peace would be a dream of the past.

CHAPTER 8

Abel pointed out the new location to Barak as they rode over a low ridge. "Up there on the ledge," he said. "There is a hidden valley and a lake beyond it, completely defensible. No one can sneak up on us and we would have the advantage being up high. There is even room to raise food and graze sheep."

"No one lives there?" asked Barak. "You are certain? Such a beautiful place!"

"We saw no evidence of anyone living there. I searched the place personally along with several of my officers and found no abandoned pots or lamps. I believe it is too remote for a village. We found it quite by accident. We were chasing a small herd of deer."

"I want to have a look," said Barak as he kicked his horse and galloped off. Abel rode after him. When Barak arrived at the site he still couldn't believe his eyes. It was beautiful with water and olive trees, and a huge flat space for the troops. It would take a little time to get the whole army here because the passages were narrow. But that would have its advantages too.

Abel went back to bring the soldiers forward while Barak stayed in the valley to explore and to arrange in his mind how the camp would look. "Deborah. How far away she seems. Was it a lifetime ago when she and Abinoam came to my encampment? We were so excited by our plans to share scripture and battle strategy. Now it is more like a dream that is fading by the day. Somehow I must find out if my father and mother are safe, and Deborah's family as well." He felt growing anger at her disappearance. How could she just abandon him?

He began to sketch out the assignments for his scouts. He needed information urgently for his army and for himself. Where were Sisera and his men? Where was Deborah? Did she get away safely? There was so much he needed to know.

Evening was falling as Barak came back to the ridge to meet the army. They were traveling slowly at night again so their whereabouts would not be revealed to anyone. Barak still could not believe no one inhabited this area, but like Abel he saw no evidence of human occupation. God had indeed blessed them.

There was rustling a short distance from Barak. He drew his knife and turned toward the noise. It was only the first of his army coming through the brush and rocks. The men struggled with bundles, animals, and equipment all night and the next few days as the camp area filled up. But spirits were high and relief shone on their faces as they approached their final campsite. The weeks of moving through mountains and forests were over for now.

*   *   *

Deborah's first glimpse of dusty little Bethel was disappointing. She had pictured Lapidoth's home as a little more grand, larger with buildings and clean streets. Bethel was mostly scattered huts, some in small groups, and not much else she could see from where they stood. She turned away so Othniel would not see the disappointment on her face.

"See, we are almost there. Now you will find your husband's people," said Othniel helpfully. "The village is small, but there are places beyond what we can see with many families."

"You go on ahead, Othniel and thank you. I need time to think. I will be alright so close to the village."

Othniel looked at her doubtfully. "No place is safe for a woman alone. Please, come with us and I will find you a place to stay. Or we will wait with you right here."

"But you cannot wait for me. Your sheep! Evening is coming. Please, go on without me."

"Joshua! Take the herd to Bethel. I will follow when Deborah decides to come with us."

Joshua blew his flute and the bellwether turned to follow him. All the sheep picked up their heads and lumbered after the lead ram, their dusty wool full of twigs and leaves. Othniel sat down on a rock to wait.

"Othniel, you are putting yourself in danger as well. Even together we cannot fight off an attacker."

"As you have said, Deborah, is it not best that we continue into the village? You can stay in my cousin's place until you make up your mind what to do. My cousin is away and will not return."

Deborah threw up her hands and agreed to go. She pulled her hood forward to cover her face and walked with her head down, praying that no one would stop them. Arriving in the village they walked among the tiny houses, dodging goats and sheep. Othniel indicated a small place near a quiet olive grove.

Deborah was still doubtful, but entering the hut she found it neat and clean. "I will bring you food and fresh straw for your pallet," announced Othniel as he turned and abruptly left before she could object.

Deborah sat down on a small wooden stool and sighed. "If only Hannah were here," she mused. "She would help me know what to do."

But Deborah knew what Hannah would say. She would say, "You are married to the man and God is still leading you. Have no fear. Continue on!"

Joshua and Othniel arrived with the straw and food. Joshua spread the straw on her bed and Othniel started a cooking fire in the crude oven. Deborah stepped beside Othniel and took over preparing the food. "Thank you. You have been most kind and I will remember your kindness."

"We are not far away. If you call we will hear you." Othniel and Joshua bid her a good night and went home.

*   *   *

Nehemiah and Lapidoth arrived in Ramah having failed to find Deborah. Lapidoth was becoming more and more alarmed. "What can I do? I have failed her! What if she was attacked and taken away? She might even be dead or worse!"

"In the morning we will go back the way we came and question everyone we see. You insisted we dash headlong and in our hurry we did not stop to inquire of others. She is somewhere close by, I can feel it," said Nehemiah.

Lapidoth paced their room at the inn wringing his hands and berating himself. "If I had stayed with her this would not have happened. But no! I had to go back! How stupid and shortsighted could I be? I should have been with her to protect her and bring her to my home. Now I cannot go home with out her because my family will see how stupid I am."

"You brought three children out of danger, Lapidoth. Do not forget that. There is no reason to claw at yourself now. You made a decision for what sounded like good reasons at a difficult time. You were running for your lives. So we go forward from here until we find her."

"But suppose she lies dead somewhere! We might be searching for weeks."

"She could be thinking the same thing of you, Lapidoth. She does not know if you are dead or alive. She has no evidence that you were not killed in Tirzah. Both of you are survivors. Have a little faith in God that she is still guided in safety as were you. Come now, have some wine and cheese, and calm yourself."

"You are probably right, Nehemiah. I just feel so guilty, so responsible if anything should happen to her. Hannah would never forgive me. She already haunts my dreams."

"We will set out at first light, my friend. Pray to God that he guides us to her and she to us unharmed. Sleep well. You are exhausted. We will make a fresh start in the morning."

Lapidoth drank the wine offered and ate sparingly. He laid down on his pallet praying that sleep would come. Fearful accusing thoughts finally gave way to disturbing dreams. Hannah was shaking her finger at him and saying words he could not quite hear. He awoke with a start when Nehemiah came back into the room.

"I left you to sleep while I prepared for our continuing search. We have bread, cheese, and figs to eat on the way."

Lapidoth shook his head and rubbed his eyes. "I was dreaming."

"Did you find her in your dream?"

"No, just Hannah shaking her finger at me."

"Was she admonishing you or pointing the way to go?"

Lapidoth had not thought about that. He was so sure Hannah was disapproving that he could not understand what she was really saying.

"She was pointing past me to the east. Was she telling me we passed Deborah and did not know it?"

"It is a good sign, Lapidoth. Let us go now and question everyone we see. It will take longer to go a distance, but the search might be shortened considerably if someone has seen her."

Lapidoth agreed and they hurried to the stable for their horses. Nehemiah's servants were instructed to go through the whole villages of Ramah and Bethel and up into the hills asking if anyone had seen Deborah.

"How could we have missed her on the road, Nehemiah?"

"She was not on that road, Lapidoth. There are other roads in the hills that the shepherds use. She could have turned onto one of them not realizing they were not the main road."

"Then she could be anywhere!"

"As you said, Deborah knows the direction and will follow the sun westward. She is not lost in the hills if she followed those paths because they all run east and west even though they wander some. It would just take longer because travel would be slower."

The servants ran from house to house and stopped travelers at the village well. They returned to Nehemiah and Lapidoth breathless. "No one has seen Deborah," they reported.

The search continued on the road to Bethel with the servants scouring the hills for shepherds. The going was slow and Lapidoth kept getting the strong urge to hurry on. But Nehemiah insisted on being thorough. "If we are not thorough and do not find her then our time is wasted. We cannot afford to be careless and miss her."

Early in the morning Othniel stopped at Deborah's hut to check on her, but she was gone. He looked around and went to the village well, but she was nowhere in sight. He asked a few of the town's people but they did not see a woman leave. He went to the sheepfold thinking maybe she had gone with Joshua or stopped to talk to him. Joshua shook his head. She was not with him.

Hannah's voice had been soft in Deborah's dream. "You have come this far. There is nothing to fear. God will lead you just as he has always done. Go now to the family of Lapidoth and wait there."

Deborah rose long before dawn, packed the remains of the food Othniel had brought, picked up her bag and set out toward the west again. "It cannot be very far. It is between Bethel and Ramah as Lapidoth said. Someone along the way must know where his relatives live," said Deborah mostly to herself.

She chose the peaceful paths of the herds rather than the main road where soldiers might be traveling. The sun was bright and the breeze cool, and Hannah's words in her dream gave her courage to go on. "How could I forget God? How could I forget all he has done for me, all of my prayers he has answered? Somehow my mission with Barak must be fulfilled and only God knows how. Barak! Where is he now? Has he avoided Sisera's men? And Moshe! He is so young and eager to join the army. If Sisera raids the village, God will surely hide him. Oh, what am I thinking? There is nothing I can do. Hannah said I must first have faith. How elusive faith becomes when there is trouble and I am so far away."

As the day brightened Deborah's step became livelier and a smile appeared on her face. For some reason she was feeling joy and happiness. The fog in her mind cleared and the future looked bright. "I must do my part and God will do his!" She asked God at every fork in the path and confidently followed the urging. She almost wanted to run, but the ground was too stony in the hills and treacherous shale covered the slopes.

She came to a stream, stopped to listen to the waterfall on the rocks, and watched it disappear into the grasses below. The euphoria came to an abrupt halt when two soldiers appeared down below. She stopped and dropped to her knees behind a rock, praying they had not seen her. The men sat down by the stream and began to eat and drink, laughing and joking. There was nothing Deborah could do but wait them out hoping they would soon leave so she could be on her way. Much to Deborah's chagrin, they lay back in the grass and proceeded to nap.

She looked round to see if there might be a way to sneak off undetected. The only possibility was to go north deeper into the wilderness and hopefully pick up another path farther on. As she started to move, some gravel slid and went clattering down the hillside. Deborah froze, her heart pounding wildly. But it seemed the soldiers were in a drunken slumber, undisturbed by the sound. She resolved to be more careful and move more slowly even thought she desperately wanted to run.

The paths became more erratic and sometimes hard to find. She couldn't tell if she was following shepherds' paths or wild goat paths. She kept watching the sun to keep her direction. As the time moved into noonday and the sun was overhead, it was more difficult to determine if she was still traveling westward. There were brambles and snares that tore at her hem and precipitous cliffs to avoid. Fear overtook her mind and she called out to God desperately from time to time. Then she sat down to rest and thought, "What did Hannah say? I must be calm and quiet in order to hear God. I cannot hear him through raging fears and terrors."

She sat quietly until she was startled by a low growl. "My God what could that be? A lion? A wolf? What?" She got up and slowly moved away from the sound. Looking back as she went she tripped and tumbled down an embankment. Her knees and hands stung from the rocks. She lay very still listening and suddenly there was the yelping of a dog above her. She tried to scramble away when a voice called out to the dog and it whimpered. The very authoritative voice came from a young woman, which surprised Deborah.

"Are you hurt?"

"Not much I think," called back Deborah.

"Did my dog frighten you?"

"I guess so. I was not sure what animal the growl came from"

"He will not hurt you. He was chasing a wild animal away from me. Can I help you up?"

"Yes, thank you." She held up her hand and a very strong hand met hers. She scrambled up the embankment and brushed her tunic around the knees. Looking up into a tanned face and friendly smile she said, "My name is Deborah."

CHAPTER 9

"**D**eborah? People have been asking all over the countryside if someone has seen you! You are the wife of Lapidoth, my cousin! My name is Rahab."

Deborah burst out laughing, mostly from relief. This was the cousin that Lapidoth told her about, the independent loose woman.

"I have heard of you, Rahab."

"I will bet you have! The family does not think highly of me and I am sure Lapidoth told you that."

"Yes, he did. But I like to meet people and decide for myself about them."

"How did you get here? I observed Lapidoth from afar and he was frantic! I would not wish you harm, but it was amusing to see him lose his composure for the first time. He is always so assured and self-contained. He can be so stiff-necked!"

They sat down together on a large rock and Deborah told Rahab the story of their escape from Tirzah.

"It is good that you avoided the solders. I saw them ride through the town and they were not anyone you would want to meet alone out here. I always carry a curved knife in my sleeve to defend myself."

"Have you ever had to do that? Defend yourself?" queried Deborah astonished at the frankness and boldness of this woman.

"Oh yes. I have not had to use it on a man. I just start to pull it from my sleeve and they walk away. However, I am quite skilled at using it. Wild animals are always threatening the sheep. That is how I practice."

"Oh, I am going to like Rahab, I am sure," thought Deborah. "Another secret I must keep from Lapidoth if he really disapproves of her. She has the courage I have always dreamed about and longed for. The courage of a warrior!"

"Would you like me to take you to our family? I am sure Lapidoth will be relieved to see you."

"Can we go slowly, Rahab? I would like to spend some time with you. If you would, please tell me more about yourself."

Rahab laughed. "We are already off course. You walked a long way north to avoid the soldiers. It will be a longer walk back. I have a place we can stay for the night. Come with me!"

Rahab ran up a goat path leading high into the hills. Deborah hesitated, but then ran after her wondering, "Can I trust her? I do not even know where I am. But I asked God for help so I must trust. Is this what Hannah was trying to teach me?"

As evening was falling they arrived at a small two-room house, much like Hannah's. There was a garden, a few small trees, and a low stone fence. "Did you do all this, Rahab?" asked Deborah breathlessly.

"Yes, most of it. It was a herder's shelter. The foundation of the house was here and I kept piling stones on it until the walls were high enough, and then I made the roof out of branches. I need a place of my own where I can be alone. That is not possible near the family. So I made this one my secret home alone and far enough away. This is why they think I am wild and a harlot because I go away for weeks at a time. Shepherd girls do it all the time. But I am not with sheep or with family men. I am with me! No one understands that."

"I think I understand it, Rahab. I never wanted to be married or have children. I wanted to live my own life and not the way someone else wanted me to. It was awful that my father began to arrange my life without even consulting me. He just took me to the home of the man he decided would be my prospective husband! I nearly choked. In fact I did exactly that by loosing my breakfast in the garden right in front of the poor young man. He confessed that he felt the same way and we had a good laugh together."

"And then what happened? How did you avoid the marriage?" queried Rahab. "I cannot believe he would not want you!"

"We had a mutual agreement. He was very sweet. His name was Ya'akov and we became friends and study companions. His father was a rabbi and agreed to tutor both of us. Ya'akov's health was very frail and after a few years he died during one really cold wet winter."

"But why on earth did you marry Lapidoth? What happened to your desire to stay unmarried? And he is not sweet! He is very rigid and controlling. Do you know that about him?"

"I saw Lapidoth being strong and in charge, subtly putting my father in his place. I enjoyed that. After we were married I saw the controlling side of him," puzzled Deborah. "At first I thought it was just thoughtlessness. Tirzah was the first time he went off and left me alone. He just handed me the reins of the mules and rode off toward Tirzah on his horse. I learned right there to handle the wagon and mules."

"Yes, that sounds like him. Completely unaware and lacking in social skills."

"Why did I marry him? He and your cousin Hannah brought us together. He heard my name in a dream and Hannah, who is a seer, knew he was coming to consult with her. She knew it was about me. My friend Ya'akov died leaving me with no defense against my father's match making. At least this one might be my choice and not his. It seemed like a plan from God."

"A plan from God? I hope God has no such plans for me!" gasped Rahab.

Rahab and Deborah talked far into the night about Rahab's life, about Ya'akov and their studies together. They ate the bread and figs Deborah had brought from Bethel, and drifted off to sleep in the wee small hours of the morning almost in mid-conversation.

*   *   *

Barak and Abel were sipping some wine with bread and cheese after inspecting the camp. Gideon, one of Barak's trusted spies, came bursting into Barak's tent. "I have just come from Gath and saw the Philistines attacking the city. Then they began to move north. I could not get close enough to know if they will turn east or if they are going to Shechem, maybe further to Taanach!"

"If they turn east we may be right in their path!" said Abel to Barak in alarm. "Do you suppose by some chance they know about this place and will come here?"

"They might go to the territory of Manasseh to Taanach. They like to stay along the coast where they can run back to Gaza when pursued. There is no reason why they should come across the passes to the east," assured Barak with more bravado then he felt. "We are far enough to the south of Shechem and the major trading center. They will be more interested in the cities they can loot."

"If they go too far north, Sisera will come after them. Perhaps they will destroy each other and leave us alone," offered Abel. "What of Naham? We have not heard from him. You sent him to Kadesh-Napthali to see about your father. I pray they do not capture him. Sisera's men will torture him and he could give away our position."

"I am not worried about Naham. He is slippery as an eel. He can blend into any background and disappear into the shadows. He will return when it is safe and will not give us away. He would rather die than do that," scoffed Barak.

Gideon moved tentatively toward the tent door, assuming he was not needed further. He did not want to hear conversations that were not for his ears. "Gideon! Good work!" said Abel. "Take your rest and we will decide what to do next."

"I will be ready to look for Naham and find out what Sisera's goons are up to. I can help you plan raids on them to defend our villages. It is about time we taught them a lesson! They burned my family's village and others as well. We have to find a way to stop them."

Barak's eyebrows shot up. He had not heard Gideon speak like this before. He just accepted his orders and brought back information. "Forgive me, Gideon. I should have remembered about your family. We will begin warfare against Sisera soon. Go now to your bed and we will summon you in a few hours."

"It would be good to send Gideon to find Naham," said Abel. "They are cousins. I can send another team to keep track of the Philistines. I think Sisera is more of a threat right now than those Philistine jackals. Philistines hug the coast and drive everyone else far into the hills. They terrorize and torture the people to make sure they will not think of coming back to their homes."

Barak scowled. "Deborah. I must know where she is . . . what happened to her after the wedding, after the attacks on the villages."

"What is it that drives you to find her, Barak? I do not mean to intrude, but perhaps I can be of more help."

"Deborah and I have a commission from God to strengthen our army. I have part of the plan and she has the other. We must work this out together. I have to find her!"

"So, you believe God has a hand in this after all?"

"Yes, Abel. Even though we marched on the Sabbath, I do believe we need God. I just do not believe God is so picky as to punish us for such a simple thing. God is greater than our small foolishness. God's plan to free our people is so large it is beyond our comprehension. Deborah is going to bring God's wisdom to us for our victory over Jabin."

"Victory over Jabin? How can we possibly defeat Jabin, the Canaanite king? Sisera is not his only general. He has other allies we do not know about."

"Do you think we can just be a gnat on Sisera's backside? Do you not think he will come after us with all his forces? Abel, we must have a decisive victory with the complete defeat of Sisera's forces, iron chariots and all."

Abel felt a shiver go all through his body. "I guess the time is coming when we will not just be playing soldier, setting up camps and practicing combat drills. We will be in the thick of it with no turning back."

"The more we 'play soldier' as you put it, the more prepared we will be for the real thing. We must be skilled and disciplined. Sisera's army will be no easy enemy. It is not like chasing off some renegade marauders. Many will die on both sides."

"Are you ever afraid, Barak?"

"As you well know, I awake in the night after dreams of battle sweating and gasping. But I only fear at night when I have no control over what my mind does. But during the day I cannot afford to entertain fears, only thoughts of victory."

* * *

In the night Gideon crept into the villages one by one and the people hid him by day. They gathered information for him that came from bandits and sheepherders in the hills. Words were passed quietly as people passed each other in the marketplaces. Damaged as these places were, they were all the villagers had to keep their commerce alive. Caravans did not travel through the provinces of Napthali and Manasseh. Instead they traveled east of the Jordan to avoid King Jabin's oppressive taxes and theft of their goods by Sisera's men.

Gideon managed to get to Kadesh-Napthali to look for Barak's father, Abimoam, and Deborah's family. The door he knocked on was that of Amri and Leah. "I am Gideon. I come from Barak to inquire about his father and Deborah. Is Abinoam still alive?"

"Come in quickly," said Amri, "and have some refreshment."

Gideon stepped inside, looking behind as was his habit, to be sure he wasn't followed.

"Tonight it is quite safe, Gideon. We do not know about tomorrow. But then do we ever know about tomorrow?" Rabbi Amri said smiling sadly.

Gideon gratefully took the food Leah offered and wolfed it down. "Forgive my manners, but I must not linger. Can you tell me of Abinoam and Sarah, and Deborah, and her family?"

"Yes, of course. Forgive me. Abinoam and Sarah are still here and unharmed. The marauders went though the village quickly as though they were hurrying to a destination farther south. There was little damage and the people were unhurt. Abinoam and Sarah are in their home as are Deborah's family. Deborah and Lapidoth were married many weeks ago and quickly traveled south to the home of Lapidoth's people in Ephraim. I pray Sisera's men did not catch up with them!"

Gideon left before dawn to return to Barak. Following a goat path into the mountains he came upon the camp of some local thieves. It was empty except for a crippled dog that was foraging for the scraps of food left by the bandits. As he circled past the camp he heard someone moaning. He stopped to listen. It was coming from a clump of scrub trees.

Cautiously he moved closer until he could see a face, a bloodied face. It was Naham!

What was he doing here? Gideon could see he was unconscious. He picked up Naham who was small of stature, and carried him away on his shoulders. He found the path by which he had come earlier and stopped at a small bubbling spring. He placed Naham carefully on a grassy bank and began to wipe his face with a piece of his robe dipped in the cool water.

Naham cried out and opened his eyes. "Gideon! How did you find me?"

"Better question, how did you manage to get yourself caught? Why are you here?"

"Barak sent me to find you. He thought I could help if you were in trouble."

"Right! If I am in trouble? Look at you!"

Naham looked suddenly embarrassed and pulled himself upright. "Yes, look at me! Will you tell Barak?"

"No, I will not tell Barak. You and I met on the goat path as I was returning, that is the truth. Nothing else need be said."

"Did you get the information Barak wanted?"

"Yes, most of it. Deborah and her husband went south, and Sisera's men after them in the same direction. I do not think they were actually after them, but I pray they did not catch up to them. I have a letter to deliver to Barak about Deborah. Can you walk?"

"Yes, I think so. My leg is a little sore and my head feels like I tangled with a mountain lion, but I will make it."

"I will find you a walking stick to lean on," said Gideon as he turned to search the area. He cut down a sapling and trimmed the twigs away to make it smooth.

Naham ducked his head into the cold spring water to clear his mind and wash away the blood. The cold water shocked him awake. He took a long drink and joined Gideon. Despite Naham's wounds and bruises they hiked for several hours before stopping.

"Philistines!" said Gideon as though a light had come on in his mind. "Those men who beat you up were Philistines."

"How do you know?"

"Fish. I smelled fish and salt water. I was near the Great Sea once and I know that smell."

"What do you think they are doing this far east? I thought they stayed near the shore and did not come this far inland."

"I do not know. But we better be more careful and get back to Barak as fast as we can. I know a trail that is shorter, but it is more difficult. We will have to climb. Can you do that Naham? Are you feeling well enough to scale some rather steep cliffs?"

"I will do it or die trying," puffed Naham.

"Here, take some of my bread and cheese. It was given to me at the house of Rabbi Amri and Leah in Kadesh. It will make you feel stronger."

Gratefully Naham stuffed the food into his mouth as they started off again. Gideon led them through a wooded area that came out near a cliff. They walked around the bottom of it until they found handholds and a footpath probably made by goats. "You go up first, Naham, and I will give you a shove if you slip. We will do this quickly so we are not exposed for too long. We do not know who might be watching."

The climb was hard, the rock ledges cut their hands, but they managed to make it without slipping or falling. Once on top they headed again for the wooded areas. They traveled on for hours, hoping to find shelter before nightfall. It would be another two days before they reached the camp and Naham was limping badly.

"Do not worry about me, Gideon. Just keep going. Even if you have to leave me behind, you must get to camp and warn Barak about the Philistines who are wandering around in these mountains."

"I am not leaving you behind, Naham! We may be able to find an animal to carry us. Some villagers might help us if they know who we are. There is a village in the hills I have visited that is not too far away. We can go in that direction and I will speak with them. If we can get animals we can travel faster."

"I am not so sure, Gideon. Animals make noise. They call to each other and may give us away if we need to hide."

Gideon frowned. "A blindfold or feed bag will keep them quiet."

They pushed on for the rest of the day, not finding the village. They slept in a crude hut made of stones and branches. It was cold, but they could not risk a fire.

They rose before dawn. Slapping their arms and legs against the cold they trudged on. At noon they heard many hoof beats. Diving for cover Gideon was ready to attack whoever it was and take their horse.

"It is Abel! He has men with him!" whispered Naham. They rose from their hiding place and ran to meet him. Abel jumped off his horse and ran to embrace them.

"Barak feared you were captured or dead! So he sent us to look for you."

"How did you know which way we would come?" queried Gideon.

"Do you remember long ago we used to follow these paths together?"

"I guess I am too weary to remember. But yes, we did travel together in these parts. We are not dead or captured, but can use your help."

The word captured made Naham snatch his breath, but he knew Gideon would keep his word.

Abel laughed as they gave Gideon and Naham a leg up onto their horses and turned to head back to the camp.

CHAPTER 10

Not finding Deborah in Bethel or beyond toward Jericho, Lapidoth and Nehemiah turned their horses north up into the hills. The shepherd boy, Joshua, told them she was in Bethel but was gone by morning. This angered Lapidoth to think she would leave the relative safety of the village to go wandering in the hills alone.

Lapidoth went over and over the conversation with Joshua in his head. "There are many paths up there because herders come from all directions to Bethel. Which way do you think she went, Joshua?"

Joshua smiled and shrugged. "I did not see her leave. It was before dawn."

From time to time they all called out Deborah's name, but there was no answer. The silence was deafening. Lapidoth felt lonelier that he had ever felt in his life. Even in strange lands he traveled as a merchant, in charge and in control. Deborah's face was before him and Hannah's scolding voice was in his ears. Nehemiah was becoming worried as well. His usual assurances became less frequent.

"I think it is time for you to go home, Lapidoth. She might already be there. Your workers can send out a search party and scour the hills. They know them better than we do."

Lapidoth nodded. "Will you come with me, Nehemiah?"

"No, my friend, I must return to Jericho. Pray, Lapidoth. Pray to God for her safe return and I will pray as well."

They embraced and parted company. Lapidoth gave one last look up into the hills before turning toward Bethel and Ramah. Nehemiah waved as he called his servants to him and guided his horse down to the main road and southeast to Jericho.

Lapidoth turned and rode furiously toward the west and his family farm. The hot mid-afternoon was upon him. Perhaps this would be one last chance to find Deborah. He knew the first trail he came to that led west would lead to his family's lower grazing fields and home. Home. That sounded strange to his mind because he hated it. Better to wander from place to place than put up with his mother, Miriam.

A family sheepherder met him but did not recognize him. "I come in peace, young herder. I am Lapidoth, cousin and more to all who live here. Have you seen a woman with red gold hair, younger than me, pass by this way?"

"No one has passed this way, man or woman."

"You are sure?"

"As God is my judge, I am sure. No one has passed this way all day."

Lapidoth puzzled about what to do next. Giving one more glance toward the hills, he slowly turned his horse toward the family village. "Someone must have seen her," he muttered.

Joab, his brother-in-law, saw Lapidoth approaching and hurried out to meet him. "Brother! It has been a long time! Welcome!"

Lapidoth slid down from his horse and met Joab's embrace. The kissed each other's cheeks and turned toward the house.

"You look troubled, Lapidoth. Is something wrong?"

"Yes, very wrong, Joab. When I was in the north I married a woman named Deborah. Our cousin Hannah knew her. We traveled south to escape the brigands of Sisera's army when the inn where we spent one night was attacked. The innkeeper helped us escape. Deborah was with other guests from the inn and they started south on the road to Jericho. Foolishly I returned to Tirzah to retrieve our wagon, animals, and belongings. I was sure I would catch up with Deborah in Jericho. But the guests each went their own way before they reached Jericho, and Deborah turned west toward our home here. She stayed in Bethel for the night and left before dawn. She is somewhere in the hills north of here, but since Bethel I have not been able to find a trace of her."

"Ah, I have an idea," offered Joab. "Your cousin Rahab often goes into those hills for days at a time. She may be with Rahab. If anyone was within a mile of Rahab, her dog would start barking and not stop until Rahab came to quiet him."

"Where does Rahab stay in the hills? Is there a house or a sheep shelter? Can you find her?"

"Yes, I know where it is. I followed her one time long ago but never let her know I knew her secret. I have told our mother and father that she goes to the city to sell her saddlebags, which is true. She is always making saddlebags to sell. They are finely made and are very popular with the merchants."

"So she really does go to the city?"

"Oh yes. But sometimes she just disappears into the hills. It makes people think she is a harlot, but she does not care. She embarrasses the family, but she does not stop. She has always been a little crazy like that."

"Will you take me to her? I must find Deborah!"

Joab looked doubtful. He did not want Rahab to know he knew about her place. He did not want to reveal it to anyone else, even Lapidoth who he trusted.

"Please Joab. I must find her. If she is not with Rahab, she could be injured!"

"We can go in that direction and see if we can get the attention of the dog. Then it will look as if we found her by accident. Let me put your horse up. He looks exhausted. We can take my asses."

Lapidoth agreed and they went toward the main house and barn. "Has there been news of Sisera's marauders this far south?"

"Not yet," replied Joab, "Jericho might look more inviting to them than our little villages. Some caravans still travel to Jericho from across the Jordan. But that will stop if Jericho is attacked."

They rode side by side until the paths became narrow. It was late afternoon and the shadows would soon grow longer, making everything look unfamiliar. After an hour more they could hear a dog barking. They stopped looking hopefully in the direction of the barking. "We are still far away from her place, so she must be close by or coming home," reasoned Joab.

Then Rahab shouted at the dog, which quieted immediately.

"Rahab? It is Joab! I have Lapidoth with me! Where are you?"

Rahab came through the trees onto the path where Lapidoth and Joab waited. Deborah followed a distance behind.

Lapidoth sat frozen unable to move. A lump in this throat prevented him from speaking much above a croak. "Deborah, thank God! I have been looking for you everywhere! Why did you leave Bethel? Why did you not take the main roads?"

Deborah shrank back. "If you remember, it was you who left me, Lapidoth! I was looking for you, too!"

Lapidoth opened his mouth to argue, but Rahab stared him down. "You have some explaining to do, dear cousin. What good husband goes off and leaves his wife on the road with strangers? You are a disgrace to your family as well as to yourself! Now we are both a disgrace! How does it feel, Lapidoth?"

Joab turned his back so they would not see him smile. "Lapidoth and Rahab never change," he thought to himself. "They have argued with each other since they were born."

Lapidoth offered Deborah the animal to ride but she walked away and Rahab after her.

Joab dismounted and walked with Lapidoth, leading the animals. It was a long walk home and the silence was deafening. Lapidoth was somewhat disheartened and too angry to talk, and Joab was at a loss. Deborah and Rahab walked a distance behind and they were quiet as well. The things they would talk about were not for anyone else's ears.

The houses of their village came into sight. Some were mud brick, some stone, and tents on the outskirts. Deborah began to wonder what her life would be like here. She was married to a stranger. Her one friend was Rahab, the outcast of the family. Hannah seemed so far away. She tried to remember some of Hannah's words, some of the scriptures she studied, the gentle face of Ya'akov, something of the plans with Barak, but nothing would come to mind. Deborah felt a bleak emptiness that had been growing since they left Kadesh.

Lapidoth turned to glance at Deborah and Rahab. He dropped back to walk beside them. Joab looked around at them and said, "I will go on ahead, Lapidoth. You know the way." He mounted his ass and trotted away toward the village.

"Deborah, you are right. It was foolish of me to leave you on that road with strangers. Nehemiah scolded me all the way up the road to Bethel."

"Who is Nehemiah?" asked Deborah.

"He is a friend who lives in Jericho. I went to Jericho looking for you. I went to his house and he sent his servants to the market to inquire if anyone had seen you. When no one reported seeing you, we started up the Jericho road and took the main road to Bethel thinking we would surely find you. His servants went into the hills shouting your name."

Rahab turned her head so Lapidoth wouldn't see her disgust.

"I was not on the main road. I turned onto a path toward Bethel when the others departed across the Jordan River. You did not say you would meet me in Jericho. You just left with a promise to catch up with us. When you did not, I had no choice but to start in the direction of your home. I was alone."

Lapidoth sighed and rubbed his forehead with his hand. Deborah reached out and touched his arm. "There is no need to scold each other. Thank God we are both safe. What did you find when you went back to Tirzah?"

Lapidoth looked up suddenly, shocked at the sudden change in the conversation. It was a cool Deborah taking charge.

"I found all of our belongings and three children. I left them all in Jericho to come look for you."

"And Sisera's marauders?"

"They were gone. There were only bodies in the streets. I went from house to house, but they were either all dead or hiding. I took the children and left."

"And where are the children now?"

"Nehemiah's household servants are caring for them. A servant will go back to Tirzah and search for their family members. Perhaps they are still alive."

"The innkeeper was so courageous to get us all out. I wish we knew what happened to him," said Deborah. "God willing they did not kill him, too."

"Here in the land of Ephraim we are safe. We cannot look back. We must establish our lives here," announced Lapidoth.

"What do you mean we cannot look back? Are not my family members still in danger? I must find out about Barak. I cannot just cut my life off and start over!"

"You are my wife, Deborah. This is how it must be. You will live with my family now. This is your new home," decreed Lapidoth.

Deborah felt cold shivers go down her spine. Her stomach felt hollow and her head throbbed. The wild adventure was over and reality began to set in. They were approaching the houses and Joab was walking toward them. Behind him was Miriam, Lapidoth's mother. She was tall and carried herself proudly, like Lapidoth.

She greeted Lapidoth coolly and turned to Deborah. "You must be exhausted, my dear. Come with me." She put an arm around Deborah's shoulders and guided her into the house. A servant brought bread, figs, and wine to the table. Deborah sat down in silence, not knowing what would come next. When Lapidoth did not appear, she inquired as to his whereabouts.

"Lapidoth and Joseph will be leaving for the coast of the Great Sea shortly," his mother replied imperiously. "They have business there that cannot wait, especially for a mere wife."

A mere wife! Deborah downed the wine and let the servant fill her cup again. "Lapidoth has told me many things, but not about this business. He did not say he would be leaving. What am I to do?"

"You will stay with me, of course. The servants will show you to your room. Tomorrow we will talk."

"We will talk? About what?"

"You will know soon enough, tomorrow after you are rested. Do not question the servants. They will not answer you."

Rahab strode through the door and said, "Come! I will take you to your new home, Deborah. I have made sure it is ready."

"Deborah will stay here tonight and until Lapidoth returns, Rahab," said Miriam coolly.

"No, Miriam, she will not. She has had quite enough exposure to craziness. Come with me, Deborah." She stepped to Deborah's side. Deborah stood up, picked up her bag, and went out the door with Rahab. This was the strangest experience Deborah could ever remember happening to her and it was frightening. At this point, it seemed Rahab was her savior and the only person she could trust.

Rahab led her to a small house a distance away from Miriam's. "I know you will want to be alone to rest, and that witch will give you nothing but grief. However, you will not be alone because I will be here with you until you get your bearings."

Deborah was stunned by the sudden turn of events. They entered the house and it was cool and comfortable. There were pillows, blankets, flowers, and two soft beds and a tiny kitchen. "Rahab, is this yours? Are these your things?"

"Yes, this is my place and now it is yours until you decide what to do. It is yours for as long as you need it or forever if you wish. I will not always be here, as you already know. But if you do not mind, it will be wonderful for me to have a friend to come home to."

Deborah burst out laughing. "Rahab, you are a wonder! And the strangest person I have ever met . . . besides myself, of course!" Rahab burst out laughing too.

Deborah slept soundly, dreaming of Barak, her mother and father, studying with Ya'akov and his father. Hannah was instructing her to find her own way. "Pray to God, be a counselor of people." Mara was telling her to walk like a queen. Sisera was bowing at her feet.

She awoke with a start, her head still full of the dreams and not able to discern where she was for a few minutes. Rahab handed her a cup of hot tea and smiled. "You were tossing and groaning last night. Busy dreams?"

"Oh Rahab, I hope I did not disturb you. Yes, very busy dreams! Hannah was telling me to pray to God and be a counselor of people. I know how to pray and I was a counselor at the village well for some years. Somehow people there trusted me with their problems. Especially the young girls. But people do not know me here."

"You pray for both of us, Deborah. I have an idea. Stay here and rest today while I go and ask some questions. I cannot explain it now, but I will when I return this evening." Rahab pulled on her robe and hurried out the door heading for the center of the village and the marketplace.

Deborah pondered the events all day long. How could Lapidoth go away without telling her? Why was Miriam so cool, almost angry with Lapidoth? What did Rahab mean about Miriam giving her nothing but grief? This time she did sit down to pray, pray long and intensely. Exhaustion was still with her and sleep was so inviting. She laid her questions and fears before God, and feeling more at peace, drifted off to sleep again.

* * *

Barak now knew that Deborah was safe in Ephraim near Bethel. He immediately made plans to put Abel in charge. "I must go to her, Abel. She carries the key to our success against Sisera."

"Barak, look at our men! Do you really think they are ready to attack Sisera, or even a small band of Philistines? We need to concentrate on training them."

"Training them will do no good if God is not with us, Abel. We need Deborah's insight when we plan our battles."

Abel shook his head. "Go if you must. I have some new training ideas and I am thinking of ways to get weapons. We need more weapons. I will begin today and hopefully have the training begun before you return. The weapons are indeed a matter of God's will!"

"Trust me, Abel. We need not only weapons and strategy, but God in our plans. Deborah knows how to do that."

Abel shook his head, started for the door of the tent, stopped and turned. "Are you in love with her, Barak?"

Barak stopped gathering his gear and looked up at Abel. "She is as my elder sister, my confidant, and friend. If that is love, then I love her. But if you mean as a man loves a woman for the sake of marriage, no."

Abel scowled and scratched his head. "That is too confusing for me. Friends are man-to-man and woman-to-woman, sister-to-sister, brother-to-brother. How can a man and a woman be friends? Would that not lead to sin? Even punishment by stoning? I fear for you, Barak. Be careful who you say these things to."

"You are the only one who ever asked me that. Am I not safe with you, Abel? Will you keep my words to yourself? I always call her not friend, but sister or cousin in the company of others. Perhaps that will ease your mind."

"I am sorry, Barak. Yes, I will keep your words to myself alone. You can depend on me to do everything needed here while you find Deborah. Avoid the Philistines. They nearly got Naham. God speed and keep you safe."

"Nearly got Naham? When?"

"Umm, just a small skirmish, but he got away as he always does. We are always in danger from them." Abel had overheard Gideon and Naham, and was ashamed that he almost let their secret slip out.

Barak clasped Abel's arms and they stood silent for a moment. "I know you will and I trust you with my life as I know you trust me with yours. Pray God that we are both successful."

They kissed each other's cheeks and Barak grabbed his gear as he trotted out of the tent. The day was young and he could make good time. His horse was eager, stamping his hooves and snorting as Barak approached him with a saddle. They tore out of the camp at a flat out gallop, heading through the pass and down the mountainside. When he slowed so the horse could steady his footing, he thought he heard someone on the path behind him. He dismounted quickly, led the horse behind some rocks and waited.

The voice came from behind him. "Barak, it is I, Gideon. Abel sent me. I am coming with you. I know the pathways through the wilderness because I have traveled them many times. Together we can move faster and have more protection than you will riding alone on these roads."

With a sigh of exasperation and some relief Barak said, "Then welcome, Gideon. I had thought to follow the sun and stars to find my way, but it is better to have someone who knows the countryside. The stars may lead me over a cliff!" He clapped Gideon on the back and they walked companionably together on the path until Gideon motioned Barak to follow him through a maze of rocks and scrub.

"Traveling south we will be moving in the direction of the Philistine city of Gaza on the west. Sisera's gangs may watch the roads to the east. The travel will be more difficult through the mountains and hills, but more secure," offered Gideon. "Of course you are the one to decide which way we will go."

"We will go as you have suggested, Gideon. I trust your judgment more than mine in this," replied Barak. "How long do you think it will take to get to Bethel-Ramah?"

"Without going out of our way to avoid Philistines or being attacked by brigands, at least two days moving as quickly as we can. I hope none of the trails have been destroyed by rockslides. That is always a danger."

Barak nodded as Gideon talked. Barak wanted to travel alone and think, but he could see the sense of having Gideon with him. Chances are he could find Deborah more quickly and avoid getting lost or being attacked. Questions ran through his mind unbidden. What is Deborah's situation? Who was this Lapidoth she had married so quickly and how was his family treating her? He could not imagine Deborah allowing herself to be enslaved or beaten.

The second day they came upon an encampment of women and children. They ran into the woods as Gideon and Barak approached. Some old people still lay in front of goatskin tents. Barak and Gideon dismounted and walked cautiously into the camp.

Gideon spoke first. Kneeling in front of the man he inquired, "Shalom, old man. Who are you and where did you come from?" Gideon suspected they were refugees from a raided village and he was right.

Seeing that Barak and Gideon were not the raiders, he spoke in a quavery voice, "I am Ezra. We are from Tirzah. Men came on horses and raided the village. They killed many, took the little livestock we had for our food for the winter, and rode away. We are the only survivors."

"Do you know who the raiders were? Were they Sisera's soldiers or Philistines?"

"They shouted 'In the name of Jabin the King!'"

"Yes, those were Sisera's men," said Barak. "Did you say no one survived? No one at all?"

"There were three children who were playing in the streets. Their bodies were not among the dead. We have not found them yet, but we sent the able-bodied men out to look for them every day."

"And travelers? Were there travelers? In an inn perhaps?" asked Gideon glancing at Barak.

"They burned the inn. There were travelers, but I do not know their fate."

Barak sucked in his breath at this news. "Did you see a woman with red hair traveling with her husband?"

"My wife brought produce to the inn each day. I heard her mention someone with red hair to her cousin. My wife and her cousin were dragged into the street and killed. I could not help them. My bones are too old and feeble." Tears came to his eyes and he turned away.

Barak wanted to question him further, but Gideon held up his hand. "He knows no more, Barak. Do not trouble him further. He is blind. Let us go on so the others can leave their hiding places and return here. There is nothing more we can do for them this day."

Reluctantly Barak mounted his horse and turned to the south again. "You are observant, Gideon. I was so worried about Deborah. I did not see that he was blind."

"My Lord, I know you fear for Deborah's life, but let us assume she and her husband escaped. It will keep our hearts steady and our eyes watchful on the journey. We might have other encounters that are not friendly like this one."

Barak heaved a sigh and agreed. "Deborah has a great mission from God, so surely he would not allow her to be cut down in the midst of it or before it is completed."

Barak sounded more confident than he felt. He began to recount the times he had not been observant of the holy laws and how he might have displeased God. In is early days as a soldier he had committed every sin he could think of. Guilt overwhelmed him and tears came to his eyes. Had he caused Deborah's death? It would be too much to bear.

"Please God, let her be safe," he prayed under his breath. "Guide us to her that we might fulfill your promise of victory for our people."

*　　*　　*

True to her word Rahab stayed with Deborah to be sure she was safe from Miriam and able to find her way about the markets.

"Tell me about Lapidoth, Rahab. I beg you. What is this business that was so urgent? How could he just leave without telling me? Of course this would be the third time. It is Miriam, is it not?"

"Yes, it is Miriam. Miriam has royal connections that no decent woman should have. She funds a foreign merchant that brings a return to our estate. He threatens to expose her to the whole tribe and have her killed if she refuses. It is a disgrace he would make public and put our family in great danger."

"And Lapidoth? What part does he have in this?"

Lapidoth sells the merchant's jewels to representatives of royal households. That is why Lapidoth travels. He compensates for our shame by helping poor people along the way. I only pray that God understands."

Deborah poured herself some wine to steady her nerves. "Is there no way out of this, Rahab? Can he not just quit and settle down?"

"Only if the merchant dies. But even then surely some of his family would continue the business. We do not know who else might know our secret and wish to profit from it."

"This is all very strange to me," worried Deborah mostly to herself.

"Deborah, you must not become involved. This is why I would not let you stay in Miriam's home. If you overheard something and she knew it, you would be in danger. She would poison you. We must find you another place to live farther away and soon."

"Will she not think you told me already?"

"No. She and the family tolerate my wanderings and I promise not to tell their secret. I am already disgraced in their eyes, so I have some power over them."

"What do I do now? Lapidoth is gone and I do not know when or if he will return. A journey back to my family would be impossible!"

Rahab poured herself some wine, too, and sat down to think. Deborah walked to the door and stared out at the hills. Mid afternoon was hot and airless. All was quiet, even oppressive.

"Here is what we will do, Deborah . . ."

Deborah stepped back from the doorway suddenly. Miriam stood before them and sneered, "What will you do, Rahab?"

Rahab stood, wine in hand, and walked slowly toward Miriam. Calmly she said, "We will go to the market and get some of the new materials that have come on the last caravan. Deborah has few things with her. Many of her belongings were lost in the raid on Tirzah. Do you wish to accompany us, Miriam?"

"Yes, I will accompany you as far as the first stall. I have business of my own. Shall we go when it is cooler? The vendors will be asleep in this heat."

"Certainly, Miriam. We will stop by your house so you can join us," said Rahab still cool and collected.

Miriam turned on her heel and left as quietly as she had arrived. Rahab and Deborah looked at each other with hands clamped over their mouths. "Do you think she heard us?" asked Deborah.

"No. That snake! We were thinking for the last little while and not saying anything. We will have to be more careful and talk where we can see if someone approaches." Rahab walked to the doorway to be sure Miriam was not lingering. "So, as I was saying, first we will find you a place to work on your own. I will go to the market and spread the word that a prophet of God and seer from the tribe of Napthali is among us and will counsel during the morning hours. That will give you a legitimate reason for being there that they will respect. It will also provide an income independent of this family. You may need it."

It was still hot when the three of them walked into the marketplace. Business was picking up as the air became cooler and the noise level heightened as well. Miriam, true to her word, abandoned them at the first stall and disappeared. Rahab guided Deborah to the cloth merchants' tents and they began to look over the goods.

"Be aware," whispered Rahab, "Miriam is somewhere near by or her spies are. So we will talk about nothing but cloth. Then we will slip away to the far side of the market to the tent of a friend to arrange for another place for you. The friend will spread the word of your counseling. The word will go out after the Sabbath after you have settled in a place."

Deborah was more baffled than ever at the rapid unfolding of her circumstances. She felt more beset by dangers than she had at Tirzah when they escaped from the raid. The more she learned about her new family the more bewildered she became. She knew of no one in her hometown, or even on the roads, that was menacing or even made her feel afraid. This kind of fear was new to her.

Several boys came running through the market waving sticks and chasing some errant sheep. The merchants and shoppers looked toward the commotion and Rahab took the opportunity to quickly pull Deborah through a tent and into a house behind the market. The house was dark and cool, and almost bare of furniture. An old woman sat in the corner.

"Mother in Israel, this is Deborah the prophetess and seer."

The old woman looked Deborah up and down, then patted the bench beside her indicating Deborah should sit there. Rahab stayed near the doorway.

"You are a student of Hannah are you not?"

"Y-Yes," stammered Deborah. What a relief it was to hear Hannah's name from this stranger. "Do you know of Hannah?"

The old woman ignored her question since the answer was obvious. "There is a place under a palm tree north east of here. You will know it by the stone altar close by. This will be your place, the Palm of Deborah. Go and stay there from daybreak to noon. Do not be there in the heat of the day or at night. You must not be suspect in any way. Go now Deborah the Prophetess and God grant you safety and good fortune. Do your work well as Hannah has taught you."

Rahab motioned to Deborah that they could safely leave. They slipped back into the marketplace crowd and to the tents of the cloth merchants. Deborah purchased some goods and plain materials that she thought would be right for her work. The merchant did his best to interest her in exotic silks, but she insisted on her own choices. She also bought herbs, seeds, oils, a pistil, some bowls, and other items for healing work.

They arrived back at Rahab's house without seeing Miriam in the market or on their way home. Deborah wondered about it but did not ask. She wanted to talk more about setting herself up here and finding the palm spoken of by the old woman.

"There will not be a problem finding the palm, Deborah. I have seen it. The stone altar is barely visible because the stones have fallen away. It was probably a tribe of Canaanites that lived here long before Joshua built it. Most people would pass by not noticing it. Will you be ready to find it at dawn tomorrow?"

"I can be ready. Rahab. What would I do without you?"

* * *

Barak and Gideon took shelter in a cave high in a cliff. The Philistines and local guerilla fighters were battling all around them. They had hidden their horses and scrambled up to a higher cave hoping to see where the fighters were. "Perhaps we can slip away in the night," said Barak. "We cannot stay here forever."

"Have patience my friend," said Gideon. "In the dark we could stumble upon them and risk capture. The Philistines will beat back the guerillas and then head for the safety of the coast. They will not stay here long. They like the comforts of their city and their women too much."

"How can you be so sure?"

"I have seen their women! And the comforts of their homes! It is a wonder they leave at all to fight. But of course the most valiant fighter gets the most beautiful woman."

"How do they know who the most valiant fighter is?"

"They get drunk and brag loudly about themselves. The loudest drunk still standing gets the woman."

Barak remembered all too well when he and his soldiers did those same things. Now he felt shame but back then it was great sport. How could he have been so taken in by the revelry, the wine, and the loose women? It held no charm for him now.

True to Gideon's prediction, there was no sign of any fighters at dawn. They kept watch for another hour before climbing down from their perch. Their horses were still where they left them. Leading their horses they walked for a distance. All was quiet.

Soon Gideon stopped and held up his hand for Barak to be silent. "It is too quiet," he whispered. He motioned they should back up and hide over the top of a ridge of rocks and trees. Quietly they turned their horses and slipped back up the trail to the trees. There was movement lower down toward the valley and then there was a war cry to their right. Warriors came rushing from the east and from the west and the battle was on.

"I cannot make out who they are," said Gideon. "I have never seen anyone like them before.

"Moabites!" said Barak. "What are they doing here? They rarely cross the Jordan!"

"Only the kidnapping of royalty would cause them to come this far into Israelite territory," replied Gideon. "They are blocking our way. If we go west we will run into Philistines and if we go east we may encounter the Moabites retreating or going home after victory."

"I would rather take my chances with Moabites. They are more likely to have inferior weapons and no soldier training," reasoned Barak.

"You mean like us?" smiled Gideon.

"It would seem to be a more equal encounter than to run into ranks of Philistines," admitted Barak. "I say we take our chances to the east. We are not their favorite neighbors, but they are usually not openly hostile to us. They will not attack us but will probably go about the business that brought them here."

Gideon sat in silence and deep thought. "If they are in retreat, they may commandeer our help, our horses, and supplies. If word of their presence has been sent north, they might encounter Sisera's men to the east before they can cross the Jordan. We do not want to face Sisera."

"Sisera is from east of the Jordan. They could be allies or perhaps the Moabites are a thorn in the side of Sisera. A nuisance. We do not know!" declared Barak impatiently. This promised to be a huge delay in reaching Deborah.

*   *   *

For a week Deborah and Rahab worked feverishly to turn the materials they bought in the market into a comfortable tent, soft furnishings, clothes, and Rahab's specialty, saddlebags to carry Deborah's healing herbs, oils, and crockery. While Rahab was busy, Deborah quietly and carefully removed the scriptures from the folds of the clothing she brought from home and tucked them securely into the saddlebags. She was not ready to share them with anyone just yet, even Rahab. She could not risk losing them because someone thought a woman should not have them, or worse accuse her of stealing them. Just the touch of the papyrus to her fingers ran a thrill all through Deborah. Vivid memories came washing over her of Ya'akov and his father, Rabbi Amri, and the study where they shared the scriptures. The memories brought waves of sadness and longing almost too much to bear.

Rahab stepped into the room to announce that they were almost ready to go to the site of the palm where Deborah would work each morning. She touched Deborah's arm. "Are you ill, Deborah? You look a little pale and sad."

"I am not ill. It is because things have changed so quickly for me that it suddenly hits me in the pit of my stomach momentarily. I am fine, really."

"It will be light soon. If you are sure you are all right, we should pack a donkey and leave now."

"I am ready," assured Deborah. She picked up her possessions and carried them out to the stable where the pack animal was tied.

Rahab skillfully hitched everything securely to the pack frame and they started out on foot leading the donkey. "We will call the place the Palm of Deborah. The old woman named it and that is how others will refer to it as well. I will come with you each morning before dawn and return for you when it is time for you to come back here."

"Do you think that is necessary? You had a life before I came here and there must be things you need to get back to."

"Everything I need to do will be taken care of. No need to worry about me. But you are a stranger here and until we are sure you are accepted and safe, I will stay with you."

"Rahab, what about Lapidoth? When will he return? What will he think about all this?"

"He is leaving you on your own as usual. I am sure he will feel guilty enough to approve, or at least accept what you must do. You have a calling from God that must be fulfilled and this must be part of the fulfillment."

"Rahab, you are so quick and clear about things. I feel so foggy and uncertain. This is not like me at all. I was willful and sure of what I wanted. Now I feel weak and foolish. What would I ever have done without you?"

"How did you handle a team of mules and a wagon with no help? How did you get from Tirzah to Bethel by yourself? You are anything but weak and foolish, my dear Deborah."

CHAPTER 11

They laughed and chatted amiably about many things as they walked along. The dawn was coming and the Palm of Deborah came into sight. It was a tiny oasis with an old well, a small pond of water, and plants growing around it. A few shepherd's paths converged there at the water's edge.

"It looks like I shall have company if the shepherds come here."

"Yes, you will not be isolated and that is good. Just as important, you have privacy here. People will respect the confidentiality of your counseling."

They set about unpacking the donkey and let him wander to the water. The tent was a struggle to erect, but with sticks of wood they brought from the family property for supports, all worked well. It eventually began to look like a suitable dwelling. They spread a heavy piece of material to make a floor until they could bring straw to place under it. Deborah brought in her belongings and began to arrange them for her work. She tucked the scriptures into the folds of her robe, not yet sure she could safely leave them in the saddlebag.

Deborah heard an earsplitting whistle and ran outside to see what it was. It was Rahab. "I am calling my dog, Kelev, to protect you until I return." Sure enough, Kelev came running down from the hills tongue and tail waiving wildly. "I just call him 'Kelev.' So if you need him, just call the word Kelev. Can you whistle?"

"I do not know. I never tried. How do you do it?"

Rahab gave a demonstration and Deborah tried, but to no avail. She could not seem to form her mouth just right to produce a whistle.

"Where did you learn it?"

"Shepherds play a flute, sing, or whistle a low tune to calm their sheep. I learned by listening to them."

Rahab bid her farewell and went on her way. Kelev sat by the tent opening like a sentry. To Deborah's amazement he seemed to know what to do.

For the first time since arriving here Deborah felt like spending time in prayer. All was in order and quiet except for the breeze in the palm tree. The palm fronds rattled against the tree trunk and occasionally one fell to the ground making a loud thump. Deborah jumped the first time, but became a little more accustomed to the sounds around the oasis as the morning went on. She slipped in and out of deep meditation. Each time she came out of the meditation, she felt more rested and centered.

Kelev gave a tentative yip and then a low growl. Deborah looked up and moved to the tent opening. A young woman was approaching. Deborah went to greet her. "I am Deborah. How can I help you?"

"I know you are Deborah. The old woman told me I might find help here. I am Keturah. I am sick in the mornings and feel tired much of the time."

"Are you married, Keturah?"

"Yes, of course. Why do you ask?"

"Could it be that you are pregnant?" Deborah looked Keturah over carefully, assessing her eyes and her skin. Then she could sense the life of the child in the womb.

Keturah was wide-eyed. "How can you know?"

"Your skin is dry and your eyes are a little red. You need more moisture in your food. Olive oil and fruit would be good. And I will give you an herb for tea in the mornings that will relieve the sick feeling."

Deborah folded the herbs into a piece of cloth and gave them to her. "Before you leave, let us pray to God for the health of the child. Let us ask God for a prosperous future for you both."

Keturah was surprised and pleased. "Yes, I would like that!"

They sat down to pray. As Keturah was leaving she pressed some coins into Deborah's hand. "You are so kind. I will send others to you. God bless you."

Deborah watched Keturah walk back toward the village and patted Kelev on his sleek brown head. He wagged his tail eagerly, licked her hand, and lay down by the door again. She went inside, took a page of her scriptures from her robe, and began to read the familiar passages. They were always comforting to her. All the confusion and anxiety of the past weeks cleared from her mind and all seemed to be right with her world again.

*　　*　　*

The only way for Barak and Gideon to go was back the way they came. As they moved back it all looked hopeless. Barak scowled darkly at the change of fortune. How could he find Deborah if their ways were all blocked or going backward?

"Why is God stopping us, Gideon? Have we again done something to displease Him?"

Gideon had no answer except to wait. "They will not tarry long, Barak. Danger always requires patience of us. My success in bringing you information is in hiding and waiting for the enemy to move somewhere. I allow them to clear my way instead of trying to clear it myself."

"What do you do when you are waiting? This drives me crazy!"

"I pray. I ask God to show me the way. I ask God to deliver me from my enemies and keep me safe. Whatever comes to mind that I need, I pray for."

"How do you know when God has opened the way?"

"When my anxieties are quiet and watching brings no fear. Then I move quietly and slowly so God can lead the way."

"How did you learn all this about God, Gideon?"

"From a dying rabbi I tried to rescue. It was too late for him. His heart was giving out, but he put his hands on my shoulders, his forehead to mine, and told me all he could before he slumped down and died."

"What did he say to you?" Barak became intensely interested in what Gideon was telling him and for a while forgot his angst at having to retreat.

"He said, 'Wait patiently for the Lord and he will give you your heart's desire.' The words came from his lips and also from his head touching mine. Everything he said was made very clear to me. I am sure his advice has kept me alive for many years. There were times when I could have been discovered and killed had I not waited, and miraculously I was kept safe."

"Then let us ask the Lord to guide us. We are no good to the army of Israel if we are foolish and dead," smiled a much calmer Barak.

Night fell dark and starless. Barak slept fitfully. While Gideon watched the skies he chewed on a piece of bread and a few dates. The moon would show itself soon and he would know what to do.

As the moon brightened the landscape, Gideon could see two men running toward their hiding place. As he watched he could see that one was chasing the other. He strained his eyes to see who they might be. Soon one man fell and the other jumped on him. A knife flashed in the moonlight. Gideon pulled his own knife from his belt and ran to where the two men were struggling. He could see the one on top was a Philistine. Gideon ran low and threw his shoulder into the man's side. As the Philistine grunted and fell, Gideon slipped his knife into the enemy's heart. Then he sprang to his feet ready for any further danger, but there was none.

The other man lay wounded at his feet. Gideon knelt down to see if the man was still alive. A weak voice came from him. "I am Ham. Please leave me to die. I am a disgrace."

"What were you doing here in the night, Ham?" asked Gideon. "What tribe are you from?"

The skirmish awakened Barak and he came quietly to join Gideon. "Who is this man?"

"I am Ham from the tribe of Gad across the Jordan. My brothers and I have been following our sister who was taken from our fields by a band of renegades. We were told they crossed the Jordan and came west. Instead of finding them, we ran into Philistines. They set upon us yesterday and killed my brothers. I have been hiding and thought to escape in the night, but they were searching for me and I had to run. Now I will die."

"You will not die," said Gideon as he bandaged Ham's wound. "It is painful but not deep. Lie still for the night and I will examine it again in the morning."

Barak kept watching the moonlit landscape for movement. "Do you think more Philistines have followed you?"

There was no answer. Ham had fallen into an exhausted sleep. Gideon and Barak did not close their eyes the rest of the night. They waited for the dawn with concern on their faces. Ham was snoring loudly and woke himself up with a start. He jerked upright, but Gideon put a hand on his shoulder and pushed him back down. "Be still my friend. You are wounded but safe."

Ham fell back with a groan, sliding his hand toward the pain in his arm. "Who are you?"

Gideon could see that he was not a man but a boy. Gently he said, "I am Gideon the scout, and this is Barak, the general of the Israelite army. We are on our way to Ephraim and Bethel-Ramah. Now that the east is clear, we will continue east until we are well past the danger of Philistines."

"I must continue to find my sister," said Ham wincing as he sat up.

"Ham, you are now one boy, not a band of brothers, and you are wounded. You cannot pursue brigands alone and weakened by loss of blood. Travel with us until you can cross the Jordan and return home."

"I cannot return home in disgrace! My brothers gave their lives and I must be successful or die trying. No, I cannot go home. You saved my life and I will be your servant until I save yours. Perhaps I will find her somewhere along the way in your travels."

"You will save our lives?" laughed Barak. "How old are you?"

Ham shrank back at Barak's scoffing. "I am the youngest of five brothers. I am fourteen years old and strong. I have fought off many jackals that threatened our livestock and I will fight those who have taken my sister when I find them!"

"Then come with us." Gideon loaded Ham onto his horse, climbed up behind him, and the three started off to the east and south.

*   *   *

Lapidoth and Joseph navigated the black markets of Ashdod, keeping their identity hidden. Their destination was the dangerous underground market of the importers of jewels. The place was heavily guarded and they revealed their identity only with a password. They were admitted to the shadowy interior of a damaged building and continued down a stairway that opened into a large room. There were wary stares from foreign merchants as they entered, but their connection greeted them with a smile and a nod. They were escorted through another dim passageway and into yet another room.

Joseph always wondered how this dangerous connection was made with Miriam's family, and how it fell to her to carry out the business. Miriam's family was aristocratic. Perhaps their wealth came from such business as this, but Joseph never knew. He learned after their marriage that he and his family were in danger if he did not cooperate. How fortunate he had felt, marrying a woman of wealth and mystical beauty, never realizing the price he would pay for the intrigue of their lifestyle. How foolish he had been to insist on this beautiful woman for his bride when his family hesitated to give their blessing.

Sitting before them in a smoky room was a merchant known only as Abdullah. He was hugely fat with a swarthy complexion. He was puffing on a bong. There were so many pock marks on his face it was hard to discern any distinguishing features.

Lapidoth set their bags of money on the table in front of Abdullah. Another man spilled it out and efficiently counted it, marking the total on papyrus. Silently a bag of jewels was pushed toward Lapidoth along with his share of the profits. Joseph took his share of the profits and Lapidoth stowed the bag of jewels under his robe. They bowed and were escorted back through the passages, up the steps, and into the glaring light of day.

The guards nodded that the way was clear and they left through the alleys of Ashdod. They moved past dark doorways and sidestepped pools of blood where local families had slaughtered goats. They moved on through the crowded main marketplace where they parted without a nod. Lapidoth was wearing the trappings of a poor rabbi. He carefully chose a caravan to join that was not too rich and was traveling north. No one seemed to notice him. Joseph met his paid guards in the market and left the city traveling toward the east and home.

*　　*　　*

Rahab came for Deborah when the sun was high, as the old woman said, "Leave when the sun is high." It seemed to Deborah hardly enough time had gone by when she heard the joyful yelps of Kelev, still by the tent opening. His tail was beating the side of the tent and his feet were prancing, but he did not leave his post.

"Good Kelev!" said Rahab as she patted his head and scratched his ears. She gave him a fresh bone and went on into the tent.

Deborah buried her utensils in a hole under the floor, gathered her herbs and went with Rahab to sit under the palm by the water. "How was your morning?" said Rahab with a conspiratorial smile. "I heard that Keturah came to visit."

Deborah looked a little puzzled. "How did you know?"

"I went to the village market to hear the gossip. Then I can be sure the right stories are being spread about you and your work here. I will know if anything is amiss. The women of the village cannot converse openly with a woman of my reputation, but they pass signals to me that others will not notice."

"How will others not notice?"

"Because the signals are the usual insults they hurl at a harlot, but they mean something different to me. They are a signal."

"What is a signal?"

"The signal is a code, a series of words and gestures that mean something else. A tug of the ear can mean danger. Harlot means yes. Bad means no. If someone does not know the signals, these things will mean nothing to them."

"Rahab, you are an amazing guardian angel!"

"Not so much an angel," laughed Rahab. "I recognized you as a sister in spirit and I knew I was to take care of you and keep you safe. Say it is my calling from God if you like."

They shared some bread, figs, and cheese before returning to the village. They passed Miriam and Joseph's house, and Deborah looked for signs that Lapidoth had returned, but there were none.

"You will wear yourself out looking for Lapidoth. He does not return for weeks or months after he and my father visit Ashdod. He will visit the homes of the rich to sell the jewels and then visit poor villages to leave them some coins. If there is trouble, the villagers protect him."

What a different picture Deborah was getting of Lapidoth. Different from when she first saw him at the village well in Kadesh-Napthali. "I was such a dreamer!" she thought to herself. "He was so attentive to me and my family, and now he must leave me for long periods of time. I cannot imagine what my mother would think of a marriage like this! But I announced every chance I got that I never wished to marry or have children. Is this how God has answered my prayer?"

*　　*　　*

Barak was relieved to be traveling again. He did not want to slow their progress by taking Ham with them, but there was nothing else to do except leave a wounded boy behind to die. Through the next day they wended their way through wilderness hills and valleys. Ahead of them were the green Jordan valley and the road to Jericho.

"Before we take the main road we must inquire at the next village if Sisera has come this far south. If he has, we should stay on the smaller pathways," advised Gideon. "We will leave Ham with someone in one of the villages near the Jordan. He can find his way home when he is stronger. The jostling of travel is opening the wound. This is not good."

Ham tried to object, but he was too weak. He wanted to prove that he was strong, but there was no strength in him. "I will catch up with you and look for my sister," he uttered through his pain in a cracking voice.

"Are you sure someone will care for a Moabite?" asked Barak.

"Yes because I will pay them and make a promise to return to check on him. That will ensure his safety."

Barak smiled. "I have learned much from you, Gideon, and much more remains to be learned, I am sure!"

"You have been willing to hear me, Barak. Not that I presumed to teach you, but other troop commanders would doubt my choices and blunder into disastrous difficulty. I am honored by your trust."

A small group of tents surrounded by sheep, goats, and children lay ahead. Gideon rose in his stirrups for a better look. "They are Bedouin and the men are lazy. They will be hospitable as long as they do not perceive an attack. If they are attacked, the men become ferocious!"

Barak and Gideon dismounted and led their horses toward the camp. Ham was swaying a bit and clung to the saddle. The children ran out to meet them shouting for their mothers and jumping up and down in their excitement. The adults slowly emerged from the tents and motioned Barak and Gideon to bring the wounded Ham into one of the tents. Gideon negotiated the price of his care with the men while the women attended to his wound.

The afternoon was hot. They accepted the hospitality offered to them and sat down with the men of the camp for food and tea. After the conventional exchanges of pleasantries, the conversation eventually turned to Sisera's threat. An older boy at the back of the tent shyly offered he had heard talk from passing travelers about someone named Sisera, but nothing about him coming here. A man, presumably his father, nodded and waved him away as if it were nothing. But Gideon and Barak heard what they came for, that Sisera was not known here.

In the early evening as the air cooled a bit, Barak and Gideon took their leave offering the usual blessings upon their camp, their health, and prosperity. They decided to take the main road toward Jericho. It was a relief from the slow and difficult plodding through rocks and vegetation, and risky goat paths that often crumbled beneath the horses' hoofs. The main road was deserted and they moved their horses along at a brisk pace to arrive in Jericho before night fell.

They stopped at an inn to lodge for the night and inquired if anyone had seen Lapidoth and Deborah. As the question went around, all were wagging their heads in the negative. A child came out of the kitchen with their food. He announced to Barak that he was Dismas of Tirzah. "I have seen the man you ask for. He rescued my brother, sister, and I when soldiers attacked the village of Tirzah and killed everyone. He left us here at his friend's house to be cared for by the cook."

"Who was the friend? Where did he go after leaving you? Do you know?" queried Barak.

"His friend is Nehemiah. They took some servants and went to look for a woman named Deborah."

"Did they find Deborah?"

"Nehemiah and our servants returned without Lapidoth. I do not think they found her."

"Dismas!" came a shout from the kitchen door. "Get in here. There is more food to be served! Everyone is hungry!"

Dismas immediately turned and ran for the kitchen.

"We must find Nehemiah," said Barak excitedly. "Perhaps he knows something more than this boy."

They went into the kitchen to ask Dismas where Nehemiah lived. The owner was not happy for the interruption but Barak gave him some coins and he agreed to send Dismas to lead Gideon and Barak to the home of Nehemiah.

They arrived at the spacious house of Nehemiah and were graciously invited in. "Yes, Lapidoth and I searched for Deborah along the main roads all the way to Bethel. She stayed in Bethel the night before we arrived according to a shepherd boy, but disappeared before dawn. The boy brought her some food, but she was already gone."

"Do you believe she is alive?" asked Barak anxiously.

"I do not know for sure, but I rather think she is. Bethel is not a place that marauders frequent. Unless she was in the hills and met with a wild animal, but that is not likely either," reassured Nehemiah.

"We thank you. We must go and get an early start before dawn," said Gideon.

"Please," said Nehemiah rising. "Be my guests. Stay here in my house tonight. There is plenty of room as you can see."

Barak and Gideon accepted Nehemiah's offer and stayed the night. The next morning before dawn they drank the tea and ate the biscuits the servant placed in their room, sent their thanks to Nehemiah through the servants, and departed quietly.

It was good to feel rested, bathed and fed. The horses, too, were eager to get moving. They stamped their hooves and tossed their manes when Gideon and Barak entered the stables. They nickered softly as blankets were thrown over their backs. As they rode through the streets the main market was just awakening and merchants were carrying goods and tents to their places along the road.

The Jericho road had few travelers and they rode quickly. The intersection of the road west to Bethel was not far. They reached it by the first full morning light when everything was brilliant and clear.

"Bethel is not far and then we can inquire as to the location of Lapidoth's family home," said Gideon breaking the silence of the morning. "After hearing Nehemiah's story of the disappearing Deborah, everyone will be talking about it at the village wells."

Barak frowned a bit at the term disappearing Deborah, but he knew Gideon meant no disrespect. After all she did seem to appear and then disappear. He had a hard time picturing this new Deborah who seemed to be not at all like the girl he grew up with. He began to worry. What if she is not pleased to see him? What if her husband accuses him of something dishonorable? It was a sobering thought. But he had to come and find her.

*   *   *

Rahab moved their beds to the roof for the refreshing cool air of the night and the canopy of stars that cast a glow over the countryside. It was a fitting end of their day to lie there and talk until sleep overtook them.

Deborah awoke in the night. She had been dreaming of Barak and battlefields. In the dream Hannah was there on the hill beckoning to her and Ya'akov was smiling at her. Deborah rubbed her face and felt around her bed to determine where she was. Then her mind cleared and she knew she was on the roof of Rahab's house. Tears came to her eyes. How she missed Hannah, Barak, and Ya'akov.

But something was changing. She could feel it. She sat up and began to pray, "Dear God, show me what you would have me do. Give me the wisdom and strength to follow the way I must go. Protect us all with your blessing and love." She sank back onto the straw pallet and sleep came again until morning. Deborah remembered the dream and over breakfast she described it to Rahab.

"What will you do? What can you do?" queried Rahab. Deep concern showed on her face. "You are here and they are so far away!"

"Each time it all looks impossible, God carries me. Each time I nearly give up, someone comes along to give me courage. That person is you, Rahab. I left Bethel because I knew I should not stay there and I ran off into the hills. Where would I be if you had not found me? And more important, you became my friend and I yours. But I am afraid I do not know enough about this place to be much help to you."

"Deborah, you are my first woman friend. You did not turn from me or judge me. You placed your trust in me, something no one else has ever done. You are more help than you can possibly imagine!"

They gathered Deborah's bundles, prepared to go to the Palm of Deborah, and begin the day. More people had been coming as the time wore on, and more tales of miracles were spread about her healing powers. Rahab no longer went away after helping Deborah set things up. She stayed closer to Deborah during the mornings now to keep people from rushing into the tent and trampling her.

More and more the elders of the villages were coming for counsel. They would find Deborah in prayer and she seemed to know their concerns before they expressed them.

They treated her with great deference and not as an ordinary woman. They brought offerings of food, goods, and coins even though she had not asked for payment. They placed them quietly at the door of the tent as they were leaving.

Deborah had less and less time for her scriptures. She missed the comforting words and mysterious passages. Was this why Ya'akov was in her dream? To remind her that her wisdom and strength came from God? And Barak! They had such plans for using the scriptures to strengthen the faith of the Israelite army. How could she help them from so far away?

When the sun was high Rahab and Deborah sat by the water and ate their figs, cheese, lamb, bread, and a little watered wine. A woman came up the road half running and half stumbling. Deborah got up and went to meet her. "What is it? What has happened?"

"I am Liliah. It is Keturah! Her child is coming and she wants you to be with her! Will you come?"

"Yes, of course. Is her labor just beginning?"

"No, it lasted through the night and we fear she and the child are in trouble. The midwife is far away at another birth and we have no one else."

"Go, Deborah. I will load the donkey and follow you," called Rahab over her shoulder as she ran for the tent.

Liliah and Deborah hurried toward the village desperately hoping they were not too late. Deborah had seen a child being born, but had not assisted. The fear of having children was still with her from her own childhood, and something within her shrank back from it even to assist other women.

Screams were coming from the house of Keturah as Deborah, Rahab, and Liliah rushed in. Servants were wringing their hands and others were cooling her brow with wet cloths. "Get a birthing stool," shouted Deborah.

A servant brought one in. Deborah and Rahab lifted Keturah off the bed and onto it. The servants held onto Keturah while Deborah felt for the child's head. It was crowning and the birth was progressing more quickly now. She caught the baby as a mighty labor contraction it pushed out. Deborah felt the exhilaration of holding a live newborn for the first time. She could not believe how beautiful it all was.

"Keturah, you have a son. A beautiful son," whispered Deborah placing him in Keturah's arms. Liliah and the servants busied themselves making Keturah comfortable and took turns holding the baby.

"Carry him outside and present him to his father, Abijah," said Keturah in a weak voice. "It is the custom."

Deborah took the child and carried him outside. She looked around for Abijah. A young man who had tears running down his cheeks stood up. "I am Abijah. Is Keturah all right? Please, she did not die did she?"

Smiling Deborah said, "Keturah did not die, Abijah. Take your son, show him to the elders as is the custom, and then come back to her."

Shakily he reached for the child and tenderly enfolded him in his arms. "His name is Moshe," he declared and walked proudly to the village square to meet the elders.

Deborah went back into the house to check on Keturah. She was sleeping. All seemed to be well, so Rahab and Deborah quietly left and started for home.

CHAPTER 12

When they were close, they could see a commotion in front of Rahab's house.

"Barak! It is Barak!" gasped Deborah. She broke into a run and threw herself into his arms. "Barak, how did you find me? Where is your army? What . . ."

"One question at a time Deborah!" laughed Barak delighted to see her. "Are you well?"

"Yes, yes I am well."

"This is my guide, Gideon. Without him I would surely have lost my way and God would be very disgusted with me."

Rahab called a boy to take care of their horses and beckoned them into the house out of the heat of the afternoon.

"And your husband, is he here?" asked Barak looking around and the obviously feminine interior of the house.

"He is away," said Deborah hoping not to have to explain his absence.

Barak noticed her discomfort and did not inquire further. He would give her time to tell him what was happening.

Miriam hurried down the road and sailed across the courtyard to find out who the strangers were and what they wanted with Deborah and Rahab. She burst through the doorway startling Barak and Gideon. "This is my mother-in-law, Miriam," offered Deborah.

"And who are you gentlemen and what is your business here?" demanded Miriam.

There was a stunned silence. Barak wondered what indeed the situation was. Here was a nasty, obviously frightening mother-in-law and an absent husband. What were they hiding?

"I am Barak, captain of the Israelite army and this is Gideon my guide. Deborah and I grew up together and I was away with my army when she married. So I came to congratulate her and her husband on their marriage. However, I have been told he is not here, but away. I am sorry to miss him."

Deborah was amazed at Barak's maturity and cool-headed response. This was not the impetuous young soldier she remembered. She beamed with pride.

"I am sure you have much to do, Miriam. Thank you for greeting our guests so graciously," said Rahab nudging Miriam toward the door. Outside Rahab said in a low menacing voice, "Remember our secret, Miriam. Keep your claws in."

Miriam turned, stormed out of the courtyard, and up the road toward her house. Rahab was eager to go back inside and hear more of Barak and Gideon's adventures, but lingered a moment to be sure Miriam did not come back. Deborah gathered food for refreshments and they all sat down to share their stories. Their conversation lasted into the late evening. Barak and Gideon left at near dark to find an inn and a room.

The next morning Barak and Gideon waited until Deborah's clients left so they could join her under the Palm of Deborah. For the first time Deborah brought her papyrus of scriptures out of hiding. Was this why Ya'akov was in her dream? To tell her it was right to share them now? These were her most trusted friends. She felt happy and safe for the first time since her wedding.

They spent the afternoon in the cool of Rahab's house going over scripture and battle strategies. Rahab and Gideon were amazed at Deborah's insights into both scripture and battle. She and Barak had an uncanny talent for putting them together in ways that made perfect sense. Their insights seemed to grow as they shared ideas.

Late in the afternoon Rahab went to the kitchen to prepare a meal. Gideon went to the well to draw water for her. "Men do not usually do women's work, Gideon," smiled Rahab.

"I am not a usual man. Please do not tell anyone," laughed Gideon.

Rahab turned away to hide the blush on her cheeks. She scolded herself for her body's response to his presence, the way his muscles rippled as he set down the water jar, his musky scent. She busied herself cutting and dropping pieces of meat, vegetables, and spices into the heating water.

*　　*　　*

Miriam paced the floor all night. There had to be a way to get rid of Rahab for good. She was grabbing power and becoming much more dangerous. She could get them all killed with that temper of hers. The right words to the wrong person would be a disaster.

Joseph arrived home in the morning. He looked worried and even haggard. "Did all go well, Joseph?" inquired Miriam with barely veiled anxiety.

"Yes, for now. I do not know how much longer we can keep this up. The authorities were very close this time. There were many more guards posted and I was not sure our own hired guards had not betrayed us. They seemed reluctant to be found when I looked for them in the marketplace." His voice rose to a higher pitch. "You have brought this trouble on us, Miriam!" shouted Joseph thoroughly exasperated.

"You insisted upon marrying me against my wishes, Joseph! I told you it would not bode well and you thought that was so alluring. You have only yourself to blame, so keep your sharp tongue to yourself!" screamed Miriam.

Angrily Joseph threw his gear onto the floor and strode out to the well to wash off the dust and the stink of Ashdod. Miriam kicked his gear into the corner and went onto the roof to calm down. It would do no good to escalate their estrangement. She had to talk to him about Rahab, Deborah, and their visitors tonight. Joseph would leave for the fields early in the morning and she wanted him to start thinking about what they must do. They must take action soon.

Rahab was on her roof when she heard Miriam and Joseph. The evening air often carried their voices when they were shouting at each other. "There is trouble, big trouble!" she said to the other three. "Deborah, we will take you to the palm and oasis. Then the three of us will go to my place in the hills. You will be safe as long as you have clients coming and going. Miriam does not know I told you about our family shame, but she may suspect anyway. I will return for you when the sun is high and we will go into the hills until I know what Miriam is planning. She is dangerous and not above having us murdered in our sleep."

Deborah froze. She had not felt she was in this much danger even from Sisera. Not even in Tirzah. Somehow this strange and dark intrigue was more terrifying by far. They left in the night, an hour before their usual time, to go to the Palm of Deborah. She was nervous all the way.

"I will not be far away Deborah. I will be hiding in the rocks and scrub," said Barak. "I will not leave you alone. I will be high enough to see if anyone approaches other than the villagers."

Rahab agreed. "I will be not far behind Barak to be sure you know the way into the hills. Gideon will keep watch with me."

Gideon said, "You will be within my sight. I will watch from a different direction than Barak so we are not all lined up like sheep going through a narrow pass."

Deborah was relieved when several villagers she knew arrived at her tent opening. All went well throughout the morning, and she was more than ready to leave as the sun rose high in the sky. She piled her belongings on the donkey and started for the hills. Barak stood and waved her to come on toward him. Gideon moved in watching behind her and they met Rahab half way to her hut.

"Come this way," motioned Rahab. "I know a place farther on. I suspect Joab knows where my usual place is and I do not know if he could be pressured into telling Joseph and Miriam where it is."

"But we have no food, Rahab. How long shall we be there?" asked Deborah.

"Do not worry, Deborah," said Gideon. "Rahab and I stole back to the house before anyone was about and brought everything to a place not too far ahead. We may not be able to return to Rahab's house very soon, if at all."

Deborah had not thought about Lapidoth for a long time. So much was happening and it just occurred to her that he must not have returned with Joseph. She did not feel married and did not have any opportunity to consider him her husband, especially since he left her alone in strange places to fend for herself.

After they were settled Gideon left to spy in Ashdod. Perhaps he could discover what was transpiring, if anything. He was known in Ashdod and had a few good hiding places from which to operate. He took the donkey rather than the horse, to seem like just another Bedouin traveling through the countryside.

Deborah, Barak, and Rahab settled down to wait. As the late afternoon came on Barak suggested they continue their studies of scripture and battle strategies. Rahab went a distance up into the rocks to watch for anyone approaching other than Gideon. She found herself praying for Gideon's safety, a surprise since she did not pray or necessarily believe. But since Deborah came into her life, she had indeed learned more about prayer and God.

Night fell and Gideon had not returned. "Do not fear for Gideon," reassured Barak. "He is more than my guide to help me find you, Deborah. He is actually a highly skilled spy and my army depends upon him for good information. That is how I learned of your marriage and who your husband is, and where you had gone to escape Sisera. I also learned that your family is still safe and the village has not been destroyed. We will wait as long as it is safe, and if we must leave, he will find us."

"You know that my family is safe? Thank you! And your father? Is your family safe as well?"

"Yes, my family is well. Sisera seems more determined to find villages that harbor so called criminals fleeing from the wrath of Jabin. There were none of those hiding in Kadesh-Napthali."

Deborah felt relieved and guilty at the same time. It was unconscionable that she could leave her family in danger, and yet she had no choice.

"What about Tirzah? They all looked like innocent villagers."

"There may have been someone at the inn. It may have even been Lapidoth," ventured Barak.

Deborah bristled. "But surely it could not have been Lapidoth, Barak! God through Hannah sent him to me. He is not even from Napthali!"

Pricked by her sudden defense of Lapidoth, Barak pressed on. "What did you know about him, really, Deborah? Were you given any information about this chosen man, about what to expect or to ask? My mother told me that many times. Not only did she know nothing about my father, but was never to ask. Fortunately my father was known in the community as a good and kindly man. Her father made sure of that for her. If your family did not know this man, it should have been up to your father to find out!"

"My father? Yes, I suppose so. But he was so glad to get me married he probably did not want to ask anything that might chase a prospect away." Now Deborah felt more angry than guilty. Her husband might be a fugitive and her in-laws were involved in some dangerous dealings. Again thinking of herself as part of the Israeli army and studying battle plans did not seem so strange. It actually seemed inviting.

"I am sorry, Deborah. I did not mean to sound so harsh. But you are my beloved big sister and my head exploded with questions and worries when I heard of your sudden marriage to a stranger. When I heard, it was too late to come to you and be with you. I told myself I was worried about the battle plans, but that is not true. I was worried for you, the beautiful intelligent girl I grew up with. I did not want to think of your life and happiness destroyed. My faith is not as strong as yours, but I am learning it slowly."

Deborah flung herself into Barak's arms and sobbed. "I have been so ashamed of myself that I did not think of you when all this happened. I was right there with you making battle plans and never thought to tell you about Lapidoth. You have always been more important to me than anyone except our families, Hannah, and Ya'akov. Suddenly everything was torn out of my life, and I just could not think anymore!"

Barak stood there holding her for a long time until her tears stopped. This was all that mattered. He and Deborah were together. While they followed the call of God he knew they would not be parted again. He had an overwhelming feeling all would be well for them.

In the morning Barak announced they would move farther north. "I had a dream during the night about a battle raging all around us and Hannah was beckoning us to her."

They agreed they should go. They packed the horses and led them farther into the hills and away from Bethel, Lapidoth's family, and the Palm of Deborah. The going was slow and difficult, and Barak kept sharp watch for any movement in the surrounding countryside. He left markers for Gideon, and wondered if he should have gone after him first. But he could not leave Deborah and Rahab. They stopped in a high cave to await the cooler air of evening and hopefully, Gideon.

Barak and Deborah continued to study and put plans in place for the army. Rahab kept watch from the top of a tree until nightfall. She climbed down and came back to the cave looking worried, but tried to keep her fears from Deborah and Barak. She never cared about anyone before, so had never been afraid before. Her life was always her own and free. Now she had feelings of fear, trust, and loyalty all at the same time. The word love was not in her vocabulary. The only mention of it was in the scripture, "Jacob loved Rachel." The story did not say if Rachel loved Jacob.

She started when she heard a snuffling sound close by. She picked up a stick to ward off any wild animal. Suddenly there was a happy "yip." It was Kelev! He did not want to be left behind and found her. She threw her arms around his scruffy neck and hugged him hard.

Barak knew his knowledge of this territory was very limited. He was not sure how far they could travel without Gideon. He planned to go more toward the east to avoid Philistines but the main road was far away. The next day they began to travel east. Again Barak left coded markers for Gideon. The hill country became more rugged and many detours confused their direction at times. Kelev trotted happily along side them tongue and tail wagging vigorously.

They stopped to rest when the sun was high. Kelev laid down too, nose between his paws, but one ear cocked straight up alert for any strange sounds. It was late afternoon when they continued on. Barak became more worried. He did not like feeling lost. The foliage was thicker which hid their presence better, but it hid the presence of dangers as well. They nearly stepped over a hidden precipice except that Kelev had blocked their way and growled. There was another reason Kelev growled. Someone was approaching. Barak crouched beside Kelev to see what he was looking at. A young man burst out of the brush. It was Ham! Barak was shocked to see him again. "Ham! What are you doing here? I thought you would be back across the Jordan by now!"

"I am still searching for my sister," said Ham resolutely. "I cannot go home without her. I told you and Gideon that."

"Yes, I remember." Barak introduced Ham and briefly told Deborah and Rahab what he knew of his story.

"Where is Gideon, Barak?" queried Ham looking around.

"Gideon will join us soon. He had some business to take care of," said Rahab who had stepped forward to more closely inspect this raggedy newcomer.

"You are worried. I can see it on your faces," said Ham.

"Yes, we are," said Barak looking off into the distance. "We thought he would be with us by now. But he is very capable of taking care of himself, and he will follow us when he can. Is there any word of your sister?" inquired Barak in order to change the subject.

"Nothing but the words of a few shepherds who thought they saw a girl being dragged along by two men, but they knew nothing more."

"The shepherds probably said something, anything, because they hoped you would pay them," scoffed Rahab. Ham dropped his head and Rahab immediately regretted her heartless words. "Tell me what she was like, Ham," she asked.

Ham gave her a description of Adah, including a scar on her forearm from a childhood fall. "She is tall, long dark hair, has an attractive face and she is very shy. Marauders took her when they attacked our village and carried her away across the Jordan."

Barak felt very sorry for Ham and his sister, but there was nothing he could do. He was having enough trouble finding his own way through the wilderness.

"Oh, but I can guide you! I know this area from the villagers I stayed with. They taught me so I could continue looking for Adah!"

"Are we near that village now?" asked Barak.

"No, actually we are quite far west of it, over several low mountain ranges. But north of us there is a high valley with an army encampment. I saw it a few days ago but did not go near to it," said Ham. "I did not know who they might be."

Barak's mouth dropped open. "My camp! We are close to my camp. Of course! How stupid of me! We have been so busy looking back for Gideon or pursuers, I did not look forward or count the hours we have traveled." Eagerly they followed Ham in the direction of the camp.

*   *   *

Gideon found Ashdod so full of guards and soldiers of all kinds it was difficult for him to move about easily. His spies told him that Lapidoth's family was in a very dangerous business. Their contacts were shadowy figures who kept to the underground traffic ways. They could not discern if there was any movement.

Gideon wrapped himself in smelly, ragged robes and went to the inns to listen. A young girl equally tattered brought him food and wine. She was frightened half to death and never spoke. He tried a few language dialects, but she did not respond. He asked his spies about her, but they did not know her. He hid for another night while they carefully looked for answers among other contacts. Nothing.

But something about her exotic looks kept nagging at Gideon. It was not attraction. Rahab filled that part of his mind completely. Then he suddenly knew what it might be. Moab across the Jordan! He told his spies to say the word "Ham" to her. If she recognized it, bring her to the ruins near the north edge of town. They nodded and left.

His friends gave him a change of clothes to use if he needed them. He took a dark robe for the girl as well. He led an old crippled mule and slowly left Ashdod at dark. Anyone would think he was a beggar going to the ruins to sleep. In the night he heard a shuffling close to him and jumped behind an old wall. Someone whispered their password and Gideon breathed a sigh of relief. The terrified girl was with them. They tossed her down in front of him and disappeared into the darkness. "Ham" whispered Gideon.

"Ham" she responded hopefully. In the moonlight she could see he was not Ham and shrank back, but then she recognized him as the beggar in the inn. She pointed to herself and said, "Adah." He set the donkey loose, took her hand, and they quietly left the ruins.

He pulled her along toward the hills walking as quickly as they could before the moon no longer lit their way.

The rocky ruins were behind to the west and a sandy plain stretched out before them. They half walked and half ran to reach the hills and safety. The plain of Philistia was a no man's land and anything but safe. They jumped into a small wadi, crouched low, and waited to catch their breath. Shortly they continued on, traveling all night moving northeast. Gideon watched carefully for Philistines, snakes, and mountain lions.

At a stream of fresh mountain water they slipped into its coolness while staying close to the brush along the bank. It washed away the dust and dirt, and their fatigue. Gideon unrolled the extra clothes and gave a tunic, sandals, and a robe to Adah. He buried their rags in a hole under a tree and they came away from the stream looking like respectable travelers.

Adah and Gideon had said nothing more than their names. As they traveled Gideon was trying desperately to recall some of the Moabite dialect Ham had used. He managed to remember the word for friend and home. She would nod but offer nothing further. The next night they stopped near Gezer in the tribal territory of Gad where Gideon had more contacts. They supplied him with food and two mules. After Gideon paid them what he could they were welcome to stay in the stable through the night. Before dawn he and Adah put their provisions on the mules and led them quietly away.

Gideon was amazed that Adah was a lot stronger than she looked. She kept up with him, never falling back or stopping until he stopped. It was better now to have the mules to ride and their progress was much faster. Soon they were past Ephraim and Bethel, taking a little used passage into the mountains toward the army camp. Gideon spotted the coded signs Barak left for him. It was a relief to know Barak, Rahab, and Deborah were well on their way to safety.

As they neared the camp Kelev came bursting upon them, jumped on Gideon, and licked his face thoroughly. Adah hung back until she saw Ham coming though the trees toward her.

He could not believe his eyes. "Adah! Adah!" He threw his arms around her and held her tight. They chattered excitedly in the Moabite dialect. Ham turned to Gideon and threw his arms around him as well. "You have rescued me twice, Gideon! Thank you, my friend!"

They walked into the camp together to Barak's tent. Adah hid behind Ham and Gideon. The encampment was huge and terrifying.

There were campfires starting to burn as far as she could see. There were guards everywhere and Barak's huge tent was fit for a sheik. Deborah and Rahab came out of their tent to welcome them. Rahab was almost tearful to see Gideon. Then she saw Adah and fire blazed in her eyes. Who was this woman traveling with Gideon?

They all sat down in Barak's tent to a meal and wine. Rahab's heart was calmed as Gideon sat down beside her. They heard the story of Ham and Adah from Barak. Then Ham began to speak. "I have not told you the whole truth. Adah is not my sister, but my betrothed. When she was abducted, my brothers wanted to help me find her quickly before my family could denounce her as dead, because then she would be unfit to be my wife. Now my brothers are gone . . ."

"Ham, I am so sorry," whispered Adah in their native dialect.

"It is not your fault, Adah. You did nothing wrong. My brothers knew the risk and chose to come with me. I told them to let me go alone, but they would not hear of it," he replied in the same dialect. They stood up and quietly left the tent to be alone.

Gideon relayed what little he had found out in Ashdod about Joseph and Miriam's connections. There was great danger as Deborah and Rahab already knew. But no one had traveled toward Bethel from Ashdod in the last few days. He learned nothing of Lapidoth. No travelers had heard that name. "Perhaps he uses another name and does not linger after business was concluded," offered Rahab.

Abel and Naham came into the tent relieved to greet Gideon. Over the meal Abel recounted all the training techniques he had employed to get the soldiers ready for combat. Naham had gone back to the region of Napthali to gather more news of Sisera's movements. Soon they were all engaged in mapping the central part of Israel and what was happening in each area. Some of the tribes were still not ready to join Barak and the army, but Naham said, "They will surely change their minds when Sisera threatens them. King Jabin is no one's friend and Sisera is his destroyer."

Deborah came to Barak's side after Abel, Naham, and Gideon left together to attend to army duties. "Barak, I have to go back . . ."

"Back to Bethel?" whispered Barak in disbelief.

"No! To Kadesh-Napthali. I have to go home and pull my life back together. Since the last time we met when your father, Abinoam, was with us, I feel like I have been on a long rough sea voyage and I am losing my way. Can you spare Gideon or Naham to take me there?"

"Deborah, I thought this would be a good time for us to continue planning. I need you here!"

"We have planned all through our journey from Bethel. We started the day you found me. You can work with what we have already accomplished and bring your army into the plans as they are now. There is already much for them to learn and do. You must teach them. I need to recover and purify my understanding of God and my place in this. I need time before I can take us further."

"Do you doubt your place with me, with the army?"

"Of course not. I did not mean I doubt God. I meant there might be guidance that I am missing and I need to reconnect with Hannah."

Again Barak admitted to himself that he was loath to let Deborah go. It was not just the planning he wanted. Somehow he needed her close to him. He reluctantly agreed that Gideon would take Deborah to Kadesh in a few days.

Deborah, too, felt a strong pull to stay with Barak. "Oh God, why do you make this so hard?" she whispered.

"Did you say something, Deborah?"

"Barak, I know now that you and I will be together forever. We have work to do, and in God we are never truly parted. I will not let fear and confusion cause me to forget you again." Tears threatened to spill from her eyes.

Deborah also wanted to say she needed Hannah, but was hesitant to have anyone else involved in that relationship. Hannah was her rock, her assurance, her mentor and spiritual guide. Hannah was her treasure. She needed to see Hannah before it was too late.

Barak looked at her with new eyes. She had verbalized his thoughts exactly. Something deepened in their feelings for each other and he knew her words were true. Gently he pressed a kiss onto her upturned face.

CHAPTER 13

Rahab sat quietly in the corner of the tent with Kelev. She looked up uncertainly at Deborah and slowly stood up. "I want to go with you, Deborah, if you will have me."

Deborah caught her breath. She had been so involved in her own next step that she almost forgot Rahab was sitting there. "Oh, Rahab, yes I want you with me! I will always want you with me. Forgive me!"

"There is nothing to forgive. I am aware of how important your calling is and I do not wish to intrude. I can always return to my home in Bethel."

"I am sure Bethel is not safe for any of us, Rahab. God has put us together and your part has been no less important than mine. Please do not go back. Let us discern together what work God has for us next."

Rahab smiled and nodded. "I will go with you and not doubt again. My faith is not very strong. I have not been accepted among people except to sell my saddlebags, but you are a great friend, Deborah. I will stay with you and learn to trust a little more."

They embraced and went to their tent. The travels through the wilderness were exhausting and it was indeed time to rest for the next day or two. They spread straw and robes over the floor of the tent and stowed their meager belongings.

"What do you know of Gideon, Deborah?" asked Rahab.

"I do not know much more than you, Rahab. I have not met any of Barak's guards except for Abel, and that was just for a moment. I believe Gideon is not just a guide, but also one of Barak's spies. He brought me news of my family. Naham is also a spy for Barak. Sometimes the two work together. But I do not know anything about their families or what villages they come from. What makes you ask?"

"Gideon is the first man I have ever been attracted to. He is loyal, heroic, wise, and I do not know what else. So many men are concerned only for their own power and riches. He seems to put other things first."

"Yes, I think you are right," agreed Deborah. "I did not know even that much about Lapidoth when I married him. I relied upon Hannah's dream and that he was her cousin. I trusted Hannah completely and relied on her wisdom so many times while I was growing up. I never even asked myself if I was attracted to him. I guess I envy you that feeling."

"No need to envy me! I saw you and Barak a while ago. I think you know very well what that feeling is!"

Deborah blushed and hastened to assure Rahab there was nothing between her and Barak.

Rahab smiled at her. "I am not sure it is a feeling to be envied. It is disturbing and raises too many questions. I am accustomed to feeling confident, clear on what I want, and what I need in order to survive."

"Well, here we are together with lots of questions on our minds. We will seek the answers together. That is what women do. Who knows what tomorrow will bring, or the day after that!" Deborah had no doubt now about her future. Her sense of assuredness and safety in God was becoming stronger by the minute.

They snuggled down into their robes and drifted off to sleep. Again Deborah was tossing in her sleep, seeing battle scenes and the faces of Amri and Ya'akov.

*   *   *

Lapidoth was fortunate to leave Ashdod unnoticed. He traveled under the business name of Marcus, a mysterious name he had heard in the far north. He chose it because it revealed nothing of his true origins. He traveled in peasants' clothing and carried an ancient sickle sword, a long curved blade, for his protection. The jewels he had for sale were sewn into the bottom of a bundle of food, salt, and flour.

After days of walking and traveling with foreign merchants he arrived safely at the seaport of Acre. Gispah, his innkeeper friend and contact, was delighted to see him as always. Lapidoth brought him business and riches. In return Gispah made appointments with houses of wealth and royalty for him and kept his identity closely guarded.

At the inn he packed away his peasant clothing and changed into the rich robes of a successful merchant. It always mystified Gispah that Lapidoth would do his business and then disappear for a few days wearing peasants' clothing. Then he would return. "I fear for your safety, Marcus. If I may ask, where do you go and why?"

"I am a salesman of a different kind of jewel, Gispah, the jewels of wisdom from many cultures."

"But I do not see any papyrus or scrolls!"

"The jewels are in my head. I teach small gatherings of people who want to be educated. I do not really sell the teachings, except to convince people they should know wisdom for a better life."

Gispah scowled and ran his fingers through his resplendent black hair. "Why? Why do you care if people want to be educated? Most do not."

"Most seem not to care about education because they know they have no chance to obtain it. They have been told it is for scholars, rabbis and priests only. I believe everyone should have wisdom and education."

"Everyone? Women, too?" Gispah's bushy eyebrows were now high in astonishment. "This is blasphemous! It is illegal! It is foolish! A waste of time! Common people have no mind for this, Marcus, and especially women. It could get you killed in those filthy alleys. And for what?"

"Gispah, my friend, I have been doing this all of my adult life. You have asked me where I go every time I stay here. This is the first time I have told you what else I do. You see I have been safe enough because I always return here."

Galina, Gispah's young daughter, came in from the kitchen when she heard Marcus' voice. She always hoped he would notice her and some day marry her, but she knew he still thought of her as a child and nothing more. Sometimes she would lower the neck of her tunic and leave her robe loose to seem more alluring, but it only brought scowls and reproofs from her father.

"Galina, you are twelve years old! You are not a woman and you are not a whore, so you will not dress like one!" This was enough to send Galina running out the back door and into the olive grove to pout.

Lapidoth was not witness to these reproofs. He could not understand why Galina would become sulky at times and stamp her feet as she walked around the inn.

His buyers were few this time and he knew he would have to continue north to Sidon to sell all of his cache. He spent only one day teaching, anxious to sell the jewels before they were stolen or lost. He kept his peasants' robes on, packed everything, and slipped out the back. He hurried to the docks and booked passage on a boat for the short voyage to Sidon with a captain he knew.

"The buyers are going farther north now. Not so many come here," said the yellow toothed captain as he waved his ale mug toward the marketplace. "There are strangers on my boat this time, so guard yourself well even though you are robed like a common man, Marcus."

Lapidoth nodded, "Thank you my friend. I will do that. But why are the buyers going farther away?"

"They find suppliers from India are more interesting, and they have more protection. There are too many raiders here, too many tribal wars. They become afraid and stay away from where there is trouble."

He nodded to the captain and boarded the boat. He found a place on deck where he could see in all directions. Pulling a wooden box closer, he sat on it and waited as the few sailors cast off and set sail for Sidon.

One passenger eyed him covertly, looking away quickly if Lapidoth turned his way. Another one stared openly at him. He wondered if they were together and plotting something. He loosened the sickle sword under his robe and left the handle partly exposed so they would know he was armed and ready for any trouble.

Winds were favorable, the Great Sea relatively calm, and mercifully the trip to Sidon was not long. Lapidoth did not relish the thought of spending a night in this situation. When they docked he disembarked and moved quickly though the wharf crowds and shops. He stopped in a doorway to see if anyone was following him. Yes, the men on the boat were lingering at a market stall not too far away, furtively glancing in his direction. Lapidoth cursed under his breath. He moved further into the doorway, unpacked his other robe and put it on over the peasant clothing. He swung quickly out of the doorway and up a road toward the rich section of Sidon. At the top of a hill he again stopped and watched for several minutes, but saw no one this time.

The inn Gispah recommended was on the other side of the hill. Night would be falling soon and Lapidoth moved in that direction on the trot. Entering the inn he gave Gispah's name to the owner. Ammiel the innkeeper acknowledged the connection, greeted him warmly, and offered his best ale to Lapidoth. Lapidoth introduced himself as Marcus and gratefully accepted the offer. He was careful to sit down near the back wall so everyone who came in would be in front of him.

Presently he went to his room at the top of the stairs and set about sorting his belongings that had become jumbled with the quick changes of clothing. He checked the jewels to be sure they were secured, tucked them under his body as he lay down on the pallet.

It suddenly occurred to him that he had not given a thought to Deborah since he was forced to leave her at his mother's house. He felt more than a little guilty not only that he had left her right away, but that he left her with his mother who was a shrew. He shuddered to think of the misery Deborah might be experiencing at her hands. But then wives were always subject to their mother-in-law's demands. He would go back in a month or two to check on her and perhaps establish a home of their own. That thought have him a little relief from the guilt.

The light dimmed into night and he began to doze. His dreams were a mix of Hannah pointing her bony finger at him and the shadowy men on the boat and in the alley. He woke up with a start as his door creaked open. He reached for his sickle sword, jumped up, and swung it at whoever might be coming through that door. There was a loud cry and a thump on the floor. Lapidoth lit a candle and stared down at one of the men from the boat who was staring up at him with blank eyes. Blood was oozing through his robe and onto the floor.

Ammiel came rushing in carrying a lantern. He nearly tripped over the man on the floor. "What has happened? Marcus, are you all right?"

164

"Yes, I am all right." Lapidoth decided not to tell Ammiel this man was on the boat from Acre. The less he knew the better. He would find out for himself why this man was following him and if he knew about the cache of jewels.

"Do you know this man?"

"No, I do not know him," Lapidoth answered truthfully.

Ammiel took Lapidoth to another room for the rest of the night. Lapidoth never asked what he planned to do with the body. He assumed the inn had a good reputation and Ammiel would do whatever necessary to preserve that.

In the morning Lapidoth dressed in his rich robe and went to the market place to find his contact. The man would be wearing an emerald earring, which Lapidoth thought would be easy to spot. He walked for a few hours before a servant approached him. He motioned for Lapidoth to follow him. They went through twisted alleys and areas reduced to rubble. The man led him to a hidden cave entrance and left him there. Lapidoth looked back over the route they had come and hoped he could find his way out. He entered the cave and followed a tunnel that twisted and turned. At last he came to a lighted area where several men were sitting. One of them had an emerald earring.

"I am Saladin." He placed a bag of coins on the table and continued, "I understand you have some high quality merchandise to show me."

Lapidoth said, "I am Marcus. This is what I have to sell." He brought out the bag of jewels from the folds in his robe.

Saladin looked over the jewels, holding them up to a light. He smiled and pushed the bag of gold coins toward Lapidoth. Lapidoth quickly counted the coins and put them in his robe. Saladin stood, bowed, and motioned him toward another room. "You can change into the peasant garb you carry. My guard will see you back to the market. It will seem as if he has captured you and is taking you against your will. And, yes, I know your name is not Marcus, but it will do."

Lapidoth's eyes widened in surprise. He dared not ask how this man knew about his clothes and his name, but there was still a chance he did not know his real name, so he remained silent. He changed his robe and sandals, secured the coins in a sewed in area of his garment and followed the guard out of the cave. They wended their way through the ruins and when they neared the market, the guard pushed Lapidoth down and kicked him.

It was a big shock, but Lapidoth stayed on the ground until the guard stalked away. He got up slowly and carefully making sure he did not rush. Men watched him but none approached. Holding his ribs where the kick landed, he limped his way to Ammiel's inn and was glad to get there otherwise unhampered. He stumbled in the back door, went to his room, changed his robe, and walked into the front part of the inn.

Ammiel rushed to bring him some ale and bread. "Are you all right, my friend? Has someone attacked you?"

"No Ammiel. I stumbled over a rock. I was looking back and not watching where I was going."

Ammiel looked doubtful but said nothing more. Lapidoth knew it was not wise to spend another night in this place. He ordered more food, finished eating, gathered his belongings and left.

CHAPTER 14

He went back to the wharf to find passage back to Acre. The boat he came north on was still tied up at the dock. He waited in the market until the captain and crew came back to the boat.

"Captain, I need passage back to Acre. How soon will you be leaving? Can you take me?" Lapidoth's anxiety was at a fever pitch.

"The tide is just about to go out. You are just in time, my friend. We are leaving right now."

Lapidoth paid him the fare and stepped on board. He watched the dock for other passengers. Two Bedouins came with large bundles of cargo. They ignored Lapidoth and went about their business of loading the bundles into the back of the boat. One of the crew cast off the ropes and they moved out into the sea. The winds were not with them as they sailed away from shore so their progress was slow. They did some tacking and some rowing. The sail went up for a while and then came back down again. The shoreline looked the same as if they were not even moving.

Lapidoth took the time to think about his life, and the danger he was always in. He thought about the danger he and his family had put Deborah in. Somehow it was no longer the exciting adventure as when he first started working with his father. He wanted his own life! But how could he do that? He determined to go to see Hannah. He dreaded her scorn and scolding when he would have to tell her how he treated Deborah, but he knew the answer might lie with her. He began rehearsing in his head what he would say to her.

After a seeming interminable voyage they reached Acre. It was late in the day and a storm was coming from the west. Lapidoth went directly to Gispah's inn. It was crowded and he might have to sleep on the bench by the wall. Suddenly he felt older and his bones creaky. Gispah gave him Galina's room and she would sleep in her father's room. Lapidoth knew he should deny the offer, but he was too tired to do anything but follow him to the room. Lowering himself onto the pallet, he put his moneybag under his arm under his robe and dropped off to sleep.

He opened his eyes in the early morning to see Galina standing over him smiling. "I have brought you fresh water," she said uncertainly.

Lapidoth jumped up and opened the door to the hall. "Galina! You should not be in here with the door closed! It is not proper!"

Galina scowled and jumped back. She turned and ran out the door. Lapidoth shook his head and went to the pitcher of water on the table. He splashed his face and arms, gathered his belongings, and went down the stairs to the room where food was being served.

"Was my daughter in your room?" asked Gispah quietly. Galina turned pale and looked at the floor.

"No, Gispah. She handed me a pitcher of water through the door for which I am grateful. I would never allow her to come into my room. I am sure you know that."

Gispah knew Lapidoth was saving face for him. He nodded and ordered Galina into the kitchen to get more food for the guests. Lapidoth finished his breakfast, paid Gispah for his lodging and left. He went directly to a livery and purchased a horse. He turned east and headed through the valley and passes to Kadesh-Napthali and Hannah's place. There had to be an answer for his life and Hannah would know it.

*   *   *

Deborah and Barak spent several days deep in conversation and prayer. Battle strategies were sketched out in the dirt outside his tent. The ones that seemed best were transferred onto pieces of papyrus. Deborah laid out the pages of scripture inserting verses and her notes about them into the training lectures. Abel looked over their shoulders in amazement. "I have never seen anything like this! I believe it will work!"

"Abel, only God will make it work. We must never forget that. Scriptures and strategies are empty without God," said Deborah.

"Yes, of course. I just meant the way you are putting it all together is amazing," said Abel a little embarrassed. "I should go."

"No, please stay, Abel," said Deborah apologetically. "You must understand these things, too. You are part of God's plan. No one is left out."

"Thank you, Deborah. I want to learn. I have loved God all my life. I just never had the chance to understand as you do." Abel sat down and listened intently. Just knowing he was part of God's plan helped him concentrate deeply and he determined to remember very word.

Early in the morning Deborah said to Rahab, "We need to leave. I must go to my family and Hannah. I miss Rabbi Amri and Leah. I even miss Ya'akov who is gone forever from my sight."

Rahab hugged Deborah and said, "I will pack everything and we will be ready soon."

Deborah went to Barak and he reluctantly agreed they should go. He would send Gideon and Naham with them. He gave them a donkey to carry their belongings. "It will be better if you do not have horses. They will make you too conspicuous. You may even have to leave the donkey if someone pursues you."

"I have become accustomed to traveling great distances over rocks, mountain passes, and through forests," smiled Deborah. "I will return to you when the time is right. Be well, Barak, and God be with you." She hugged him tightly and turned to go. Gideon, Naham, and Rahab joined her. Barak and Abel watched until they disappeared over the ridge. Sensing Barak's feeling of emptiness at Deborah's departure, Abel said, "We have much work to do, my lord. Shall we begin?"

Barak turned to Abel, clapped him on the shoulder, and agreed, "Yes, let us begin. Our journey will require much of us all and we must be prepared."

Gideon set a brisk pace, which pleased Deborah very much. She was finally on her way home and it was exhilarating. Rahab walked with Deborah and Naham led the donkey. The animal was a willing little beast, as if he knew he was part of a great journey. He walked briskly sometimes passing Naham and pulling him along. The day was uneventful but Gideon and Naham were not lulled. They kept constant and careful watch.

*   *   *

Hannah's old bones were feeling the onset of the cold weather. Slowly she gathered the last of her herbs and roots into a basket to store for the short winter. Wrapping her robe tighter around her shoulders against the cold wind she went inside. She started a fire in her oven to heat the room, hung the herbs from the beam, and placed the roots in a cloth bag in the next room.

There was a rapping on the door. Hannah was surprised. She had practically no visitors these days since Deborah had married and moved away. Her occasional visits to the market would bring questions about her well being in a lonely place in the hills. Each time she considered living in the village, the answer in her mind was "No, I am better off where I am."

Hannah pulled the door open a crack and peered out. "Lapidoth! Lapidoth, come in!" Her face brightened. "Is Deborah with you?" she said leaning out to see.

"Greetings, Hannah," he said as he stepped through the doorway. "Deborah is not with me. She is still in my family's home. I came alone on business."

Hannah narrowed her eyes and scrutinized his face. "Lapidoth, you are not lying to me, I know. But you do not know the truth."

Lapidoth's brow furrowed. "I do not know the truth? What are you talking about, Hannah?"

"Deborah is not in your family's home. Barak rescued her from dangers there. Dangers you knew about. Did you tell her about your business, Lapidoth?"

Lapidoth was astounded. How could Hannah know about these things? And how could she know something about Deborah even he did not know?

"Where is she now, Hannah? Do you know that too?"

Hannah watched him carefully. "I do not know where she is. More importantly, you who are supposed to take care of her do not know. How can this be?"

There was silence. Lapidoth wanted to just get up and leave, but he had come here to find an answer to his own life. He had come here to seek advice and knew he would be on the spot about Deborah.

"Hannah, there has been much trouble. I have dreamed about you so many times pointing your finger at me. Perhaps I should start from the beginning."

"Yes," agreed Hannah. She poured him some herb tea and gave him a chunk of bread. She placed some cheese and a few figs on the plate and set it before him. "We can accomplish nothing without that."

Lapidoth started from the night of the raid at Tirzah. He left nothing out. Hannah sipped her tea quietly and nodded occasionally. He told how he had left Deborah with other inn guests and then lost her. How he and Nehemiah had searched, and finally found her with Rahab in the hills north of his home. "That day is the last time I saw her. My father ordered me to immediately accompany him to Ashdod. We left abruptly without a word to anyone, even Deborah. I was sure she was safe and my mother would take care of her. After that I do not know what happened." Lapidoth hung his head and ran his fingers through his hair.

"I know something of your mother. How could you think Deborah would be safe with her? Word came to me quickly that she was in danger. Fortunately Barak found her and took her away from there. I know nothing more."

"How does this word come to you, Hannah?" asked Lapidoth suspiciously. "Do you have spies? Did you dream it? Did God tell you?"

"What does it matter, Lapidoth? When you find Deborah she will tell you the rest of the story. Why did you come here? Surely not to salve your conscience! What do you want from me?"

"Because of my mother's scandalous connections and my father's determination to keep the family safe, my life has not been my own. I have done my father's bidding to get the business completed even though it always put us in danger. I have been followed, attacked at night in a room at an inn, and met shady merchants in filthy caves surrounded by guards. I have tried to do some good by going to the poor in the villages to teach them wisdom and something of money, although they rarely have any. I have given them some of my funds to help them. I feel trapped by my mother's evil past. I want an answer. I want to know how to live my own life. So I came to you."

"Have you asked God, Lapidoth?"

"I have no knowledge of praying or of God's will. My family is not observant. My mother is a heathen and my father fears her."

"Then let us begin with prayer," said Hannah. She put an old prayer shawl over her head and handed one to Lapidoth. Clumsily he fumbled with it and managed to cover his head as she began.

Darkness was falling as she concluded the prayers. Without a word Lapidoth rose and went out into the cool evening. He untethered his horse and rode slowly to the village of Kadesh. Hannah watched him from her doorway until he disappeared down the path to the road. She was troubled for Deborah and decided to continue her prayers until her heart was calm again.

Hannah slept a troubled sleep. Dreams and images came to her. In her dream there was darkness in Ephraim and danger all around. Deborah was scrambling up a hill reaching out for something. She awoke in the middle of the night, started a fire in the oven, and heated water for tea.

"What is it, God? What do I need to understand? What do I need to do? Indeed what can a gnarled old woman do?"

The next morning Hannah packed some herbs in a small bag, wrapped her warmest robe around her, drew up the hood, and started for Kadesh. The wind had not yet picked up and the sun was bright. The earth was not so soft under her feet as it was a few weeks earlier. She knew what she had to do. She first needed news of Deborah.

Judith, Deborah's mother, opened her door at Hannah's knock. "Hannah! Welcome! Are you well?"

"Oh, yes. Yes, I am well enough. And you? Are you well?"

"Yes, not too bad. Come in. I have a cough but it is not very bad."

"I have brought some herbs for your tea, Judith. You will want to be well when Deborah arrives."

"Deborah is coming? Here? How do you know?"

"I have spies," smiled Hannah.

"Your first spy is God, is it not, Hannah? You always seem to have an inside track that could only be a miracle of God. I am certain you could part the Red Sea for Moses or anyone else who needed to escape from Egypt!"

"I am glad you have your sense of humor back. That alone tells me you are indeed well."

"But what do you know of Deborah? Why would she come back here? Is she not with Lapidoth's family?"

"No, she is not. There was danger and Barak, the young commander, rescued her somehow. I do not know the details or where she is now, but I am sure she will be coming here to see you."

Judith gasped and sat down on a bench. Hannah trudged into the kitchen to prepare some of the herb tea she brought. "What kind of danger?" asked Judith with alarm. "Surely Sisera has not gone as far as Ephraim yet."

"The danger is not from Sisera but from evil closer to Bethel. I saw the darkness to the south in my dream." Hannah handed the cup of tea to Judith and sat down. "I thought I might go to the market this morning. Perhaps there will be some news there."

"Do you think the merchants would know something?" asked Judith.

"I doubt the merchants will know anything. It is not to the merchants I am going. There are others," whispered Hannah. Hannah decided not to mention Lapidoth just yet. She was still too disturbed about him. Let him confess his own neglect to care for Deborah and to keep her from danger.

The market was busy which made Hannah happy. She would be less noticeable in a crowd. She wandered along the market stalls until she could find a moment to slip into the back alley and await the elderly cripple who always came to sit in the doorway. He had been a friend of her husband and kept the information flow from breaking down after Hannah's husband died.

Presently he appeared and settled down on a stone doorway sill. "Shalom, Laban. How is your leg today?" queried Hannah.

"Ah, I could do with a few more of your healing herbs, Hannah," he replied in a gravely voice. "Have you brought some for me?"

"Of course I have, Laban. I never forget your kindness when my husband and your friend died. When all turned away and forgot me, you remembered me. For that I shall always be grateful." Hannah kindled a small fire in a stone lined hollow, warmed some water, and made his tea. He sipped it with slurping sounds of relish until it was gone. Then he leaned back with a sigh and closed his eyes for a moment.

"You are seeking news of Deborah, are you not?" he asked without opening his eyes.

"Yes, have you heard anything of her whereabouts? I had a dream of darkness in Ephraim."

"Indeed there is an evil there. It comes from the Philistine coast on the great sea."

"And Deborah?" Hannah asked after a few moments.

"She is safe for now. God willing we will see her soon enough."

Hannah knew not to press. She sat beside Laban for a while, fixed him a little more tea with herbs especially for the circulation in his legs, and went back into the marketplace. She spent a little more time there and then walked slowly back up the road to her home. If Deborah were coming back, she would surely seek Hannah's counsel and Hannah wanted to be home when she came.

Hannah prayed for her safe arrival. "She is the daughter of my heart, O God. She is your willing servant destined to do great things in your name. Watch over her and keep her safe, for your holy work is still before us. Amen."

CHAPTER 15

Gideon, Deborah, Rahab, and Naham stopped for the night in a cave hidden by thick foliage. Kelev went foraging for his dinner in the surrounding area. Naham unburdened the donkey and set about to make a small fire. The ceiling of the cave was high enough to let the smoke rise. He was careful to collect only dry tinder of the kind that would produce little smoke. As the fire kindled he went about the area to be sure the smoke would not be seen.

Deborah went over her scriptures until the light was almost gone. She sipped a little tea and wrote some notes. When it was dark she shared in the repast of bread, lamb, figs, cheese, and wine with the others. All was quiet and they kept their conversations low. Voices traveled far at night and although they had not yet encountered anyone, still they were careful.

Rahab stretched out on her sleeping mat and watched Deborah until her eyes closed. She began to dream of fire, chariots, and Gideon. She woke with a start when Deborah shook her arm. "Rahab," whispered Deborah. "You are almost shouting in your sleep."

Rahab rubbed her face. "I was dreaming . . . there was war and fire!" said Rahab.

"Who was in your dream?" queried Deborah.

"Gideon and a lot of soldiers. He was the only one I recognized."

"What do you think made you shout?"

"I could not reach him. I wanted to tell him you and Barak were coming to help him. He did not seem to hear me. I kept shouting his name, but he did not stop. What do you think it means? Am I to lose him in a battle?"

"I think it means your head runs ahead of your intuition. You are very good at thinking familiar things through, but that goes just so far. You must learn to trust your God-given wisdom more."

"Oh, thank goodness! I was afraid it meant something worse."

"It could if you do not heed its message," laughed Deborah.

"You are joking, of course . . ."

"No, Rahab, I am not. Pray on it. Pray for God's wisdom to be clear and ask how to follow it without fear."

Kelev heard the commotion and crept whimpering into the cave to be close to Rahab. "I will . . ." yawned Rahab, and drifted back to sleep. At dawn she and Deborah were jolted awake by Gideon and Naham's hands over their mouths.

"Shhh! The Philistines are close by. Come with me," whispered Gideon.

The four crept out of the cave, listened, and began to gather brush to fill the mouth of the cave. They piled it to the ceiling and retreated farther back into the recesses of the cave, taking their belongings with them. They covered their foot tracks by sweeping the floor with a leafy branch behind them as they went. Then they waited barely breathing.

"They will find the animals," whispered Deborah.

"I untied them before dawn and they wondered off to find grass. That is when I sensed we were not alone. Then as the sky grew lighter I noticed there were no birds singing. All was too quiet," whispered Gideon in reply.

"Are you sure someone is out there?" asked Rahab in a hushed tone.

"Yes, I am sure. I stay alive by knowing these things and paying attention to my gut."

Rahab pulled her hood around her face and commanded Kelev to stay quiet. He lowered his head to the ground. She patted his head and hugged her knees. The back of the cave was cold and damp and she shivered.

The daylight barely penetrated the foliage and the cave was very dark. It seemed that hours passed as they sat in utter stillness. Deborah sat a small distance from the three to concentrate her thoughts on prayers. She kept the hood of her robe pulled close around her face, and her bundle of scriptures and notes tucked securely into an inside fold.

Presently there were voices outside. They seemed far away at first, but then up close. The branches at the entrance shook as if someone or something were pawing through them. There was a groan. The four came to immediate attention. Kelev perked up his ears and the hair on his back stood up but he kept still. He sensed the danger and stayed silent as Rahab commanded.

Gideon tapped the other three and pulled them with him. "Come," he whispered. "Hang on to me." Slowly he moved them farther into the cave feeling along the walls as he went. Kelev went on ahead snuffling at the ground as they walked. They stumbled over rocks and stepped into holes in the pitch darkness, but they hugged the damp wall of the passage and kept moving. Sounds from outside the cave slowly disappeared as they went deeper. They clung closely together, their fears growing. Suddenly there was a light. Gideon had lit a candle that dimly illuminated the walls. "There is water ahead," he whispered. "It is a water fall. Pray it is falling from above which might mean a way out."

"And if it is falling below?" asked Rahab shakily.

"Then walk carefully," said Naham as he took her arm more firmly.

Rahab knew what Naham meant without asking further. A waterfall down would mean a deep hole, a lake or underground river. There would be no telling how far down the drop might go. She had seen this in the hills north of Bethel. She had followed streams to their underground beginnings in caves and looked up in astonishment at waterfalls coming from far up but still under the ground. She never ventured further than the light from outside would let her see. This was very different. Even though Gideon held a candle high, she could see very little. Terror kept creeping into her thoughts making her knees weak. Her comfort was in knowing that Kelev was looking out for them.

The path sank downward now. They moved on slowly, Gideon checking step by step for a drop off. There was a sudden flapping of wings rushing by them. "Bats," said Naham. "That means an opening to the outside may be near. Look to see where they are coming from. They are coming in now that it is growing light."

Gideon blew out his candle and gazed upward. There was a pinhole of light ahead. He could not tell how far away it was, but the floor of the cave was now rising under his feet. "We are going up," he whispered. "Step carefully."

The light was not growing larger. The sound of falling water was closer and then seemed farther away. It began to echo as if they had entered a large cavern. Deborah bumped her head on something hanging down from the ceiling. Gideon grabbed her arm to keep her from falling. "There will be many of these as we near the water. The water drips through the stone and forms these hanging sickles."

They all crouched low and held an arm up to protect their heads. The path was becoming slippery and the air more damp. As they rounded an outcropping of stalactites, the light suddenly became brighter and revealed a huge room with a small stream running from somewhere above and disappearing somewhere below. It shimmered and sparkled making light patterns dance on the walls.

"It is beautiful!" breathed Rahab. Deborah stood speechless at the wonder of it all. Stalactites were everywhere making lattice like shapes. Stalagmites were rising from the floor created from the dripping sickles in the ceiling. Kelev was licking them vigorously as the water dripped down.

"Where do you suppose we are?" asked Deborah in a low voice.

"Likely we are on the other side of the ridge of hills, maybe a little to the north. We must be quiet. We could still be right in the middle of the Philistines," cautioned Gideon.

The hole in the ceiling proved to be far above them. Their hopes of it being a way to escape were dashed.

*   *   *

Lapidoth was at loose ends. Hannah continued to admonish him to pray. He found it difficult to concentrate on God up there somewhere when the answers he needed were down here on earth. How could God give him answers?

He went to the inn for wine and to think. He couldn't imagine what life held for him with Deborah. He hardly knew her. Would someone from his family eventually find him and force him back into the life of danger? Would the jewel merchant's thugs come after him? He still had their money. They were waiting for him in Ashdod but not for long. There seemed to be no safe place for him to go.

He fell into an exhausted and troubled sleep over his wine. Dreams of being pursued by someone or something dark and evil assailed him. He woke with a start when the innkeeper tapped him on the shoulder. He saw it had indeed become night. The innkeeper offered him a filthy room behind the kitchen, but he preferred the stable. No one would be looking for him in a stable. At least not yet.

The light was coming through an opening in the roof of the stable and Lapidoth woke to see Hannah standing over him. "Come with me," said she tersely. Then she turned and walked out into the crisp morning.

Lapidoth shook the hay out of his hair and brushed his robe. He checked the moneybag in the lining. It was still there. Then he followed Hannah. She did not look back but walked on into the market and began looking over the merchandise in the stalls. He did the same but stayed a distance away. She walked into an alley and he followed. The old man, Laban, was sitting in a doorway with a small fire burning at his feet. Hannah sat down near him and began to make more tea.

Lapidoth stood uncomfortably in the alley, looking warily from side to side, and then leaned uneasily against the stone wall of the building. Except for the three of them the alley seemed to be empty. What could she want with this old man and what did it have to do with him?

The two drank tea together and then the old man nodded in Lapidoth's direction. Some words passed between them that Lapidoth could not understand. "Come and sit, Lapidoth," beckoned Hannah. He found a place on the doorsill beside her and carefully sat down.

"He knows nothing of Deborah as yet. He will send his cousin into the hills for any word of her."

"Why did you bring me here, Hannah, if he doesn't know anything?"

"He wanted to see your face, to know if you are sincere. He has decided to help you. Do not let looks deceive you, Lapidoth. God uses many people to do his work regardless of their station in life."

Lapidoth looked at the old man again. "Is this how God brings his answers to earth?" wondered Lapidoth silently. "How does Hannah know what people God uses?"

He stood up, graciously thanked the old man, and walked cautiously to the mouth of the alley. Hannah rose and followed him.

"You will stay in the home of Rabbi Amri and Leah, the parents of Ya'akov," she quietly instructed him. "Stay inside and do not show yourself until we know if someone pursues you. You will be made to look like a student of the scriptures and you will speak to no one."

Lapidoth opened his mouth to reply, but she was gone. He drew his hood over most of his face and walked toward the stable. No one seemed to notice him. As he reached the stable his mind was still in turmoil.

"Can I trust Hannah? She is so shadowy. I may even put Ya'akov's family in danger. Deborah would never forgive me," he reasoned. "I could leave now and go to the other side of the Sea of Galilee into the land of the Midianites. It is dangerous, but I can follow the Jordan down into Moab, and pose as a trader. Perhaps I will find a caravan and travel with them."

He could not think of Deborah now. He had to find a way to extricate himself from his mother's evil. Then he would find Deborah again. He bought supplies, paid the stable owner to tell no one, mounted his horse, and headed east at a fast pace.

*　　*　　*

Miriam waited until Joseph came in from the fields, hoping she could talk sense to him about Rahab. She took his bag from the corner where she had kicked it and placed it on a stone shelf. While she tidied up the place she rehearsed what she would say. Rahab was their niece and Joseph would always defend her. But he had to know how precarious a position they were in if she talked to anyone, and there was reason to think she would. Rahab hated her with a passion for all the trouble she brought with her to the family.

Evening was falling and Joseph came in from checking their livestock. "I have been waiting for you, Joseph," began Miriam calmly. "Rahab is gone again."

"Rahab comes and goes as she pleases," growled Joseph.

"This time it is different. Deborah is gone too. And there were strange men, two of them, at Rahab's house. One was a soldier. We are in trouble, Joseph! I can feel it. My skin crawls every time I think of it."

"I will speak to her when she comes back. She always shows up sooner or later," replied Joseph attempting to escape Miriam's questions.

"The four of them went away together, I am sure of it! Rahab threatened me with telling our secret when she drove me out of her house."

"She has threatened before, usually when you are screaming at her. Did you see them leave together?"

"No, I did not see them leave at all. They must have gone in the night. You have to do something!" Miriam felt her fear rise and the pitch of her voice along with it.

Joseph reached for his bag to check its contents. "I have other things to worry about. I have not heard from Lapidoth since we left

Ashdod. I never know if he is safe until he returns. Your friends, the merchants, will want their money and will send someone here for it, I am sure."

"My friends! They are not my friends. How dare you call them my friends!"

"Well, they certainly are not my friends," shouted Joseph. "I will go to see Joab. Perhaps he knows something." Quickly Joseph turned and left the house, pleased to make his escape.

Joab had just come in from his fields as well. Wearily he listened to Joseph's story. "I do not know what I can do. Do you know where Rahab goes? Do you know where she might be? Miriam believes she is angry enough to tell someone about the merchant dealings and our involvement."

Joab thought for a moment. He had never revealed the location of Rahab's place in the wilderness to the north. He simply could not bring himself to do so now.

"I will ask about her tomorrow when I go to the market. Someone may have seen her. They all know her. And Deborah, is she gone too?"

"Yes, Deborah, a soldier, and another man who visited Rahab. All are gone according to Miriam."

Tamar, Joab's wife, came in from the chicken yard. "Tamar," said Joseph, "do you know where Rahab and Deborah might be?"

Tamar was startled. Joseph rarely spoke to her other than to grunt or complain about something. "I have not seen them, but then they do not visit me. I know nothing."

"Are you sure? Are you covering for Rahab?" barked Joseph menacingly.

A shocked Tamar looked at Joab and back to Joseph. "Yes, I am sure." She turned abruptly, walked into the kitchen, and yanked the curtain across the doorway behind her.

"What is this about, Joseph? Why the sudden concern? You know how unpredictable Rahab is. And Deborah . . . is she perhaps at her place under the palm at the oasis? That is where she goes every morning."

Joseph sat down, his head in his hands. "She is sure they are up to something. Miriam will be waiting for me, expecting some news. As always she will accuse you and Tamar of aiding Rahab in her wayward behaviors. The fight will last into the night."

"Please, Joseph, stay the night here. Your shouting can be heard everywhere. Get some sleep and we will talk again in the morning."

Joseph was grateful. This was not the first time he had stayed at Joab's when Miriam was on a rampage.

Reluctantly Joseph went home in the morning. Miriam was waiting at the door, hands on her hips. "Well? Do they know anything?"

Joseph shook his head.

"Of course not," retorted Miriam. "They never know anything. They are covering or they are just more useless than stupid burrows. I suspect they are covering something."

Joseph turned and headed for the well and Miriam followed him. "If we do not take care of Rahab we could be in great danger," she snarled.

"Oh? And what do you suggest, Miriam?"

"She could have an accident. You are the head of the house, Joseph. You can do what needs to be done without questions from anyone."

Joseph was incredulous. "An accident? Murder my own niece? Are you crazy?"

"I am not crazy! She hates me. She hates you. She could destroy us with that temper of hers."

"Yes, she hates you. Have you ever given her reason to feel otherwise? You have hated her from birth! She has cunning like you, Miriam, but fortunately she also has the heart of her mother. Something you seem to be missing!" Joseph jerked the bucket up and dropped it into the well. Furiously he drew up some water, splashed his face and arms, and stalked off toward the sheep shed.

Exasperated, Miriam sat down by the well to think. "I must take care of this myself. That much is clear. Joseph is all but useless, but I know who will help me." She went to the house, grabbed up a bag and began to pack belongings. Then she went to the barn, threw a harness on a mule, hitched it to a cart, and started on the road toward Ashdod. Rahab! Deborah! Lapidoth! She would take care of them all.

*   *   *

It was relief for Miriam to arrive at the cool halls of her childhood home. The midday heat was becoming intense. Servants greeted her, took her bag, and escorted her to the atrium. Omar, her cousin, was enjoying wine by the pool. Omar was her confidant and partner in many shady and exciting dealings. Omar's late wife had been a sullen, dull-witted woman who kept her distance from Miriam.

Omar was Miriam's childhood love and her first sexual encounter. Being forced to marry Joseph was punishment inflicted by her father when he suspected the liaison between the two of them. Miriam stirred up trouble wherever she was and the family was glad to be relieved of her constant nasty temper. Degraded and angry she was swept off to Bethel and the life of a herder. Her hatred of it and the promise of revenge continued to burn hot and unabated over the years.

Omar rose to greet her and kissed her on both cheeks. "What brings you here, my she-bear?" he said in his smooth baritone voice. "Have some wine." A servant rushed to fill a goblet for her.

Miriam sat down beside him, sipped her wine, and plucked a few grapes from a bowl. "Rahab. I found her plotting with Deborah, Lapidoth's wife, and two strange men, one a soldier. She has to be stopped before she does some damage."

"I am glad to hear your family relations are going so well! I thought you would have killed her or Joseph by now. I applaud your restraint."

Miriam began to boil, but fought to appear calm. These were Omar's usual taunts, designed to spark a rage that would draw her into his bed for a time of violent sexual passion.

"She has threatened to reveal our business secrets on many occasions. Recently she drove me from her house with these threats and now she is gone."

"Gone? Not unusual. Who did you say the men were?"

"I do not know them. But they seemed not to be strangers to Deborah, Lapidoth's new wife."

"Ah, so stiff necked Lapidoth married! And you are now the jealous mother-in-law, Miriam. Did he get your consent? I am sure he did not. Is that what is angering you?"

"Omar, do not taunt me. This is not about me or my family resentments. This is serious. I tell you she was angry enough to do something foolish and she must be stopped!"

Omar shifted in his chaise to look at her more directly. "What exactly does she know? What did you tell her?"

"I told her nothing, but she saw through my lies about where Joseph and Lapidoth would go. She has spies in many places. When she suspects I am keeping something from her, she has other ways to find out hidden things. She is wild and dangerous. Since she disappears so often, someone could find her and make sure she never returns."

"And Joseph? What is his part in this to be?"

"Joseph is useless. He loves Rahab. He will never hurt her. He would never discipline her or force her to marry. He is not a man."

"Ah," said Omar nodding, "she is the woman Joseph hoped you were when he had what he thought was the good fortune to marry you. Sad for him you were not. Now you want to be rid of her? Of course you do."

"I warned you not to taunt me, Omar!"

He burst into laughter. Miriam could contain her rage and frustration no longer. She snatched up a fruit knife and swung it at him, grazing his arm. He grabbed her wrist and twisted it making her drop the knife. She cried out as he threw her down on the chaise and tore her tunic away. He pinned her arms down and entered her roughly. She struggled, spat and cursed him, which only heightened his desire. His breathing was ragged and hot on her neck. She gave one last shove to dislodge him, but he rolled her off onto the terrazzo floor, moaned loudly as his excitement heightened. His violence brought him to his last brutal thrust, and finished he dumped her into the lily pad pool. She splashed and floundered in the water still sputtering threats and curses.

"You look like a drowned rat, Miriam!" and he laughed even louder through his gasps to recover his breath.

Miriam climbed out of the shallow pool, threw her wet body on top of him, and pounded his chest with her fists. "I came here for your help you fool! Stop this and listen to me!"

He pushed her off and rolled on top of her again. He pinned her arms down until under his weight she could not breathe and fell limp. He got up leaving her gasping on the marble floor.

Servants came out to the atrium with fresh robes for them, and disappeared as quickly and quietly as they had come in.

"What on earth do you want me to do, Miriam?" spat a menacing Omar.

"I want you to have them tracked down and killed. Find Lapidoth and bring him back here with the money for the jewels before we are all killed," shrieked Miriam.

"I think you are in a panic for nothing. All this is your imagination. What is your proof that Rahab has ever betrayed us or that Lapidoth will not return as he always does when his business is done? Kill them? I am a lot of things, but I am not a killer, Miriam, nor do I order such things."

"You lie, Omar. Do not patronize me. I know you. You have no such scruples. You are capable of anything when it suits you."

Omar turned and waved his hand toward the door. "Go home, Miriam. I will make some inquiries."

"Will you send word?"

"That depends on what I find, if anything. Now go." He smacked her on the buttocks and left the atrium.

Exasperated and angry, Miriam snatched up her bag and stalked out of the house to the stable to fetch her mule and cart. She beat the animal mercilessly all the way home.

CHAPTER 16

Gideon and Rahab followed her faithful dog, Kelev, toward a tunnel near the waterfall. Kelev ran to the mouth of the tunnel, sniffed the air, turned to give a low woof and then ran in. Naham and Deborah came cautiously behind Gideon and Rahab. The tunnel was cold at first until it took a sharp upward angle. A dim glow lit their way. The higher they climbed the warmer the air became. Kelev was waiting at the top, tongue hanging out, anticipating their arrival.

Rahab threw her arms around Kelev. "Good dog! Good Kelev!" she whispered. Gideon cautioned them to remain there and quiet while he went out to determine what side of the ridge they came out on.

In a few minutes Gideon was back. "We are most fortunate! We are on the edge of a cliff where we can see if anyone approaches."

"Are we far enough away?" asked Naham.

"Just barely. But we are aimed in the opposite direction of their travel. So we will climb down into the valley and find a place to hide until evening. I will scout the area and we can decide what to do next."

The climb down from the mouth of the cave was slow. As they reached the bottom of the cliff, Kelev darted away into the trees and was gone. Naham and Gideon paid no attention to his sudden departure. Deborah and Rahab gazed in that direction for a while.

"Does he usually run off like this?" asked Deborah.

"Yes, all the time, but not when danger is close by."

"Then it must be we are safe, at least for now."

"Perhaps. He left suddenly as if he had a mission of some sort," said Rahab.

"A female?"

"Or lunch!"

The four sat down in a glade to rest. Deborah bent over her notes and continued her work. "If we blow the trumpets too soon, the enemy will know we are coming. We must use surprise. Their surprise will be God himself is coming! We will not march in straight lines, but scatter in the wilderness as we did coming out of Egypt. At just the right time the trumpet will sound and cause all the soldiers to remember God.

The trumpet will give them assurance that God is with them."

"We must come out of the wilderness from different places shouting. It will sound like there are many more soldiers than we really have. We will drive Sisera into the swamps of the Kishon valley. His chariots will be useless! We will slaughter them before they can get out."

"We must be sure to time this when the Kishon floods. If it does not flood, that is God's message to wait," wrote Deborah in her notes. "And if the Kishon does not flood for another year or two? Then we must wait upon the Lord as Hannah always tells me."

There was a low bark and a nicker from the trees. Kelev was nipping at the heels of the pack animals as they came trotting out into the clearing. He ran right to Rahab, tail wagging, anticipating her appreciative pat on his head.

Naham grabbed the rope halters of the animals and pulled them quickly into a grove of trees and behind some rocks. Gideon herded everyone deeper into hiding. "We must lay low until we are sure they were not followed. Rahab pulled Kelev with her by his ruff and dropped down behind the rocks. "Quiet," she whispered to him and he dropped to the ground too.

Naham and Gideon quietly circled around to get a better vantage point. "Over there . . . coming around those rocks," whispered Naham. Gideon drew his knife and moved forward, Naham behind him. "There are only six of them."

There was a low growl behind them. It was Kelev, the fur standing straight up on his back and his fangs bared. He charged past them. There was a cry of pain very close to them and a man jumped up, cursed, and ran from his hiding place back toward the others. There was laughter and the group turned continuing away from Naham and Gideon.

There was a very low whistle behind them. It was Rahab. Kelev came trotting back from rousting his prey, tail and tongue wagging. Deborah stood up beside her. "Who were they?"

"Renegades, robbers, or thugs," said Gideon. "There were not organized. If they were they would not have been chased off by Kelev or laughed at their man. I am sure they were not part of a larger contingent. Let us keep going."

* * *

Miriam was in a foul mood and berated Joseph for not doing something about Lapidoth. "What do you mean, Lapidoth always comes back. The difference is now he is married! Who knows how that will change him? Perhaps he will try to run away! He has money and a wife!"

Joseph wanted to avoid an argument about Lapidoth. "Where did you go? Did you need to run that animal nearly to death? He is barely alive from the heat and exhaustion."

Miriam was not about to be deflected. "Since you will not do anything, I went to Omar. He will track them down, Deborah and Rahab as well."

"Track them down and do what? What kind of foolishness is this?"

"Foolish am I? Track them down and kill them! Do you want our secrets exposed?"

"Are you crazy? Do you want him to kill me too? Perhaps he will get rid of you instead."

Miriam scowled at Joseph and spat, "We will be rid of the danger and continue our business as usual. He will find Lapidoth and the money."

"I pray that Omar has more sense than you, Miriam. He has never been one of my favorite people, always scheming, but he is not a killer." Joseph turned to leave. He gathered some belongings and walked out. Rahab's house was empty and he would occupy it for now. Tomorrow he would pay Omar a visit.

*　　*　　*

Hannah's bones were creaking and her fingers felt numb. She warmed her hands by the oven to chase the evening chill and the aches it brought to her joints. "That foolish Lapidoth is gone," she muttered to the flames as they danced low. "He must not bring disgrace or disaster to Deborah. We have much to do. God send me a sign!"

The next afternoon she walked to the village to meet Laban in the alley. Again she kindled his fire and made his tea. They sat for some time together saying nothing. He would know her concern and would tell her when his old brain organized the thoughts enough to be told.

"There are four, Deborah and three others. They are closer, but they are not safe. Their path is full of dangers," said Laban slowly.

"Do you know who is with her? Is it Barak?"

"A soldier and others, but not Barak. Ephraim holds great darkness." Laban closed his eyes and sipped his tea.

Hannah knew that was all he could tell her today. She put more kindling on his fire and walked back out into the market. What was the threat from Ephraim? What was this darkness? It could not be Sisera. I must be someone else. Hannah sat down to think in the shade of a kiosk with an old woman who bought her herbs. She stared at the hem of her sleeve and then she knew. "Miriam!" she said aloud.

"What is it Hannah? You said 'Miriam' out loud."

"It is nothing. Not yet," replied a startled Hannah. She gathered her robe about her and hobbled quickly away toward Judith's house.

Judith was in her garden and looked up pleased to see Hannah as always. Rising she said, "Greetings Hannah my friend! What brings you to the village?"

"Have you heard from Deborah or Barak?"

"There have been no messages. Why? You look worried."

"How can you tell I look worried with all these wrinkles? I must naturally look worried all the time," smiled Hannah. "I guess I was missing her especially today."

"Come in for tea. I have fresh bread just out of the oven."

Hannah followed Judith into the house, turning over in her mind what she should tell Judith, if anything. They chatted amiably about the town folk, their own aging bodies, and the weather, which would turn cold soon. Finally Hannah got up to go home, having decided to say nothing of Laban's words just yet. The sudden realization that Miriam was the darkness from Ephraim troubled her greatly. But how would that manifest? Was Deborah still in danger from Miriam? Is that why Lapidoth disappeared? Such vague information would only worry Judith and why should there be two worrying when one was quite enough.

*   *   *

Deborah was exhausted but heart pounding with excitement as she stood on tiptoes to glimpse Kadesh-Napthali. It seemed like an eternity since she left with her new husband. Her brows furrowed at the thought of Lapidoth. She was married and abandoned in a short time. "Where could he be?" she thought. "Is he looking for me still in Bethel? Should I have stayed there? No, I could not. Miriam! Who knows what she is capable of? No, I had to go on. God has a purpose for me and I must fulfill it the best way I know."

Rahab came to stand beside her, the breezes blowing her robe and hair. Kelev nuzzled Deborah's knee and pushed against her leg for a pat on the head. Gideon and Naham were scouting the area before they ventured closer to the village.

"I need to see Hannah first," declared Deborah. "Before I can go to my family home and speak with anyone else, I need to talk with her. What can I say about Lapidoth not being with me? Why am I back so soon? Have I come home because I am in disgrace? There will be a hundred questions, if not spoken, at least filling their minds and gossip circles."

Deborah longed to see her mother and Ya'akov's family, but suddenly coming home did not seem to be the wisest thing to do. "Let us wait until the sun goes down," suggested Rahab, "and we can to go Hannah's without anyone noticing us."

"We might frighten her coming in the dark," said Gideon. "Let me go now to tell her. No one knows me."

"Good idea," said Naham. "We will wait here until it is almost dark."

Deborah sat down on an old rock wall and pulled her notes from her robe. Rahab sat down beside her. "These are almost complete. The presence of God will be in the minds of our men wherever they go, in battle or not. They will not be defeated," said Deborah quietly. "Let us give thanks to God Almighty who gives the victory."

*   *   *

Joseph left Rahab's house early to pay a visit to Omar. He was not fond of Omar, finding him oily and devious, but he was sure Omar would not give into Miriam's demands for murder. A servant met him at the gate to Omar's palatial home and graciously escorted him to the atrium. "My master will be along presently. Please, may I bring you some wine and refreshment?"

Joseph nodded and sat down to wait for Omar. The coolness and peace of the atrium was welcome after constant strife with Miriam. "How can this place feel so cool and peaceful and still harbor the evil that emanates from it?" whispered Joseph.

"Ah, welcome my friend!" sang out Omar as he swept into the atrium, his voluminous gold embroidered robes billowing out behind him. "I hope your journey was pleasant and I see my servant has taken good care of you."

Joseph was always put off by Omar's effusiveness, but he had urgent business on his mind and overlooked it. Omar collapsed onto a lavish purple couch and took the wine his servant offered. With a deep sigh, he said, "I am sure I know why you are here . . . Miriam's visit to me! Is that not correct? I was so fortunate that her father chose you and not me to be her husband. I am certain she has made your bed full of nettles."

Omar's inscrutable placid smile irked Joseph, but he was still determined to keep his composure. "Miriam seems to have murder on her mind with you as the perpetrator. Yes, Miriam is a trial to be sure, but I have not thought of her as one who would go that far. I was wrong. What I need to know is whether you are in collusion with her."

"I told her I would look into her concerns," soothed Omar. "I will send a trusted servant to discern if there is any danger to our family fortunes. I trust Lapidoth. He has been faithful, he is intelligent, and succeeds. I do not know Deborah. Perhaps you can tell me about her. Is she a danger?"

"Deborah is a quiet person devoted to her scriptures and her god. She is resourceful. Lapidoth left her on the Jericho road after a raid on Tirzah, promising to catch up with her after he went back to Tirzah to recover his belongings. She found her way to Bethel on her own over shepherds paths. Rahab found her before she reached our home. Miriam was her usual grating self in greeting Deborah, and Rahab spirited Deborah away to her own house rather than leave her at the mercy of Miriam. But is Deborah a danger? No."

"Fascinating, Joseph! A truly fascinating story!" said Omar thoroughly amused. "I like stories about plucky women."

"She is not a plucky woman as you put it. I am sure it was the first experience in which she had to survive on her own. She was most fortunate to get through the difficulty."

"And where was Lapidoth all this time?" cooed Omar, offering his wine goblet up for a refill.

"Not finding Deborah on the Jericho road Lapidoth sought the help of a friend in Jericho. The man and his servants rode out immediately with Lapidoth to find her. Once he brought her to our home, we had to leave immediately for Ashdod."

"This is a pity. Is she beautiful?"

Joseph was speechless for a moment.

"Come, come, man. You surely noticed if she was beautiful," laughed Omar.

"I was busy with my sheep and crops," stammered Joseph embarrassed. "What difference does that make? Is she to be your quarry for murder or something else?"

"I have not decided. I would have to see her. Unfortunately Rahab has always eluded my overtures. She has Miriam's cunning and her dead mother's decency. What a woman!" Omar's face was flushed with the wine and perspiration was breaking out on his brow.

"Will you grant Miriam's odious wishes or not, Omar?!"

"Have no fear Joseph. I am not a foolish man, nor do I bend to the whims of women. Miriam's rage fuels her irrational fears. She wants to control everything and is terrified when she thinks she does not. I will obtain information about Deborah and Rahab, and will call for you when I have it. There is nothing about our business that can be known to cause much difficulty. Even you know only surface information, a cover story. Nothing more."

Chastened, Joseph got up to leave. "I must return to my sheep and crops before nightfall."

"Your wife left here a happy woman, Joseph. You should keep her at home," sneered Omar.

Joseph stared at Omar silently for a moment. "It seems you enjoy nettles, Omar. I do not." He turned and walked away.

Joseph was watering the sheep when Miriam descended on him. "You went to see Omar did you not? And behind my back!"

"I do not recall that you got my permission to visit Omar, Miriam. It seems you received at least a portion of what you went there for."

Miriam raised her arm to strike him, but Joseph caught it midair and pushed her onto the ground. Miriam gasped and struggled to get to her feet. Joseph pushed her down again and stood over her. "I am a mild man, Miriam. Perhaps you hate that about me. But be careful you do not push me too far," said Joseph in a low menacing voice.

"And what will you do?" spat Miriam defiantly, "beat and rape me?"

"I will leave that to Omar. It seems he is more practiced than I." Joseph walked away and left her seething on the ground.

"You will tell me what Omar said!" shouted Miriam at his back.

"Ask him yourself. I give you permission to go back to him. You do not have to sneak away," he said turning toward her. "Go to him and stay. You need not return here."

"I will go and I will return whenever I please. My money built this place, bought your flocks, and fed your children. You are nothing," growled Miriam rising and shaking the dirt from her robe. "Do you hear me? You are nothing!"

"I am glad to be nothing according to your world, Miriam. Remember that when you come crawling back." Joseph turned again toward the fields and strode quickly away.

CHAPTER 17

A s evening came, Gideon approached Hannah's house. He sat afar off and watched for a while to be sure there was no one else around.

Hannah lit a lamp inside and the soft glow shown dimly through the window coverings. She stepped outside and looked around for a moment. "Whoever you are, you may come in. The house is safe and the way is clear."

Gideon rose from his hiding place and walked toward her. "You knew I was here all along, Hannah. Thank you for the welcome." He kissed her on both cheeks. She took his arm and drew him inside.

"I knew you would come back. Barak sent you some time ago to speak with Leah and Rabbi Amri to inquire of Deborah."

"Yes, it seems long ago now. I went back to Barak and we went south immediately to find her. When we did find her, Lapidoth was gone and she was in danger. However, she was safe with Lapidoth's cousin, Rahab. The four of us departed the Bethel home, traveled to Barak's encampment, and at Deborah's insistence, started for here to see you. Deborah is near. She wishes to speak with you tonight."

"She will not go to her mother first?"

"She will not wish to face the questions she will be asked about Lapidoth and why she is coming back alone."

"Wise. We offered Lapidoth a place to hide until we could discern what he could do to free himself from certain intrigues, but he took his horse and fled. Perhaps he did not want to trouble us or something happened to make him leave quickly."

Gideon went out onto the path and gave a low whistle for Kelev. It was the signal that all was well. Kelev got slowly to his feet, ears pricked forward, and his muzzle close to the ground. Seeing Kelev react Deborah jumped up, gathered her robe around her, drawing the hood over her head and close around her face. Naham and Rahab rose from the hiding place as well. That is the signal, a whistle only Kelev would hear. They started through the rocks and brush to Hannah's place.

"Come in my dears, I have tea and bread to refresh you. Come and sit." They filed in the door, glad to be sheltered from the night air. Deborah rushed to embrace Hannah. Naham shyly kissed her on both cheeks. Kelev lay down just outside the door, his head resting low on the cooling grasses, eyes alert.

"And you are Rahab, Lapidoth's cousin," said Hannah with a kindly smile.

"Yes. Did he tell you of me?"

"He did."

"Not a very complimentary picture of me, I am sure. My family does not approve of my choice to be independent of them."

"My dear, God chooses our path in life, and yours is not to be judged by me. After my husband died, it was my choice to be alone. No one approved, but I knew it was right."

Rahab smiled and held out a cup for the tea Hannah offered. "Your kindness is rare among our peoples. I thank you."

"Hannah, my beloved mother in spirit," said Deborah quietly. "I have continued my studies. Barak and I have created many battle plans according to Scripture. I am not sure what comes next. What else am I to do? Have you a vision? A prophecy?"

"The day is coming," began Hannah, "when I will no longer be here for you to depend upon for visions and prophecies, Deborah. My life will end and you must go on without me. Before that happens, let us pray together that all wisdom given to me is now yours."

"Shall we stay, mother Hannah?" asked Gideon. "Do you wish to be alone with Deborah?"

"Stay! Please stay, all of you, if you will. God's wisdom is open to all and needed by all. I had hoped your cousin would stay, Rahab, but he fled in fear. We will include him in our prayers that he is safe and will return to take his rightful place in his family." Deborah was busy with her thoughts and did not catch that she meant Lapidoth.

Hannah gathered robes and blankets for them, placed more kindling on the fire in the hearth, and they all settled in for a long night's meditation and prayer. Hannah began with a chant in her high reedy voice. They all joined with a low hum. When they were again quiet, Hannah began to sing an invocation for God's presence to be welcomed in each one and his wisdom to fill their hearts. The prayers continued through the night. An hour before dawn a cock crowed and Kelev let out a muffled bark.

Hannah arose, placed more kindling on the faintly glowing coals in the hearth, and heated water for tea. Deborah, Rahab, Naham, and Gideon rose stiffly from the places where they had sunk down onto straw mats and drifted off to sleep.

Making a place for them beside the warm oven Hannah said, "Come, let us speak of our dreams."

Rahab rubbed her face and moved sleepily to a bench near the table. Deborah followed her. Gideon and Naham went outside to splash water on their faces at the small well. Kelev was already out on a hunting foray for his breakfast.

"I believe I have been in a battle all night," said Deborah. Large numbers of troops were coming down hillsides into a valley swarming like locusts, covering it completely. I have had that dream before. I was hoping for guidance to know the steps to get to that place."

"There will be a call to sing your song, Deborah, to sing out to your troops to remember God in battle. Perhaps you have done all that needs to be done just now."

"I heard your song in my dream, Deborah. It was a rallying cry and all who heard were victorious," said Rahab, her thoughts clearing from sleep to awakening.

"We are going back to camp, just Naham and I," said Gideon glancing at Rahab. The air was electric between them. No words of love had been spoken, but he could not imagine being without her. Yet, it must be. She must stay with Deborah.

"Am I to stay here?" queried Deborah. "And do what? Just wait?"

"Go back to Rabbi Amri and Leah to study," said Hannah. "There is more to this part of your journey. The battle is not yet. When Lapidoth was here, I arranged for him to stay with them because I thought the message was about him. But it was not. It was about you, Deborah."

"Lapidoth? Lapidoth was here? When?" asked a wide-eyed Deborah.

"I am sorry, Deborah. I told Gideon and did not recount it to you. Yes, Lapidoth came to me asking how he could be free of his mother's intrigues. I could see he was frightened for his life and desperate. I quickly arranged for him to hide at Leah and Rabbi Amri's, but he fled on horseback. I do not know where he went. The stable boy said he took the road riding east. I charged the stable boy severely never to reveal that to anyone else."

"Was it ever God's will that I should be his wife? Nothing has gone right since our wedding. Even the night we might have consummated it, Sisera's men attacked and we were spirited out of the hotel into a wadi and we ran toward the Jericho Road. I did not see him again until we met in Bethel. But he immediately left me again, and that is the last I saw him. What a strange union that is not yet a union and may never be."

"Are you grieving this, Deborah?" asked Hannah gently after the men had gone outside again.

"Hannah, you know I never wanted to be married, or have children. I agreed because Lapidoth came out of nowhere into your dream and to your house. I thought it must be God's will to marry him and I am ready to do God's will. But to be truthful, I am not grieving. I have not known Lapidoth as a wife knows a husband, and I am not with child. I am . . . I am relieved."

Hannah put her arms around Deborah and held her tight. "We can discern God's will day by day. But we cannot see the whole path we will walk. We can see only to the next turn. Be at peace, Deborah. God knows your heart's desire and will honor it as you honor him."

Rahab sat thinking about Gideon. Would the desire growing in her bosom for him be honored as well? Could they ever really be together? She wanted to ask Hannah. To her surprise, Hannah said, "No, Rahab, you will not marry Gideon now, but you will be together throughout the battles, and in the new day for Israel. You are independent, Rahab. Not common for a woman, but God will lead you to the fulfillment of your heart's desire. Do not force anything, and do not be afraid."

Rahab embraced Hannah and then drew back, not sure that was the right thing to do. Hannah smiled and pulled her back into her arms. "It has been too long since you felt the embrace of someone who loves you. You are my daughter in spirit and I will always love and embrace you."

Rahab broke into uncontrollable sobs. All of her pent up pain from years of enduring Miriam's hatred and the loss of her mother came gushing out. Hannah and Deborah helped her to a sleeping mat where she laid sobbing and shaking for what seemed an eternity. Deborah lay down beside her and held her beloved friend close.

Midmorning, Hannah said, "It is time to go to see Judith, Deborah. Take Rahab with you and say simply that Lapidoth brought you and left. Nothing more. Then go to see Leah and Rabbi Amri. No questions will be asked of you there. Ask for more studies and for Rahab to join you. The next step will be revealed to you."

To Deborah's relief Amram was away. Judith looked a bit puzzled at Deborah's brief explanation but did not press her daughter. She was delighted to meet Rahab and they sat down to talk of events in Kadesh-Napthali.

"I would love to see Abinoam and Sarah again," said Deborah. To Rahab she said, "They are Barak's father and mother."

"Oh, you shall see him!" said Judith. "He brings a bit of grain for me, but mostly wants to talk about how proud he is of Barak. He should be here soon. This is the time of day he comes."

Deborah lowered her eyes. She could not tell Judith that Barak did not come. She did not want to break Abinoam's heart by telling him Barak would not visit him. Somehow she had to signal Rahab not to reveal anything. But Rahab seemed to read her thoughts and nodded almost imperceptibly.

True to Judith's prediction, Abinoam arrived at the door. He embraced Judith and then saw Deborah. His face was alight with a wrinkled smile. "Deborah. I did not think to see you ever again.

God is so good!" She smiled back, touched his arm, and introduced Rahab.

"Tell me what has been happening in your life father Abinoam," said Deborah, hoping to pre-empt any questions from him. He regaled them with his aches and pains, and his wife's health. He spoke of his dreams of Barak and victory. But he asked nothing.

Deborah and Rahab got up to leave, mentioning they would visit Rabbi Amri and Leah, and Abinoam followed them out the door. A distance from the house Abinoam said, "Fear not, Deborah. Naham and Gideon were on their way to visit me with a message from Barak when they saw me on the road near Hannah's. They told me everything. I will say nothing. Know that you and Barak are always in my prayers, and I am eternally grateful to you for going with me to Barak's camp to help him. God go with you, and if it is God's will I will see you again. Shalom. Shalom."

"God's words travel fast!" said Deborah smiling at Rahab. "First you read my mind and then Abinoam already knows everything. It makes me dizzy!"

"We are given the message not to worry or fear, and yet we cannot seem to help ourselves," laughed Rahab.

"What did you think of Hannah's prediction about you and Gideon?"

"I am content to know we will somehow be together. I, too, never wanted to marry. But he is the only one I would want if it comes to that. I do not want to be without him, whatever it takes."

Leah was at her door and ran to meet Deborah and Rahab. She kissed them soundly and ushered them inside. Rabbi Amri looked up from his scrolls and broke into a wide smile at the sight of Deborah. He came to embrace her and Rahab.

"We are here to continue my studies, Rabbi, if you are willing," said Deborah.

"It is God's will! How can I not be willing?" answered Amri joyfully.

"You will stay with us. Your room is prepared for you. We always knew you would come back. Judith knows you will be here. I have told her if you and . . . Lapidoth . . . ever came back, we have room where she does not. Alas, Lapidoth did not come to us."

"I know," said Deborah. She did not know what Leah and Rabbi Amri knew, so she smiled and they sat down to some wine, cheese, bread, olives and figs. To be truthful, this was more home to Deborah than with Judith and Amram. Afterward Rahab moved to help in the kitchen, but Leah said, "Oh, no dear. You are to study with Rabbi Amri and Deborah. A servant will take care of everything here."

Rahab was a little self conscious and apologized to him that she was not schooled in the scriptures. He smiled and said, "Every student who comes to me is not yet schooled in the scriptures. That is why I am here! To see they become so."

Their studies began happily and Deborah could only think how happy she was to be home. Rahab, who always had to make her own home, was graciously allowing Leah to fuss over her. Any discomfort she might have felt quietly disappeared.

*　　*　　*

Naham and Gideon thundered down through the hills into the encampment. Abel, Barak's aide, greeted them enthusiastically. "I heard of some delays you encountered along your way. I prayed you were safe! What would we do without you?"

"How did you hear of these delays, Abel?" asked Naham.

"When I heard brigands might be in the area I sent a shepherd to spy on you," said Abel smiling mischievously. "Of course I know you and Gideon can handle any trouble, but I did not want to miss out on the fun!"

They laughed, embraced in the way soldiers do, and went to Barak's tent to hear all the news. A soldier brought them food and spirits immediately and departed.

"Have you heard any news of Sisera?" asked Abel.

"We visited Barak's father and he told us what he heard. Sisera has turned from his campaigns to go to the north and east of Hazor, and is looking to the south for his next conquests. His men have raided in the south from time to time, to get the lay of the land, but the big battle is not yet."

"It seems he is waiting for us to come and beat him into the dust," boasted Abel. "We are ready. Training has been relentless and our soldiers know what to do. Our weaponry has increased many fold. We managed to borrow more than a few weapons from the Philistines," he smiled. "Of course they did not give them up without a fight!"

Gideon's eyebrows shot up. "Abel! You have been very busy! I knew I could trust the encampment to you." Barak sat back and laughed loudly. It felt good to be able to laugh heartily. Tension and serious work had occupied them for so many weeks. The two went out of the tent to walk around the camp.

"Gideon, you look glum," said Abel.

"Huh? Oh, I must be tired. I will go to my tent."

"He is not tired," chided Barak. "He is in love."

"What is love? What to you mean?" said Abel. "In love how? Tell me!"

209

Gideon batted Abel on the shoulder and walked away into the encampment. He was eager to see the soldiers, trade stories, and gamble with them to keep his mind off Rahab.

"Rahab! He misses Rahab," guessed Abel. "I cannot blame him. She is a lot of woman. I always wanted to catch him jumping on her, but never did. Would like to do that myself."

"Better watch how you talk about her around him. He will slit your gullet! She is not a whore."

"Oh? I do not understand all this, but I will say nothing more," acquiesced Abel looking a bit disappointed. He was looking for the usual rowdy conversations of the soldiers about women.

Barak had changed since Deborah and Barak's father came to see him at the former camp. Abel shrugged, left Barak's tent, and went out to join the troops in their training exercises.

*　　*　　*

Miriam paced in her house for what seemed to be hours. "What can I do now? I must find out what Omar has planned, if anything. But how? He will only mock me. I must find some way to threaten him. I must learn something I can hold over his head. But what?" She paced some more. Then she hit on a thought, "His servant, Ahmed! Ahmed must know something. I cannot bribe him, but I may be able to bribe a beautiful woman to seduce him. This will take time, but I must try something!"

Joseph came into the house later to get some food and found Miriam furiously grabbing at threads from the tapestry on her loom, unraveling row after row. "What are you planning now, Miriam. You never touch that loom unless you are working out a plot of some kind. Omar will not help you with any murderous scheme, nor will I. I do not understand what makes you so vicious. Deborah knows nothing and Rahab would have told what she knows long ago if she had a mind to. I think the two of them just want to be left alone."

Miriam threw her shuttle onto the floor and angrily rose to face him. She raised her hands, fingers like claws, toward his face. He stepped back, sure she would scratch his eyes out. But instead she went rigid and dropped stiffly to the floor where her shuttle had landed. Her mouth was open and one eye drooped. She lay twitching and then was still. Joseph was shocked. He knelt down to shake her shoulder. There was no response except a low moan. He ran from the house shouting for Joab to go into the village to fetch the physician.

Back in the house, Joseph covered her with a fleece robe and patted a little water onto her face. She was ghostly pale. Her face was contorted and her breath came in low rasps. Presently an old woman came in the door with a bag and knelt down beside Miriam.

"I sent for the physician! Who are you?" demanded Joseph.

"I am Ana. The physician has gone to Gaza. I am a healer and midwife, but I see nothing I can do for this woman." She sadly picked up her bag and started for the door. She turned and said, "You have done all you can, Joseph. Keep her warm, perhaps a little weak wine later on, and wait."

Then she left. A stunned Joseph watched her walk away and then turned back to Miriam. He picked her up and laid her on a sleeping mat, covered her again, and called out the door for Tamara. Tamara, Joab's wife, could look after her while he thought of what to do.

"Father Joseph! Father Joseph! I heard you calling! What has happened?" shouted Tamara. She stopped inside the door and saw Miriam lying on a mat twitching and breathing loudly. "Oh, may God preserve us! What has happened to her?" The horror on her face brought Joseph to her side to keep her from falling too. He led her back out the door and seated her on a bench.

"It struck her suddenly during one of her fits of rage. She has been screaming for days. I am not surprised that something exploded inside of her. How can a body bear so much anger? How much evil can one contain and not be harmed? Will you look after her, Tamara?"

"How will I be able to do that? She has always hated me and wished me dead. I am afraid she will rise up off that mat and claw at me."

"I do not think she will be rising soon, if at all. But it is only for a short time. Soon I will take her to Omar and his physician. Do not fear her. I will be close by."

Tamara looked at him doubtfully, got up from the bench and went back into the house wondering if she could bear to stay there with Miriam, even if Miriam were dead.

CHAPTER 18

Akhmed rode into the town of Kadesh-Napthali and looked around as if searching for someone. His bearing was regal and his eyes were a snapping black. Village men stared back at him because he wore strange clothes and his horse was an expensive breed not seen in small villages except in the rich caravans.

The women at the well stared from behind half closed hoods and whispered, "Who can this be?" as he rode by. "Is he from Sisera or King Jabin?" A small crowd, especially children, began to gather and follow as he continued to the inn.

"Innkeeper! I seek the woman, Deborah. Do you know of her?"

The innkeeper continued to sweep the floor without looking up. "Who are you?"

"It is not your business who I am. Do you know Deborah the seer and prophet?"

"I know of no seer and prophet," mumbled the innkeeper who kept on sweeping.

Akhmed looked around but no one else was in the room. He stormed out of the inn and into the village square. He pulled from his robe the scrap of parchment Omar had given him. The words were carefully penned, "Deborah, seer and prophet, wife of

Lapidoth. Comes from Kadesh-Napthali. Father Amram." He took his horse to the stable, paid the stable boy to take care of him, and went back to the square to wait and think.

The innkeeper sent a boy with a message to Amram and Judith that someone was looking for Deborah and to hide her. Judith carried the message to Hannah in the hills and they sat down in prayer together. Presently Hannah went into the courtyard and piled some stones on the wall behind her house. It was a signal. They waited.

Soon a shepherd boy came by to water a few sheep. "Go to Rabbi Amri and Leah and tell them to hide their guest. Be careful you are not seen. There is a dangerous man, dressed in rich clothes, in the square. Avoid him and remember you are a dumb shepherd boy. If anyone approaches you, you know nothing. You know what to do." The boy gave her a nod and a big grin. She tucked some bread and fruit into his bag and sent him on his way.

Evening came and Judith made her way back down the hill toward home. She entered the door and looked for Amram. The house was quiet. She prayed Deborah was safe. Soon Amram came in the door and nodded curtly to her. "I have been to the inn. The man still waits in the square. He will surely come back to the inn for the night, so I did not stay long. What does he want with Deborah? He would tell the innkeeper nothing, not even who he is. What has she done?"

"It is about Lapidoth, not Deborah, I am sure," whispered Judith. "There has been only mystery and trouble since he came into her life. They are after him. We should have learned more about him before we consented to her marriage to him. What did we know? She does not know where he is. He is running away from someone."

"Who?" half shouted Amram. "For God's sake, who?"

There was a sharp knock on the door. Judith and Amram fell silent. Amram went cautiously to the door and opened it slowly.

"You have a daughter named Deborah," said the man with a strange accent.

Amram and Judith just stared at him.

"I know you have a daughter named Deborah, and I must find her."

"And who are you? You have failed to introduce yourself," replied Judith stepping in front of Amram with her chin held high.

"I am Akhmed, emissary of Omar of the family of Miriam, mother of Lapidoth.

I seek Deborah because Lapidoth has not returned and his life may be in great danger."

"She is not here. She has not seen Lapidoth since she left Bethel-Ephraim," blurted Amram.

"So you have seen her and she has told you this?"

"She sent us a message. We do not know where she is or where the message came from," hurried Judith in reply.

"As I said, his life may be in great danger. I will be here one more day and I urge you to contact her. Be assured she is in no danger from me." He turned on his heel and left. Judith and Amram watched him leave their courtyard and disappear out of sight. They shut the door and together heaved a nervous sigh of relief.

"Perhaps I should seek out Rabbi Amri and tell him what is happening," said Amram.

"No! You will lead this man right to her if she is still there. Hannah has already sent word to Amri and Leah. Let us just wait and do nothing. That would be best." In the night they sought their sleeping mat, but sleep came to neither of them until very late.

Deborah and Rabbi Amri were in his study when the shepherd boy
came to their window. Amri went to the window and leaned out to
hear what the boy had to say. Then the boy disappeared as suddenly
as he had come.

Rahab set the scroll she was studying down. "What is the matter?"

"There is a foreign man here asking about Deborah," replied Rabbi
Amri. "He is perhaps Egyptian. He is wealthy. We are to hide you,
Deborah. It came from Hannah. That is all."

"Miriam!" said Deborah and Rahab together.

"Miriam has a cousin who is part Egyptian or connected through
her family to them. Probably Miriam has asked Omar to send a spy
to find us or worse," whispered Rahab.

"And Hannah said to hide," said Leah. "Perhaps we should do
that right now. The root and wine cellar is a good place. Let us go
quickly."

Rabbi Amri pulled coverings over the windows. They took lamps
and lamp oil to the cellar. "I will bring mats and bedding, and
some food," said Leah as she turned toward the kitchen. A servant
brought Deborah and Rahab's belongings to the cellar as well.
Rahab fingered the curved blade that was sewn into her robe. It
gave her some comfort to know it was there as always and close at
hand.

Amri and Leah went back to the study after moving a bookcase in
front of the door to the cellar.

*   *   *

Barak and Abel were hard at work enlarging the encampment and
finding sources for more sophisticated weapons and tools. Their
army was increasing rapidly while at the same time Sisera's men
attacked and looted villages and farms. "It will not be too long

before Sisera knows we are here. We must be ready," said Abel as he squinted toward the pass in the low mountains. "Word will get out one way or another as they capture and torture people."

"We need to find Deborah. I am afraid something may have happened to delay her," worried Barak. "Where is Gideon? I have not seen him for a few days."

"When he came back after Deborah got to Kadesh I sent him north to find weapons, or steal some, whichever works."

"If he steals them from the wrong people, they will come looking for us! It could mean war. It is too soon."

"You know Gideon, Barak. He is the best. He knows his craft. Did you not tell me God is on our side?"

"God is on our side so long as we have Deborah with us," answered Barak. "I am not sure how I stand with God. We cannot go into battle without her. Where is Naham?"

"Naham is across the Jordan north of the Sea of Galilee spying out Sisera's camp. He should be back in a day or two."

Glancing up Abel saw a signal from the hills. He jumped up from his campstool and grabbed Barak's shoulder. "Someone is coming through the pass, and it is not Gideon!"

Barak jumped up. "It is a marauding party or an army! No mere raiding party would attack an army camp this size. It could only be Philistines!"

Abel sent out the call to battle. Everyone in the camp grabbed a weapon and ran to the training grounds. They divided into three parties and headed for the mountains surrounding the pass. Barak and Abel set out for a high point to determine how many were coming.

Two men came with them to send up flaming arrows as signals. One arrow signaled a raiding party. Two signaled an army. Abel shouted down from high in a tree, "Two!" The men lit the arrows and fired them high into the air. All was eerily quiet as Abel and Barak made their way toward the pass. When they got close, a huge shout arose from the Barak's men and the battle was on. The Philistines were surprised and held at bay on the other side of the pass. The Israelite army defended the pass for two days. Then suddenly the Philistines disappeared.

Barak was puzzled and sent men to watch for another attack, but none came. The next day a caravan of farm wagons strung together drawn by oxen came through the pass. It was Gideon. Barak and Abel took some men and hurried out to meet him.

"Look under the hay! All these wagons are full of weapons! I see you all have been busy getting some battle experience," grinned Gideon.

"You must have seen the Philistines, Gideon. Where did they go?" shouted Abel.

"Yes, I saw them. I got these weapons from the Hivites up north and they have been chasing me ever since. Just as they were about to catch me they ran into the back flanks of the Philistines and became engaged in battle. They had to forget about the wagons and me. The Philistines being attacked from two or three sides turned and attacked the Hivites instead and drove them back to the north. They are probably still killing each other. We were lucky."

"Lucky indeed! We have some wounded but no dead as yet," said Abel who began a tally of the troops, "unless some of them die from their wounds in the night."

"Gideon, it may be known that we are here. We need to prepare to move into battle soon. We have to find Deborah."

"You have not heard from her?"

"No. Neither she nor Rahab have sent word. I am concerned that she has been detained somehow."

"I left them at the home of Rabbi Amri and Leah, the parents of Ya'akov. I am sure they will keep them safe, but someone may have come looking for her from Bethel or Ashdod. I will go back to Kadesh before first light," said Gideon.

"You need to know that Naham is in the land near the Midianites spying out Sisera's movements. Midianites are not exactly friendly."

"Good information! Things are becoming more and more dangerous according to some of my contacts and moving messages is more difficult. I will determine where he is without exposing him."

*   *   *

Gideon left before first light and made his way through the mountain pathways toward Kadesh. At dawn he could see smoke rising from a Canaanite village. Was it Hivites on their way home to the north or Sisera pushing south? He climbed a tree and waited to see if anything would stir. He waited for an hour, climbed down, and headed east to avoid any inhabitants that might be hiding close to their village.

A heavy hand fell on his shoulder and he jumped sideways. A badly wounded man fell beside him almost taking him to the ground. Gideon knelt beside him and found his water flask. He touched the man's lips with water hoping to get information about his attackers, but he did not revive. He was dead. Gideon pushed the body into a small ravine and covered it with stones and dirt to prevent vultures and dogs finding it. The dogs would follow him because the dead man's scent was on him. Those who knew the village dogs would be able to track him by following them.

He turned back north and saw smoke again. He knew the Hivites would not come this far east and common thieves did not usually burn a village. It must be Sisera's marauders. If he went north again would he find more burned villages? Was he too late?

* * *

Hannah kept busy sending and watching for messages. Shepherds came only by night now but their visits were getting fewer. She knew the window of safety was closing for them, so she determined not to burden them further. Canaanite villages had been burned and trouble was on the move.

Judith refrained from visiting Hannah or Leah. The stranger was gone from the town square, but she did not feel it was safe to openly venture out. Amram frequented the inn for news but no one had seen the man for a few weeks. His horse was gone from the stable.

Hannah ventured to Kadesh one morning to visit her friend in the alley. She made his tea and sat down on a doorstep saying nothing. "He is still here," he mumbled. "Be watchful." Hannah got up after a few moments and left the alley, moving behind the merchant's tents. She pulled the hood of her robe closer around her face and walked to the south, the opposite way from her house in the hills. Worry crowded her thoughts. If she were followed, she would lead him away from her home. She decided to walk to the next village where her late husband's elderly cousin, Asshur, lived. Perhaps she could find news there.

* * *

Deborah came up from the cellar every morning, but this time she said, "I must seek out this man and discover what he wants. It is foolish to involve and frighten the whole town. I need to know his intention."

"Are you sure, Deborah?" asked Rahab. "Omar is a mysterious and changeable man. He cannot be trusted."

"It is Lapidoth they seek, not me. They do not know if I have knowledge of the family business. But you, Rahab! They know you do. They may be looking for you as well. Perhaps you should stay in hiding until I learn of this man and what he wants."

"But no one has seen him for many days," said Leah.

"If I come forth, he will surely appear," answered Deborah with assurance. She left the house and walked first to Hannah's. Discovering that Hannah was not home she continued back into Kadesh and the village square where she sat down by the well to wait.

This place at the well brought back so many memories of her girlhood. But instead of disturbing or distracting her, they seemed to stiffen her resolve to stay in fearless command of her mind and her life, giving it only into God's care.

After a few hours she was ready to give up when the stable boy came to her with a message. "Come to the inn. Do not fear. I mean you no harm."

So Deborah gathered her robe around her, drew her hood in close, and walked down a small hill to the inn. She walked in and sat down in a corner. The light was very dim and she could not see if anyone else was present. Someone came to her table and sat down on the bench opposite her.

"Are you looking for me?" Deborah's voice was steady. "I am Deborah."

"I am Akhmed sent by Omar to find Lapidoth if he is still alive. Have you knowledge of him?"

"The last time I saw Lapidoth was when he left me in Bethel the day I arrived there. He gave no explanation. He did not even bid me farewell. His mother, Miriam, said he had business to attend but she did not tell me anything more. I heard that he came here some weeks ago, was offered sanctuary, but refused it and left immediately. This is the extent of my information about him."

"He shared nothing with you before your wedding or on the road to Bethel?"

"Nothing. We fled Kadesh and Sisera's marauders immediately after the wedding. When we arrived at the inn in Tirzah we were exhausted. The town was attacked in the night and again we fled. The innkeeper led us through a back tunnel from the inn and into a ravine that led to the Jericho Road. Lapidoth turned and went back to Tirzah, promising to catch up with me and the other guests. I did not see him until that day in Bethel when we met and he left without a word."

"And may I ask where you were and who you were with between the time he left to return to Tirzah and when you arrived in Bethel?"

Deborah's eyes began to blaze. "No you may not. That is between my husband and me, and has nothing to do with you or your mission!"

"Should I take the word of a mere woman?" asked Akhmed smoothly with a rare smile.

"You will take the word of a woman, prophet and seer, and be glad to have it," replied Deborah in a cold steady voice.

Akhmed sat there staring at Deborah for several moments. This was not the direction he expected the conversation to go. He had underestimated her. He rose slowly and said, "We will meet again, I am sure."

"Is it your intention to find Lapidoth and bring him back to me alive, Akhmed?" asked Deborah as she also rose.

"Alive, yes, but not to return him to you. I will return him to Omar who wishes a conversation with him. What he does from there is up to him."

"If you do not bring him back to me, then I assume we will *not* meet again. Will you now leave this town in peace?"

"I will leave your town in peace, be assured. I am a man of my word."

Deborah wanted to say "Omar's word" but she kept her silence and he left.

She left the inn after a short time. As she walked out of the inn she heard the clatter of horses hoofs and saw Akhmed riding away to the east.

The next day Deborah went to her parent's home to reassure Amram and Judith they were all safe.

"We have nothing to fear from Akhmed, father. He is looking for Lapidoth and I believe I convinced him that none of us know where he is."

"Do you know where he is, Deborah?" demanded her father.

"No, I do not. I believe he is in trouble and is hiding east of the Jordan, but I have no evidence of that. I think Akhmed already suspects he has gone east. Probably the stable boy told him."

Deborah went back to Rabbi Amri and Leah's to tell them what happened. Rahab was relieved to see her. "I was afraid someone would snatch you. Omar is no one to trifle with. Gideon was here. He brought news of a battle with Philistines and Hivites, and Barak is anxious that you return to the camp."

There was a rap on the door and Hannah walked in. Deborah ran and put her arms around the frail old widow. "I heard about the visit of Akhmed," said Hannah. "I did not wish to lead him to my house, so I went to see my late husband's cousin, Asshur. He often has news. Jabin's army is on the move. They are not coming this way yet. They are amassing somewhere east of the Jordan with Sisera as their general. The time is coming, Deborah, when you will lead the army against Sisera. That time is not just yet, but any further preparation you need to make should be done soon."

"Lead the army!" exclaimed Leah. "What is she talking about?"

"Deborah is chosen of the Lord to assist Barak when he goes against Sisera," said Hannah calmly. "The Lord led her to study the scriptures with Ya'akov and to study battle with Barak. Thanks to Ya'akov and Rabbi Amri she was able to learn scriptures, help Barak teach them to the soldiers, and make battle plans accordingly. Barak and Deborah grew up together and will stand together in battle. God will lead them and Israel will be successful."

Leah reached for a chair for support. A puzzled Rabbi Amri invited them all to sit down in his study. "Deborah, did you know of this when you began to study with Ya'akov? Was this your purpose in being with him and with me?"

"Beloved rabbi," said Deborah, "I have not used you or Ya'akov. In my childhood I had dreams at night of being in battle. I did not know why. I could not tell anyone but Hannah because it sounded so absurd that a girl should dream of battle. Perhaps it would even be thought of as heresy. I studied with Ya'akov because I quickly came to love him and wanted to be close to him. Studying with him under your guidance was a beautiful way to do that. Neither of us thought marriage was right for us at that time. He knew his health might not hold out long. It is God using us to save Israel. But it was not my intention to use anyone for myself."

Rabbi Amri sat back and thoughtfully pulled at his beard. "Go on, Deborah . . ."

"I was told that Barak was falling away from God. His father came to me to help him bring Barak back to God. By then Barak had become a soldier and a leader. It was in talking to him that God's plan unfolded for us. Barak would teach me battle strategies so I could match them with scripture and the army of Israel would become the army of God."

"Is Lapidoth involved in your plans? Is this why someone came looking for him? Why he rode east across the Jordan?" asked Leah, still mystified.

"Lapidoth is involved in a secret family business that I know nothing about. Something has happened concerning that business, but I do not know what. I understand he came here, but then fled by night."

Rahab cleared her throat and began to speak. She was hesitant because to safeguard her own life she had never spoken to anyone about the family business activities. "The family business involves the sale of black market jewels. I do not know where they come from, but Lapidoth is the distributor of them and his father, Joseph, as well. Lapidoth travels as a pauper when he carries them, then changes his robes to those of a wealthy merchant, and sells them to the rich and powerful. It is a dangerous business. I agree with Deborah, something must have happened. Akhmed is probably right. His life may well be in danger, but not from the man who sent him, my half cousin Omar."

Hannah shifted in her seat. "Lapidoth came to me saying he wanted his own life. He wanted to sever connections with this business, but he did not know how. There were several attempts on his life before he came here. We offered to hide him until he could sort it out, but he would not stay. I understand Akhmed is gone now, perhaps to continue his search for him."

Shifting the focus from Lapidoth to the coming battle, Deborah said, "Perhaps it is time to go back to the camp. Where is Gideon now?"

Rahab was anxious too. "He has gone to find news of Naham. Barak sent Naham to scout out Sisera's movements. Gideon will be back soon because Barak sent him to bring us back to the army camp. Perhaps the skirmishes with the Palestinians and the Hivites have caused Barak to be anxious for your guidance."

*   *   *

Naham wrapped his robes closer about him as night came on. He followed the Yarmuk River to the east of the Jordan and turned north into the low mountains above the Sea of Galilee. The Midianites were to the southeast and Sisera dead ahead to the north. He kept to the forested areas until he got closer and waited for his contact in a certain cave known to both of them. Night fell and all was quiet until he heard a stone drop and then a second one. Naham threw two stones at the entrance. It was the signal and Shem, a herder, slipped into the cave.

"Have you news?" said Naham in a low voice.

"Yes," was the whispered reply as Shem crept into the light of a very small fire. "Gideon just arrived in Kadesh. He sent word asking about your progress. He is returning to Barak soon."

"Send word that the camps are growing larger and there is much stirring in them. New soldiers are arriving every day. Couriers are running from camp to camp. Weapons are coming in from the north. They are preparing for more than small attacks on villages."

"I will carry your message across the Sea of Galilee. I will go with a fisherman. There is the smell of storms in the air and I dare not wait until they come down from the mountain and make the waters rough and impassible."

Naham nodded and extinguished the fire. The two slept briefly and Shem departed in the middle of the night.

*   *   *

It was a few hours before dawn when Kelev began to growl softly. Rahab got up and went up stairs to see what disturbed him. She opened a shuttered window and leaned out.

"It is I, Gideon."

"I will let you in the back door," whispered Rahab. She pulled her robe close around her and went to the door. "Did you see Naham?"

"No, but I know where he is. It would be dangerous for him if I went any closer. But I know he is alive and he left information with a trusted friend who passed it onto me. Barak will be glad I found you and Deborah. We must leave soon. I will grab a few hour's sleep and then we will go."

Rahab brought him robes to sleep on and tiptoed back to the wine cellar where she and Deborah still stayed. Deborah did not awaken. Rahab lay awake until Gideon came down the stairs. Deborah sat up and looked startled at Gideon. "Is everything all right, Gideon?"

"There has been a battle, but we survived thanks to a bunch of Hivites that were after me. They drove off the Philistines. They must have taken their battle toward the Great Sea and we were left alone. We must leave for Barak's camp now before anything else stirs. He needs you and has asked me to come for you," said Gideon in a low voice. "He fears the big battle with Sisera will come too soon and he will have to fight without you."

"If what the Lord has told me is true, he will not have to go into battle with Sisera alone, without me. Tell him to have no fear, Gideon. God will send Barak himself to me when the time is right," said Deborah with assurance. She smiled at Gideon and touched his arm. "Now go and deliver my message. Take Rahab with you if she wishes to go. Moshe is ready to join Barak as well. He is young, but he needs to learn the ways of men to make him strong. Take him too. He is your surety that I will return when Barak comes for me."

Rahab's eyes darted from Deborah to Gideon and back to Deborah. She wanted so much to go with Gideon. But Hannah said not to force anything concerning Gideon and she did not think she could bear to leave Deborah. "I must stay here," she said with some regret. "I will return with Deborah and Barak when the time comes."

Gideon hid the disappointment in his eyes by turning to Deborah and quickly asking about Moshe. "Where will I find Moshe? Is he in the fields with the flock?"

"Yes, and there are cousins with him. So he will not leave the flock unprotected. I will send a servant to find him and bring him here," replied Deborah.

Moshe arrived out of breath and wide-eyed with excitement. "Is this true? Am I to go to Barak's camp and learn to be a soldier?"

"You will make a good soldier as long as you do not forget the Lord your God. And I will be with you soon, Moshe," said Deborah affectionately.

The life of a shepherd was solitary and lonely. Moshe was often at a loss for words or appropriate actions in the company of those older than himself. He ducked his head to hide the embarrassing flush he always felt when he was excited or when he did not know what to say. His complexion was that of a red head like Deborah's and to his embarrassment, flushed easily.

Rahab watched from the roof of the house as Gideon and Moshe rode away. Her heart rode away with them. Her allegiance was to Deborah and to run away with a man not her husband could subject them both to punishment. Some day in the right way God would send Gideon to her again and she would wait for that day.

CHAPTER 19

L apidoth traveled into the desert of Arabia beyond the Midianites. He purchased an old camel from a caravan and a Bedouin tent from a tent maker on the outer edge of a bazaar. His plan was to travel north and cross the Jordan again above Lake Semechonitis to reach Sidon on the coast of the Great Sea. It would be a long lonely trek, but he could see no other way to regain some kind of life in familiar territory and, yes, find Deborah. He still had no sure answers and spending time alone would give him the opportunity to clear his mind and think.

He tried to remember what Deborah told him of her childhood with Barak and God's plan for her. "It sounded so strange when she spoke of leading armies. This could not be and yet she was so sure. God had led her to study the scriptures in unusual circumstances. What would my part in her life and she in mine possibly be? What exactly drove me to seek out Hannah, who is a cousin I do not know? How did it happen that I came to abandon Deborah on the Jericho road? What strange power drew me into this circle of people and then spewed me out again? He felt a rage burning within him, and in his dreams his mother, Miriam, was laughing at him."

He traveled at night in the cool air by the light of the moon and slept in the heat of noonday. The questions buzzed in his head like insects that refused to go away. "Hannah said she would pray. Can I also pray? Can I receive answers from God, as Deborah seems to be able to do? Where do I find that kind of faith? God, why am I out in this wilderness with no clear direction and no home? Do you have a plan for my life? If you do, reveal it to me! If you are God, reveal it to me now!"

Before turning west and leaving the desert, Lapidoth sold his old camel and bought two mules. He loaded his tent and provisions on the smaller one and rode the larger one. Somehow this felt right. It felt like going home even if he was not sure where to find a home in this difficulty. As he rode west he calculated his chances of picking up the threads of his old life and perhaps discover if someone was looking for him. He would start with Ammiel at the inn in Sidon. He could make discreet inquiries. If he heard nothing, he would start for Acre to determine if anyone had inquired about him there. After that he was not sure what next step to take. He dared not seek out Deborah until he was sure it would not put her in danger.

*   *   *

Barak was fuming as Gideon and Moshe slipped back into the camp. "It has been weeks! What has taken you so long? The food supplies are dwindling and the men want to go home. We cannot fall apart now!"

Abel was pacing the tent floor. "We could let the men go to their homes a few at a time to see their families with the promise they would come back within three days."

"These are soldiers! They cannot just leave! What if they are captured and forced to reveal the location of our camp? They could give Sisera vital information!" shouted Barak. "What if we are attacked while they are gone?" He wheeled on Gideon and Moshe. "Where is Deborah? Why did she not come with you?" Then he noticed Moshe and in his frustration blurted out, "Why are you here?"

Shaken, Moshe stepped back behind Gideon. Gideon moved forward. Clearly the tension and waiting had gotten to the whole camp. "Barak, my captain and my friend, please let us sit down to talk. I have much to share with you."

Reluctantly Barak nodded his agreement and they sat down around a table. Abel poured wine for each of them and sat down. "First, Deborah said she would be here when God calls her and God will send you to fetch her. These are her words:

"If what the Lord has told me is true, he will not have to go into battle with Sisera alone, without me. Tell him to have no fear, Gideon. God will send Barak himself to me when the time is right."

"She has sent Moshe to you to be trained as a soldier. He has grown strong and is eager to be in your army, Barak."

Barak thought for a few moments and turning to the shaken Moshe he softened his voice. "Do you really want to be in the army, Moshe?"

"Yes, sir! I have always, always wanted to be a soldier and serve you, Captain Barak!" said Moshe enthusiastically. Then remembering his place, he flushed and ducked his head.

"Perhaps Moshe is just what we need," said Barak. "We will divide the camp into two factions, younger men who need seasoning and older soldiers who can train them. Those who have younger brothers at home or know of young boys in their villages may go home to be recruiters. Moshe will be the orderly for the younger group and infuse them with his enthusiasm. Are you willing, young Moshe?"

Moshe's head popped up and his eyes were wide with astonishment. He jumped up and exclaimed, "I will do my very best, sir!"

"Now Gideon, what news from Naham? Is he still alive?" asked Abel eagerly.

"Indeed he is still alive and has passed information through his contacts to me. I did not approach him because he was too close to one of Sisera's camps. If I were spotted it might compromise his position. Here are the dispatches giving the numbers of Sisera's forces, their equipment, and a sketch of their camp locations and plans." Gideon laid the sheaf of papyrus he carried in his robe on the table before Barak and Abel.

Presently Gideon whisked Moshe off to a place where Gideon could draw the plan of the camp in the dirt. When Moshe completely understood the layout of the camp, two guards took Moshe to a tent on the far side of the camp where he could stow his gear and sleep.

When Gideon returned, Barak and Abel were hard at work drawing up new plans for the camp, training, communications and recruitment. Abel set up the new division in the camp and made plans for training. Gideon set up plans for soldiers to safely go to their villages to find young soldiers. He would go with them and find food as well. Barak began to review the plans and scriptures he and Deborah had put together anticipating the Lord's battle.

*   *   *

Deborah and Rahab took advantage of a cool morning to walk to Hannah's place. "I heard you in my prayers, Hannah. I heard you call to me," said Deborah.

"Indeed I did," replied Hannah. "Sisera is on the move. I received news from Naham."

"Have you seen him? Has he met up with Gideon?" asked a breathless Rahab.

"I have not seen or heard from them, Rahab. I know your heart is with Gideon. Keep your faith, cousin. Things may not turn out the way you hope, but perhaps much better. We must look farther into the future as well as seeing what is at our feet."

Rahab looked down to hide her disappointment. Her greatest fear was things would not turn out as she hoped.

"Must I get news to Barak to be ready to go against Sisera?" asked Deborah, eyebrows furrowed. "I have no urging, no message from God as yet."

"The time is not yet, Deborah. You must know where Sisera intends to go. He and his army must be in exactly the right place. God has a plan," reassured Hannah.

"I cannot help wondering where Lapidoth is. What is he doing? Is he dead or alive?"

"Lapidoth is a very resourceful man," offered Rahab. "He manages to slip through knot holes of difficulty and always emerge triumphant. Believe me I know. Miriam and her family used him unmercifully. He had to learn to survive on his own."

"Why do you think he allowed himself to be pulled into their intrigue?" asked Deborah truly puzzled.

"Lapidoth was very young when it all started," answered Rahab thoughtfully. "To him it was exciting, like your brother, Moshe, playing soldier and dreaming of leading armies. Lapidoth did not dream of leading armies, but of international intrigue and danger. To him it was a game. He did not know their evil would suck him farther and farther into their blackness until there was no way out. I suspect he is trying to find the way out and cannot send messages or show up again. If Miriam sent someone to find him, it would be to kill him. She cares nothing for him, his father, or the rest of the family. She is evil itself. Even her cousin, Omar, keeps her at arms length. He is the kingpin in the smuggling business. He is no angel but he is not stupid."

"I must find him," said Deborah suddenly. "He is still my husband and I cannot ignore that. His riches are my riches, and his troubles are my troubles. If Miriam seeks to kill Lapidoth, she will do the same to me and perhaps to you, Rahab."

Hannah looked up in shock. "Are you sure, Deborah? What about God's call?"

"God can call me wherever I am and when I hear that call, I will answer it. I cannot sit idle and wait. Everything depends upon everyone and everything else. How can I answer the great call if I do not pay heed to the smaller call of my life and Lapidoth's? I must go."

"How will you know where to start?" asked Rahab with a worried look on her darkly beautiful face. "He could be anywhere!"

"I will start with the Egyptian, Akhmed. I will follow his steps beginning from the stable and the stable boy who kept his horse. I made my way to Bethel alone, and I can do it again."

"This time you will not be alone. I will go with you. We can send a message to Naham. He may be able to help us," responded Rahab in a determined voice.

Deborah turned to Rahab in surprise and pleasure. "Now you sound like the Rahab I first met in the hills above Bethel! You are no longer a follower, but your true independent self! We will go and God be with us!"

"God is with you," celebrated Hannah in her high rusty voice. "I can feel it! This is right and you must go, Deborah! And you, Rahab. Do not think your role in this is feeble. God drew you and Deborah together for a purpose. God always has a purpose and it is not small, but great! Go! I will pray."

Deborah and Rahab walked and half ran to the stable. The stable boy was a little startled by their sudden and dramatic appearance. "The Egyptian road away on his horse to the east," stammered the boy. "He said nothing to me. He just paid for the keep of his horse and left. He did not even leave me money for myself."

"To the east. That could only mean the land of the Midianites across the Jordan, unless he traveled north close to the coast and slipped past Jabin and Sisera. They would not bother an Egyptian, especially if he promised them trade," mused Deborah. She asked to buy two pack animals, paid for them, and asked the stable boy to hold them ready for a journey.

The stable boy's eyes were aglow. He already sensed the intrigue and excitement. "Perhaps I can go with you! I can care for your animals and help track the Egyptian. You would not be in so much danger as traveling alone without a m . . . without company of a male."

"You are but a boy," snapped Rahab. "How will you protect us? With sticks and stones?"

"I am thirteen years of age. I look like a mere boy because food has been difficult for me to get. But still I can fight, and I speak the Egyptian and the Midianite languages. My father was Egyptian and I was carried off during a raid on our home. We camped in Midian for a year and then I was dumped at this stable. My captors rode on leaving me to be a starving stable boy. Please, let me go with you. Please!"

Deborah and Rahab looked at each other in astonishment. "God is with us," smiled Deborah. "You may come with us and we will be glad for your presence."

The boy glowed with pride and excitement. "My name is Astennu, after the god of the moon. I see well in the darkness of the earth and the souls of evil men."

Rahab raised one eyebrow at Deborah, they burst out laughing, and went to the market to buy provisions. They went to the home of Rabbi Amri and Leah to collect their belongings and bid them farewell.

"Two women and a boy? You will be a target for thieves!" exclaimed Leah. "And how will you find Lapidoth if you do not know where to look?"

"We know he went east. Naham is east of the Sea of Galilee. We may find him or someone who encountered Lapidoth. They may have seen the Egyptian. They would not forget him!" reasoned Deborah. "God will lead us. We have been blessed by Hannah and her prayers will be with us."

Rabbi Amri laid down his scroll and invited them to sit down with him. "The land beyond the Sea of Galilee is filled with enemies. You do not know their language or their customs. You will need to go to their markets for food. It is very dangerous as Leah has said."

"The boy knows the languages. He can get food for us while we wait in hiding," ventured Rahab.

"Is this the boy from the stable? No one knows if he is trustworthy. He was brought here and abandoned. He is part Egyptian. This is his story but you do not know if it is true. If you give him money for food, he may run away. Or he may rob you as you sleep. Please think this through carefully," advised Rabbi Amri. "If you reject him, God will send you another."

Rahab withdrew the curved knife from her robe and said, "I have lived alone most of my adult life and I know well how to use this." Kelev came trotting in tail wagging and nuzzled her knee for attention. "And Kelev here is a good protector. He helped bring us through the wilderness up from Bethel."

Rabbi Amri scratched his beard thoughtfully. "Travel up the west side of the Sea so you will not be trapped between the Midianites and Sisera. Ask shepherds along the way. They look isolated and alone, but they have ways of communicating and know more than they let on. Can you agree with this plan, Deborah?"

Deborah and Rahab looked at each other and nodded. "It sounds wise. We will stay near our own people first. Perhaps we will learn something and not need to go into enemy territory," said Deborah.

They took their belongings and started back toward the stable. When they arrived only one mule was there and the boy was gone.

Rahab fingered the knife in her robe and vowed, "I will skin him alive when we catch up with him. We bought those mules he took and he will answer for his slimy lies, too!"

A man came into the stable and Deborah recognized him as the inn and stable owner. "Can I help you?"

"We bought two mules from your stable boy and he ran off with them and the money," spat Rahab.

"You gave him money? Of course he ran off! I let him clean stables because I felt sorry for him, but he is always stealing something from strangers who come here and I have to empty his pockets. Wait for me. I will get him." The owner mounted a horse lodged at the back of the stable and went galloping away.

Deborah and Rahab just stared wide-eyed at each other and then turned to look in the direction the owner had ridden. "Maybe there are things we need to learn," said Deborah. "Maybe Rabbi Amri was correct. We need to stay among our own people and not invite anyone to go with us."

"A lesson learned! We will surely do better on our own! That seems to be our best way!" exclaimed Rahab.

They sat down to wait, their bundles on a pile of straw near by. When they were about to leave and return to Rabbi Amri's house, they heard the clatter of hoofs on the hard road. Rahab laughed out loud when she looked out the stable door. The owner on his horse was trotting toward them with two mules in tow and the stable boy tied and strapped to the back of one of them. When they stopped she pulled her knife from her robe and tapped Astennu's nose with it. "Shall I cut off your nose, thief? Perhaps cut off your hand as the Egyptians do?" she said through a triumphant grin.

Astennu squealed and tried to jerk away, but Rahab laid the knife at his throat. "What is your real name boy?" she demanded.

"Astennu, I swear it. I have told you the truth!"

"Yes, that is what he told me his name is and I saw the travelers who left him. That much is true," verified the owner as he yanked Astennu off the mule and dropped him into the dirt. He tore off the boy's robe and retrieved the money. Then he kicked him and snarled, "Now get out and do not come back!"

"Please ladies, take me with you or I shall starve here! I have learned my lesson. I will not steal from you again!"

The owner snorted, dragged Astennu out of the stable by his hair, and threw him into the street. "That is how we take out the trash here!"

The owner counted the money he had taken from Astennu. It was more than a fair price for the mules. He handed the halter ropes to Rahab and Deborah, gave them a small sack of coins, and went back to the inn. They loaded their supplies and belongings on the mules and started out to the north, the way Rabbi Amri suggested.

They stopped by Hannah's for a moment for tea and to tell her the story of the stable boy. She whooped and laughed. "Well now, that was an auspicious beginning! Now you know the Lord has mysterious ways to keep you from stumbling and lead you to your destination. God has willed it! Go in peace and do not forget to pray lest a worse thing befall you!"

Rahab and Deborah kissed Hannah on both cheeks and started for the hills overlooking the west coast of the Sea of Galilee. It was hot and breezy with clouds overhead. Late in the day they found a sheltered place and pitched their tent. The mules were happy to stop and graze, and Kelev crouched down in the grass to watch them and be sure they did not wander off or run away.

* * *

Lapidoth rode slowly north along the west side of the marsh of Lake Semechonitis. The insects buzzed around him in swarms driving him west toward the desert mountains and dryer land. He wandered alongside wadis to keep his direction and eventually came back down to lower land and green meadows to feed the animals. The town of Dan was just ahead and he decided to stop there for rest and provisions. The city gate was still open. He passed through the second wall to the marketplace. It was near the time of closing when he arrived but a few stalls were still open for business. After picking out dates, cheese, grapes, lamb, and bread, he sat down near the village well to eat some of his purchases. A man appeared before him with a dipper of water. "May I serve you, Lapidoth?"

Lapidoth jerked himself up and was facing a smiling Akhmed. "You are in no danger from me, my friend," said Akhmed, "but we must find a place to talk. I have some wine. I see you have bread. Perhaps we could meet at the small oasis west of the town. I am sure it will be quite deserted."

Lapidoth squinted at Akhmed. Slowly he recalled seeing him at the house of Omar. "Who sent you? Omar? Miriam?"

"Actually Miriam implored Omar to send someone to find you, Deborah, and Rahab. She wants you all killed. Omar is not a killer. He does not wish you harm. But he does want what you owe the smugglers so they do not kill him and his household."

"And my mother, Miriam? She wants me dead?"

"Most definitely! But you have nothing to fear from your mother. She became quite ill suddenly, paralyzed completely on one side. She is unable to walk and barely able to speak. Your father said her anger finally got the best of her. She was in one of her wild rages when it happened."

"Are you the only one looking for me? Or are there others? I was nearly killed in Sidon probably by a man who was on the ship I sailed on, heading up the coast to Sidon. I thought I had eluded him in the streets, changed my clothes to make my sales. I did not look like the poor beggar he saw on the ship. But still he came to my room at the inn in the middle of the night. I sleep lightly with a curved dagger near my pillow. When the door creaked open I lunged at him and killed him. I do not know who he was. Perhaps he just smelled money and came after me to rob me. The innkeeper disposed of the body to save the reputation of his inn. I sailed for Acre the next morning."

"Fascinating story! I know of no one else who is coming after you. Perhaps it was a robbery. Did you see his robes or his face?"

"No. It was pitch black. I could only hear him coming but the smell of the ship was still on him. Thankfully I surprised him before he could kill me."

"What will you do now?" asked Akhmed, genuinely concerned.

"My plan was to start at Sidon and ask the few people I know there if they know of someone pursuing me. If there is nothing, I will go down the coast to Acre and inquire of a friend there. My informants are more plentiful in that area."

"I know it is presumptuous of me to ask you to trust me since you do not know me, but I would like to travel with you. I promised Omar to protect you as best I can if you will allow me. Otherwise I will be forced to follow you from a distance to fulfill my promise."

Lapidoth sat quietly in thought, sipping the wine. "I suppose I do not have a choice. You are here and you know where I am going. I would rather have you with me than wonder where you will turn up next," said Lapidoth with a faint smile.

"I must tell you I was in Kadesh-Napthali and spoke to your wife, Deborah. She did not know of your whereabouts and when I challenged her, she skillfully rebuked me, as I richly deserved. She is very strong and forthright, far beyond the ordinary woman."

"Truly, she is no ordinary woman," replied Lapidoth with a sudden pang of guilt and loneliness.

"I see the pain in your eyes. I will not pry into your business, Lapidoth. Let us plan how we will resolve your difficulty and free you from the past that encumbers you."

"How can I repay you for this service?" asked Lapidoth looking around the oasis as evening was falling.

"There is no need. Omar will settle with me handsomely. You did not ask me to come. He did and the debt is his."

"And if you are not able to take me back? What then?"

"Then, my friend, I will be deprived of a fortune. So you see it is in my best interest as well as yours that we work together, get whatever debt that is owed resolved, and we both go free."

"Free! It seems I have not been free since I was ten years old. Tell me, Akhmed, what is it like to be free? Surely there are some restrictions upon you. How free can we really be?"

"Alas, freedom is in the mind," mused Akhmed. He shifted in his seat to face Lapidoth more squarely. "First you decide what it is you want to be free of, and then you plan your movements to make it so. My wish has always been to be free of fear. When my mind is free of fear, I do not act in fearful ways. I exude confidence as well as kindness and patience. It has a good affect on the people with whom I must deal and makes things go more smoothly than if I acted like a chastened slave or an arrogant bastard."

"It seems I have played the role of the arrogant one when I am selling to the powerful and played the chastened slave when dressing like a beggar to move from place to place. When I approached Deborah and her father, I found myself confused. Neither way was satisfactory for that situation. I soon found myself following Deborah's lead because she seemed to know what came next. She is so sure of her calling from God and let's nothing turn her away from it. I have not seen a woman like her except for Miriam, and Miriam does it with angry demands and vicious threats. Deborah does it gently with assuredness."

The evening was turning to night as Lapidoth and Akhmed returned to Dan for supper and a night in a comfortable inn, just before the city gates closed.

CHAPTER 20

Face down on the ground Naham struggled against the bindings of his captors. A small band of brigands ambushed him thinking he was one of Sisera's men. "Do I look like one of Sisera's soldiers you idiots? I am on your side. Untie me immediately and help me. We cannot stay in this place long!"

One was about to cut his throat but the other grabbed his arm. "No!" he whispered urgently. "Sisera's men are close by and he does not call out. He speaks the truth and I fear we are in danger ourselves. Let us leave now."

"What about him?" asked the others.

"Bring him. Throw him over your shoulder. We will carry him to a safer place to question him. He might have information we need."

The band of four took Naham to the east over hills to a desert oasis. They removed the gag from his mouth and gave him water. "Who are you?" sputtered Naham. "You nearly got us all killed!"

"You sound like a Hebrew. You smell like a camel! What are you doing here?" demanded Jarib.

"Pardon, friend, but your smell is also disgusting," retorted Naham.

Mishma stepped forward to strike Naham, but again he was stopped mid swing by Jarib. "If his tongue is loose, perhaps we should keep him talking."

"Unbind me. I am not your enemy. No reason for you to be mine," said Naham in a calm voice. "I am Naham. What information do you seek? Perhaps we can help each other."

The leader said, "I am Jarib. This is Mishma, my second. These are Tema and Sabtah. We are from Midianite territory but we are not really Midianites. We were taken as small children and became slaves to a Midianite master for twelve years until we killed him and escaped. We have been searching for our families, asking everyone we meet if they know of four children from the same village who were taken from their parents. But it is difficult to know where to look since we do not know where we were taken from."

"I do not have the answers to your questions but if you wish to fight against Sisera and other oppressors, I invite you to join the Israelite army of Barak. There are many with him who are from families all over Israel and from across the Jordan. You may find someone among them who has knowledge of you."

"Let us eat and drink," announced Jerib. "Then we will take council among ourselves and give you our answer."

*   *   *

The Israelite soldiers were preparing to go to their villages and had explicit instructions to return in three days with recruits and food. Gideon quickly trained them in ways to slip through fields unnoticed, and to recruit by night in their villages. It was risky but it had to be done before Sisera mobilized. The soldiers eagerly agreed and promised to return.

Gideon climbed to the summit overlooking Barak's encampment and scanned the valley and hillsides wondering if Naham was safe.

He received no messages from him in many days. He decided to travel in the direction Naham was last known from his messages.

Abel and Barak kept track of the men who left and where they were going. If they did not return on time, a scout would be sent to find them. They kept busy inventorying the weapons, inspecting the living quarters, and checking on food supplies. Two days went slowly by and Barak was pacing more than usual.

At last Abel hurried into Barak's tent and announced that three men had returned with recruits, some young, some older. The word was spreading among the villages that the choice was to fight or become slaves to Jabin. The women not wishing to be prostitutes for Sisera's army urged their brothers and husbands to join Barak. During the next several days men were streaming into the camp, bringing with them food and provisions of all kinds. Barak couldn't believe his eyes. Scribes scrambled to keep track of everything and reported that all who left returned safely. Only Gideon and Naham had not returned.

*   *   *

Hannah was in her garden when Gideon came down out of the hills. She stood up and shaded her eyes with her free hand. Her eyes were not as strong as they used to be, but slowly she recognized him. He moved quickly in her direction, hood over his head. Open spaces were not his favorite place to be.

"Gideon! Come into the house. What brings you here?"

"Have you heard anything about Naham? It has been many days." He sat down and reached for the tea, bits of lamb, and bread she offered. "When I sense he has been gone too long, I start looking for him."

Hannah smiled. "How do you come to care so much, Gideon?"

"He is my cousin's son. We did not grow up together. Then we met when we become spies for the Israelite resistance. He is a little younger than I am. Just a kid really. I watch out for him I guess. He takes too many chances and gets into trouble. I found him tied to a tree once. But he is getting better at watching out for himself."

Hannah laughed out loud. "The Lord blesses those who are after his own heart! Let me meditate on this for a little while. You go ahead, eat and wash up." She went into her bedroom and sat down on her sleeping mat. Gideon went out to the well and drew some cool water to splash on his face and arms. He sat down in the garden by the wall to rest and wait for Hannah.

Evening was coming on when Hannah came out of the house. "He is not alone. I sense a little danger around him."

"Do you know where he is?"

"He has not moved. That is all I can see."

"Thank you, Hannah!"

"Thank the wisdom of God, Gideon. It is not I! Wait there is more . . ."

But Gideon was already sprinting across the fields and heading north. Night was coming on, but at dark he could see well enough by the moon when he got to the road to keep moving. Some time before dawn when the moon was no longer visible he stopped to sleep for a few hours.

When he started out again he found a mule wandering in the hills. He thought it was strange because the mule had strap marks in his fur. He captured it and rode on north. In the evening he stopped at an inn for food. Before he went in he watched the inn for a time to be sure there were no soldiers around. As he came out of the inn a dog ran up to him and pulled on his robe. "Kelev! My god, where is Rahab?" His heart and stomach seemed to collide when he realized she must be in trouble. That surely meant Deborah was in trouble too.

He led the mule and followed Kelev into the hills. It seemed they walked all night, Kelev constantly running forward and running back for him. He tried to keep up as best he could. Then he saw it, a fire burning low in a crude camp. He stopped, hobbled the mule's front feet, and motioned Kelev to the ground. He drew his knife and crept slowly to the edge of the camp. Two men were asleep. He couldn't see anyone else. Then he saw the edge of Rahab's colorful headscarf under a scrub bush.

There was no noise, not even snoring. Gideon crept closer. No one stirred. The men were not sleeping, but dead. Gideon reached for the scarf and drew it out of the brush. It was whole. "Kelev, find Rahab!" ordered Gideon. Kelev sniffed the scarf and ran off toward the east. Gideon ran after him. It seemed forever before he heard Kelev's excited bark. In the morning light he crested a hill and saw Rahab and Deborah by a stream washing clothes and bathing. They looked up when Kelev came up to them tail wagging. They threw on their tunics and Rahab drew a knife.

"It is I, Gideon! What has happened?"

Rahab rushed into Gideon's arms and Deborah came close behind her. "We are well," said Deborah. "Two men attacked us on the road."

"The ones I found dead at a campsite?"

"I do not know. What did they look like?" asked Rahab turning away to bend down and pick up her robe.

As she turned again to face him Gideon smiled, reached into his robe, and pulled out her headscarf. "I think you left this behind."

"Oh! It must have blown away." She did not ask where he found it, nor did he ask where she lost it.

"We have been gathering up our belongings. One mule is missing," said Deborah.

"Yes, I found and hobbled him. I will go get him," replied Gideon. When Gideon returned they set about repacking their supplies.

"Where are you going? Why are you here alone?" queried Gideon greatly concerned.

"I have decided to find Lapidoth," said Deborah resolutely.

"Do you know where he is?" asked Gideon more puzzled than before.

"We do not know where he is, but he left Kadesh-Napthali going east. He was fleeing because he thought someone was pursuing him. It seemed right that we should travel on this side of the Sea of Galilee and not the Midianite side. He will surely come back across the Jordan and we may find word of him," replied Deborah.

"Great and holy god, Deborah! You do not know where he is! You travel alone! You do not know who might be pursuing him, or whether he is alive or dead! How can you go into this so calmly? Is it another of your God leadings?"

Deborah scowled at him. "Hannah has given us her blessing and she would not do that if she thought it was wrong," she retorted. "If I am to trust God to lead me into battle against Sisera, then I can surely trust him now to find Lapidoth and guide me wherever else I go."

"But Barak and I have been with you since we left Bethel. This is different. Now you are alone."

"Do you not remember how I found my own way to Bethel? I was alone then. And Rahab has lived alone as well!"

Gideon sat down on a flat rock and scratched his chin thoughtfully. "Yes, you have. I guess the question now is . . . how do we proceed from here? I have come seeking Naham. When I stopped to see

Hannah, she did not tell me about your plan, so seeing you here is a complete surprise."

"How could it be that Hannah did not tell you? There is nothing to hide!"

"I seem to remember her shouting something after me as I crossed the field. I thought she was just saying 'goodbye' but maybe she was trying to tell me about you. I guess I was in such a hurry to find news of Naham, I did not stop."

*   *   *

Naham was ready to believe the four men would not return. He had to find a way out for himself. Sisera's camp was too close. The binding was not strong and began to give as he quietly rubbed his wrists against the edge of a rock. He was almost free when he heard footsteps. He was about to roll closer to some bushes when Jerib appeared quite suddenly. He took out his knife and cut Naham's bonds.

"We wish to join Barak and his army if he will have us. Will you lead us to his camp?"

Naham got to his feet quickly rubbing his wrists. "I will lead you there. Right now, be aware when you grabbed me I was observing Sisera's movements and we are in great danger here. We must retreat quietly and carefully down through the hills to the water, but stay hidden away from the shore. There are many crevasses and hiding places. Come this way."

Jerib was not happy to follow another's lead. Jerib was the leader and the three had always followed him. He would rather rely on his own wits. It was clear Naham expected them to follow him. This was a challenge for the four.

Mishma saw Jerib's hesitation. "Do not be concerned, Jerib," said Mishma in a low voice. "We still follow only you."

"We do not know this man. He has not attacked us and he is not afraid of us either. Stay alert," whispered Jerib. "He is our best chance right now."

Naham took a leafy branch and dusted it across the area where they met and had them drag branches behind them until rocks were under their feet and no footprints would be visible. They walked on crouched low for some distance until their backs were aching.

"We will stop here in a cave just ahead. I have a little food. There is water near the cave. Wait here," cautioned Naham, "while I make sure no one is there."

Jerib grabbed Naham's shoulder. "I will go with you."

"As you wish, Jerib. I assure you I will not run off and leave you. Come with me."

Tema and Sabtah, nodding to Jerib, sat down to wait and watched the trail behind them. Mishma began to follow but Jerib motioned him to go back. Reluctantly Mishma sat down behind a rock to watch. Naham and Jerib scratched their way up a high cliff where the air was much cooler. With a little difficulty Naham found the entrance, which was well concealed by overhanging grasses. With relief they determined the cave was unoccupied, undisturbed, and the food was still there. Jerib gave a low whistle like a bird, and the others followed. The cave was pleasantly cool and they all stretched out gratefully on the sand of the cave floor. Naham went to get water and motioned for Jerib to join him.

"How far away do you think this army of Barak is?" asked Tema, his eyes adjusting to the darkness of the cave. The others did not answer.

Eventually Mishma answered. "If it is hidden from Sisera's movements, it must be far away. We will be traveling many days. We need animals to carry us and provisions when we are far enough south to cross the Jordan."

"And if Naham does not agree?" queried Sabtah.

"We will hear his reasoning," answered Mishma. "We will be in a strange country, his country, and we must heed his wisdom."

Jerib gave a low whistle to let them know they were approaching with the water. Together they drank and brought out what food they carried. It was not much, but adding to what was stored in the cave by Naham, it would sustain them for more than a day.

"We must be on our way. When we reach the Jordan I will be more sure of our safety and our travel may be easier, God willing," said Naham.

They picked up their belongings and crawled out of the cave. They moved into a clump of small scrub trees and sat quietly for a moment to listen for any movement below or around them. All was quiet except for the sound of birds and gurgling water. The sea glistened quietly in the late afternoon sun. They moved quickly, following Naham's lead. The going was arduous because of the rugged hills and steep cliffs, but they pushed on without stopping again. Naham wanted to be across the Jordan and into familiar territory before nightfall.

*　　*　　*

Lapidoth and Akhmed rose before dawn. Lapidoth packed the mules and led them quietly toward the gate of the city at first light. Akhmed led his horse. The city was quiet and the clip clop of the animals' hooves echoed through the streets. The city gates were still closed, but the guards were just now coming to open them. Merchants were gathered outside waiting to enter and set up their bazaar in the market area. As the gates rumbled open they allowed Lapidoth and Akhmed, who were on their way out, to pass through first. One merchant looked curiously at the pair, one in Egyptian clothing leading a horse and one dressed as a peasant, leading mules.

The merchant stopped in front of Akhmed and looked at Lapidoth. "One moment, my friend! I believe I recognize your servant." Lapidoth pulled his hood over his head as he slowly turned to adjust the bundle on one of the mules.

"I believe you are mistaken, friend," said Akhmed with an imperious clip to his words. "What would a rich merchant like you have to do with a lowly servant?" He swung up onto his horse and motioned to Lapidoth to follow. The merchant turned toward the open gate, glancing back only once before he moved through it.

The sun was rising behind them as they turned west toward the Great Sea. "Did you recognize him, Lapidoth?"

"No, I did not give more than a glance to his face. A servant would not stare. I have traveled with many caravans along the Great Sea dressed like a peasant. He could have been in any one of them."

"Could it have been one of the men on the ship you took going to Sidon? Could one of the ones who were paying particular attention to you possibly be the one who attacked you in the night?"

Lapidoth rubbed his beard and thought back over that voyage, trying to call up the images of those men to his mind. "None of them was a rich merchant, as you called him."

"These were not rich merchants but common thieves selling their booty. I called him a rich merchant to turn his interest from you to me and to throw him off guard. I forced him to act the part. Nevertheless, we will watch for anyone following us. You were wise to pull your hood close around your face. He may not have had a chance in that brief moment to confirm his suspicion."

"I will go to Acre to check in with my friend the innkeeper there. He may have news. Depending on what I hear, I will take the same ship to Sidon. I want to question the captain of the ship. He may know something. Do you wish to take that journey with me?"

"No, Lapidoth, I think it might be advantageous if I continue directly to Sidon and meet you there at Ammiel's inn. My presence might be a hindrance in Acre. I traveled through it and asked for information about you from a few people there. They pretended not to know you. I bribed a stable boy and he pointed to the east."

"We will part near the coast. It is a long journey to Sidon. Perhaps you can find a vessel out of the Port of Tyre."

"Perhaps so," said Akhmed as they arrived at the top of a high hill and got their first glimpse of the Great Sea. The vast expanse of blue water beckoned them to stop for a moment and just gaze at it. The cool breezes were refreshing as they made their way slowly down to sea level. With a nod of farewell, they turned in opposite directions, as agreed.

*   *   *

Deborah, Rahab, and Gideon trekked past Hazor, careful to stay a distance away in the fields. Hazor was bristling with rooftops and city walls. It was a little unnerving to know King Jabin and his guards were so close. Gideon turned to see a large dust cloud coming toward them. "Jabin's guards! Keep your faces covered and look at the ground, not at them."

"I will do as you say unless they try to touch us. Then I will carve them up in small pieces," breathed Rahab defiantly. She fingered the curved blade under her robe to be sure it was accessible.

The guards galloped up and stopped their horses short. "Where are you going?" shouted the first one.

"To see the widow of a cousin, Captain. Can we be of service to you?"

The ploy worked. The guards thought they were loyal to King Jabin since Gideon offered to serve them. "Long live King Jabin!" the captain called back and they rode off.

"Very good, Gideon," laughed Deborah. "You always have your wits about you!"

"Let us continue before they think better of it and return," grumbled Gideon.

Rahab looked a little shaken. "Perhaps we should continue west to Acre, Gideon. My cousin mentioned doing business there quite often."

"That sounds right," said Deborah, looking toward the west for a path they could take.

Gideon looked around desperately. He had not found any trace of Naham as yet and felt drawn to return to the Jordan. He was sure in his gut that Naham would not be anywhere near Acre.

"I will go with you as far as the Acre seaport and leave you with my friends there. Then I must go back to the Jordan for Naham."

"How will you know where to look for him?" asked Rahab.

"If he is alive, he will head for Barak's camp to report."

"He sends messages through trusted couriers, does he not?" asked Rahab.

"Yes, but couriers can be caught and killed. Or they may be so delayed that the information is no longer useful. So he always comes back to the camp within a certain time to confirm and wait for new instructions."

Deborah had been walking a little ahead to give Rahab and Gideon a little precious time to be alone and talk. She kept up a conversation with God as they climbed the steep path into the hills. She felt a strong pull toward Acre as she walked. "Dear God, you must guide me because I barely know this man whom I have married and rarely seen. Show me why it is right to seek him at this time. What is our purpose together or do we remain apart?" she prayed in silence. The quiet of the hills and the cool breezes were comforting and refreshing.

* * *

Naham led the four across the Jordan south of the Sea of Galilee and continued south. He was headed for a small village where he knew they would be welcome. He could always depend upon the people for food and lodging for the night. Most important, they could be trusted to warn him if there was danger.

Jerib and Mishma looked warily around as Gideon found the path off the main road along the Jordan. A group of Sisera's soldiers were coming up from the south dragging and prodding a group of peasants. They were women and old men. Gideon motioned to Jerib to crouch low in the rocks. "Let them pass, for now," whispered Gideon. "They will camp outside of Beth-Shan and we will fall on them there."

"What? You want us to take on soldiers for peasants? Are you crazy?" gasped Jerib.

"No, I am not crazy. I am an Israelite and I take care of my people," replied Naham with an air of finality.

"But they are just peasants!"

"Yes, our people are peasants and possibly yours are as well. They know we will take care of them if we can. That is what makes us strong, Jerib. That is why we will be welcomed at the village tonight and be safe. That is what Barak is fighting Sisera and Jabin for! If you are not with me, you can return to the Jordan and be on your way."

Jerib did not care to be dismissed in such a fashion. It showed him to be a coward, or worse, unworthy of Barak's army. "Forgive me,

Naham. I did not understand the ways of your people. We will stay and fight with you."

They waited until dark and went to Beth-Shan to find the people. As they crept up on the camp they could hear soft weeping. It nearly broke Naham's heart to realize what was happening to the women. Jerib tapped him on the shoulder and pointed to a place where the bushes were moving. Naham nodded. Jerib pulled out his knife and crept toward the sobbing. A soldier suddenly stood up laughing, his back to Jerib. Deftly Jerib jumped on him, his knife finding the throat before the soldier could make a sound.

He pulled the girl up from the ground and carried her away to safety. He set her down where she would be hidden. She was light as a feather. Jerib realized she must be not more than ten or eleven. A flash back came to him of his own abduction and his heart melted. "Sit here and do not move. We are here to help you. I will find your people and come back for you," he whispered in a gravely voice. He gently covered her trembling body with his robe and left to find Naham and his three friends.

Mishma met Jerib in the brush and they went closer to the soldiers who were finishing some skins of wine and bedding down for the night. The soldiers looked around for the one who had dragged a girl away for some sport and began to call for him. Sabtah positioned himself on a rock and jumped the soldier as he passed. The soldier cried out before Sabtah could stop him and the others were alerted.

"How many?" asked Mishma.

"Five," whispered Naham. "Two are down. Now go!" They rushed into the camp and attacked. The fight was short lived. Mishma, Naham, Jerib, and Tema were quick and in seconds the other three soldiers lay dead.

The peasants had crawled into the bushes, their ankles hobbled. "It is I, Naham, my friends, and I have killed the soldiers that took you.

Come out quickly so we can free you and take you home to your village."

The people hobbled out of their hiding places, looking ragged, bloody and beaten. Tema cut their bonds and picked up an old man who could not walk.

"We must leave quickly. How many are you?" asked Naham.

"There are nine. I will count them . . . there is a girl missing!"

"Yes," said Jerib. "I found her and she is safe, if she has not run away in fright. I will go and get her."

"Naham, my friend," said a swollen battered face, "you cannot recognize me in the dark looking like a battered old rag. I am Zillah."

"Zillah! We were coming to your village tonight. What has happened? Is anyone left alive there?"

"I pray they are, but I do not know. The soldiers rushed in and grabbed some of us. It was all so quick I could not see if they hurt anyone else."

Jerib returned with a very frightened Milcah. Milcah ran into Zillah's arms and cried.

"Hush, child. All will be well. Whatever has happened I will take care of you. Hold onto me."

They walked throughout the night in the hills toward Shechem. They did not stop for fear of more soldiers coming to look for their companions and finding them dead. There would surely be an immediate search. They had to be far way by dawn.

Just before first light Naham hid them in a cave that was a short distance from the village while he and Jerib went to scout the area.

When they determined there were no soldiers, they crept quietly into the village. There was some low moaning and a few children starting to call for their mothers.

"Noah! Noah, are you here? It is I, Naham!"

"I am here, Naham," replied a quavery voice.

Naham rushed to the animal pen where Noah lay, badly beaten. "Noah, my friend. How bad are you?"

"Oh, just battered. I will live. They took . . ."

"Yes, we know. We attacked and killed the soldiers who took them. The villagers are not far from here in a cave. Is anyone else alive?"

"If they are I am sure they ran to hide in the caves not far from here."

Jerib went through the village and found the children and their mothers hiding in fear. "We are friends. I have come with Naham," he said to them. Slowly people began coming out into the street.

"Where are your young men, Noah?" asked Jerib slightly puzzled and looking around.

"They are not here. They have gone to fight along side Barak in the Israelite army. I suppose that is what the soldiers were looking for . . . our young men. They were enraged when they found none. So they took some of my people to torture them for information I am sure."

The mention of Barak brought back the flood of thoughts Jerib had about joining him and perhaps finding their families and homes. Jerib gave one of his bird-like whistles to signal the others to come into the village. The people began to trickle back helping or carrying the injured and feeble. They looked around at the destruction to see if their houses still stood. A few of them were undamaged. They checked on their families and neighbors to see if all were alive. One elderly woman was dead but she seemed not to be battered.

"She was dead before they came," said Zillah. "Her heart gave out. I am glad she was gone before all this happened."

Naham and Jerib decided to go on to Barak's camp alone and leave Tema, Mishma, and Sabtah find food and to help the villagers clear the debris out of the village. "We will bring back our solders to rebuild the dwellings," promised Naham. "They will not be long in coming. They will say, "Moses is our father" so you will know they are Israelite.

CHAPTER 21

Gideon left Deborah and Rahab at an inn near the marketplace in Acre. He gave them the name of a man in Acre who could be trusted to help them or get word to Barak if they ran into trouble.

They settled themselves in their room and sat down to rest. "Where do we start, Deborah?"

"We will start with prayer and then go to the well near the city gate. Lapidoth and I first saw each other near the well in Kadesh-Napthali. We will be there among other women and we can listen to their gossip. If Lapidoth is here, he just might glance toward the well."

"We might also check on our pack animals at the stable. That would not cause a stir," added Rahab.

"We could ask if Lapidoth stabled his animal there."

"We could," said Rahab, "but he travels under another name . . . Marcus, I believe. It could raise suspicion if we used the wrong name."

Deborah agreed. They prayed together, ate some of the figs and cheese from their pack, and set out for the village well. It was hard for them not to be noticed. Deborah had strawberry blonde hair and a regal carriage. Rahab had a dark defiant look. The other women around the well drew away, so Deborah and Rahab sat down and remained quiet.

Finally Rahab put a smile on her face and went among the women. She told them Deborah was a very well known seer from Ephraim of a good family in Kadesh-Napthali. That sparked some interest as they talked among themselves. One woman approached Rahab and asked to be taken to Deborah. Deborah smiled as the woman curtsied politely and asked for her advice.

The rest of the day was spent at the well speaking with the women who wanted her counsel. Soon a few of the male leaders of the community came to her as well seeking her advice about their concerns. They found her counsel quite satisfactory and rewarded her handsomely.

As evening came on they returned to the inn for a meal and wine. "What a day!" exclaimed Rahab.

"Did you hear anything about Lapidoth, I mean Marcus?" asked Deborah in a low voice.

"No. But I did not ask. I thought it was too soon. I wanted to let you establish yourself before we began asking questions."

"Good thought," replied Deborah, taking a sip of her wine. "I become impatient when I lose the sense that God is leading me forward. Right now things seem to be standing still. I can hear Hannah telling me when that happens, it is time to wait."

"Shall we go to the well tomorrow?" inquired Rahab frowning slightly.

Deborah laughed. "I know this was not an exciting day for you, sitting by and being my guard. I think tomorrow I would like to go to the shore and be near the water. I want to see the Great Sea and let its rushing waves calm my soul. Perhaps we could find a spot just a little away from the seaport where it is not so busy."

* * *

Lapidoth arrived in Acre and went to the inn immediately to speak with Gispah. Gispah knew nothing but promised to keep his ears and eyes open for anything that might help. Then he went to the seaport to find his ship captain. The departure time was an hour away. He found the captain and they sat down on the dock to talk and drink some imported brew. "What is this drink? It is quite strong!" exclaimed Lapidoth coughing loudly.

The captain laughed in amusement. "I think it is made of foreign grains and other things. I do not know just what they are, but this drink will leave you feeling fine, sleeping well, and no headache in the morning." They boarded the ship while the crew was preparing to set sail as soon as the tide was right.

"I have some inquiries to make of you if you are agreeable," ventured Lapidoth.

"Certainly. What do you want to ask?"

"Do you remember the men who were watching me the last time I sailed with you?"

"Yes, I do. I was also watching them to be sure none of my cargo walked away with them!"

"I believe I saw one of them again in Dan, but I am not sure. He may have recognized me. Do you know if I am being pursued?"

The captain scratched his head and looked around as others boarded the ship and cargo was being stowed. He stepped over ropes and boxes to take the wheel. Lapidoth followed him.

"We have many strangers traveling up and down the coast pretending to be merchants. I think their business is theft or they are killers for hire. Honest merchants smell better. Is there a reason you think someone might want to kill you?"

"It is a good possibility. My mother is from a family that lives on the edge of that kind of intrigue. My father and I were forced to work for her family under threat from her import business people. I have recently married a wife and I cannot put her in danger, so I am trying to escape that life. But I need to return to square my debts with the importers. I am trying not to be murdered before I can accomplish that," confided Lapidoth.

"Ah, my friend, I am sorry to hear of your troubles. You have always paid me well and been fair with me. I will help you. I have contacts who can inquire in such dangerous places as you and I do not care to know about. Have you money to pay? They may require a price."

"I have resources, Captain."

"Very good. Keep them hidden and yourself safe."

The ship slowly moved away from the dock, hove in the direction of the tide, and began the trip north to Sidon. Lapidoth breathed a little easier. For a time he felt a little safer on the water than on land. His mind turned to finding Akhmed in Sidon.

*   *   *

Barak was relieved to see Naham coming into his tent. Naham told Barak how he met Jerib and his three companions and about the attack on Zillah's village. "My three companions remained at the village to help clear out the debris left from the attack," offered Jerib. "They need help to reconstruct the buildings quickly."

"Can we spare some men to help?" asked Naham. "The soldiers tried to get information from the peasants about the location of our camp and the size of our army. Of course the people said nothing. The soldiers dragged some of them away and began to beat them. Fortunately we rescued them before the soldiers killed any of them."

"And these soldiers of Sisera, where are they now?"

"Dead. There were five. None of them got away to go for help. We cut their throats so fast they could not make a sound."

Barak went to his tent door. "Abel! Send some men with building experience to Zillah's village. They were attacked on account of us and they need our help."

"Right away!" Abel set off at a trot to the tents of the soldiers to secure the needed help.

"Jerib and his men wish to join our army," continued Naham. "They were taken from their homes as small children and made slaves of the Midianites. They do not know their origins. We may be able to help them while they help us."

"I am not sure we can help them, but they are welcome to make their home here with us if that is their wish."

Jerib grinned, saluted Barak, and turned to join the soldiers going to the village.

"Do you think they are telling the truth, Naham?" mused Barak.

"They jumped me while I was observing Sisera's movements in his camps. They thought I was one of Sisera's men. They tied me up and hauled me away. I asked them if any of Sisera's soldiers were dressed in peasant clothes like me. I convinced them we were in danger by being so close to Sisera, and that they needed to unbind me and plan a route of escape. I told them of your army and since they had nowhere to go, they asked to join us. So far they have been faithful to their word. They helped me kill five of Sisera's soldiers and free the villagers. They carried some of the badly beaten ones to the village on their backs and immediately began to help."

"There is always a question of loyalty, especially when it comes to wanderers," said Barak. "But as you say, they have been faithful to their word so far. They proved they are willing to stand and fight when they are outnumbered. We will assign some guards to secretly keep an eye on them until they prove themselves further when we meet larger forces in battle."

As they were talking Gideon appeared at the doorway of the tent. "Naham! Thank God you are here and safe! I went looking for you," said Gideon clapping Naham on the shoulder and hugging his neck.

"Yes! Well you did not find me tied up, the victim of renegades this time! But I did run into four men who jumped me and nearly exposed us all to Sisera's guards. You will meet them shortly and we will tell you the story over some food and wine," replied Naham grinning.

"Where have you come from, Gideon?" inquired Barak.

"As I was starting to search for news of Naham, I came upon Deborah and Rahab traveling north by the shore of Galilee. They were going to find Lapidoth whose whereabouts are unknown since they saw him in Bethel."

"Traveling alone?"

"Yes, Barak, traveling alone. When I found them, they had dispatched two robbers and were just gathering up their packs and mules. I pity anyone who tries to give them trouble!" laughed Gideon.

"They killed them?" asked Naham.

"Well, I found them dead. How they died, I did not inquire," replied Gideon coolly.

"Where are they now?" asked Barak becoming highly concerned.

"I escorted them to Acre. That is where Deborah felt she should go. You know Deborah. She has mystical resources and she follows them faithfully. I left them at the inn of my friend Gispah and paid him to look after them."

"Did you tell Gispah why they were there?"

"No. I did not think he needed to know. I am sure they will tell him if the need arises. I do not want to interfere with God's business."

"So you think this is really God's business?"

"If it concerns Deborah, you must know the answer to that!"

Barak smiled a worried smile, shook his head, and got down to his own business, discussing plans for the army and their next moves.

*   *   *

The ship on which Lapidoth was traveling docked in Sidon after negotiating some rough seas. Lapidoth had never experienced seasickness before this voyage and was very glad to be on land. He held his bundle of belongings close as he walked around Sidon for a few hours to get his bearings and settle his stomach. He walked through the marketplace looking for familiar faces, especially the ones who were on the ship last time, as well as the one they met in Dan. As he covertly glanced at men, no one seemed interested in him either, which was good. He thought he might run into Akhmed somewhere. Finally he climbed the hill toward Ammiel's inn. It was empty except for Ammiel who was sweeping the floor.

"Ah, Marcus my good friend. May the blessings of all the god's be upon you," said Ammiel in greeting. "I am very glad you have returned. I was afraid after the trouble you experienced here, you would find another inn!"

"You served me well, Ammiel. How could I think of going anywhere else!" exclaimed Lapidoth sitting down on a bench. "Please, some of your excellent wine and cheese, if you have them. I am starved after a passage over rough waters."

Ammiel shouted at someone in the kitchen to bring food, and sat down with Lapidoth. "Someone was looking for you," he said in a low voice.

"An Egyptian?"

"Yes, I think so. But also another man, the unsavory sort."

"Tell me about them. Can you describe them?"

"The Egyptian was well dressed, polite, and revealed nothing except your name. The other was not with him, but came in after he left. This second man was shifty-eyed, with bad teeth, dark skin, and smelly robes. The kind of smelly that comes from sleeping with camels. He called you by another name."

"What name?"

"Lapidoth, I think. Has he mistaken your for someone else?"

"Perhaps. Thank you, my friend. You have been most helpful." Lapidoth paid him handsomely for the food and information and went out into the brilliant sun of the afternoon to continue his search. He must find Akhmed before this other pursuer found him. What could he be facing now? How many were there? Was Akhmed also in danger?

Sidon was large and sprawling from the busy north harbor to the south harbor and to the east. There were markets where workmen plied their trade in shaded streets with many alleys and doorways, streets leading away, winding and twisting through the city.

Lapidoth moved quickly and carefully, stopping often at a merchant's stand or in a doorway to watch. At one point a young boy came out of an archway and tugged at his sleeve. Lapidoth jerked around ready to defend himself. The boy motioned him to follow. They turned down several alleys and then into a doorway. He stopped to be sure Lapidoth was behind him, and quickly opened the door.

Lapidoth stepped in to see Akhmed leaning against the wall inside the door.

"Akhmed! What has happened? Were you attacked?"

"Yes, my friend. I am afraid I was careless. But it is a slight wound on the leg and I will be fine thanks to this generous family who took me in."

Lapidoth looked around and recognized the family members sitting at the back of the room. He had visited them in the past when he came to teach. But they lived in Acre when he saw them. They all embraced him and Lapidoth asked, "How is it that you are here in Sidon? Is not your home still in Acre?"

"It is in Acre, Marcus," answered the man. "We took the money you gave us and came to Sidon to escape King Jabin's men. They are harassing the people in the poorer neighborhoods trying to get information about any secret uprising that might be coming against the king.

"Were they looking for someone?" asked Lapidoth. He was thinking about Barak and Deborah. Had they been discovered?

"No one person that I know of. No names were ever mentioned. I would know if there had been."

"How did you come to be here, Akhmed? It is amazing that you stumbled into the house of my friends, especially since they do not really live here at that!"

"I was evading someone I thought was following me, and another jumped out from a doorway with a knife. We struggled for my purse and I managed to overpower him. He ran but not before he pricked me with the knife. We singed the wound. It is small but the knife could have been poisoned or used to carve an animal."

"And the boy found you?"

"It happened just a few feet away from the doorstep of this house. Most fortunate. These good people took me in immediately."

For a few minutes Lapidoth sat looking at the floor trying to take in all he had heard. The last thing he expected to see was Akhmed injured in an alley. Was he telling the truth?

"Perhaps I should be going. I would like to speak again to Ammiel," Lapidoth said quietly.

"It would be better if we stayed together, Marcus. Being alone in this city is dangerous. I am easily able to walk, even run if necessary."

"I welcome your company," replied Lapidoth.

"Do you think it would be better if you wore your merchant robes? We are conspicuous together as it is, and more so if people think you are a peasant or slave. They will begin to offer money for you and I may not be able to resist if the price is high enough," said Akhmed with the first grin on his face Lapidoth had seen.

Lapidoth was shown to another room where he changed his attire and packed away the peasant robe.

They thanked the family profusely for their hospitality. Akhmed left them a gift as they took their leave. Lapidoth noticed but thought nothing more about it. They made their way back into the market place watching carefully as people jostled them to get closer to the merchandise stalls.

"Thank you for remembering the name I use when traveling, Akhmed. I am sure it would be well for us to continue using it until we return to the places where I am known as Lapidoth."

"Yes. I agree, my friend. I must tell you more about the attack in the alley. A young boy came to me in the market and whispered that you were injured. He pointed to the alley and then disappeared. I should have been suspicious, but instead hurried directly there expecting to find you lying in the gutter. It was careless of me. How did this boy know that I was looking for you? How did he know we were connected?"

"How did he know me at all? Someone must have sent you into the trap. If they knew it was not me they were trapping, how indeed did the boy or anyone else know?" puzzled Lapidoth.

"Someone paid the boy to do this and it happened he was of the family who helped me. He showed his father the money and his father ran into the alley. He was looking for whoever paid the boy. That someone could only come from your family. Surely Omar would not do that but . . ."

"Miriam! Not Omar. My mother."

Akhmed stopped by a booth to browse through the merchandise and think. "Omar sent me to find Lapidoth. Why would he or Miriam try to kill me before I delivered Lapidoth to them? It must be someone else."

They went back to the inn and secured rooms for the night. Ammiel could tell them nothing more, but sent a servant to the harbor to watch and listen. The servant returned after an hour and reported a strange acting man who was giving money to a boy. The man did not look like a prosperous merchant. He was lodged in a run down harbor inn for the night.

"Did he see you?" asked Ammiel.

"He did not see me," replied the servant. "I played the drunk and went to the run down temple of a forgotten god, and stayed there until I was certain I was not noticed or followed."

Lapidoth and Akhmed ate dinner mostly in silence and went to their rooms. "Bar your door," warned Lapidoth.

"Keep your blade in your hand," said Akhmed. "Ammiel will set a servant by our doors."

"I am sure he will," whispered Lapidoth. "He remembers the last time I stayed here. I killed an intruder to my room in the middle of the night. He had a body to dispose of before dawn. His other guests would have been most unhappy to see that."

*　　*　　*

Deborah and Rahab continued to walk around Acre. Kelev followed behind busily exploring the booths and sniffing the tent poles. They found no information about Lapidoth. Deborah was puzzled. "How could this be?"

When they returned to the inn a man was waiting for them. He was short and powerfully built with a balding head and a large abundant black beard. He carried a black cane. "I am Heber of the Kenites. I come seeking Deborah the prophetess."

Deborah looked at Rahab and back to Heber. "Why is it you seek this woman?"

"I have an urgent message. Are you Deborah?"

"Yes, I am Deborah. What is your message?" she asked hoping it was news of Lapidoth.

"Jael the priestess, who is my wife, has need of you and asks that you come to her. I am here to guide you to her tent, which is north of Kadesh-Napthali. It is urgent."

"How did you know where to find me?"

"I am a trusted friend of Rabbi Amri of Kadesh-Napthali. He sent me to Hannah the seer, who sent me north along the shore of the Sea of Galilee and west to Acre."

"Will you give me a few moments to regard your message and confer with my cousin?" asked Deborah.

"Yes, of course. I will go to the market place for some supplies and will return shortly. Please know this is not a small matter. Jael is most anxious to speak with you." Heber turned and left. Deborah and Rahab sat down together and ordered some wine and bread.

"Have you heard of Jael the Priestess?" asked Rahab.

"No, but Hannah will know her if she is a seer. She is sensitive to impressions. I cannot question that, although I have not heard of her. Amri and Ya'akov did not speak of her. But there was probably no reason to. There was a mysterious looking woman at Ya'akov's burial, but I did not think to ask who she was. It could have been Jael. If Heber was with her, I did not see him."

"Is it enough that he names Amri and Hannah? Is that enough for us to trust him and go with him?" pondered Rahab.

"I must pray. Let us go to our room. Gispah will send a servant when Heber the Kenite returns." They went to the room and sat down to await the word of God.

Deborah was still deep in meditation when a knock on the door startled her. Rahab opened the door and a servant girl motioned them to the front of the inn. Rahab nodded and Deborah motioned to her to close the door.

"I was in a battle, much like the ones I dreamed of at night. Barak was there and also a woman I do not know, but now I am sure it must be Jael. I believe we are to go to her."

Rahab began to gather their belongings while Deborah went to meet Heber. Kelev was at Rahab's heels. She patted his head pushed him out the door. He trotted through the inn, out into the bright sunlight, and ran directly to Deborah. He was protective of her and wary of this stranger.

"We will go with you. When do you wish to begin?"

"It is urgent that we start now, if you are ready," replied Heber.

"We are ready."

Rahab and a servant brought their belongings, and joined Deborah and Heber in front of the inn. They went to the stable to retrieve their animals and started for the tent of Jael the Priestess. Deborah looked back at Acre from high in the hills wondering if Lapidoth had been there and wondering if she did not look hard enough to find him. There were many conflicting thoughts in her mind. She wondered if there really was a call from God to find him. Surely they would have been successful if it were a true call. Why had they traveled all the way to Acre, braving dangers, only to return to where they had begun? It just did not make sense. Then Deborah remembered they had turned toward Acre without guidance. She had made that decision on her own after Jabin's guard questioned them. She wanted to get away from Jabin's territory. It was not God's guidance, but fear and guilt.

"Perhaps, Rahab, I brought you all this way in error. I did not stop to ask for guidance before I made the decision to turn and go west to Acre. I am almost sure God sent Heber to fetch us and get us on the right path again."

"If it was an error, at least you know Lapidoth is not in Acre. We walked everywhere and asked anyone who might have seen him. Surely someone would have come forth with information."

"It is difficult to know if they would approach strangers and women at that. Notice how many people did not look at us when we questioned them. Either no one knew or they all knew and were not going to tell us anything."

They traveled as quickly as the terrain would allow. Kelev was happy to be traveling again and bounded up and down the trail ahead of them. When they stopped to rest for a moment at the top of a hill Deborah said, "Heber, tell me about Jael."

Heber was silent for a few minutes and then turned to Deborah. "Jael is a priestess and a seer. She sees a connection with you that is crucial in the coming battle with Sisera. She must take counsel with you and only you."

"And her connection with Amri and Leah? Did she know Ya'akov?"

"She is their cousin. Yes, she knew of Ya'akov and also of the friendship the two of you shared. But since we moved from place to place, we rarely saw him."

"Are you shepherds that you move from place to place? Nomads?"

"We are the hands and feet of the Lord our God. We go where we are sent, where the Lord knows we are needed."

Heber turned his attention to the road again and they continued on. It occurred to her that she and Rahab had been doing the very same thing. They went where they were guided. Again she felt the weight on her heart of making what she thought was a wrong decision. Jael's tent was north. She wondered how far north. Had they passed it? Had the turn to Acre prevented a meeting with Jael that would surely have taken place? But Deborah remained silent and did not question him further. How she wished Hannah were with them now. A sudden pang of homesickness swept over her. Perhaps tomorrow or soon after, she would again see Kadesh-Napthali and her mother.

Jael the Priestess was a tall woman with raven black hair that hung to her waist. Her eyes were dark and deep set, and her nose and chin were prominent. She wore a long black tunic that stood out in stark contrast to the bleached white tent and white rugs that were her dwelling. Deborah and Rahab stopped in their steps, awe struck by this vision of power and mystery. Heber whispered to Jael, then collected the animals and led them to a small pool of water where they drank deeply.

"Welcome Deborah and Rahab. Please come in." Kelev was ready to approach Jael with a dog's usual curiosity, but Rahab motioned him back. He obediently lay down outside the tent door, his eyes shifting back and forth from Heber to the tent door. Heber brought him a bowl of water, let him sniff his hand, and Kelev relaxed.

Deborah, Rahab, and Jael sat down together and a servant girl brought food and wine. "I have much to share with you. Since the time is short I will begin immediately. The victory over Sisera will be in the hands of two women, Deborah. Yours and mine. At the perfect time you will lead Barak to the battle. The battle will be decisive and Sisera will come to me for asylum. He will burst into my private quarters instead of my receiving tent where I will be obligated to kill him for the trespass."

Deborah and Rahab sat stunned at this revelation. Jael gave no more details. "The timing of these events is up to God. We will be guided at the moment action is needed. You need not be concerned."

"Do I have a part in this?" asked Rahab quietly.

"Rahab, my dear, you saved Deborah from death. You have always been God's handmaiden, following an inner guidance you thought was from your own mind. But you have always been and are still in God's plan. Have no fear."

They stayed in Jael's tent that night. Deborah had a powerful dream, but not her usual one about battles. A strange woman appeared with a large sword standing over a man who was asleep or drunk. She announced, "I am Judith of Bethulia. Death to Holofernes!" and the sword came down. Deborah awoke with a start. It was not yet morning, but she got up and went outside for a breath of cool air. The dream had left her gasping, as if her own head were severed. Jael came out of the tent as well.

"Deborah, you had a dream, did you not?"

"Yes! How did you know?"

"I saw the dream in my sleep. I share a spiritual communion with only certain ones. I allow them to sleep in my tents. I see their dreams and their thoughts."

"Do you know what my dream meant?"

"Oh yes. You saw the future. In wanting to know how the battle with Sisera would go and how he would die, you saw much farther into the future! You saw four hundred and fifty years into the future where another such slaying will take place. You saw the result of a threat by General Holofernes to Judith and her city. No man threatens a great high priestess of God such as Judith and lives."

Deborah shivered and drew her robe around her.

"Come back into the tent. We will share some tea and you will sleep."

The tea was soothing, but Deborah was still full of questions. "But why did that dream come to me? Why so far into the future?"

"To help you understand greater mysteries and to help you know that you are not out of place as a prophetess, seer, and warrior. You are part of a holy sisterhood that has existed since the beginning and will exist forever, and your destiny is ordained, not accidental. You have felt alone all your life except for Hannah, who had the wisdom to understand and nurture you. Your destiny is something greater than mere womanhood. Now you have seen that you are not alone at all."

The effect of the tea took over and Deborah drifted off to sleep again, this time dreaming of Ya'akov and their sweet times together.

CHAPTER 22

Deborah, Rahab, and Heber arrived at Hannah's. Heber greeted Hannah, spoke to her privately for a few minutes, and then bid them all farewell.

"Can you not stay and rest for a while?" asked Rahab. "You look tired."

"Indeed at this age of life, I am usually tired and look even more so. But there is important work to be done, and I will rest at home with Jael while we look into the future together." With that he turned, tapped his walking stick on the path, and walked toward home.

"Hannah! Is Heber blind?" asked Deborah with great concern.

"Ah, so you have not noticed until now!" laughed Hannah. "Yes, he is nearly blind, but he uses his second sight, which is far more perfect. He sees much more than sighted people do. Because we have physical sight we are distracted by physical appearances, and often do not look more deeply for the truth."

"I thought Kelev did not like Heber because he kept an eye on him. But Kelev knew there was something different about him and was watching over him," said Rehab. "Indeed, even Kelev sees more deeply than I do!"

Hannah laughed and invited them in for a meal. Her foods were limited to the breads and fruits of a small household, but her expert use of her herb garden to season food made it all taste like the richest feast. Deborah told her of her dream about Judith and Holofernes.

Hannah frowned. "I do not know those names . . ."

"They are far in the future, Hannah. I have seen an event that will happen four hundred and fifty years from now." Deborah related all that Jael told her.

"You are progressing well, Deborah. You must trust these sightings more and share them only with prepared minds. Do you understand?" Both Deborah and Rahab nodded.

"I am glad you understand as well, Rahab," whispered Hannah as she patted her hand.

"Oh, I understand! Deborah is the seer, I am her body guard," laughed Rahab. "She will save us all and I will see that no one stands in her way!"

"And so you have been her guard all along and a very good one. Your services will continue to be needed. Harder times are coming. A war with Jabin and Sisera is inevitable. There will be the bloodshed and tears that war always brings. But, enough talk of those things. Deborah, your mother awaits you."

"Does she know I am here?"

"No, she does not. But she awaits your return every day."

"Then I must go to her."

"She has not been well lately. You will notice the changes in her. They are subtle now but they will increase slowly with time."

"And my father? Does he see them?"

"He sees nothing except his political position with the elders of the city. He blames you that he has not progressed, but it is his own stubborn ways that are his problem. Not you. He has not changed, nor will he. Love them they way they are, my dear."

*   *   *

Miriam was slowly regaining her speech and mobility. At first her body shook violently and refused to obey her. Her speech was slurred and saliva ran from the corner of her mouth. Joseph was increasingly absent, leaving her to curse the very walls and Joseph's god that she believed did this to her. She kept her Canaanite idols close around her, alternately demanding their help and cursing their silence. She forced herself to walk outside very short distances, first once and then more times a day, collapsing in exhaustion after each time. Anger drove her on and the promise to herself that she would regain control of everything, including Joseph and Omar. She would see to the demise of Rahab and Deborah. She would make Omar pay for mocking her and Joseph for leaving her in such a wretched state. "I will repay you all," she croaked furiously. "Every last one of you!"

Joab and Tamar were concerned about Miriam's growing viciousness. She shrieked for them at all hours of the day and night. She cursed them for not coming to her aid faster and repeated how she hated them and their stupid dull lives. Joab and Tamar had two sons, Jahdai and Caleb, who kept their distance from Miriam and ran away into the fields or the village marketplace when she began screaming for them.

Joseph returned to care for the livestock and assist Joab with the fields. "How good that your sons are grown enough to help in the fields. They are blessings, indeed."

"Yes, and they do good work. They like the farm very much. Tamar and I will be well cared for in our old age, God willing, and if Miriam does not kill us all first."

"Has Miriam extended her hatred to your sons as well?"

"Oh yes! They pretend they do not hear her and run away when she screams for them. I know it is a sin to resist taking care of her. But God help us, we dodge pottery that she throws at us as well as curses. She pulls out her hair! She is insane!" said Joab throwing up his hands in helplessness.

"She has always been insane, Joab. Her craziness was slight and attractive at first, but it has grown in her mind like the tares that ravage our fields. Her illness has made it much worse. I do not stay in the house with her in order to preserve my own life. She would kill me in my sleep, I am sure."

Joab was relieved to have Joseph spend some time with him. "Tamar does not talk to me about this because a daughter is supposed to be subject to her mother. It was difficult to persuade her to ignore Miriam's ranting. She told me she could ignore the screams but not the throwing of good food on the floor. Tamar is terrified of her mother. Perhaps you could talk to her," said Joab.

"What can I say to her? I gave her a terrible mother," replied Joseph.

"You can encourage her to stand up for herself. Tell her it is not a sin. She may believe it if you say it."

"I will speak with her, Joab. First I will speak to Miriam. Hitch the mule to the cart and bring it around front."

Joseph entered the house and pushed aside the trash on the floor with his foot. "Miriam, when are you going to act like a civilized person?" he shouted.

Miriam came limping into the front room leaning on a stick, eyes blazing. "It's that lazy Tamar. She is good for nothing. You tell her to get in here and clean this up!"

"Tamar is not lazy! It is you who broke all this stuff." Miriam swung the stick at him just grazing his arm. He grabbed the stick out of her grasp and broke it in half. She shrieked and lunged at him. He caught her and quickly wrapped a robe around her pinning her arms at her sides. She spat and struggled, but Joseph did not let go. He carried her outside and put her in the cart.

"Where are you taking me?" she demanded.

"Home in disgrace. It is still a husband's right to give his wife back to her family if she displeases him, and you displease me," he said quietly. He climbed into the cart beside her and smacked the mule's rump with the reins.

Miriam was quiet for a while. Then she said, "Joseph dear, I am so sorry. Please take me back. I promise to be a good wife."

Joseph broke out laughing long and loud. "It is a bit late, Miriam. You should have said that on our first day of marriage and meant it. No one is fooled by your promises, especially me."

Miriam struggled and tried to kick herself free from the robe. Joseph pushed her down on the floor of the cart and put his foot on her back.

They arrived at Omar's palace and servants came out to meet them. "Our master is not at home," said the head servant puzzled.

He dumped Miriam out of the cart onto the ground and instructed the servants to take her and lock her in a room. She began screaming that she would kill them all. The servants shrank back a bit so Joseph motioned a guard to come and assist.

"Give Omar a message for me," he said to the guard. "Miriam has disgraced her family and she is not to return to my house. She is a danger to us all. He can do with her whatever he will." Then a grim-faced Joseph threw his sandal down to finalize his rejection of her as was the custom, climbed back into the cart, turned the mule toward his home and snapped the reins.

*   *   *

Lapidoth and Akhmed were up with the sunrise. The night was uneventful and they were grateful. But the city was far too quiet, lacking the usual morning commotion.

"Sidon might prove more difficult and dangerous than I thought," said Akhmed. "Perhaps we should confer with Ammiel. He would surely know what we are walking into. It may not be about us at all."

"I agree," said Lapidoth. "I have not been able to figure Sidon out at all. Not the last time I was here and not now."

Ammiel was quiet and secretive. He looked around warily as he spoke. "It would be good for you to leave while you can. There are many who would capture Sidon for its riches and its seaport. They may come from the north, or it may be Jabin from the east. But there is much fear and unrest. Go by sea if you can reach the seaport safely. Go now. Take the alley behind the inn, go south and then turn toward the sea at the fabric market. Time is short."

Lapidoth and Akhmed were stunned by this information. "So perhaps it is not Miriam at all, but something else," said Lapidoth. They gathered their belongings from their rooms and started for the seaport. The alley was narrow and filled with garbage and feces. They hurried trying not to slip on the wet paving stones. They stopped at the fabric market. The merchants were not yet there. The place was empty. The streets ahead were empty.

"This makes my skin crawl," said Akhmed, out of breath. "Keep your knife close to your hand." They ran on toward the seaport and stopped behind a building near the dock.

"There are no ships! No boats!" exclaimed Lapidoth. They both shrank back into a building. It was dark and filled with bales of goods. "If we start for the south port, we may find a way out," whispered Lapidoth. "There is a little used port at the south end of the city."

They took advantage of the shadows of early morning to make their way south along the shoreline. Then came the sound of marching feet and orders given in shouts. They stopped and crouched low. "Jabin's guard. They are on the docks," said Akhmed.

"This is not an invasion, but King Jabin going somewhere. A ship is anchored at the mouth of the bay, hard to see in the mist," said Akhmed in a low voice. "If we wait until they board, if that is what they intend, it might be easier to get out of Sidon."

"Or it might be better to keep moving. If all the guards do not accompany King Jabin, they might scatter throughout the city bars for the night before they return home or leave for somewhere else. Or maybe King Jabin is not here with his guard."

"Let us continue," said Akhmed. "I always feel safer on the move. Being in one place makes me feel like a trapped animal."

They went cautiously from building to building until the south port came into view. There were a few stone buildings near the shore and a deserted jetty. "Nothing here."

"This is so strange for even this little port to be deserted. The smaller boats come and go here constantly," said Lapidoth. "Unless there is a blockade somewhere. If the focus is on the seaports, we should try to get out by land."

"I still have a horse at the stable on the road to the east," said Akhmed. "Let us make our way there. Or else we will be on foot all the way to Acre."

The city was waking up around the outskirts. Cautiously merchants with oxcarts were bringing produce and goods to the marketplace. Akhmed and Lapidoth purchased two peasant robes from one of them and slipped away into an alley to pull them on. They traveled through filthy alleys to the stable. The stable man accepted payment from Lapidoth for a second horse. They led the horses into the yard, tied on their bundles, mounted, and rode away to the south through the hills.

"Do you think Ammiel really thought we could beat the guard to the docks? Or do you think he sent us into the path of the guards so we would be caught?" mused Akhmed.

"If he sent us into harms way, he was threatened or paid. Our concern is not Ammiel but who got to him," answered Lapidoth. "Miriam. I still think it is Miriam."

"And a better question would be who else. When we get to Acre, we can set a trap for whoever is pursuing us," said Akhmed. He turned to Lapidoth. "Do you think about Deborah? Do you think she is in danger?"

"Yes, I think about her and the farther I am away from her the safer she is. If she and Rahab are together, they will be more than a match for anyone who accosts them. I hope they are in Barak's camp by now. When she goes after Sisera, when her god tells her to, no one can protect her but her god and I pray he will."

The breeze was still hot when they entered Acre. It had been a long ride and both men were exhausted and glad to have arrived at last. They stabled the horses and went directly to the inn of Gispah. It was cooler inside and the brew was welcome refreshment. Galina smiled broadly when she saw Lapidoth, but her smile disappeared when she saw Akhmed. Her father sent her back into the kitchen so they could talk.

"Ah, Marcus, my friend, it is good to serve you in my establishment again. And Akhmed! I see you have you found answers to your questions!"

Akhmed lowered his voice to nearly a whisper. "Some of them, Gispah. We have more. Has anyone been asking for Marcus? Or a man named Lapidoth?"

"There were two women here. Galina said they were asking at the well for a man named Lapidoth. Do you know him?"

"Gispah," said Lapidoth quietly, "I travel under the name Marcus for safety. My name is Lapidoth."

Gispah's bushy eyebrows shot up and he gasped. "Thank you for telling me. But you can be certain I will tell no one. You are still Marcus in this house."

"Thank you, Gispah. What were the names of the women who were here."

"Are they in trouble?" asked Gispah.

"We hope they are not. One is my wife and the other, her cousin. What can you tell me?"

"Gideon brought them here and left. They were here a few days and another man came for them."

"Who was the second man?" asked Akhmed.

"I do not know. Since he was not staying here, I did not ask his name. The women seemed not to know him, but they were willing to go with him."

"And their names?" asked Lapidoth, fairly sure that he already knew.

"Galina! Come here!" shouted Gispah. Galina came running in looking from one to the other. "Galina, do you know the names of the two women who stayed here?"

"Certainly, Papa. Women always know each other's names," she said triumphantly, happy to have some secret knowledge that she could impart to men.

"Well, are you going to tell us or just stand there gazing at Marcus?" demanded Gispah.

Galina's face reddened and she spat, "Deborah and Rahab." Then she turned and ran into the kitchen to hide her tears and embarrassment.

"Do you know where the second man took them?"

"To the east!" shouted Galina from the kitchen.

Gispah began to feel bad that he had mistreated his daughter, especially since she seemed to have more information. He excused himself and went into the kitchen.

"Galina, I am sorry I embarrassed you. Please come back in and tell us what you know."

"I know nothing more, Papa," said a tearful Galina. She picked up a bin of scraps for the animals and hurried out the back door.

Lapidoth sat down, bewildered. "They came looking for me! Deborah was asking about me! What do I do now? How can I find her?"

"Not finding you, she has gone on. We must continue to Ashdod, my friend. You have a mission to complete, and I as well. She is continuing on her journey and chasing after her will not benefit any of us just now. Perhaps a time later when the stars are aligned."

"Stars? Aligned?"

"Obviously they are not aligned now or the two of you would have met, not missed."

They set out for Ashdod the next morning, Lapidoth reluctant to face whatever lie ahead, and Akhmed eager to return and receive his remuneration for a mission completed. Ashdod was a week's ride to the south through Philistine territory. They would join a merchant caravan to lessen the chance of being attacked and robbed.

*   *   *

Deborah and Rahab went to the home of Rabbi Amri and Leah. "We need to summon Gideon to take us back to the camp," said Rahab hopefully.

"I will send the message to Barak," offered the rabbi. "I know he is waiting and an escort will not be far away."

Deborah went to see her mother, perhaps for the last time. She sensed that time was growing short and she needed to return to Barak's camp quickly. The time of battle may be nearly upon them.

Judith lay on her bed, and rose slowly and painfully when Deborah came in. Her voice was weak and raspy. "I am so glad to see you, daughter. I thought I might not see you before I die. The Lord has granted my prayer."

Deborah was shocked and pained. The mother who was so strong now laid on her bed a shadow of her former self. Deborah reached for her and hugged her tenderly. "Has Hannah been able to help you?"

"Oh yes. Her herbs have eased the pain as it grows worse. When my body began to swell I thought I had another child in me. But now I know it is not a child."

"And Father? How is he?"

"Your father is afraid. He is afraid for me, afraid to be left alone, afraid of Sisera's threat. He stays among his sheep or sits many hours with the elders and listens to their fears, which add to his. There is nothing I, or anyone, can do for him. He closes himself off and lives in his own tortured world."

"And you, Mother, are you afraid?"

"No, my dear, I am no longer afraid of anything. I will soon sleep and not awaken. It will be a blessing. I know the Lord guides you in what you must do and takes care of you much better than I could."

Tears sprang to Deborah's eyes. "You always knew I was different and you shielded me. You let me run to Hannah without ever complaining. You must have thought I deserted you."

"You always came back to me, my daughter. You would bring me flowers and I knew they were from your heart. I often longed to be to you what Hannah was, but I knew that was not to be. I am content to be your mother. I will pray for your victory and your happiness."

"Happiness," repeated Deborah shaking her head. "Happiness is fleeting. The more I search for it in Lapidoth, the more I think of Ya'akov. The more I believe I loved him, the more I miss him."

Deborah put some water over the fire to make some tea. They sat together in sweet silence for a while, each lost in thoughts mixed with blessings and regrets.

The abrupt entrance of Amram broke the silence. He stopped and looked from Deborah to Judith and back. Then he turned and retreated out the door. Deborah set down her tea and hurried after him. She reached for his arm and he stopped not looking at her.

"She needs you, Papa. And so do I. Please do not turn away. Please?"

Slowly he turned to her, eyes full of tears he hoped to hide. She threw her arms around his neck. Hesitatingly he put his arm around her shoulders. "I turned away from you all your life. I never knew what to say to you."

"I was not an easy daughter, Papa. Sometimes I did not know what to say to myself."

"You should have married Ya'akov."

"Yes, I have often thought the same thing. I wonder if he would have lived had I done so. But we agreed to be friends, strange I know. Men and women are not encouraged to be friends, but that is what we thought was right for us. You chose him, Papa, and I came to love him. You gave me that gift."

Amram stared at her bewildered.

"You do not have to say anything, Papa. Just know that I love you. I must go now and Mama needs you."

He hugged her briefly and went back into the house without looking back. Deborah stepped into the house, kissed her mother, and left.

Rahab hurried through the marketplace to find Deborah. It was late morning and the vendors were loudly hawking their merchandise as Deborah made her way back to Rabbi Amri's house. They spotted each other as they neared the well.

"Barak and his men are here to take us to the camp. Can you be ready to go shortly?"

Deborah heaved a big sigh and sat down in the grove of trees where she sat so long ago with the other young girls of the village. "My mother is dying and I shall never see her again. My father is lost in grief and fear of the future. I need to clear my mind and get back to God. Go with me to Hannah's for a little while."

"Do you think we should tell Barak or Rabbi Amri?"

"We will not be gone long. But you can go back if you wish." Deborah looked up and smiled at Rahab. "Um, is Gideon among them?"

"I wish he were! There are four men with Barak. None of them Gideon."

"Let them rest. I want to spend a little time praying with Hannah. That always calms and clears my crazy thoughts."

Hannah was delighted to see them, as always. She hobbled down the path to meet them and kissed them soundly on both cheeks. "How is your mother today?"

"She is very weak and close to death. We bid each other farewell."

"And Amram, did you see him?"

"Yes. I spoke to him openly for the first time in my life. He is frightened, very frightened. I know there is nothing more I can do for them. Help me clear my sadness and turn my mind to what God would have me do next."

"That I will gladly do. Come in and have some tea, both of you. You have been on a long dangerous journey, I know."

They sat down together and Hannah poured tea. Then she handed teach one a polished smooth white stone. The stones glittered with silvery specks. "These stones represent the morning star, the divine within us. They hold no magic of their own. They reflect only blessings that come through you."

Deborah and Rahab closed their hands over the stones and closed their eyes. Hannah's crackly voice led them into the silence and in a moment led them out again. "Now, go, find Barak and his guard. Keep the stone to remind you that a moment in the silence is all you need. God is complete. In God there is no time."

Deborah and Rahab rose from their places, kissed Hannah, and trotted down the stony path to the road. There were soldiers on the road. Deborah noticed they were not Barak's guard. They pulled up their hoods and pretended not to see them. Rahab took Deborah's arm as they hurried their step, giggled and chatted with each other as though they were sharing girl's secrets.

Kelev ran out to meet them barking and wagging his tail. He stopped abruptly. The hair on his back stood up. He turned to the soldiers and lifted his upper lip, baring his fangs. Rahab took hold of his ruff and pulled him beside her. The soldiers consulted each other. They looked again at the women and the dog, and turned decidedly toward the inn and the wine they were looking forward to.

*   *   *

Miriam hobbled out into the courtyard and sat down heavily on a bench. Her breathing was ragged and she was hunched over like a vulture. "Omar! Omar! Where are you? Your physician is driving me crazy!"

"May I serve you?" inquired an elderly servant of Omar's. "My lord has gone and will not return until this evening."

"Gone? Where has he gone you old fool? I must speak with him!"

"I am sorry, madam. My lord did not tell me. He often does not say where he is going."

Miriam threw her cane at him. "Be gone you useless old goat!"

The servant ducked, picked up her cane, and placed it out of her reach. "As you wish, madam." He stared at her for a moment, eyes piercing hers. "Will that be all?"

"Go away!"

Omar's physician, Rajnish, swept out into the courtyard with a flourish. "Madam will please return to her treatment! Do you wish to remain a cripple and die?"

Miriam turned on him with a vengeance, but he sidestepped her lunge and pinned her arms behind her. "My orders are to use force if necessary. Please do not make it necessary."

She bared her yellowing teeth and spat. "That for your treatments! They are doing me no good. You are a fake. I will tell Omar to dismiss you when he returns."

"Omar will not dismiss me, Madam. Have no hope of that. Your healing will take time. You must continue to do what I tell you, even if there is pain. Your outbursts of rage only make you worse. You will have another stroke in the brain if you do not control your temper! I am sure your temper and screaming caused the first one."

Miriam relaxed into a sulk. He took her arm and led her back into her chambers. At his signal his slaves began again to guide her limbs in a regimen of movements. Hot teas and compresses were prepared, and a potion was poured into a goblet for her to drink. When she was completely exhausted, they carried her to her bed and covered her with a robe.

Omar returned in the evening. He went to his own rooms and did not inquire about Miriam. He had Akhmed on his mind. A courier came in late with a message. "Akhmed and Lapidoth are alive and travel with a caravan coming to Ashdod, my lord. They will arrive tomorrow and will surely seek an audience with the traders to settle Lapidoth's debt."

"How did you come by this news?"

"A rider, who is my brother, has traveled ahead of the caravan and is lodged in Ashdod."

"Bring him to me at first light."

"It shall be done, my lord." The courier bowed and left.

"Did I hear you speak of Lapidoth, Omar?" Miriam's voice was growly and menacing.

"Guards!"

Omar's guards come on the trot.

"Return Miriam to her room. Drag her if necessary and lock her in!"

Miriam was about to scream at them, but she remembered Rajish's words. She went immediately quiet vowing to herself, "I will await my chance. I will be well and I will repay them all."

CHAPTER 23

Rabbi Amri was at the door awaiting Deborah and Rahab. He was relieved when he saw them coming up the road.

"Rabbi! I wish to speak with you," called Deborah panting as she approached the house. He beckoned the two into the house. "I need to know about some scriptures that are puzzling me, if you are willing."

"Of course I am willing. Come into my study and sit down. We will see what we can discover."

"I wish to speak with Barak," said Rahab, excusing herself. She went into the garden where the soldiers waited.

Barak jumped up. "Is everything all right? You two have been away so long and there are troop movements not too far away."

"We are fine. We saw no troops. We went west to Acre."

"Why did you go there?"

"Deborah felt led to look for Lapidoth. She had the feeling he was there. Gideon was with us."

Mysteriously Barak's heart sank. "And did you find Lapidoth?"

"No. Heber the Kenite, husband of Jael the Priestess, came to us in Acre saying Jael urgently needed to speak with Deborah. So we went back with him toward Dan to her tent. We were there over night and came back here today. We met with Hannah and then came here. There were two soldiers on the road from Hannah's but Kelev scared them off."

Barak chuckled. "How do you get a wild dog to be your body guard? Where did you find him?"

"He found me. He was hurt and hungry. I fed him and put ointment on his wounds, so he stayed around. Sometimes I think he reads my mind."

"I have seen your hand signals to him and he obeys. Did you train him?"

"Not really. We just seem to be able to communicate. That is why I said he reads my mind. He might have been someone's herding dog and his master died or was killed. But he found me and stayed with me."

It was evening when Deborah emerged from the rabbi's study. Her face was full of resolve. She had gathered strength from Jael, renewed trust in God from Hannah, closure from her mother, and deeper understanding of the scriptural message from Amri. It had all come together within a few days in a way Deborah had not thought possible. She was ready.

They gathered for a last supper together. A sharp knock on the door startled them. Cautiously Amri opened the door. Gideon was standing there. "I hope I am not too late for dinner," he said mischievously.

"Gideon! Come in. We have saved you a place at the table. You are always welcome."

Amri, Leah, Deborah, Barak, a delighted Rahab, and Gideon sang the prayers and then it was quiet. Even the servant was careful to place the food on the table without any noise. They ate in silence as if the moment was too holy to interrupt with conversation. Their eyes met from time to time across the table, but no words were necessary. When they arose from the table, the servant brought a bowl of warmed water and a cloth. Amri dipped the cloth in the water and washed the hands of each one and bade them good night. Deborah stepped forward to wash Amri's hands feeling how incredibly precious this moment was. As he kissed her cheeks she looked into his face and saw the face of Ya'akov.

"Go my daughter and rest. Your victory is assured."

*   *   *

The caravan moved slowly. Even though Lapidoth and Akhmed wore peasants clothing, they were suspect because they rode horses. No one else was riding a horse. Akhmed let the word spread that they were bringing the horses to their powerful master in Gaza who had purchased them. It was enough to keep curiosity seekers at bay for now.

"There are only two of us, Akhmed. They may decide to attack us anyway. They know the horses are valuable."

"Then they will kill each other for them," snorted Akhmed. "However, we will need to leave this caravan tonight, gallop down the shore close to the water where the sand is wet and hard until we see a way into the hills. The Philistines and other brigands will have small campfires and we can more easily avoid them."

Lapidoth shuddered at the thought. If only he knew where Barak's encampment was. They would be safe there and perhaps Deborah would be there. But he had no idea where it might be. "How thoughtless of me not to ask Hannah before I left."

There was dust and sand blowing into the air ahead. "Brigands!" shouted Akhmed. They turned their horses toward the hills and spurred them into a full gallop across the plain. A good distance away Akhmed shouted, "We cannot go on blindly! We must turn back to the north and find another way!"

They slowed to a walk when the lathered horses could no longer sustain the speed. The promise of shelter in the rocks came into view. They stopped and listened in case someone else had the same idea. A goat burst out and scrambled up to a higher safer perch.

"Careful," whispered Akhmed. "Something frightened the goat and it was not us."

Two boys came out of the rocks and waved at them. "We are not far from home. Will you take us home on your horses?"

"It is a ploy, a trap that robbers use to lure travelers," said Lapidoth. "Ride on quickly!"

They turned away and headed north and then east toward Megiddo. Lapidoth had a sinking feeling he would not soon be able settle the business with the underground merchants in Ashdod and be free. His hope of starting a new life of his own choosing was fading.

Akhmed was thinking out loud. "We are no closer to Ashdod. We cannot go back to Acre. The plains are too open. Even the caravans take a chance traveling them. Most travelers in the caravans are willing and ready to fight, but we cannot afford to do that. Our best chance might be to stay in the mountains. Perhaps Megiddo will be safe enough for us to get food and lodging while we decide what to do. There may be news as well."

"We could cross the mountains to the Jericho road, but it will take a long time to get back to the coast. We could be too late," worried Lapidoth.

"Too late for what?"

"I am not sure. I have this foreboding as if we are running into obstacles because we have not followed . . . guidance. Do you think Deborah's god would be willing to be our god as well?"

"You are talking like a man who has had too much desert, too much sun. If I had a god or gods they would be Egyptian, not Hebrew, and they would help me not bar my way. We are running into obstacles because there are plenty of them out here. Brigands, Philistines, Sisera's goons, and who knows what else? They are all on the move and it will take great care and patience to avoid them." Akhmed was becoming impatient and was eager to set a course and move on. A large sum of money awaited him when he arrived at Omar's with Lapidoth. "Let's get to Megiddo."

*   *   *

Barak, Deborah, Rahab, Gideon and the other of Barak's men started out before dawn for Barak's encampment. "There is still time to cross the Kishon River without getting mired in a swamp," said Gideon. "Megiddo would be a good place to refill our supplies. There may be news there of any troop movements or other disturbances in the area. I have contacts there who will be glad to receive us."

One soldier told Deborah and Rahab to stay in the midst of them so they would be protected. Rahab laughed out loud. "I am as good a fighter as any soldier! You may need *my* protection!" The young man reddened and walked away.

Gideon heard the conversation and clapped the young man on the shoulder. "She means it, brother. Be glad! We will need all the help we can get."

Deborah looked out over the terrain as they traveled. The Kishon River seemed to have a strange attraction for her. When they stopped to rest, she pulled a fresh piece of parchment from her robe and began to sketch a map of the area. Barak moved closer to her to see what she was sketching. "What is this?"

"I guess you could call it a picture of the way from Kishon back to the camp. I have been making notes should we come this way again."

"Good! May I help you with some of the military details? There are passes that will not accommodate an army and equipment and some that will."

Deborah eagerly agreed and they sat close together talking and marking places on her growing map. She soon noticed Barak's closeness, the fragrance of his body and the comfort it gave her. Together they seemed to work as one, breathe as one. She snapped her mind back to the task at hand, but the feeling did not go away. Her body wanted to lean toward him. Her mind and sense of duty tried to pry her away.

They continued on the path and Rahab walked beside Deborah. "I saw you and Barak. You look like you belong together," she teased.

"We grew up together and we are in God's plan together, that is all. I am married as you well know!"

"Yes, and where is that idiot cousin of mine? He has not been with you since you left Tirzah! God did not see fit to bring you together in Acre. You are a passionate woman, Deborah. You deserve better."

"I am passionate for the plan of God and for the wisdom to carry it out. That is my only passion!" Deborah was beginning to flush, an embarrassing characteristic of people with reddish hair and freckles.

"Let your hair down a little, Deborah. Allow yourself to feel something. You loved Ya'akov and he is gone. You tried to follow a spiritual leading when you married Lapidoth, but you do not love him as a woman loves a man. Barak is a healthy man, real, alive and he loves you."

"Rahab, stop! Please."

"It is hard to see you stay behind that veil of purity. Deborah the woman is already waging war with Deborah the chaste. Who will win?"

"I do not understand what you are talking about and I do not like to be teased, even by you, my dearest friend."

"I am teasing only a little, but serious about the woman part. War demands a great deal of passion. Battle excites the body. It is not just a case of cool planning and execution. You will need your whole self to face Sisera and his army, use everything God gave you."

"How do you know this? How have you become an expert in the ways of war?"

"I lived near Miriam, remember? It was a battle every day to survive her evil. It took all the passion I could muster to keep her at bay so I could live. Lapidoth did not have that kind of passion. He succumbed to her every demand of him. And now he is surely running for his very life. He will soon know he cannot be free of her by running. He will only be free by standing up to her and destroying her hold over him."

Deborah wanted to shy away from this conversation, but she knew Rahab was right. Lapidoth lacked passion for her and whatever life they might have together. Their hurried marriage came about through fear of Sisera. The whole focus was to get to Ephraim and be safe. She started to laugh, quietly at first, and then a bursting laughter that would not stop.

Rahab looked at her in amazement. "I do not know what has made you laugh, but it is wonderful to hear it! You have not laughed like that since we met. Life has been so serious that we have almost forgotten how!"

"I was just recounting my reasons for marrying, when I really did not want it. Fear of Sisera, to please my parents, to do what our culture expects of a woman, curiosity about who Lapidoth was, and Hannah's urging. No! That is wrong. She did not urge me. In fact she was sure she had argued with God against it so long that God stopped listening to her. It was not the joyous anticipation a young woman feels when thinking of marriage. I had accepted an abbreviated ceremony so we could get on with the journey! Tired of fighting it, I gave in."

There was silence between them until they came to another resting place.

"I did not mean to pry. Forgive me."

"You pried open the door to my womanhood and I am grateful. I refused to think about it all these years and now the truth is coming to clear my confusion. When I sit beside Barak, I feel like I am about to explode, lose control, and spoil everything. If I refuse to acknowledge my womanhood, I will surely explode. Or it will explode regardless of how hard I try to deny it."

*   *   *

"When will Lapidoth arrive?" demanded a crooked faced Miriam. "He is my son and I have a right to know, Omar!"

Omar ignored her until he finished writing in his account book. Then he slowly lifted his head and looked over his shoulder at her. "You were never a mother, Miriam. Your demands are meaningless. Leave me."

She stood there seething and her legs threatened to give way. She clutched her walking stick with both hands and brought it down hard toward Omar's head. As if he had eyes in the back of his head, he moved aside and grabbed the stick. She shrieked in shock as he broke it in half and threw it into the corner of the room.

"Guard!"

A guard came running into the room, accustomed to Omar's shouts. Omar never shouted for his guard unless it was urgent.

"Take her back to her room and bar the door from the outside. Bar the windows. Instruct the servants to ignore her yells and serve her no food for three days. Anyone who disobeys will be severely punished. And call Rajnish the physician to me."

The guard hastily bowed and took the snarling Miriam limping back to her room. The physician came in presently. "What does my lord, Omar, require of me?"

"Is Miriam improving?"

"No, my Lord. She insists upon fighting us at every turn. Every outburst of rage endangers her further. Healing of the brain comes through calm and quiet. She is never those things."

"I have confined her to her room again, and ordered that no food be brought to her for three days."

"I do not know which will kill her first, my lord, the lack of food or the unabated rage that goes on within her. The damage may be causing her insanity and the insanity is preventing healing."

"She has always been insane. If she lingers, I will send her to an asylum in Gaza. My servants fear for their lives when they have to attend her. I will not have her threatening my household. Do you have any other suggestion?"

"No, my lord. I long for peace and the joy of my medical studies. It will be as you command. How long will you keep her here?"

"One week. No more."

"As you wish. I will prepare for her departure, however it happens."

The shouts and threats abated on the third day. She quieted to whimpering. Rajnish and the servants unbarred the door to bring in food. She did not look up when they came in. She had soiled the place everywhere and torn what few furnishing there were to shreds. The smell was overwhelming. The servants placed the food inside near the door and ran. She pounced on the food after the guard closed the door and barred it again.

Omar sent word to Ashdod inquiring about Lapidoth. Had he and Akhmed arrived? There was no affirmative answer. The caravan was attacked not too long after they left Acre. Many were killed but there was no sign of them in the carnage.

Days went by with no change in Miriam. Omar signaled the servants and guards to prepare for her departure. They gathered her and some meager belongings into a cart, stowed the pouch of money Omar had given them for her keep, and set out for the asylum at Gaza.

*   *   *

Lapidoth and Akhmed spent the night in a cave in the hills and rode into Megiddo just after dawn. The city gates were opening and merchants were pouring through them to get a place in the market area. Lapidoth was wary now of these groups of merchants since their encounter with the one who recognized him at the gates of Dan. They went immediately to an inn and secured a room. They changed into their merchant robes and emerged to get wine, food, and supplies. Lapidoth quizzed some of the men in the bar about any disturbances, robberies or attacks. They all shook their heads. One told him to check at the guardhouse near the gates.

Akhmed went to the guardhouse, but no one was there. Then he went on into the market to ask among the merchants who were still unpacking their wares. One man said he saw Philistines farther west, but nothing to the south. He helped the man set out his merchandise while they discussed possible routes to the south. When Akhmed settled on a road through the mountains he went back to the inn to get Lapidoth. On his way out of the market he was sure he recognized Deborah and Rahab moving through the stalls. He ducked behind some tents to avoid being seen by them and hurried back to the inn. Lapidoth would certainly want to see Deborah and he wanted no more delays. So he did not tell him. It was later in the morning when they mounted their horses and headed south.

"I thought your plan was to stay in Megiddo for a day and leave in the morning when we had more information."

"I did not expect to get the information we need so quickly. There is no reason to stay here. We do not want to risk running into the merchant who recognized you in Dan."

Lapidoth thought something was odd. Akhmed sounded eager to leave after being in such a hurry to get to Megiddo. Why would that merchant show up here? Before he could ask these questions, the conversation quickly turned to plans for Ashdod and freedom. Akhmed showed Lapidoth the map he had drawn and pointed the way to the mountain road they would take.

* * *

Rahab tugged on Deborah's sleeve. "I thought I recognized an Egyptian man. He looked like one of Omar's mercenaries." They hurried in the direction Rahab indicated, but lost him. "He has hidden himself. Now I am more sure than ever it was Akhmed."

"Akhmed? That means Lapidoth might be with him!" exclaimed Deborah.

"Either Lapidoth is with him or Akhmed is looking for him. Megiddo is a strange place for either of them to be. It is far out of the way. So Lapidoth must surely be with him! The question is, are they hiding from someone or riding south to Ephraim avoiding the coast?"

"I do not know what to do. I cannot seek him out if he is hiding from someone. It might endanger us all. And I cannot be drawn away from joining the Israelite army now. The battle is too close and time is short."

"Deborah, you have looked for him many times at much risk to your safety. It is time you let Lapidoth seek and find you. Let God bring him to you if that is the true plan."

Rahab was right. Deborah was surprised at the relief she felt. She was free. It was not her place to keep running after him. "It is still a mystery why I came to marry him at all. Was he really sent to Hannah? Was the purpose really to find me?"

"Do not let this hinder you. I am almost sorry I mentioned seeing Akhmed, but I was so shocked that I could not think. Meeting him just now might have meant disaster to us and to all of Israel. Come! We have some shopping to do, supplies to gather, and great men await our return. They will fight for us if there is trouble. Enjoy it! God's plan is not only for blood and death, but for life and happiness!"

Deborah looked completely amazed at Rahab. "Good to hear you talk positively about God's plan! I have been so driven I could not see the gift of happiness in it. Here in this moment, Rahab, we should gather all the joy it holds. Tomorrow is another day and Sisera will get his reward in due time."

They went through every stall in the market just for the joy of seeing and touching the goods, laughing and commenting on what they found. Their baskets were full to overflowing when Gideon came to find them. "We thought someone had carried you off! But no, here you are playing in the market like girls seeing one for the first time!"

Rahab whirled on Gideon and was about to object to his evaluation of them when she saw his grin and the twinkle in his eyes. Her reaction melted away as she handed him her basket and fell into step beside him. Deborah leaned against a tent post soaking in the pleasure of watching lovers walk together. She felt a tug on her basket. A thief? She jerked the basket away, turned and saw Barak standing there.

"Were you about to hit me with a tent peg?" he laughed. She burst out laughing with him. He took her basket and gave her his arm.

"God has given me this moment," she thought. "The commission to wage battle was so ominous it occupied my every waking moment and crept into my dreams." A great relief rolled over her body and mind. "Thank you God for this little oasis of happiness, for this man who has loved me all his life."

*　　*　　*

The trek through the mountains was long and difficult. Akhmed and Lapidoth said very little to each other, keeping careful watch and listening for noises above the hooves of their beasts. Akhmed was focused on Ephraim, Ashdod, and the riches he would use to buy a slave woman. There might be one in the slave market from the north who would look something like Deborah, fair with red hair, but with a more compliant temperament.

Lapidoth felt his emptiness keenly. What would there be for him after Ashdod? How would he avoid being conscripted into more of his mother's evil schemes? He would not go back to Bethel. Traveling alone again would be his lot until he found Deborah. But where on earth would he look for her now? And if he found her would she be truly his to command? Would she obey him as a wife should? Or would she be killed in the battle for her god and people?

After many days, they crossed back to the west and the golden sands of the coast appeared. The sprawl of the dusty, sand-laden buildings of Ashdod were before them and the bright blue sea beyond. It all looked so peaceful and innocent. Both men knew it was not as it appeared. It was the underground for smuggling slaves and goods, high stakes business interactions, and great danger. Always danger.

"Where is the money for the jewels? Do you have it?"

"It is in a safe place, Akhmed. Why do you ask?"

"It is dangerous in Ashdod. It would be safer with me."

"It has been perfectly safe with me for many years even until now. It is my debt that must be paid. I will continue to safeguard it."

"As you wish, my friend."

Lapidoth had no doubt that the word friend went only one way if at all. Something happened in Megiddo. He was more certain than ever. Had Akhmed another plan in mind? What did he really know about this man who claimed Omar sent him?

"I suggest we go to Bethel so my father knows I have returned. He will know how to approach this."

"I do not think that is a good idea. How do you know he is there?

"Then perhaps we should go to see Omar first. Omar will know."

Akhmed sensed Lapidoth's wariness and agreed to pay Omar a visit and get his advice. He still could not figure out where Lapidoth hid his money. He had seen Lapidoth's garments and bags and saw nothing of it. Was he lying about having it? That could mean big trouble from the underground in Ashdod.

They arrived at Omar's villa late, but Omar was still in his library. The servant announced them and motioned them to step in.

"Welcome! I have been concerned about you. I heard about the attack on the caravan."

Akhmed smiled and said, "We saw the dust rising ahead and assumed it was a raid so we galloped off across the plain. We thought the people in the caravan were ready to kill us to steal the horses, so it was timely. The attack took their eyes off us."

"We went to Megiddo and then south. It was safer than traveling the coast but it was longer and harder. Do you know where my father is?"

Omar pulled at his beard and signaled the steward to pour them all some wine. "Things have happened since you have been gone. Your mother fell and was partly paralyzed. The physician calls it an accident in the brain. She became ten times crazier and more enraged that ever before. Joseph brought her here and threw his sandal down denouncing her, which he has a right to do. My physician tried to help her, but she attacked the servants and scared them half to death. I finally had to send her to Gaza to the asylum there. I am sorry, Lapidoth."

"There is no need to be sorry on my behalf. I was sure she sent someone to kill me. I have been running all over the country trying to pull my life back together, watching my back all the way. I was nearly murdered in Sidon. Now I just want to pay off the black market and be done with it all."

"Yes. I understand you have a wife now. Where is she?"

"She is going about God's business, something about defeating Sisera. Rahab is with her."

"How do you know Rahab is with her?"

"They were living together in Rahab's house. They were driven away by Miriam, as you probably know. When Deborah returned to Kadesh-Napthali I hear Rahab was with her. I know nothing more."

"I understand you abandoned Deborah on the Jericho Road. Is that right?"

"It is a long story, Omar, and the hour is getting late. I want to go to Ashdod in the morning and settle my debt."

"Yes, yes of course. My servants have prepared your rooms. You are most welcome here. Please accept my hospitality."

"With pleasure," sighed a weary Akhmed. Leaving Omar and Lapidoth to conclude their business he followed the servant out the library door.

Omar motioned Lapidoth to stay. "Paying off your creditors will not be so easy. The merchant we normally deal with, Abdullah, has been murdered. I do not know who is now taking his place. There have been fights over it and several others have tried and died. Your father, Joseph, has gone back to Bethel to tend his land with Joab. Please tell me all you know."

Lapidoth and Omar talked late into the night. In the morning Omar, Lapidoth, and Akhmed were seated in the atrium of Omar's palace. There were pieces of parchment with numbers spread before them. Omar was writing on a blank one.

"There is no longer a reason to bring Lapidoth back except to tell him of his mad mother and the death of the merchant. Lapidoth has turned the money for the jewels over to me. I have given him this document saying his debt with the merchants is now transferred to me."

"Akhmed, I will pay you as promised. You did your work well."

The disappointment showed on Akhmed's face. He hoped to handle the money so he could broker a better deal in Ashdod. He had hoped for a more lucrative settlement, but it was not to be. "I will go now and leave you to family business."

"Akhmed, may I call upon you again?"

"Yes, of course. You have been most kind."

"Thank you, Akhmed, for helping me return safely." Lapidoth was about to say Akhmed could call upon him if he needed assistance but thought better of it. That would keep him on a tether that would surely draw him right back into the black market business or something worse. No, he was now free and would begin by going to his father and Joab.

Akhmed departed, claiming business to attend to. Lapidoth stayed on to hear more of what happened with Joseph and Miriam. He recounted to Omar his travels and his reason for taking so long to get back.

"How do I get started on a life of my own, Omar? How does one recover such a vast amount of time wasted? I am no longer so young, my wife is at the head of the Israelite army facing Sisera and may not return alive."

"Start from home, Lapidoth. Go back to Joseph and Joab. Rest there until something appears in your mind and then pursue it."

CHAPTER 24

B arak, Deborah, Gideon, Rahab, Kelev, and the small company of soldiers arrived at the Israelite Army encampment early in the day. Deborah and Rahab went to their tent to sort their purchases and rest. A young soldier bringing food for them tapped on their tent and entered. He placed the food on a mat and looked around with great curiosity. Then he remembered his mission and announced, "Ladies, you are requested to be at Barak's tent early at sunrise." He bowed, his face reddening, and retreated backing through the opening.

Deborah and Rahab could not stop their giggles at the embarrassment of the young man. "He probably has never entered the tent of women. I wonder what he expected to see when he looked around. We should not laugh." But they could not help it. They were too tired to control it. They ate and slept. Kelev guarded the door.

A trumpet blast awakened them just before dawn and the camp sprang into action to begin the day. The makeshift kitchens were busy and the soldiers lined up for the meal. The night guards retired and the morning guards came on duty. Other tasks around the camp were done and the training commenced. Deborah was at work reviewing scriptures and battle plans. Soldiers from the Kishon valley area were called in to discuss the annual flooding of the Kishon River and the valley that becomes a swamp each year. Barak and Abel gathered information and sketched crude topographical maps of the place where Deborah was sure they would engage Sisera.

Deborah watched as Abel and Barak studied and discussed their approach strategy, soldiers, equipment, weapons, animals, and transport carts. Abel was the classic soldier devoted to duty and to his leader. His intensity filled the space around them. He was small and wiry with black hair, steady eyes and muscular shoulders. He described various parts of the organization with his hands, creating imaginary pictures in the air.

Barak watched and listened intently asking questions about everything. He had a strong, handsome profile, great bone structure to his face. His whole body was well proportioned and he carried it like a taut bowstring, ready for action.

Deborah wondered at the growing attraction she was feeling toward Barak. Her mind kept flashing back to their times sitting by the well in Kadesh-Napthali when he was just a young village boy. How could her perception of that relationship have evolved and changed without her realizing it? Had she changed the perception of herself as well? Had she allowed herself to grow up into a woman in her own mind, or did she see herself unchanged from those early days? Rahab's observations had shaken that innocent image of long ago. She saw Rahab as a powerful mature woman. Why had she not seen herself that way as well?

Barak glanced up. "Deborah, come sit beside me so we can trace the routes we will travel. We need to know them equally well should we be separated."

Deborah was shocked out of her reverie at the sound of his voice. The man had called to the woman, not a boy to a girl at the well. Equally he said! Hesitantly she got up trying to shake off the oscillating images in her head and moved closer to where he was sitting. She sat down and gazed over the parchments that were spread out before them.

Slowly it all began coming into focus. The words of Scripture, the movement of an army, the purpose each Scripture would serve along the way. She marked the location of Jael's tent knowing somehow this was a necessary image. It gave Deborah a visible anchor to the woman who would play a great part in history. She could feel Jael's energy reaching out to her, encouraging her and it sent shivers down her spine. Deborah murmured the words of Jael, "The victory will be given into the hands of a woman."

Barak glanced at Deborah and wondered at these words she spoke. Abel looked on with interest but asked no questions. Deborah was a mystery to him and he did not care to understand it.

*   *   *

Lapidoth was grateful for this unexpected release from the black market ties. He still did not feel quite safe, but perhaps with time he would release the dark nightmares of being pursued.

Joseph and Joab were just coming back from inspecting the fields when Lapidoth arrived. They all greeted each other with kisses to both cheeks. "Come into the house and let us have refreshment together," hailed Joseph.

Joab wanted to go to his house and Tamar, so he declined saying the other two had business to discuss that did not include him. The absence of Miriam had changed Tamar from constant bitter agitation to a peaceful attractive woman. He found himself longing for her body as never before. He and Lapidoth embraced again. "It is good to have you safely home, brother."

It was strange to walk into the house without the screams and reproaches of Miriam bouncing off the walls. "How did you accomplish this, father? Or maybe the question should be, why did you wait so long?"

Joseph smiled. "It is easier to transport a disabled or dead tiger than a live healthy one."

"How did she do this to herself?"

"An escalating rage simply destroys the body. The physician said it will cause the brain to bleed and do harm to the heart. I do not understand it as he does, but I can certainly see what led up to it and the result he described. Now, tell me what has happened to you."

"I have been running for my life. I was nearly murdered after I sold the jewels in Sidon. I did not know whether to trust this Akhmed who was sent by Omar to find me, but I had no choice. I was trying to get free of my debt and begin to live my life as I wanted it to be."

"I am grieved that I gave you such a terrible mother. She was the source of all our troubles."

"I wanted to come here and Akhmed wanted to go to Ashdod. I suspected he had other plans when we got near Ashdod, so I insisted we go to Omar's. Omar has the money I was carrying and has given me a letter saying my debt is now transferred to him. The merchant in Ashdod was murdered and he did not know with whom he would be dealing now. I could see the futility of waiting there for a resolution. It could be years."

"And your wife, Deborah? Where is she in all of this?"

"Fortunately her only involvement was to meet Akhmed when he was looking for me. She could tell him nothing and stood up to him when he became a little threatening and pressed her."

"I hope Omar settles the debt before they decide to kill him. I hope that written agreement will keep you safe. But I fear it will not be honored. We are honorable men, they are not."

"Do you believe I have been unwise?"

"I believe you did the only thing you could. Your safety would be in danger either way, and Omar knows the ways of black market business. He has connections. Again what of your wife?"

"She has followed the guidance of her god since childhood and continues to do so. I have not been with her enough to know if I am part of her god's plan or not."

"Have you spent a night with her. Have you consummated your marriage bed?"

Lapidoth turned away in embarrassment. "No. The one opportunity I had was in Tirzah, and we had hardly settled down for the night when the raid happened." He did not mention they had separate accommodations at their other stops as well as at Tirzah.

Joseph looked askance at Lapidoth. "How is it you did not plan for your marriage? A man must do his duty to his wife as well as to himself. Did she reject or refuse you?"

"Everything happened so fast there was no time to plan. We fled Sisera's raids and nearly got caught in one."

"I understand about the raids, but you were here with her. Could you not have returned from Ashdod with me to attend her before you traveled north?"

"I have no answers to your questions, father. It is not her fault. I did not approach her and I do not know why."

"And I should not pry, but your standing in the village or wherever you are will be damaged. Do you wish her to remain as your wife? She is not with you. You could divorce her and save yourself from ridicule."

"That would place her in danger she does not deserve. I am the one who kept leaving. She even came looking for me in Acre but I did not arrive there until after she left. Again this is not her fault."

"It pains me to say I understand. I did not have a conventional marriage to Miriam. She did not want to marry me, but was forced to. I was blind, seeing only the glamour of her exotic beauty and fascinated by her unpredictability. I thought her independence would dissipate when you and Tamar were born. I thought she would settle down, but she did not and actually got more adamant and demanding. I thought it was my fault but in later years I could see that it was not. So I claimed my right to dissolve our marriage by dumping her at Omar's door and throwing my sandal down in front of witnesses. Other than the birth of my children, that was the happiest most satisfying event of my life."

"Do you know where she is now?"

"I have not asked. Why would I want to know unless she was planning to come storming back into our home."

"Omar did not put up with her for long. She refused treatment by Omar's physician. He said she got more enraged every day and the physician said she would damage herself again. When she terrorized his house he had the guards take her to the asylum in Gaza the day before I arrived. I doubt she will come storming back here."

Joseph heaved a sigh of relief. "What will you do now?"

"I will stay with you for a year. I will work the land with you. I will not do anything about my marriage for now. Deborah is fated to somehow lead the Israeli army against Sisera. There is no use in trying to interfere with the plan of her god. I have already been prevented by circumstances from being any influence at all against that."

"This is an unusual story! Is she with the army now?"

"I do not know."

"She is in the company of men unescorted and without her husband!"

"I am sure that is the case. Of course Rahab is with her. Deborah will fight beside her life long friend, Barak ben Abinoam. The prophecy is she and Barak will defeat Sisera together and save Israel."

"This is beyond me. You are welcome to stay here and work the fields with us until you decide what to do next. I am pleased you have come home. I have spent many years praying for your safe return."

*   *   *

With great effort Hannah traveled north to the tent of Jael. "Good afternoon, my sister in the spirit of the Holy One," said Jael taking Hannah's arm. "Come and sit down. The servant will bring us tea. When you are refreshed, we will pray."

Hannah and Jael prayed far into the night, envisioning the battles to come. They carried questions into their meditations. Answers would come in the form of visions and symbols. At dawn they spoke of the revelations they had seen and heard, and agreed that Deborah was in the right place at this time. They saw Sisera running from his defeat to the place of his demise.

"Will Deborah and Barak be spared?" asked Hannah quietly.

"I see much death as always in war, but I do not see their deaths," replied Jael. "Fear not, Hannah, the battle will not be prolonged. A defeated Sisera will come here to my tent and I must be alone when that happens."

"Will he try to kill you?"

"No. He will believe he is safe. He will be grateful for my hospitality and for his demise at my hand. I am his only chance for redemption and freedom from Jabin's diabolical plans. Only his soul knows this. His soul will bring him to me for release."

"What must I do? What will be my part?"

"Go to Judith and attend her passing. She is near the end and you will hold her high in the consciousness of spirit. Her husband is not capable of this and will be absent. Remember to bless him with strength as Judith goes to sleep with the Mothers."

Hannah and Jael ate a morning meal together. Heber joined them and then prepared to escort Hannah to her home. He brought two donkeys from the field, put a small frame on their backs so he and

Hannah could ride. Hannah was increasingly unsteady and Heber's vision was greatly lessened when he was tired. Hannah gathered some herbs and spices from her stores. Heber waited and they set out for the home of Judith and Amram.

*   *   *

Miriam lay on a filthy mat hardly able to move her limbs. The ride to the asylum had nearly pounded the life out of her. A bowl of thin gruel was left beside her. There were no attendants, just howls, moaning, and occasional screams from somewhere close by. The smell of death, vomit, and feces was overwhelming.

Words came through her injured brain in fits and starts. "I . . . repay . . . all! Repay! Repay!" She made an attempt to move and discovered she was tied down and restrained. She wanted to rage against the bonds, but her body would not obey her. She remembered the words of Rajnish the physician. "The quieter you are, the better your chances to recover." And so she determined she would recover and willed her mind and body to be still.

A servant came by after what seemed an eternity. She lifted a spoon of the cold greasy gruel to Miriam's lips. Miriam wanted to gag and scream, but she obediently opened her mouth like a baby bird in a nest and received spoonful after spoonful. Her stomach wanted to revolt. She kept the urge at bay by thinking with every spoonful, "I will recover!"

*   *   *

Gideon and Naham left to again spy out Sisera's movements. Word came from one of their shepherd message carriers that Sisera was in Jabin's palace in Hazor. "Probably conferring about where to attack and when," said Naham.

"We might need to know exactly where," said Gideon staring intently at the sky to the north. "We do not expect Sisera until spring when the Kishon creates a swamp in the valley. Deborah's guidance says the same thing."

Naham was accustomed to watching the Canaanites in their military camps. "It would be certain death to try to get near Jabin's palace. It might better serve to see what Sisera's troops are doing while he is away. Do they maintain military discipline or do they lapse into disarray? Do they become drunk? Do they let down their guard? This would be useful to know."

"Their chariots and iron weapons are of great concern. We must somehow disable them, make them useless. We cannot use the Hula marsh. It is too far north. The swamp of the Kishon River during flood season is a good choice. We will tell Barak to draw them further east and south."

"If the soldiers are as undisciplined as I believe they are," responded Naham, "they might be foolish enough to charge right into the muddy low land thinking the horses could pull the chariots through it. But the iron wheels are heavy and cut deep ruts wherever they roll. Pray the chariots will sink quickly up to the axles in sucking mud and be rendered useless."

"The chariot drivers and warriors will also be stranded in the swamp. Sisera has been so proud of the chariots that he nearly abandons the use of foot soldiers, the backbone of any army. It will be interesting to see where he places the foot soldiers. Will they come at us first clearing the way for the chariots, or will they come last only to be barricaded by the fallen chariots and forced to stay back?"

Gideon and Naham watched Sisera's camps until they had enough information to be satisfied. They turned back to the Israelite encampment and traveled with haste especially while they were close to Sisera. They watched for marauding groups of soldiers lest they be trapped between the two. The Kishon River was ahead of them, giving them the opportunity to determine the deepest part of the river and the widest part of the flood plain. The river was deceptively small at this time, not giving a clue to the torrent it would become.

* * *

Barak eagerly awaited the return of his spies. He still had many questions about the enemy. "Answers! I need answers!"

"Do not be so worried, Barak. We will have the answers and guidance we need," said Deborah trying to calm the ever-growing anxiety that was beginning to affect the entire army. "We will need clear minds and courage to receive it. Worry will block it."

"I know you are talking about God who has never failed you, but is God able to speak to an entire army?"

"Do you no longer trust my word? Are you beginning to doubt me? Doubt God? If so your army will begin to fear and doubt as well. We cannot let that happen now when the time is so close."

Barak studied Deborah's face as though he were trying to remember something. "I have not doubted you since I was a child. No, I am just a military leader trying to be sure he has everything he needs for success, the defeat of Sisera. I do not want to fall short because I missed something important."

Deborah touched his forearm. "I do not doubt you and God does not doubt you. That is why we are here, why we were chosen."

"Chosen!" Barak repeated. "I have not thought of myself as chosen, or even of enough importance for God to notice me, much less choose me! What did I do to deserve it?"

"How can we question this? God has chosen me, a woman, even though women are not chosen to be military leaders among our people. We are not to be educated. We cannot inherit property as sons can. We cannot choose to live without marriage. If we do we are considered harlots. If we do not bear children we are a disgrace. And even though our people give women the lowliest regard, God has given me the highest. I never wanted marriage or children. So God has given me a husband who is absent. I did not know how to live as an independent woman, so God gave me Rahab to teach me and walk that road with me. I did not know how to be friends with a man, so God gave me Ya'akov, who was not willing to be married because of his health. But he gave me the opportunity to learn Scripture with him and be educated at the table of his father. Everywhere I go there is God opening the way. If I lost my way, there was God speaking through Hannah. My list of blessings and unexplainable attainments goes on and on. You are one of those blessings, Barak. Where else could I have learned military ways? Who else would stand beside me or let me stand beside him?"

Barak listened in wide-eyed amazement. "Deborah, you have opened my eyes to so many things. I have not considered the plight of women. I thought the laws protected them. Now I see women are considered only property, to be beaten into submission, killed, or cast out. I cannot imagine going into battle without you, but surely there are many men and women who think this is abhorrent. It can only be God who could transcend the foolishness of people and show them what is right and just."

They sat together for a long time in silence, taking in the words they had spoken. Barak slowly turned and looked at Deborah as if seeing her for the first time. He saw the serious look of her face and realized how he had come to trust her dedication. There was the red-gold of her hair curling around her temples, and the graceful flow of her robes as she walked. Immediately he stopped his thoughts. He dared not go deeper and discover his feelings. He was afraid of what he might find there. A shout from Abel told him Gideon and Naham had returned. Together they walked out of his tent into the warmth of the sun.

*   *   *

Lapidoth worked several weeks in his family fields. He took produce to the market and helped Joab repair the family homes and animal shelters. Joseph was aiding a widow who had no male relatives to help her. But Lapidoth's mind was on Omar's promise and the piece of parchment he kept sewn in the hem of his tunic. Was he really free?

Joseph scrutinized Lapidoth's face and looked into his eyes. "It is good to have your help, Lapidoth, but I see you are still troubled. What do you want to do?"

"I want to see Omar again. I want to ask him if we are really clear of Ashdod. I have dreams at night that I continue to be pursued by a dark shadow."

"I will go with you," said Joseph. "Since the murders in Ashdod, it is not safe for one man to travel alone. Even if no one is pursuing you with purpose, it is dangerous."

They set out before dawn on borrowed asses. The asses were larger, faster, and stronger than small donkeys. Arriving at the gate to Omar's palace the servant met them and said in a worried voice, "My master is away."

"How long has he been away?" asked Lapidoth.

"One week, my lord. I do not know where he is."

"Is this unusual for him to be gone so long?"

"I suppose so, my lord. In truth I have begun to fear for his safety."

"Which way did he go?" demanded Joseph becoming agitated.

"To the west, my lord. I do not know if his destination was Ashdod or Gaza. He took an ass rather than a horse and was dressed in plain Bedouin robes."

Joseph shot a worried glance at Lapidoth and said, "We must lose no time!" They turned and rode west. "Why would he go to Gaza? It is far away over dangerous Philistine territory. Surely he went to Ashdod to learn what has become of the black market and who is taking the murdered Abdullah's place."

"There would be no reason for him to visit Miriam in Gaza. He would send a servant if something was needed for her care. This must be something bigger and much more dangerous."

As they hurried on Ashdod rose slowly on the western horizon. It was brown with sand and deceptively quiet on the outskirts. Closer to the inner city there were children, goats, and sheep running in the alleys. Markets were teeming with merchants and shoppers. Down by the shore were bobbing boats, a jumble of warehouses, and men sitting in doorways keeping watch from various vantage points. Joseph and Lapidoth could feel many pairs of eyes following them. They secured their animals at a small stable and went on foot to the wealthy homes. As they inquired about Omar from one house to the next the inhabitants all shook their heads and shut their doors quickly. When they were about to give up and try something else, a small boy appeared at the corner of a house. He beckoned to them and disappeared.

"It is a chance," whispered Joseph. "This could be a trap or the last chance to find Omar."

"It could also be that we are sticking our noses into Omar's delicate negotiations," worried Lapidoth. "He will not welcome us if that is true."

"His servant is worried. His absence is of an unusual length. I say we go in."

Lapidoth and Joseph quietly disappeared around the corner of the house, down an alley, and through an open gate into a walled courtyard. The gate was quickly closed behind them and the boy beckoned to them again. Glancing warily around the empty courtyard, they followed him. The interior of the house was dark and cool. They were shown down a steep stone stairway. At the bottom the boy pushed aside a ragged drape and revealed a tunnel dimly lit by lamps sitting in niches in the wall. It went on for what seemed like several blocks and finally led to an open chamber.

"Come. This was Abdullah's place!" said a guard beckoning them forward. Joseph and Lapidoth stopped before the great table where they had examined jewels for selection many times. In the dim light through a swirl of smoke from a bong, they saw Omar sitting on Abdullah's cushions.

"Welcome friends! Have you come to continue our business? We have much for you to sell. Come and sit down. I would hate to lose such faithful partners."

Lapidoth and Joseph were shocked to a stand still. Lapidoth's heart sank. Was he trapped again?

*　　*　　*

The physician, Rajnish was right. Miriam felt a little stronger each day. She even managed a crooked smile at the obese male attendant who fed her. The attendant eventually untied her bonds. "We were afraid you would fall out of the bed and injure yourself. Perhaps if you stay calm and cooperate, the bonds will stay off."

Miriam wanted to claw out his roving eyes, but she merely smiled and said, "I thank you. You are most kind." As time went by, Miriam offered to assist the overworked attendants, and fed some of the other patients. Her limbs were a little more responsive each day and her determination to be well increased.

To her surprise the obese attendant found special more nutritious food for her one day. She thought it was because she was helping. But that was naïve. He said, "If you will let me know you better, I will make certain you get better food than the asylum gruel."

She knew what he meant. Trying not to show her revulsion, she concentrated on "getting well and repaying" those who thwarted her. "Yes, I am willing," she barely whispered and looked away. When darkness came, she woke to the sweaty smell of him as he knelt down, pulled up her tunic, and threw his heavy leg over her body.

"You will be quiet and do what I want," came his harsh whisper. His hot breath was on her neck and he rolled onto her nearly crushing her. As she fought for breath he became more excited. His thrashing became more violent. Again and again he tried, but was not successful. He punched her and pinned her arms above her head and pounded frantically, but he could not make his manhood obey. He cursed her and staggered away in the dark.

"You promised better food. This is gruel!"

"You put a curse on me last night. We will try again tonight and you will pray Allah that you will be successful in lifting the curse!"

Miriam sat up and looked around. She had to get out of this place. She was strong enough to walk now, but where could she go? She would go south along the coast to Gaza City. There were Egyptians with whom she did business residing there. She would find them.

When darkness fell, the attendant came again, pulled her up by her hair, and tore her tunic away. "We will fix this now," he grunted. He dragged her outside and dropped her on the ground beside a shed. In the dark she grappled, feeling frantically around for a weapon. She needed a sharp stick or a rock. She found a stick and hid it beneath her. The attendant dropped his garments, and knelt down over her. As he cursed and fumbled with his manhood she withdrew the stick and rammed it into his eye with all the strength she could muster. She pushed it upward into his brain and he died with hardly a sound. It took all her strength to push him aside as he fell so she would not be pinned under him.

She got painfully to her feet, picked up his robe, shook it out, and threw it around her. Her stomach churned at the smell of it, but it would keep her warm and shield her from being recognized. It was pitch dark yet so she walked quickly toward the sound of the Great Sea. She turned south, picking her way by feeling the soaked sands and the edge of the water lapping at her feet. At times she tripped over rocks and fell to her knees, but hope and determination were rising like a tide in her body and mind, increasing her strength.

*　　*　　*

Barak's forces swelled. They were too many for the area and too vulnerable altogether. He and Abel decided to divide the camp into cohorts of 600 men each. "There are too many trained in only one or two battle skills. We must train some as archers, some as lookouts, some as builders, and whatever else we will need to support the invasion. Splitting the camp will enable us to determine the talents of the men and place them in advantageous positions. Anyone coming to attack us will not see the real size of the army and cannot surprise all of us," said Barak running his finger over a crude topographical map.

"I sent Naham and Gideon out to find other places to make camps. We will move the cohorts out to establish them when the two return. The men will take supplies with them and plans for the campsites. In time we will have camps spread out like a chain toward the north of us so our troops will have safe places to stop, re-supply or, God forbid, to fall back to."

Deborah and Rahab saw that women were coming to the camp a few at a time to find their men. They began gathering the women into their tent to speak with them. Rahab's voice was gentle and sympathetic. "You cannot live with your soldiers, making lonely men jealous. They will fight among themselves at a time when they must be in harmony as soldiers with a single purpose. Thinking you are harlots some may even attack you and cause great dissension in the ranks. Our food supplies are not great and we cannot feed you."

The women bowed their heads in disappointment. "We have always followed our men. There are the same problems in our villages when we stay there. What shall we do?"

"Here is what you can do," began Deborah. "Our army needs good food to stay strong. You can gather food and bring it to us. We will set up kitchens with ovens to cook it and root cellars to store it. You will be a great help to your men and the others. The war with Sisera, God willing, will not last long. But Israel will need a standing army to protect the people from other invasions. Are you willing to help?"

The women talked among themselves for a few moments. The excitement was building. They could be part of the army! Eagerly they all assented and set about making plans.

Rahab was thoughtful. "We will need protection for them. Guards to be sure no one tries to assault them in the night. We must speak with Barak and Abel about this. We will need their cooperation."

"I will go to Barak and explain our plans. I am sure he will see the value of this," replied Deborah with a little more assurance that she felt.

Barak turned from his maps and lists of men when Deborah came into his tent. "You know there are women in the camp, do you not?"

"Yes I know. We have tried to send them home but they come back. They could cause us serious trouble among the men."

Deborah set out the plan for the women before him. He was doubtful at first. But he could see the possibilities of keeping them around, relieving some of the men from the task of gathering food. "We have some pretty bad cooks among the men. They tend to spoil more then they save. This is unheard of, but I believe we have no choice."

Naham stood at the door of Barak's tent. "I do not mean to listen, Captain, but could not help it. I have a suggestion."

"Name it, Naham. I need all the help with this I can get!"

"Sisera's encampments have compounds, places that are somewhat walled in. They enclose the tents of the officers and generals, hospitals and other things that need protection and privacy. We could build such a compound here and in each new camp. It could also enclose the women who are working for the army."

"Good! Yes, excellent idea. We will begin immediately to build one. Deborah, is this well with you?"

"All is well with me, Barak. I think this is one more step in strengthening us against Sisera. The taking of Sisera will not be that difficult if our men are well fed and not afraid. They will sense the good organization of the troops by the leaders, and their confidence in God will be great."

"We have long been behind in the ability to protect our lands. Other kingdoms know all these things already. It is good that we learn from them. Naham, please find Abel and tell him what we plan. I am sure he has men with building knowledge."

As Naham left the tent, Barak sat beaming at Deborah. "How could we have known it would be like this? You and I have progressed far from the visits at the well as children to this!"

Deborah felt the tingle throughout her body. She smiled back, but found no words to offer in reply. They were all bound up in emotion and she could not speak. She feared the tremendous urge to be in his arms. Barak walked to the tent flap and pulled it closed. They were alone. He drew her upward into his arms. She melted against his body. He held her tightly only a few moments and released her as she pushed back.

"Barak, we cannot become distracted. We cannot . . ."

"I know," said Barak as he turned, raised the tent flap, and tied it securely. "Forgive me."

Her heart was pounding and her legs shaking as she walked out of the tent. She was glad no one was nearby to see her distress.

However Rahab was watching, took her hand, and led her to a small grove. "The fight with Sisera will be nothing compared to fighting your heart. I know. I want Gideon to carry me off to some distant world where no one knows us and we can be together. But that is not our situation. We cannot disappear because of something forbidden we want so much."

Deborah drew in a deep breath. "You are such a gift to me, Rahab. I cannot imagine how I would handle this without you. Doing God's work has always been such a powerful force within me, I thought nothing else would compare to it! But here I am mooning like the young girls gossiping at the village wells!"

"Are you afraid you will thwart the will of God? Might it not be that God has given you this gift as a reward for all the hard work you have done? Israel will not fall because you are in love with Barak. If God is love, might we also be love if we are God's image and likeness as you have told me?"

"Now I really am confused! What do I do?"

"If you do not fight it in your mind, you will make wiser decisions. You will see more clearly what you have to do. Struggling against it makes everything harder and the problem larger. The desire will only continue to rise and become stronger. I have discovered that. Every time Gideon goes out, he may not come back. I want him to lie with me before he leaves. I have to turn my mind to things that will help us, things that will insure we will be here for him to come back to, God willing."

"Yes, it is all God, is it not? Hannah kept saying that to me. But it was easier to live by it until I began to see Barak in a different way."

*　　*　　*

The walk was long and difficult. The sky was becoming illumined by the approaching dawn. Just when she was about to collapse in the wet sand, Miriam saw a cart that seemed abandoned by the roadside. She climbed into it and covered herself with the attendant's voluminous robe in order to rest for a while. She was so exhausted she did not awaken when the cart began to jerk. Donkeys were being hitched to it as she slept and were led slowly toward a road. Dawn streaked the eastern sky as a man climbed into the driver's seat and clucked the team into a trot. Miriam's head began bouncing against the floorboards and she turned to cushion her head. Then she woke up. She raised her head to see they were following the coast to the south. Laying her head down on her arm she smiled. She was rescued! Someone was unwittingly carrying her into Gaza City.

* * *

Akhmed returned from Egypt and traveled north along the coast to Gaza to meet with his contacts. He was looking for the merchant who asked for his courier services. He took his horse to a stable in the city and walked down the familiar alleys to the meeting place. A donkey and cart were parked across the alley. Akhmed's curiosity was stirred. He reached into the cart and picked up the robe that covered Miriam. He decided someone must have been summoned to pick up a dead body and was carting it away. Then she moved.

"You are alive!" said a startled Akhmed.

"Yes, I am alive you fool. Do you have any food or wine? I am starving!"

Akhmed pulled a flask from his robe and handed it to her. "Keep it. I have no food." He abruptly walked away wanting nothing more to do with this filthy whore, or whatever she was.

Miriam smiled her crooked smile and drank deeply from the flask. It was strong drink and she felt slightly dizzy immediately, but it warmed her and slowly brought life back into her limbs. She clambered out of the cart and headed down one of the alleys leading away from the center of the city. She was close now to her cousin's house. Iscah would take her in, she was certain. They had not seen each other for many years, but they had been childhood companions.

A servant cautiously opened the door and gasped at the sight of Miriam. "I must look frightening, but I am Iscah's cousin, Miriam. Please may I come in?" The servant closed the door leaving Miriam standing outside. She pounded on the door again and a voice said, "Go to the servants' entrance and we will give you food."

"Well, that is a start," thought Miriam as she limped her way around the walls to the servants' entrance. An elderly man let her in and helped her into a small kitchen. "May I wash? It has been a difficult trip."

The elderly man brought a pitcher of water, rags and pulled a curtain across a corner of the room where she could privately wash herself. How good it felt! To her surprise, a fresh tunic and robe were handed to her. She dressed and pushed the curtain aside. "Where are my filthy clothes?"

"Burning with the rubbish, madam. They were not fit to use again."

"Indeed they were not. Will you tell Iscah that her cousin, Miriam, is here?"

"She has been told madam. She requested that we offer you refreshment from your travels immediately. Please sit at the table and the cook will bring you food."

A bowl of bits of lamb in broth was placed before her. She wanted to gobble the food, but she knew that would not be wise. It had been some time since she had eaten decent food, so she forced herself to eat slowly. When she finished the elderly man led her to a side room with a cot and bid her rest herself. Miriam wanted to resist, but could not muster the energy. She lay down and was fast asleep immediately.

The house lamps were lit when she awoke and Iscah was by her side. "Miriam, what has happened to you? Where is Joseph?"

Wearily Miriam recounted her illness and how she was rejected by Joseph and Omar, and taken to an asylum to die.

Iscah was wide-eyed. "I cannot believe this of Joseph! How could he do such a thing?"

"It was Omar's idea. My marriage has been difficult and they plotted to do away with me."

"You must stay here until you are stronger and we will decide what to do!"

Safe, fed, and cared for, Miriam began to slowly recover and even thrive. Once again she felt she could do anything, accomplish whatever she wanted. The old spine of steel that had always characterized Miriam was returning and her mind was clearing little by little. Iscah wanted to send a servant to Omar, but Miriam begged her not to. "Please Iscah, I am not strong yet and I fear for my life. The asylum was a hellhole and I nearly died there. May I impose upon your hospitality a little longer?"

"Of course you may. As long as you need. A proper room will be prepared for you. It has been a long time, Miriam. I look forward to being with you again and hearing of your experiences. You were always the aggressive one, while I was shy. You told me exciting stories of things I hardly dared dream of!"

Miriam smiled her crooked smile and patted Iscah's hand. "You are a good friend, my dear cousin. I will repay your kindness some day."

Iscah was still beautiful and Miriam was always jealous of her. Iscah was the attractive one, the fair one, and men flocked to visit her father just to get a glimpse of her. Where she, Miriam, was dark, dangerously exotic, and was married off like a chattel to the eager Joseph. She felt a rage building in her, but remembered the physician's advice and quickly calmed herself. "There will be time enough to repay them all," she thought, "and I will repay."

*　　*　　*

Deborah found it more and more difficult to keep the women in the camps happy as well as separated from the men. There was discontent fomenting and she needed to do something. But what?

She and Rahab puzzled over this until Rahab said, "They are all ignorant of the scriptures. They cannot read. They have never been educated except in cooking and having babies. What if we offered to educate them?"

Deborah snatched her breath. "Surely the men will not allow it!"

"We will not tell them! It will be a secret among the women. They love secrets. You are educated and you have taught me. I can teach. Let us ask them!"

Word was quietly passed from woman to woman, cousin to cousin, and a thrilling sense of conspiracy grew among them. Classes took place late in the evenings and everyone attended. Deborah had not realized how hungry they all were for the scriptures, the interpretations, and the ability to write the words for themselves. They made soft clay tablets on which to practice sketching the letters. The tablets were kept wet so they could be smoothed and reused.

Barak complimented Deborah on how well behaved all the women were. He could see a transformation in them, but fortunately was too busy with the army to think about what caused it.

The women learned quickly and created a system of exchanging places with women in the new camps so eventually the educated ones could carry on classes in all the camps. Deborah was the busy bee her mother predicted she would be. She held classes for the leaders of the soldiers during the day, and oversaw the women's classes at night. A guard escorted Rahab to the new camps ostensibly so she could assist the women in setting up the kitchens and storage places, and see that the men built a suitable wall around the women's compound. Still they did not suspect Rahab's real reason, the women's classes.

On her way back to the main camp Gideon caught up with them. With her guards present Rahab tried not to show her delight at seeing Gideon. He began to chat with them about the placement of the string of camps and the success of getting new ones started. Rahab was grateful for what she considered "men's talk" to learn what Gideon had been doing. The guards assumed she was not interested but Gideon knew better so he described the new camps in great detail.

*   *   *

Lapidoth recovered from his shock at Omar's presence in Abdullah's place. "I thank you for your most gracious offer, cousin. As I said to you when we met at your palace, I wish to pursue my own life now as a teacher. I will not betray you. I have kept the promise not to reveal our sources and I intend to continue to keep that promise."

Lapidoth turned to leave but two men stepped into his way. Lapidoth looked from them to Omar to Joseph. "What is this? Are you keeping me prisoner?"

"Prisoner? No, of course not. I am saving your life!"

"How is it you are saving my life, Omar? I have not asked for your protection. I intend to go and leave all this behind," said Lapidoth sweeping his arm across the table.

Joseph stood mute and motionless. Lapidoth turned to him. "Was this a plot between you and Omar, Father? Is that why you insisted we come to find Omar?"

"No, my son, I had no such plot. Do you remember your words before we entered here, that we might be rescuing Omar or be sticking our noses into his business? It seems you were correct about the second part. We have indeed stepped into a viper's nest."

"How do we gracefully bow out, Omar?" growled Lapidoth becoming agitated. "Surely you did not expect us to come back into this business. We will leave by the way we came in and not return."

"Do you still have the parchment I gave you relieving you of the debt?"

Lapidoth fumbled in the folds of his robe and found the parchment. "I have it."

"My dear Lapidoth, it is worthless to those who cannot read it, true? Those faithful to Abdullah might think it was you who killed him and seek your life in return! You are safer under my protection, Lapidoth. Stay with me. I will make you a rich man. That is my promise."

"And my father? Will you make him rich as well? I remember these promises years ago and we are not yet rich. Why should we believe you now?"

"You will believe me because it is I, not Abdullah, at the head of this business. I have not done you wrong, Lapidoth. It was your mother's doing, not mine. I, too, have no choice. I either take Abdullah's place or I die as well. I choose not to die."

Lapidoth looked at Joseph who had sat down on a cushion near the table. "Speak to me clearly, Omar. Is my father also under your protection?"

"If he should desire it," answered Omar glancing at Joseph. "He must think about the safety of his family in Bethel. What good is it to protect you if he and his family are not safe?"

"You speak in riddles, Omar!" Lapidoth advanced upon the place where Omar was sitting. Again someone stepped in to block his way.

"My influence goes only a small distance. Your family is everywhere. Your cousin, Rahab, and your wife, Deborah, are somewhere in the tribal territory of Napthali, your sister and brother-in-law are in Bethel, your mother is in Gaza if she still lives. Her cousin, Iscah and her family are in Gaza. I will do what I can. If you help me and our power increases we can do so much more. So stay with me, Lapidoth, and we will work this out together."

Lapidoth shoved the man out of his way. The guard drew his knife, but Omar waved him back.

"Surely you can see the sense in what I am saying. Have I been plain enough? We work together, we become strong and rich, we rule the markets, and we live. Otherwise we die."

"Will you give me a moment with my father?"

"Yes, of course. Go into the room beside me and draw the curtain."

Joseph and Lapidoth slipped into the room and faced each other. "Father? What is your wisdom? What do you say?"

"It is your life too, my son. If you see a way out, tell me, because I do not. I have struggled to remain as far away from Omar as I could get, but that was nearly impossible with Miriam at my throat. I could not protect you from her either. Rahab is the wise and strong one. She managed to stay out of Miriam and Omar's clutches. I pray she and Deborah are still together. That is the only way Deborah will survive. She cannot survive with you, Lapidoth. Had you consulted me before you married, I would have warned you."

"Then let us find our way out from inside the business, rather than running away. We will only be pursued. Sometimes the only way out is in and through. Nothing worse can happen to us than has already transpired."

Lapidoth and Joseph returned to Omar's presence. "I hope you have seen the good sense of my offer?" Omar announced and asked at the same time.

"We are not sure what is good sense at this point, but yes, Omar, we are with you," replied Lapidoth in a strong convincing voice.

Omar clapped his hands, ordered the guard to bring his best wine, and proposed a toast to their success.

*   *   *

Sisera stormed back into his main camp. His guards scattered to call the troops to attention. He looked around with satisfaction at the polished chariots and the arms ready for battle. He stepped up to a podium and shouted, "The glorious King Jabin has ordered me to subdue the territory of Napthali and prepare to invade Ephraim! We will drive right down through the middle of the land and not stop until we have taken it all!"

Cheers roared up from the soldiers. They were tired of small war parties, skirmishes against defenseless villages, looting, and killing old people. They wanted a real war!

The word came to Jael of the danger and Heber carried the message to Hannah. Hannah piled stones on her garden wall to signal her shepherd to come and carry the message through their communications relay to Barak and Deborah. Heber convinced Hannah it was no longer safe for her to stay alone in the hills. Reluctantly she agreed to return with him to Jael's tent to stay until the battle was over.

"Has Judith passed?" inquired Heber gently.

"Yes. I closed her eyes not long after you left to return home. I sent word to Amram who sits at the gate with the elders. He, Rabbi Amri, and Leah came immediately. I sent word to Deborah and Moshe that there was no need for them to make the dangerous trip home. We can mourn her passing together when the time is right."

"What of Abinoam and Sarah?"

"They are quite frail and prefer to remain in their home. I gave them some herbal remedies for their bones and asked Amram to promise me he would look after them. He seemed relieved to have something useful to do and agreed. I sent that message to Barak and Deborah as well."

Heber helped her onto his donkey and they made the trek north toward Jael's tent. A group of soldiers rode past them heading north, but paid no attention to two seemingly insignificant old people and a plodding donkey. They were in a great hurry. For that and Jael's prayers Heber was most grateful. Travel on the roads was becoming more risky by the day.

*   *   *

Iscah's husband, Ehud, returned home one evening with a guest, Akhmed the Egyptian. Miriam could hear the voice of the man who lifted her cover in the cart and gave her his flask. She knew that voice from somewhere else as well, but could not place it. When Iscah asked Miriam if she would come meet their guest, Miriam complained of not feeling well and declined for that reason. Iscah was not surprised. Miriam's recovery had been long and slow. She often had spells of feeling faint and took to her bed for a few days at a time.

Miriam needed time to let her damaged brain recall the memory that floated just beyond her immediate reach. She sensed it held either great danger or great advantage, she could not tell which. She knew if she coaxed it gently, it would come like a slow dawn to her conscious mind.

Akhmed and Ehud were chatting when Iscah joined them again. "What is your cousin's name?" inquired Akhmed politely.

"Miriam, cousin of Omar," replied Iscah.

When Akhmed raised his eyebrows, Iscah wondered if she should have mentioned Omar.

"I seem to remember a Miriam at Omar's palace several years ago. Do you think she would receive me for a moment?"

Iscah became wary. This was a most unusual request, to intrude upon a woman's privacy. "Perhaps some other time. She has been quite ill and any stress would be harmful."

Ehud signaled the servant for more wine. He was anxious to get back to their business discussion. "What interest do you have in Miriam?"

"Really none that I know of. I just have a memory that is not quite clear. I am sure it is nothing." Akhmed waived it off and was also eager to get back to business.

Iscah went back to Miriam's room and whispered, "Do you know an Egyptian man named Akhmed?"

Miriam started at the name. "I do not know. There is something that will not come to mind. I need time to let it come through. Is he here?"

"Yes, he came with Ehud. I told him you have been ill and cannot see anyone."

"He knows I am here? Who told him?"

"Ehud. I do not know why. He knows your name and that you are connected with Omar."

"Iscah, I cannot let him see me until I know who he is and why his name is familiar. My life has been endangered more than once and I do not know who else might come for me if they know I am alive."

"Perhaps he will tell Ehud why your name is familiar when connected with Omar. If he does I will tell you what he says."

"Be careful, Iscah. Give nothing more away."

"I will say nothing. I will listen." Iscah turned and went out of Miriam's room, back to the main room. Ehud and Akhmed were deep in conversation, so she sat down at her loom and began to weave. She heard only talk of business, nothing more about Miriam.

It was late and the lamps were lit when Ehud invited Akhmed to be their guest for the night. Akhmed gratefully accepted. Iscah instructed the servant to show him to a room at the other end of the house, away from Miriam's room.

In the morning Akhmed left without inquiring about Miriam. Ehud went about his business for the day and Iscah busied herself with the servants, planning the meals and the purchase of food. Miriam stayed in her room and Iscah brought her a light breakfast and water.

"How are you this morning, Miriam?"

"I am well enough but the memory I seek has not yet spoken to me. Is this man, Akhmed, gone?"

"Yes, for now. He did not ask after you again."

"He will. Thank you, Iscah, for shielding me. I will not be a burden on you for long."

"You are no burden, Miriam! Where will you go? Please stay with me. I love having you here."

Miriam smiled her crooked smile and patted Iscah's hand. "I will sleep now."

Miriam kept a knife from the kitchen under her bedding. As Iscah left the room, Miriam touched the knife to be sure it was still there where she could reach it. She ate a few more bites of her breakfast food and went sound asleep.

*   *   *

Deborah emerged from her tent dressed as a soldier. She marched into Barak's tent to announce it was time to call upon the leaders of the tribes of Israel and Judah to send their quota of able-bodied men to join them against Sisera. Barak was a little taken back at the sight of her in battle garb. Suddenly she was a warrior queen! She had the demeanor of a leader rising to lead her people to victory.

"You will surely be with me, Deborah? I cannot go into battle without your blessing, your presence." She smiled and came to stand by him over the maps of the territories.

"I will, Barak. Fear not. We should count the tribes that will surely come. There will be those who are more remote and will not respond to the call to battle."

He smiled and quickly agreed. "Word has come from Hannah that Sisera is mobilizing. We will gather from the tribes a great army and I will move them to Mount Tabor to guard the northern entrance to the plain. The tribes of Zebulun and Napthali will already be there with me and Issachar will come." He traced the territory northward with his finger.

"I will send out the call in my name as judge and prophetess of our God, a Mother in Israel. I will send word to the tribal league of leaders for their quota of soldiers to join us immediately. Since I am now of Ephraim by marriage, they will come. And Benjamin too. Small as that tribe is, they are faithful. And Machir who is near them will come."

"Reuben is weak, still clinging to the life of the sheep herders of long ago, and Dan is on the coast southwest of Ephraim, often defending us from Philistine invasions. Asher to the north of Zebulun on the coast of the Great Sea sits by his landings and does not move, content to trade with the Canaanites. The Gileadites do not cross the Jordan, acting as if they are not part of God's promised land."

"If they are attacked, they may change their minds!" smiled Barak. "The Hebrews followed the pillar of light through the desert. They were wise. Some do not move until they feel the heat and then it might be too late."

Barak was acutely aware of the change in Deborah. He was not accustomed to responding to a soldier who was a woman. It threw him a little off balance, but he hid his uncertainty by studying the maps and checking Abel's lists of soldiers, animals, and supplies.

Rahab came into Barak's tent with a list of the contents of each new camp. The camps seemed to grow in strength and resolve by the day. "The women have been able to gather supplies and store them in greater quantities now that they work together. They are proud to have a part in defending Israel and they thank you for that opportunity," said Rahab with pride. Rahab was now dressed as a soldier as well and Barak could hardly believe what was happening. His army was stronger because of women!

Then he remembered Deborah saying to him that God would give the victory into the hands of a woman. He tried not to let that hurt his pride. Certainly it would take an army to be victorious. What could one woman alone do? He looked at Deborah for a moment and the heat began to rise in his loins. He shook his head to clear his thoughts. "Come Abel, let us find Gideon."

Deborah was deep in thought and did not notice his abrupt exit.

* * *

Lapidoth and Joseph set about pulling together the trade lines that had broken because of Abdullah's death and Philistine infiltration. The merchants recognized them and were eager to continue the business, but the Danites and the Philistine raiders battled sporadically along the coast. The Philistine raiders had pushed more deeply into the hills of Danite territory and the men of Dan were banded together to push them back to the coast. The battles regularly disrupted the trade routes along the plain and coast between the north and south. They would erupt without notice. Travelers were robbed and killed. Caravans were scattered and looted.

Lapidoth and Joseph began to make a plan. "I will go south into Egyptian territory to find mercenary guards who will travel with us," said Lapidoth somewhat doubtfully. He remembered how the mercenaries nearly deserted them the last time they started out of Ashdod.

Joseph thought for a moment. "While you engage them, I will travel to Dan in the hills and ask the Danites for their help. They are not very friendly to us because they have always been jealous of Ephraim, whose tribe was given a much larger territory. But they might be willing to trade information about the north for information about the south and give us protection. We can help each other."

Joseph bid him God's protection and started for the hill country of Dan. Lapidoth began the lonely and dangerous trek south toward Gaza. But then Lapidoth's second thought was to go to Omar's palace. Since the servants had taken his mother to Gaza, they would know the safest route and people who would help him. Also they might know something about the mercenary, Akhmed, through whom he could find others.

"Yes," said Tebah servant of Omar setting wine and sweet meats before Lapidoth. "We took the lady Miriam, your mother, to the asylum north of Gaza. I am sorry, Master, she was very ill."

"There is no need to apologize for doing your job, Tebah. I know what my mother was like and I am surprised it did not happen years go."

"Thank you, Master. The way to the north of Gaza is no longer open. Renegades are using it and they will kill us if we try. Perhaps you remember that your mother has a cousin in the city of Gaza. It might be better to travel in the hills until you are south of Gaza and return by the Egyptian road north into the city."

"Ah, yes, I remember Iscah and Ehud. I have had no contact with them for many years. I do not know where they live in the city."

"If you will allow me to accompany you for your protection, I do know where they live and I can take you there."

"Can you leave your duties here?"

"Oh yes, Master. My son is grown now and he has been under my instruction to take over. Master Omar will approve, I am sure."

Lapidoth thought for a few minutes. It all sounded too quick and easy. He decided to stay at the house of Omar for the night and speak at length with Tebah in the morning. What are his skills as a bodyguard? Why does he seem eager to go to Gaza?

Tebah was up before dawn and prepared them for the trip. Lapidoth heard the rustling about and got up immediately, calling for Tebah.

"I did not wish to wake you, Master. However, your breakfast is ready. Shem will bring it to you." Tebah bowed and went out.

Lapidoth dressed and ate quickly. Tebah appeared again and announced they were ready to go. He handed Lapidoth his robe and bowed.

"Where in Gaza does Iscah live?"

"In the southern part where the wealthy people live, Master. Her house is marked in blue around the doors and windows."

"Thank you, Tebah," replied Lapidoth with some relief. Any suspicion of secrecy on Tebah's part was lifted. "If we should become separated, I will be able to find it."

"Yes, indeed, but we will not become separated. That would be dangerous for both of us. The roads are too hazardous for even lone robbers, so they stay in the protection of the city slums and prey on individuals in the marketplaces."

They started out together through territory Lapidoth did not recognize. He felt for the curved blade he kept close to his body making certain he could get to it quickly. He thought about Deborah, wondering where she was now. He inquired about Sisera's movements as they went through villages and met a traveler or two, but there was no news this far south. Was she really going to lead troops into battle? It seemed inconceivable. His marriage to her seemed more like a dream that was fading slowly. He struggled to remember her face.

*   *   *

Gideon and Naham once again prepared to travel into Napthali to assess Sisera's movements. Jerib came out of the camp to Barak's tent. "Sir, I wish to go with Gideon and Naham. I am skilled as a spy and wish to help my friend Naham who rescued me from making a deadly error close to Sisera's camp. We have begun to hear the scriptures here and I can see God's hand in Israel. They bring back memories of my childhood when someone read scripture. I cannot remember who read it or what the scripture was, but vague memories dance in the back of my mind each time I hear them. I wish to serve you and Israel with skills that kept me alive and brought me here."

Barak turned from his maps and frowned at Jerib. "Have you found any information about your origins? Where your family lives? What tribe you are from?"

"I have not sir, but I know God will reveal that to me when the time is right. I do not have to spend valuable time pursuing it. My purpose now is to serve God by serving Israel, if you will allow me."

Barak paused for a moment. Abel was at the tent door and nodded to Barak. Barak went out to speak with Abel. "He and his friends are already great assets in our army. I trust them completely."

Barak stepped back into his tent and faced Jerib. "We are honored to have you, Jerib. It is up to Gideon and Naham if they will take you. Go to their tent. They are preparing now."

Deborah and Rahab prepared to ride with a company of soldiers to the other camps. "I want to start with the farthest camp to get as close as I can to the battle field. I want to see for myself one more time what the land looks like."

"I want to see it too. How close are you planning to go?" questioned Rahab.

"Gideon and Naham will be back and stop at the last camp. We will wait for them to come back before we move any closer."

Rahab smiled at the thought of Gideon returning.

"I know that smile, Rahab," laughed Deborah. "You do not smile like that for anyone else!"

"I hope you are the only one who notices," returned Rahab laughing as well.

The company of soldiers was ready. Deborah and Rahab, in soldiers clothing, took their place in the middle of them.

"The territory is more dangerous than ever," advised Barak. "Please be careful . . ." His words trailed off as he met Deborah's gaze. "I know God will take care of you."

Deborah stepped forward and touched his arm. "Thank you, Barak. I am sure God speaks through you as well. I will be watchful."

The electricity between them was palpable. They found it difficult to break away.

"Oh!" Rahab bent down and brushed a twig from the hem of her robe, hoping to draw the attention away from Barak and Deborah for that moment. The soldiers immediately turned to Rahab and the moment passed.

The trek through the hills and over goat paths was difficult. It took more time as the scouts went ahead and reported back. Passing the fourth camp, the scouts went out and did not return.

The captain of the small guard said, "We must retreat to the fourth camp. If the guards do not come back it will not be safe to continue on."

Deborah scowled. "Do you mean you will leave the scouts to fight alone? Barak would never countenance that! We will find a place to hide our gear and go to look for them!"

The captain laughed. "And are you going to be the one to go after them? You, a mere woman!"

"I believe you are new here, Sir," whispered Rahab stepping up to his back and pushing the point of her knife into his ribs. "It seems you are the one easily overtaken."

The soldiers near by chuckled and instantly stopped as their captain turned to face them. There was a deadly moment of silence until Deborah spoke. "You are quite right, Sir. I am a mere woman and an emissary of our Lord, the most high. I am also a prophet, seer, and warrior. And as you can see by the knife in your back, my good fortune is better than yours. I will lead this army along with Barak and you will see the hand of the Lord for yourself. Meanwhile, I will lead the search party if you are too afraid!"

Rahab withdrew her knife and placed it under her robe in an accessible place. The red-faced captain wheeled on Deborah speechless.

Deborah stood her ground and looked upon him with resolve and compassion. "It was not my intention to insult you, Captain, but you forced me with insults of your own."

She turned to the men around them. "I ask you not to laugh at your captain now or ever. I suggest we show respect for God and each other, unless you want to be dead under Sisera's chariot wheels. Through God and mutual respect, we will win this war!"

He was about to make a grab for the power again until he looked at the expressions of admiration on his men's faces. "Our apology, Captain. We were caught by surprise. We meant no disrespect," said one of them.

"Then let us not be surprised by Sisera! We will continue to the fifth camp and look for our scouts," announced the captain.

Deborah whispered to Rahab, "Did you not think I would be victorious?"

"Oh, I knew you would be! I just wanted to be part of the fun! I wanted them all to know we are more than just two women without means. We are a team, a powerful and dangerous team. I have something for you and I would be grateful if you would accept it."

Rahab pulled a knife with a curved blade from her robe and handed it to Deborah.

"Rahab! I do not know what to say! I have never carried a knife. What will you do without it?"

"Oh, this is an extra one I picked up along the way. I have been saving it until I was sure you would not only be heavenly enough to trust God, but earthly enough to know God has ways of insuring the success of his chosen."

"I welcome you, team member! I am fortunate to have such a capable partner and friend, and one who has her own understanding of God. You are wise where I am lacking, and I am glad to learn."

"Let me show you how to hold it to best advantage, and how to thrust at just the right moment."

Deborah took a deep breath and turned the knife over in her hands. "Is it anything like preparing lamb for the spit?"

"Yes precisely, except your opponent may not be a lamb. Follow my movements and imitate them exactly."

Deborah and Rahab set about practicing and sparring. "Someone will think we are having a quarrel!" exclaimed Deborah.

"Let them think what they will and beware the power of women."

They set out again looking for signs of their scouts. Kelev had followed them even though Rahab had given him orders to stay in the main camp. He came abruptly out of the woods and nuzzled Rahab's hand.

One man had his knife drawn. "Do you know this animal?" he asked in surprise at the familiar greeting.

"Yes, he is my companion. Although I ordered him to stay in camp, my orders seem to last only an hour before he breaks and comes after me. I should have known he would do the same now."

"Why did you order him so?" asked Deborah.

"I thought with the spies and scouts being gone, he could help guard the camp. I guess he decided he was not needed there. I forget he has a mind and wisdom of his own. Captain, do you have any possessions belonging to the scouts?"

"Yes, we have their packs of belongings."

"Would you be kind enough to get them for me?"

The captain ordered the packs to be brought to Rahab. She beckoned Kelev to pick up the scent. With a low bark, Kelev ran out ahead of them.

"He will pick up the scent of the scouts and follow it until he finds them."

"How do you know this?" asked the captain completely puzzled.

"Dogs have sensitive noses and can follow a scent trail for miles. If the scouts do not cross water the scent will remain. If they do cross water, he will cross to the other embankment and look until he picks it up again. We must hurry after him. If there is danger for us he will stop and warn us."

"It seems I am learning new things by the hour. First women and now dogs!" The captain ordered his men forward to follow Kelev.

Kelev took them into thick brush and down steep cliffs. He growled at the base of trees and tore on when he found the scent again. When the soldiers got behind, he came back and gave a low bark as if to say, "Hurry up! This way!"

Hurrying through the dense undergrowth, Rahab stumbled over something. She parted the brush and discovered a barely alive scout, one of the two. Kelev pulled at Deborah's sleeve. She dropped down by Rahab's side.

"He is breathing. Let us find the wound," she whispered gently turning him.

"Here, on the back of his head. He may have struck his head falling. Let us see if there is another that caused him to fall." There was a slight wound in his leg. Fang marks.

Rahab immediately pulled out her knife and cut above the marks. Deborah reached into her herb pouch and brought out something that she packed into the cut. "I do not know if it is too late, but the blow to the head may have slowed his heart and breathing, and the spread of the poison as well." Hannah had taught her to find the pulse that came from the heart.

The men came back and stood over the scout.

"Do not move him," instructed Deborah, "until his breathing is stronger. That will be a sign that the poison will do no more damage."

"Kelev, go!" ordered Rahab. Kelev turned again toward the other scent and enthusiastically continued his hunt, the men pursuing him. Two men stayed with Rahab and Deborah, even though Rahab insisted they were not needed.

An hour later a triumphant Kelev emerged from the wood followed by Gideon. Naham and Jerib were dragging the second scout between them. They laid him down in the shade and he did not stir. Deborah went immediately to his side. "Where is he injured?"

"He was shot through with an iron tipped arrow. His blood was drained before we could stop it."

"Yes, I see he is dead," whispered Deborah berating herself for staying behind. "I might have saved him."

Gideon squatted down beside her. "No, Deborah, he was gone when we picked him up, else we would have carried him, not dragged him. There were sounds all around us and we needed to move back quickly. There was nothing anyone could do for him."

He rose and turned to look at the other scout. "Is he alive?"

"Barely," replied Rahab hugging Kelev. "He has a poison snake bite and a head wound. We will know in an hour if he will live."

Gideon watched Rahab tend the young scout. Strong and tough as he was, he suddenly longed for the tender ministrations of this woman. He abruptly turned himself away from her toward the immediate requirements of their situation. He strode over to the captain and shared his assessment of their situation. "We are closer to Camp Five, but we may encounter the enemy getting there. We could retreat to Camp Four, but then we would leave Camp Five without intelligence of the enemy."

"I will go to Camp Five and bring help," offered Jerib.

The captain agreed immediately. "Go. When you return we will either be able to move this man, or he will die and we will bury him. We must move on."

Jerib sprinted off into the wilderness. He held his head low and he made not a sound.

*   *   *

Joseph struggled against his bonds. He had not convinced the Danites his story was true. "You are a spy for the Philistines! Tell us their plans!" Someone kicked his leg.

"I am Joseph of Ephraim, father of Joab and Lapidoth. I have come here to ask your help and offer payment."

Word went out among the Danites until a man came to look at Joseph, and verified that he was indeed of the tribe of Ephraim. "I have seen him leaving Ashdod headed toward Ephraim. He may be a thief or be working with the Egyptian black market. What is his business? What does he offer?"

Another who seemed to be their leader said, "What do you think the tribe of Dan, given the smallest territory, can do for the great Ephraim?"

"We are your brothers, not your enemy. The territory was given long ago, and we did not have a choice in the matter. The Philistines have caused battles to occur on the trade routes, and we ask your help in guarding those roads to keep them open."

"And you offer us money? We are herders. What need of money have we?"

"You also defend all of our lands from the Philistines. Money would buy you better weapons and more information. You may be a small territory, but you can be a mighty tribe as well."

"Unbind him!" ordered Manoah, leader of the camp. Others jumped to cut Joseph's bonds. "The call has gone out from Deborah the judge in Israel for the league of leaders to send their quota of troops to aid Barak. We have not responded to the call, but other tribes have. Soldiers are going north now to join Napthali and Issachar against Sisera the Canaanite. There is to be war! Who will keep the Philistines at bay if we go, too?"

Joseph's eyes widened. "Deborah? Who is this Deborah you speak of?"

"She is a prophet of God anointed to lead the armies against Sisera in the battle to come."

Joseph took a deep breath and forcibly returned his mind to the matter at hand. "All the more reason for you to help us. Our world is changing and you will need riches and weapons of a more sophisticated nature.

"What is it you wish us to do?" questioned Manoah.

"My son and I are traders. We need to know when the Philistines are present on the road. We will fight with you in order to get our goods through to the north. Your part will be a tenth of our profits."

Manoah was doubtful, but looked over his men and noted their shepherd's rags. With a few crude weapons they barely held out against the Philistines in the last attack, but they might not hold out for long.

"Where will we buy arms with iron tips, as you say?"

"We will bring them to you and teach you to make them yourselves."

"What is the danger?"

"The danger is what you have always faced, the ever stronger Philistines who will bring more weapons like these and one day will overrun your lands."

"Can you be sure of getting these weapons for us? Where will you find them?"

"You have already told us there is a war to come in the north with the Canaanites. The general, Sisera, prides himself on having such weapons. The northern tribes are terrified of him. As God is with us, there will be spoils left on the battlefields. Some will be gathered by the peasants and traded among themselves, some finding their way into the coastal marketplaces. There will be more than one source."

Manoah scratched his chin and thought for a while. "It will be done. We will send word. You will draw the marauders out and we will attack."

Joseph had not intended himself as bait for the attacks. It was a surprise, but he was sure it was the best agreement he would get.

He made his way back to Ashdod to confer with Omar on these plans. He was not sure Omar would be pleased to have his trade exposed, but Omar did not have an army of his own. It seemed to be the best outcome. "Deborah!" he repeated to himself. "My son is married to the leader of the Israelite army! Does he know this? Does he know of the battle she is about to wage against Sisera?" It boggled his thinking.

CHAPTER 25

Miriam began walking to the market with Iscah each morning to strengthen her legs. She still walked with a limp and her mouth was still crooked. But she did not care. She had a goal, to make them all pay, and what did she care about her appearance. She needed to be strong and independent.

With each step she would silently say their names. "Joseph, Omar, Rahab, Deborah, Lapidoth and all Omar's servants." It gave her pleasure to remember their names and list them in her mind over and over.

She fingered the cloth at the merchants' booths. "I must regain my fortune and I will purchase whatever I want. I will be beautiful again. I will have clothes, cosmetics, a jeweled cane, and my foot on the neck of Omar that traitor. I will settle with Joseph once and for all time." The merchant noticed she was mumbling and shooed her away thinking she was drunk.

Seeing the merchant's reaction Iscah stepped in. "Anything you want, Miriam, just let me know. I will pay. You must have clothes and jewels. You must have face creams and colors."

"You are so kind, Iscah. I will repay you when I regain my fortunes," said Miriam barely concealing her disgust that she was reduced to begging from relatives. She picked out cloth and cosmetics, and jeweled sandals. Iscah's servant came behind her and paid the merchants.

The servants rushed the cloth to the seamstress to be designed into beautiful garments. When Miriam tried them on she was surprised at the perfect fit. She slipped her feet into the jeweled sandals and looked at herself approvingly in the reflection pool in the inner courtyard.

"Are you pleased, Madam?" inquired the seamstress. "I can change anything that displeases you."

"You have done well," said Miriam flatly. "I am pleased." Miriam never before said that to a servant but it seemed to roll out of her mouth unbidden. She dismissed the seamstress and sat down to think.

"Miriam, you look beautiful! May I send in some tea," inquired Iscah.

Beautiful? Iscah was still beautiful. She was not, but she did not care. "Yes, please do, Iscah." Miriam knew she had to get strong enough to leave and get about her business. She fought to remember what the physician, Rajnish, told her to do in order to heal. She could feel the fury rising within her but pushed it back down. She dared not let it injure her again.

*　　*　　*

Lapidoth hoped to meet Akhmed at an inn on the edge of Gaza. He sent a message to Akhmed through a village slave. It worked. Akhmed came.

"Omar needs your help, Akhmed. He has taken the murdered Abdullah's place and the trade routes are so populated by brigands and marauders we would not make it past the first village out of Ashdod."

"Did Omar send you to find me?"

"Not exactly. My father and I are working for Omar."

"I thought you wanted to be free of this business!"

"I did and I do, but I find myself hopelessly ensnared again. There seems to be no way out at this time. So I have decided to continue until the next opportunity to be free presents itself."

"Be careful, Lapidoth. You may be telling me too much."

"How so? I have confided much to you over the past months. Do you wish me harm?"

"No, I do not. But I am an impartial mercenary for hire to the highest bidder."

"I see."

"What do you need me for? Why now? Or should I ask, what does Omar want of me?"

"I want to say I need a friend, but that is not realistic. I need a body guard and guide, much the same as you have been to me before."

"And what of your father?"

"He has gone north to engage some of the Danites since they have many skirmishes with the Philistines and know the territory."

"Has he been successful?"

"I have not heard from him. They might kill him. The Danites and the Ephraimites are not friends. There is much jealousy on the part of the Danites. It is a chance he decided to take."

"Yes, I have heard about those two tribes and the uneven distribution of the territory. Can you pay me?"

"I can pay. I have kept funds stored in various places over the years."

"I will give you my answer tomorrow. Meet me at the home of Ehud and Iscah. I believe you know them."

Lapidoth's eyebrows shot up. "You know my mother's cousin?"

"Yes. I have business with Ehud. Again be careful. I believe your mother is lodging there after an escape from an asylum. I understand from a servant girl that she is recovering from an illness under Iscah's care. She is still a danger to you. The servants say she talks in her sleep and repeats over and over, 'I will repay them all.' She speaks your name, your father's, and Omar's. Probably that includes Deborah and Rahab as well."

"Does she have someone who will obey her wishes? Someone who will carry out her retributions?"

"I am not sure. She seems financially dependent upon Iscah. But if she has resources, I think she would try to engage me if she learns who I am. So I have not spoken to her, but I am sure Iscah innocently told her I was there with Ehud."

"Is it then wise for us to meet at Ehud's home?"

"She and Iscah go to the market every morning. But if she is there, perhaps you can get a better read on what she plans. Do not be shocked when you see her. I understand her illness is of the brain and it has altered her face and lamed her body."

"My father lamented that her illness made her more enraged than ever. I cannot imagine how anyone could be any worse. She can be more dangerous than a mob of Philistines! I must get word to Omar and my father that she is not dying or dead, but very much alive and on the move."

"Tomorrow morning then?"

"Yes, tomorrow."

Lapidoth hired a surefooted ass and rode quickly to the family farm where he had a cache of money. He dug furiously near the corner of the family house and was relieved it was still there. It took all day and night to get the money, and ride back to Ehud's home for his meeting with Akhmed. He was early and waited in an alley nearby. Presently Iscah and Miriam emerged from the gate and walked toward the market. It was indeed a shock to see Miriam. She looked even more evil then ever. Her face was lopsided and her gate was halting.

"Amazing she has survived," said Akhmed coming up to stand by his side.

"Her ravaged body is a slave to her will, as is everyone around her," growled Lapidoth.

Once inside the courtyard, Ehud emerged from the house and greeted them. "Lapidoth! This is a surprise! Welcome to my house. What brings you? Surely you are not here to take your mother home."

"I am not here to take her anywhere. She seeks my life and my father's. Akhmed and I have some business to transact and then I will be leaving. I would be honored to spend more time speaking with you, Ehud, but not here."

"I understand. Come in, Akhmed. You can meet in the back of the house and leave by the back gate. Be advised the servants listen at the walls and doors. Sometimes I think they have a gift to hear thoughts before they are spoken. I will advise you if the women return, but they usually take their time. Miriam must rest frequently. She is still weak and cannot walk too far."

Akhmed and Lapidoth went to the back of the house and sat down to settle the details and finances of their agreement. For a few days Akhmed would continue to visit Ehud and glean what he could about Miriam's plans. Ehud would help. Lapidoth would stay in Gaza and try to determine Omar's connections to the Egyptian smugglers. He would have to step carefully and not expose himself as a spy.

*   *   *

Sisera preferred to be the general of his army rather than be a king, even a minor king. In his absence Sisera's mother, Ashubaal, commanded the palace household, the business of their Canaanite territory, and the religious observances.

Sisera was away at his encampments or visiting other Canaanite kings for much of the time. She enjoyed his absences as well as his presence. When he was absent she could be in complete control. Her word as a Queen Mother was law. The kingdom would be in no danger should he be disabled and unable to rule. She would rule for him as regent. It suited her well.

"Oh, yes. I enjoy his return from battles, especially from rich nations," she thought as she fingered the fine veils, gowns, robes and coverlets that adorned her dressing rooms.

"I do not know why he desires to attack these backward Hebrews from Israel and Judah. They have nothing but stone huts and sheep dung. It makes me furious to think he would endanger his own life for that! If only he would listen to me. There is far more to be gained in the east. But no! He is fixated on this rabble for some reason. They are no match for his charioteers. What could the fascination be?"

Lilah, one of Ashubaal's ladies of the court, was a favorite of Sisera.

"Perhaps she would know what it is," frowned the Queen Mother. "I shall ask her and if she does not know, she must find out!"

Lilah came at Ashubaal's bidding. "How may I serve you, Lady?"

"It seems my son is fixated on war with the rabble Hebrews. Do you know the reason?"

"He has said nothing to me. He has been here so seldom, there is not time to talk. He does not want talk from me. I will inquire where I can and will bring you any news."

"There must be a reason. They are of no account and will increase neither our power nor riches. I must know why!"

She turned suddenly to Lilah. "Take a guard with you and go into the city. Question people without raising suspicion."

"I am not sure I understand, my Lady. Suspicion?"

"You do not need to understand, Lilah. Go and see what you can learn."

Lilah was a little hurt by the rebuke but dared not show it. She curtsied and quietly left to find a guard to accompany her. At the taverns where she inquired they laughed and called out to her, "Everyone knows it is not the Hebrews but their god who hates us all!"

"Tell me what you know of this god. Why does he hate us?"

"Their god is Yahweh who takes as consort our Asherah and defiles her. We would rescue Asherah and destroy this god. Then Asherah will bless us with riches!"

Lilah frowned. "I have seen no statues of this god."

"He is the invisible god!" laughed one man. "Who ever heard of an invisible god? Is he ashamed to show himself? Does he not have fine clothes? Baal is not afraid to be seen!"

"If he is invisible, how can he defile Asherah?" asked Lilah completely puzzled.

"I hear her altar stands captive beside Yahweh's. They share the worship of the people, Yahweh being higher."

"How do you know so much?" demanded Lilah's guard.

"I am a merchant and I travel the country north to south, east to west. I hear many things. Perhaps you should go see for yourself!" Everyone in the tavern laughed uproariously.

Lilah and her guard departed. She hurried back to the palace to report to Ashubaal what she had heard.

"That is absurd. Why would Sisera care about the gods?"

"He thinks only of you, my Lady. He knows you hold the love of Asherah in your heart and perhaps believes she will bring you more riches if he destroys the people of Yahweh."

"I thought it might be a queen or princess he desires. But there are no kings among the Hebrews, so there would be no queens or princesses. It still sounds absurd, but what other explanation could there be?"

Lilah stood quietly by, trembling a bit at the thought of Sisera desiring a foreign princess and abandoning her. At length Ashubaal dismissed her.

"Yes, I have the love of Asherah and I know her power. But it is a mistake to attack another nations' god. It makes the people many times stronger when defending their god. Even a ragged people like the Hebrews can show amazing strength. That is what makes Yahweh strong, the passion of his people. I must speak to Sisera and soon."

Ashubaal sat by her window and gazed through the latticework out onto the hills. She could not shake the feeling of doom that grew in her heart and made her shiver. A servant brought her a robe and placed it around her shoulders.

"My Lady? Are you not well?"

"I am well. Send for the guards to ready my chariot. I will go to Sisera's camp! Go quickly!"

The road to the camp was rough and Ashubaal clung to the side of the chariot. She demanded to the driver, "Go faster!"

He shouted over the rumble of the iron wheels and the clatter of the horses' hooves, "But my Lady, we will both be thrown from the chariot! Sisera would have my head!"

She tightened her grip. "Go faster!"

*   *   *

Deborah stood in a high pass overlooking the Kishon Valley. Her robe was blowing in the wind and her hood fell back revealing her vibrant red gold hair. She was every inch a commander. The strength welled up in her body and her resolve grew into a driving force thinking of God's command that she and Barak defeat Sisera.

The river would be rising and soon it would spill over most of the valley. God would tell her when the valley floor would be soft deep mud, when the time was right.

"This is the pass I will come through when Barak and his army are in place," she said to Rahab. "We will show ourselves to Sisera when he is nearly into the mud of the valley. He will charge into the swamp toward us and Barak will attack them from Mount Tabor. His soldiers will throw down hundreds of branches in front of the army so they will not sink when they go after Sisera's foot soldiers."

Rahab caught her breath at the sight of this transfigured woman. It seemed that Deborah grew taller, larger than life, for the moment. Then she turned to Rahab with a smile, and she was again the familiar friend and confidant. They turned to go back to Camp Five. Jerib met them and guided them through the forest.

"The spy is still alive," he whispered. "The women at Camp Five are ministering to his wounds and caring for him."

Arriving at the camp Deborah and Rahab went immediately to the women's compound to the mat of the spy. Deborah touched his forehead. "He is cool. His body is no longer fighting, but healing. This is good." She took the blood soaked herbs from his wound and replaced them with fresh ones.

Gideon stepped up beside Rahab and whispered, "A wonderful idea to bring the women to serve in the camps."

Rahab was startled and whirled to face Gideon. "It is you! I thought someone was sneaking up on me."

"You could say I was sneaking up on you, but that is nothing new. In my heart I have been stalking you. Since I first saw you I have thought about you day and night. At your home in Bethel I was sure you would gut me with your knife if I made a move toward you."

Rahab could not keep from laughing out loud. "Indeed, I might have done that, and a good job of it, too!"

He stood there for a moment inhaling the perfume of her body. His passions began to rise. He turned and glanced around for a place where they might be alone. When he looked back toward her, she was gone.

Then he saw her colorful shawl hanging from a low branch. He circled around behind the compound wall. Making sure he was not seen he moved quickly toward the bush. Taking the shawl, he disappeared into the woods. He knew she would be waiting for him in a hidden glade beyond the camp perimeter. Excitement rippled through his body as he slipped soundlessly through the trees. A whiff of her perfume was in the air, and suddenly she leaped out at him like a cat and brought him to the ground.

He rolled over on top of her, pinning her arms to the ground. "No one has ever surprised me like that and lived! You could be dead!"

"I am anything but dead," she whispered.

*　　*　　*

Miriam thought the house felt strange, like something was going on behind her back. Ehud seemed nervous and left abruptly on an errand. He drew Iscah out to the gate with him, leaving Miriam standing alone. She turned to see Lapidoth standing in the doorway glowering at her.

"Mother, I see you are recovering," he said coolly. "If you wish to continue in good health, I warn you not to send someone to murder me, Joseph, Rahab, Deborah, Omar, or anyone else. Enjoy what you have left of your life and do not mess it up again. The next trip to the asylum will be to a locked cell underground. Do I make myself clear?"

Miriam's mouth quivered and she stumbled backward. She caught herself on an urn and landed against the wall. "You bastard! What do you know about anything! What are you accusing me of?" she sputtered, the panic rising in her voice.

"Do not play innocent, Mother. You have been killing the whole family one way or another all our lives. And now you plan actual murder, do you not? Or so Omar told me. I believe you are crazy and the whole family will agree. So behave yourself unless you enjoyed life in the asylum."

Miriam's eyes were wide with rage. She threw a piece of pottery at him and stumbled from the room. Collapsing on her bed she gasped for breath. "I must remain calm," she desperately told herself. Soon her breathing was easier but she was terribly thirsty. When she reached for a goblet of water the room began to spin. The goblet smashed on the floor and she lost consciousness.

Lapidoth looked in on her and then left the house. He went to the inn to change into peasant robes and headed for the port taverns. The black market trade always came through the ports and the taverns were dens of merchants and thieves. He walked through the alleys and onto the docks. He did not question anyone, just listened to the conversations hoping for hints of Omar's connections. Not much was revealed and he sensed he was being followed. He fingered his knife and stepped behind a tent in the marketplace. The man came by close enough for Lapidoth to see his face. He recognized him as one of the men from the ship to Sidon and also at the gate of Dan. Following the man behind a warehouse, Lapidoth grabbed his head, pulled it back and cut his throat. He threw the body into an empty corner of the warehouse and slipped away into the alleys.

He decided it was time to leave Gaza and head north to find Joseph. Hopefully his father would have good news about the Danites. The trade routes would be safe again and they would be in business. He found a small caravan going north and joined it as unobtrusively as possible. He kept constant vigil around him in case anyone else was following him.

*   *   *

Ashubaal arrived at Sisera's camp. The men were shocked to see their queen arriving in a chariot at full gallop. "My Lady, King Sisera left for King Jabin's palace two days ago. Then he planned to come straight home to your palace. May we escort you back home while it is still daylight?"

Disappointed she ordered her driver to turn around and accepted the escort.

Sisera returned home before Ashubaal got back. He was in a great mood when he came into the palace. He leaped up the steps two and three at a time. "Bring me Lilah, food, and wine!" The servants rushed to open the drapes in his chambers to let in the cool evening air.

He sipped his wine and eyed Lilah's lithe body. "Did you miss me, my dove?"

"You are always gone so long," she pouted. "Perhaps I will find another to amuse me."

He pulled her down onto the bed, brushed her hair back, and began to pull up her tunic. "You will not find a lover such as I, my dear, and you know it. Do not threaten me. It is useless." He dropped his robe on the floor and rolled on top of her, the heat rising in his loins.

She ran her fingers through his hair and moaned. "And you are hopeless."

"My son has returned! Where is he?" demanded Ashubaal.

The servant lowered his head and glanced toward the door to the private quarters.

"Never mind. I know where he is. Summon him to the great hall when he is . . . free."

"Yes, my Lady." An embarrassed servant scurried away to find the chamber servant who knew how to do this task without causing shouts and curses from Sisera. He did not savor another beating for his missteps.

Ashubaal paced the hall from window to window, waiting for Sisera. She knew he would take his time, and he knew she would wait.

"Mother!" He strode confidently across the distance to her side. He kissed her cheeks and embraced her. "What do you want of me so late?"

"I want to know why you must battle the Hebrews. What do they have that you want?"

"For one thing, they continue to attack the Canaanite villages and encroach upon our territory."

"That is a lie, Sisera. They seem to live quite peaceably with the Canaanite villagers until soldiers interfere. Tell me the truth. Or do you know the reason why at all?"

"It is King Jabin," he sighed impatiently. "He demands that we destroy them and stamp out their belief in this invisible god, Yahweh. They become arrogant when their god is insulted and it makes them increasingly dangerous. King Jabin believes they are building an army. They have been spying on us from the heights."

"And if you think this is true why do you not capture the spies and force them to tell you what they know of this army?"

"How much of an army can they have? They are untrained peasants with no metal weapons! They would be fools to attack us and if they do, will surely go down in defeat the first hour of the attack. It is a nuisance, but it must be done to appease King Jabin. Asherah forbid we should ignore Jabin and he be proved right!"

"Be careful how you use Asherah's name, Sisera. Have you made the proper sacrifices at her altars?"

"The sacrifices have been made, Mother. Our victory is assured." Sisera kissed his mother again and returned to his quarters where Lilah awaited him. He looked forward to entering her warm body again, more wine, and a good night's sleep.

*   *   *

Barak rode into Camp Five with a large army of Ephraimites. They were eager to see their leader, Deborah, and Barak was also eager to see her. He went right to the women's compound to find her. Deborah greeted him at the gate of the compound. "One spy is dead from a metal tipped arrow. The other is injured but will recover. He was bitten by a snake and fell hitting his head on a rock."

Barak turned from joy at seeing Deborah to sudden concern for the spies. They went into the compound together to see the recovering spy. Barak knelt down beside him. "Did you get any information on Sisera's movements?"

"Yes, Captain. You will need to move the armies from Issachar and Napthali quickly to the east and take them with Zebulunites to Mount Tabor before Sisera can cut them off from us. Sisera will come at us from the west through the territory of Asher."

"Thank you, soldier. You have done a fine job."

"I want to be with you, Captain, when you attack Sisera. It might be many more days before they come at us. I will be well enough by then. I must avenge my partner's death."

Deborah leaned close to the spy. "God will surely avenge his death and reward your faithful heart. God will care for him and all of us better than we can."

Barak smiled at Deborah and touched her arm. They walked together in the direction of the camp sergeant's tent. He was pleased to see how well organized this camp was. Being the farthest from the main camp, it needed a good leader and Abel had chosen well. It was almost ready for the battle to come. A tent was set up for Barak and a soldier brought the packs from the pack animals to him. This would be the first staging area closest to the battlefront.

Deborah helped him unpack and sort out the plans while he organized weapons and other gear. He seized a moment before the tent flap was tied up to pull her to him and kiss her passionately. She melted into the power of his arms and the masculine fragrance of his body. She could not stop herself until the words of Rahab came to her mind. "You will have a greater battle against your own passions than with the whole army of Sisera." She was a married woman and could not give into the fire in her body. Slowly she pulled away and turned to go.

369

"Deborah, I think more about you than I do the coming battle," panted Barak.

"This is our present battle and perhaps our most difficult one, Barak," she whispered breathlessly. "Sisera will come in his own time and we will think about him then. Now I must remember I cannot return to my husband pregnant with your child."

The words jolted Barak back to sanity. Yes, she was married. He tied the flap back and carried the pack harness back to where the animals were pastured. He stayed there for a time to clear his head. He knew Deborah was right. It would mean the end of all that was good in their lives. Near some trees he knelt down to pray asking with all his heart for strength and wisdom. He was now sure God would not grant them victory over Sisera if he defiled Deborah and himself in the heat of the moment.

*　　*　　*

Late in the afternoon Iscah went to Miriam's room to check on her. There had been no sounds from there all day. She found Miriam on the floor, the smashed goblet near her head. Iscah rang furiously for the servants who came running. They lifted Miriam onto the bed. When they turned her over she began to regain consciousness and looked wildly around.

"What happened? Why are you all here?"

"Miriam! You were unconscious on the floor. Do you remember what happened?"

Dimly she remembered Lapidoth confronting her, but she decided not to reveal it until she was sure what took place. "I . . . I am not sure. I remember reaching for the goblet of water. That is all."

"We must have stayed at the market too long and tired you too much. I am so sorry, Miriam."

"Do not blame yourself, Iscah. It was I who insisted on staying longer. This is only a small set back like many I have had. I must keep trying. I will be stronger soon."

The servants brought watered wine and bread to Miriam in her room. She was grateful for something light to eat and to have a reason to stay in her room. Her mind was slowly clearing and she remembered more of what transpired between her and Lapidoth. It was shocking. She had never seen him like that. Was he deliberately trying to provoke her into another stroke? Perhaps he thought it would be a way to kill her without delivering the blow himself.

*   *   *

Omar decided to close up shop and return to his palace. Until the trade routes were safe to travel again, he could only wait. From a distance he could see dust rising ahead of him. As he got closer a large crowd came into view. His servants ran out to meet him.

"Master! Lapidoth, Akhmed, Joseph, and a large group of Danites are at your gates."

Omar smiled broadly. He knew Joseph and Lapidoth had done well. "Welcome them, Tebah! Good fortunes are smiling upon us!"

Manoah, leader of the Danites, approached Omar immediately. "We have been promised a tenth of the profits. Is this agreeable? If it is not we will return home."

"Yes! Yes! Come into my home and be welcome. There is room for all of you. We shall work out the details tonight. First you must have a good dinner and good wine!"

Manoah was wary. Effusive greetings always made him suspicious. Omar looked like a fat slippery Philistine to him. Joseph assured him that Omar was definitely not Philistine.

Food and wine calmed some of their doubts. Akhmed turned into a skilled ambassador and spoke with everyone. Omar, Joseph, Lapidoth, and Manoah sat down together to hammer out a satisfactory agreement.

Later in the evening Lapidoth sat down with Omar and Joseph. "Miriam is not at the asylum, nor is she dead. She somehow escaped into Gaza to the home of Iscah and Ehud. Iscah has been helping her recover. I confronted her when I was there. I told her if she wanted to continue to recover and live a comfortable life, there had better not be any more attempts to murder any of us. She was her usual enraged self and threw pottery at me. Then she stumbled into her room. The last I saw of her, she was face down, half off her bed, and a broken water goblet was on the floor."

"She survived that hell hole in Gaza?" Omar shook his head. "If anyone could, she could do it. I will speak with my physician about it. He may be able to tell us if she is likely to continue to survive.

Lapidoth turned to his father. "Father, I hope I did not shock you. I was a little abrupt. I should have given you more of a warning."

"No warning is necessary, Lapidoth, unless she is actually coming to kill me. Then I would like to know ahead of time."

Lapidoth looked at his father with interest. He did not know Joseph had a wry wit. It was a pleasant discovery. Their lives had been so filled with angst and danger there had been no opportunity for that to come forth.

Omar burst into laughter and toasted them all. "To long life and great riches for us all!"

CHAPTER 26

Deborah set about dusting a robe with yellow saffron and crystals of mica to be sure Sisera would see a golden light shining from her. "Sisera must see me as the light of Yahweh blazing before him. He might even think I am Asherah coming to fight for Yahweh!"

Rahab helped her roll the robe inside out to preserve the dusting. "Remember your knife. If any of that rubbish makes it through the swamp and past your soldiers, you know what to do."

"Do you think God intends for me to physically fight, Rahab?"

"He may grant you the status of a hero by sending you one of the enemy on whom to blood your knife."

"Blood my knife?" To change the subject quickly Deborah asked with a sly smile, "Did I not see you and Gideon coming from the forest? What were you looking for?"

"Berries," replied Rahab with her chin held high.

"Do you want to tell me more?" teased Deborah.

"No, I do not. Even though I am a single woman and thought to be a harlot, I could still be stoned to death. So I will not even speak the words."

"That is a wise choice!" laughed Deborah. "Then there is no one to overhear and no temptation to tell another."

Turning from the subject again, Rahab smoothed the robe and asked, "Do you think this robe will entice Sisera? He is no fool."

"I hope it will frighten them all. They might hesitate for a moment and cause their own demise. If they stop their chariots to look at me, the chariots will sink and his foot soldiers will run right into Barak's advancing army."

"A great plan. Um, Deborah, have you thought perhaps Barak might be killed in the battle?"

Deborah heaved a heavy sigh. "I have tried not to dwell on that. When it worries me, I pray for his safety."

"And do you think God will grant you his safety?"

"His safety is between him and God. Barak is the one who must ask. Praying soothes my fears and reminds me of my faith that has brought me this far."

"I am always confused about that," said Rahab sitting with her chin on her fist. "How does God decide which favor to grant? If God does not give me what I ask for, what point is there in asking at all?"

"The point for me is to align my mind between God and what I ask. Then I let go of the request and return to faith in the right outcome for all of us. I have to believe in that even if things do not happen as I desire. God created the world. I did not. And even though there are times I am arrogant enough to think I could do a better job, I know that is foolishness."

"It sounds like a frightening mystery! We have no control over anything. How do we know what we are being faithful to?"

"It is a mystery and I cannot know it all, so I ask for deeper understanding of my place in it. Somehow it always soothes my fears."

"That sounds like the advice Hannah gave me, that Gideon would be in my life, but perhaps not the way I am thinking right now. A mystery indeed!"

*   *   *

Deborah met the leaders of the Ephraimites in Barak's tent. They looked worried and expressed doubts about this battle. She began to talk to them about scriptures. "Does it ever trouble you that Ephraim was given so much more territory than some others? Or have you just puffed yourselves up and looked down upon those with smaller territories?"

The worry on their faces changed to guilt.

"My brothers, we are engaged in a battle for the Lord, not just for ourselves. We could go on letting Sisera grow stronger, conquer more territories, and eventually find his way to Ephraim. If we do not gather together now to resist, they will run over us one by one and Ephraim will not be safe. Do you want to see statues of Baal in your cities and villages? Do you want Sisera's chariots to destroy your fields? Your sons will be killed and your daughters defiled by his soldiers. I know you thought it would be safer to remain in your own territory because you have seen no trouble as yet. But if you do, it will not be yours for long!"

There was grudging agreement as they talked among themselves.

"The day is coming when all God's tribes will join as one and become a great nation. Is that not what God promised Abraham? God knows we cannot survive divided, each one alone. Are we not all followers of Yahweh? Have we not come out of Egypt following the pillar of cloud by day and the pillar of fire by night? Joshua was given victory and we settled in a great land."

"But Joshua did not conquer all the land! There are many Canaanites and Philistines yet to fight!" shouted the leader.

"Do you expect one man to do all the work for you? Did you not think there would be continuing effort needed to carry on God's work? Abraham and Joshua were only the beginning of a great nation. We carry on the work. Our sons and daughters, our grandchildren and their children, will do so as well."

In the following days as Deborah walked among the soldiers she shouted, "Who is on the Lord's side? The Lord who grants us victory?"

There were shouts of assent. "The song of Deborah is great! We will follow her battle song! We will fight for the Lord! Victory! Victory!"

*   *   *

Lapidoth, Joseph, and the Danites started north on the main trade route with a caravan that had been stalled because of the danger. They moved as quickly as possible keeping watch every step of the way.

"It is as if the Philistines knew of our plans," whispered Joseph to Lapidoth. "Do you think there is a spy among us?"

Manoah rode up beside them. "What do you think?"

"We were wondering if they planted a spy in the caravan to learn our plans," replied Joseph being careful not to accuse and alienate the Danites.

"My men will walk among the members of the caravan and find who is alone, not traveling with companions. A spy would keep to himself. We will be discrete and not arouse suspicion. We cannot afford to be divided. If we find the spy we will deal with him quietly when we are out of danger. He can do no further damage now."

Lapidoth remembered how he traveled as a loner, dressed in peasant robes and keeping to himself. "I will help you, Manoah. I have traveled as a loner in the caravans many times, but I was not a spy."

"Good! You and two of my men can go without causing a stir. Tell them what you are looking for and make a plan among you."

Lapidoth's mind flashed back to the two men on the boat and one at the gate of Dan. "Could it be that his partner is still following me and saw me join this caravan? What does he want? Is he just a jewel thief or is there something more?"

*　　*　　*

Miriam waited impatiently for news from her spy and had almost given up. "This is my one last chance. I must find him or he must find me." After several days she insisted that Iscah take her to the market again.

"But you are unwell!" exclaimed Iscah.

"You do not understand. I must keep moving. If I lay here, it will make things worse. This is the advice of Rajnish, Omar's physician. Just a short trip to the market, Iscah, please. It will do me good."

Miriam's spy, Alvah, had been trying to find her for many weeks, but when he went to her home in Bethel to report, a man told him she was gone. He tracked her to Gaza then lost the trail. He waited and listened. Then he spotted her in the marketplace with another woman. He bought several lapis necklaces and approached her posing as a merchant.

"May I show you a necklace that belonged to a pharaoh, my Lady?"

Iscah was about to shoo him away, but Miriam held out her hand for the necklace. It constituted an agreement to purchase. Miriam

377

said to Alvah, "Meet me here in three days and I will settle with you for the necklace."

Alvah bowed and watched Iscah lead her away. He followed them at a distance to Iscah's house and then departed. Miriam hung the necklace in an outside window of her room so he would know where to find her. Nights went by and she waited impatiently. At last the necklace disappeared from the window and Alvah slipped in.

"Are you unwell, Miriam? You look quite ill."

"I have seen better days. Tell me about Deborah. Where is she? What is she doing?"

"You assigned me to follow Lapidoth, my Lady, which I did."

"Why did you not kill him as I ordered?"

"I sent a man to kill him in the night in Sidon, but he was armed and ready. From then on he traveled with an Egyptian who protected him.

"Do you know this Egyptian's name, Alvah?"

"Akhmed, I believe. Employed by Omar."

"Why did you send an incompetent man to kill him instead of doing it yourself?"

"I am a spy, Miriam, not a killer. Had I tried to do it myself I would be dead and unable to bring you the information you request."

"And Deborah? She is Lapidoth's wife you know."

"I did not know. There is a war coming and word is that a woman called Deborah the prophetess and seer is leading the troops against Sisera."

Miriam burst out laughing, her crooked mouth more ugly and pronounced than ever. "Are you mad? Women do not lead armies!"

Then she hesitated, "But Deborah did practice counseling when she was in Bethel. Rahab helped her get set up and brought clients to her until she was established. I wish I had paid more attention."

"Something else you might be interested in, Miriam. Omar has taken the murdered Abdullah's place as head of the black market jewel trade in Ashdod."

"Aha! You must take me to Omar and soon."

"That may be a great danger for you. He already left you for dead once. He will do it again."

"I will take care of Omar, Alvah. You just get me there. I have information he needs that will make him my ally. I have been saving it for a time such as this. Come for me in one week with a cart."

Alvah was puzzled but asked nothing more.

"Remember! One week. I will put the necklace in the window."

Tossing the necklace onto Miriam's bed, he quietly slipped out the window.

*　*　*

The Danites found the invading Philistines more quickly than Joseph and Lapidoth could have imagined. There were ten coming across the caravan road just as Lapidoth grabbed the arm of a suspicious loner in the caravan. The man cried out, "Allah is God!" and tried to wrench free, but Lapidoth held him fast while he slipped his long curved blade between the man's ribs. By the time Lapidoth went to assist Akhmed, the marauders were all slain.

"I found the spy and he is dead," reported Lapidoth. "I see you have slain many to my one!"

"Ah, but the one you caught would have brought many more upon us. It is good you found and silenced him. His cry nearly warned the Philistines, but he was too late."

They pushed on through to Ashdod uneventfully. Perhaps the word was out that the caravan was heavily guarded. The Danites camped outside Ashdod as Lapidoth and Joseph entered the city to find Omar. They followed the alleys to the gated courtyard where the same boy once again beckoned them to follow him.

Omar again sat in the murdered Abdullah's place. "Welcome friends! I have something very special for you. They are crown jewels taken from Pharaoh's personal collection. They will bring a great price."

Joseph was stunned. "Pharaoh's collection? His soldiers will be upon us before we can get to Acre!"

"Pharaoh has so many jewels! Unless he looks for specific ones in his collection he will not know they are gone. The thieves know which ones to pick. Now go! Choose carefully who you inform of their presence in your possession."

The Danites agreed to escort them as far as Acre and would wait for them just south of the city.

Joseph glanced around with a worried expression. "We must be watchful of the Danites. They could just as well slay us and return word that the Philistines killed us. They are with us for the money and not because of brotherly love. They were about to refuse to help us until I mentioned money."

Approaching the gate of Acre they changed into rich merchant robes. Akhmed went ahead of them to search the city for dangers.

"Remember to call me Marcus, father. That is how I am known and we will find assistance and welcome among those who recognize that name."

"And I am Adnan," whispered Joseph.

They entered the city and went immediately to Gispah's inn. It was crowded as were the markets, which was a good omen. There would be much commerce and they could sell the jewels quickly. They paid for a room and headed for the market. They stopped short at the harbor's edge and their breath froze in their throats when they saw an Egyptian galley coming slowly to the dock. Many men gathered on the shore to stare in awe.

"This does not bode well," whispered Lapidoth. "We will have to be very careful. We cannot move further north to Sidon because the galley takes up much of the harbor and other boats may not be able to set sail until they leave."

"Let us go into a good tavern near the docks. Someone may know why they are here."

They moved quietly to the street with the better taverns, where their merchant garb would not stand out, and waited. As ale and wine were consumed the customers' voices became louder and more excited. Fingers pointed toward the harbor.

"Marcus!" a man called out. "Come and join us! And bring your friend."

"This is my friend, Adnan," began Lapidoth making up a story in his mind quickly. "He is a fellow merchant. We have known each other for many years."

Joseph nodded in greeting but said nothing.

"Have you heard why the Egyptians are here? They are nearly swamping the boats in the harbor!"

"We are wondering the same thing, Marcus. We thought you might know something."

"Indeed not," returned Marcus feeling a little exposed. He wanted to escape the tavern and move to the eastern part of Acre, but could not think of a way to leave politely.

Akhmed came in from the back of the tavern. He did not acknowledge Lapidoth and Joseph, but kept an eye on everyone who came in the door.

"Then we will just have to wait until someone comes in who knows," said a barmaid as she delivered wine to the tables.

* * *

Deborah heard someone calling in the night. She sat up abruptly and looked around in the darkness. Nothing was moving. From the sound of Rahab's breathing she was asleep.

So she lay back down and drifted off. Again came the call and again she awakened. Hannah. It was Hannah's voice. What was she trying to tell her? She wrapped a thick robe around her and went out into the night air.

Kelev came from behind the tent with the fur standing up on top of his neck and growling low. There was movement outside the compound wall. Deborah called for guards but no one responded. Barak came out of his tent and called to her. "What is it?"

"There are no guards! Kelev senses something wrong!"

Kelev was crouching and his teeth were bared. He charged toward the entrance to the compound and leaped into the darkness. There was a cry of pain and then another.

Deborah went to the gate and shouted, "Ephraim, the enemy is upon you! Rise up!"

There were shouts from everywhere. Torches were lit revealing the soldiers of Sisera by their gleaming helmets. Now the whole camp was involved in the skirmish. Barak ran out of the compound to join his troops and assess the attack. Deborah closed the compound gate just as someone was climbing over the wall. Rahab was right behind her and dispatched the intruder. The women in the compound rushed to guard the walls.

"Let none of them escape!" shouted Barak.

The skirmish was short. The gleaming helmets easily identified the enemy and all were killed.

Deborah came out of the compound and walked among them. "Take their weapons and armor, and anything else of value to us."

Barak stepped to her side, "There may be clues as to how they found us and if anymore are coming."

"There will not be any following them. This is not the place of our final victory battle."

"Indeed, it looks like a scouting party. But who sends out a scouting party in full armor? One would think they would require stealth and silence, not clanking armor."

"Their arrogance is about to be their defeat, Barak. They fear no one and believe they are indestructible. Their foolishness is our advantage."

The wounded were coming into the compound, either staggering on their own or being carried by comrades. The women rushed to wash and bind their wounds, each hoping her husband or sons were not among the wounded or dead.

Rahab looked for Kelev first inside the compound and then in the battle area. She whistled for him but he did not come to her. Then she became quite worried. Tears began to roll down her cheeks. She wiped them away furiously. When had she ever cried over anything? But then when had she ever loved anything other than Kelev?

The leader of the Ephraimites came to report to Deborah and Barak. "All were killed. If they left a scout behind to report back regardless of the outcome, we did not find him."

Rahab rushed up to Deborah and Barak. "I cannot find Kelev!"

CHAPTER 27

Again Miriam hung the necklace in her window. When Alvah arrived she sent him to petition Omar for the return of her dowry from Joseph. "I will get my inheritance if I have to steal it!"

She wrote on parchment that she would either receive her funds or would move back to Omar's palace and bring guards with her.

Alvah took the parchment and eagerly set out for Omar's palace. He knew his own fortunes depended upon it. It was a long rough ride to Omar's from Gaza. He took a cousin who owed him money with him for protection. He kept the parchment hidden even from his cousin and did not tell him the reason for the journey.

Omar looked at the parchment and laughed. "And will you two steal the money I will send to her?"

"Oh, no my Lord! We are honest men," said Alvah eyes cast to the ground.

Omar put the parchment in the fold of his robe. "You go back and tell Miriam to come get it herself. Then I will know for sure where the money went. Guard!"

The guards came on the run.

"Throw these two out and never let them in again!"

Alvah and his cousin found themselves thrown into a dry stream and their animals scattered. Bruised and battered they climbed up to the level ground.

"What do we do now?" asked the cousin with fists clenched.

"We wait until the old buzzard leaves for Ashdod. Then we kill whoever is left, gather his gold, and ride east into the foothills. I will give you half."

"If we kill everyone, why leave? We can wait until Omar comes home again and kill him too! Then we can live in a palace instead of a goat skin tent."

"Everyone knows Omar, you fool!" snarled Alvah. "Shall we say he sold the place to us, or that he owed us money? Shall we parade in his robes and talk like the beggars we are? Oh no! It is better for us to take what we can and disappear quickly."

"And what about Miriam?"

"If we have the money, who needs her?"

*　　*　　*

Joseph went back to the Danite camp outside Acre. "Be patient, Manoah, we must wait until we discover the mission of the Egyptian galley in Acre or wait until it leaves the port. If they found Omar and are looking for more Egyptian black market traders, we will be discovered and killed."

Manoah thought for a minute. "I will send two of my men into Acre to the docks. They will not be suspected of anything. You and Lapidoth lay low for a while. Those galleys move from place to place quickly. They will not stay long in one port."

Lapidoth went back to Gispah's inn to wait for Joseph. He sat near the back door should he need to escape. He could not imagine the Egyptians would come this far into the city unless they were looking for someone.

Galina fancied he sat there to be close to her. She paid extra attention to him, flirting in her girlish inexperienced way. Gispah growled at her to stay in the kitchen and tend to business. She flounced away looking coyly back over shoulder at Lapidoth as she went.

This was drawing too much attention from the others in the inn, so he went up to his room to think. Wanting to believe this was an invitation to follow him, Galina found an excuse to go up to the rooms. She slipped her blouse down leaving her shoulders and most of her small breasts bare, before she boldly opened his door and walked in.

"Galina! What are you doing?"

She closed the door and leaned back on it provocatively. "I am in love with you, Marcus! I knew you would come back for me. I am no longer a little girl, you know." She moved forward, pressed her body to his, and clung tightly to him.

"No, Galina!" He struggled to free himself from her embrace. In the struggle her blouse fell away leaving her naked and she ran her hand down his torso. He moaned as his manhood responded and his breathing became heated. She wrapped her leg around his knees and pushed him back onto the bed. Sitting on him she reached for his manhood and guided it into her.

When they were both spent, she retrieved her blouse and went to the door. "Perhaps I will now carry your child, Marcus, and you will marry me." She smiled and left.

Lapidoth was still in shock when Joseph came in. "Have you learned anything?" Joseph inquired.

"Only that a bar maid is hot after my manhood," said Lapidoth grimly.

"You always draw them like flies," laughed Joseph. "They are always eyeing you."

Lapidoth cared to say nothing further about it and was relieved when Joseph changed the subject. He told Lapidoth about his conversation with Manaoh. They would wait for word from his men.

Lapidoth waited uneasily and stayed close to Joseph. He ignored Galina when they went downstairs for a meal. She was cool and business like when she brought their food. When had she grown into a woman of wiles? Was it not a year or more ago she was a child? Lapidoth tried to turn his mind from thoughts of her and his eyes from the sway of her hips.

One of the Danite men came into the inn looking for Joseph. He whispered, "The Egyptians were indeed looking for smugglers and it seems they have caught two men and taken them onboard. The galley is backing away from the dock as I speak."

They heaved a collective sigh of relief. "Now we can be about our business," said Joseph. "Go back and tell Manoah we will be there shortly if the Egyptians have not scared away our buyers."

"It looks like they carried off our competition. Perhaps that means we can command higher prices," commented Lapidoth.

The Danite departed and they set off to find the buyers from the kingdoms of the far north and east.

*   *   *

"I must go to Omar's immediately," said Miriam. "Something has happened and I need to go there."

Iscah tried to talk her out of it, but there was no reasoning with Miriam when she made up her mind. Reluctantly Iscah hired a wagon, mules, a driver and a dozen guards for Miriam. She also gave her a pouch of money so Miriam would be free to make her own decisions.

"If you need me, Miriam, send word. I will help you any way I can."

Miriam's tone softened, "You have saved my life and given me so much, Iscah. How I deserve such a friend I will never know. I have loved and trusted no one in my life except you."

Iscah kissed her cousin on her emaciated cheeks and bid her farewell. Miriam sat tall in her wagon seat and rumbled out of sight. She wrapped the cushions and robes tight around her to dull the jolts of the wagon over the rough road.

Late in the evening not too far from Omar's Miriam heard a voice call out. She ordered the driver to stop. "Alvah? Is that you?"

"Yes, my lady! Please help me!"

The guards found him and helped him onto the wagon seat.

"Have you the money? What has happened?" demanded Miriam.

Alvah told her the story of being thrown from the gate into the ravine. He told how they planned to attack and kill all the servants. Omar's servant Tebah was well prepared in case of an attack and drove them off, killing his cousin.

"So you got nothing?" shrieked Miriam.

"Nothing," Alvah said with head bowed in shame.

She pushed him out of the wagon onto the ground. "Guard, this man is a thief. Kill him!"

The guard immediately ran his knife through Alvah's heart, checked his robes for money, and threw him into a ravine for the jackals to feast on.

They drove on with haste to Omar's palace. Indeed the guards were on high alert. Tebah came to the gate. "Who goes there?"

"It is I, Miriam. We caught a thief coming from here and have sent him to his grave. Is all well here? Let me come in, Tebah!"

"Miriam? You are still alive!"

"I am very much alive! I have come to retrieve my dowry Omar paid to Joseph. Then I will be on my way."

"How do I know you did not send this thief?"

"Tebah, I have come myself! What do I need with a common thief?"

"Wait while I have my counting clerk look at the records. He will see if anything is owed you."

"Of course there is something owed to me, you old fool!"

"But Joseph has denounced you legally, Madam. I was a witness. This may forfeit any dowry or inheritance."

"Listen you old goat, it was my money from my father. It was taken from me without my consent when I was forced into marriage. Now that I am free of that hideous marriage, it is mine! Return it to me at once!"

It was midmorning when Omar arrived. Miriam had slept in the wagon and her guards had slept on the ground close by. Tebah came out of the gate and whispered to Omar.

"I will send funds to Iscah for your keep but that is all. If I give you more you will only wage war on Joseph and Lapidoth, my most valued employees. I cannot have you interfering in my business. Now go back to Iscah's, Miriam, and do not bother me again."

Miriam gathered all her strength, slipped a knife out from under the seat of the wagon, and sprang at Omar's throat. "You are interfering in *my* business!"

Despite his effort to fend her off, Miriam viciously slashed his throat and blood spurted everywhere. A surprised Omar fell to the ground. Tebah ran toward him, but Miriam's guard ran him through.

A blood spattered Miriam hobbled triumphantly through the palace gate with her guards. They rounded up the other servants and slew them before they knew what was happening.

"Now the palace is ours! Two of you go back to Gaza and recruit servants and guards. I will pay you all handsomely now that I am rich and in charge."

She gave them each a pouch of coins. "There will be more for you when you return. Be quick!" Delighted with the turn of events they rode toward Gaza in haste.

The guards set about exploring the palace and especially the kitchen and the wine stores. One of them made a plate of fruit and bread, poured a goblet of wine, and brought it to Miriam.

Miriam smiled to herself. "They thought I would die! They thought I was this feeble old cripple! They thought they were safe from me and my threats were idle ravings. Well I am showing them now! The repayment has begun!"

*　　*　　*

Ashubaal sat on her throne brooding. She could not shake the black mood that came over her. Something was terribly wrong and she could not decide exactly what it was. Each time someone mentioned the Hebrews, her blood ran cold. She stepped down from the throne and rang for a servant.

"Yes, my Lady?" said Lilah.

"Have the guards prepare my chariot. I wish to be taken to visit the priestess, Jael."

"May I go with you, Lady?"

"Yes, you will come with me. Bring my robe."

It was late morning when they reached Jael's tent. Heber met them and escorted them into the outer tent. "Jael will see you now, Your Majesty." He bowed and pulled back the drape to the inner sanctuary.

Ashubaal stepped imperiously into Jael's presence. Immediately she felt somehow diminished before Jael, but she kept her chin up. Then Jael smiled and invited her to sit down on one of the plush cushions.

"How may I help you, Majesty?"

"There is a dark cloud over my palace. I want to know what it is. Will the palace be attacked?"

Jael breathed deeply and sat with her eyes closed for a few minutes. Slowly she opened them. "There will be no attack on your palace, Majesty."

"And will my son, Sisera, be killed on the battle field?"

Jael said quietly, "No, Majesty, he will not be killed on the battle field."

Ashubaal breathed a sigh of relief. She left a handsome payment with Heber, summoned Lilah, and returned to the palace.

"You are smiling, my Lady. It has been many days since I have seen your smile. Did the priestess's answers please you?"

"Yes, Lilah, they did. But the darkness is still hanging around the edges of my mind."

"Perhaps tomorrow we could visit your favorite shrine and pray to Asherah."

Ashubaal did not answer. She went to her private quarters and did not emerge for the rest of the day.

Before retiring Lilah inquired at her door and was invited in. "Are you well, Lady?"

"Yes I am well but I am disturbed. I asked the priestess if Sisera would die on the battlefield. I did not ask if he would die or where he would die. It is not what I asked that troubles me, but what I did not ask. Perhaps I do not want to know anything more."

A chill went down Lilah's spine. Speaking of Sisera's death in this way made her very uneasy. Ashubaal had never been this disturbed about Sisera's campaigns. Why now?

"Is there anything more I may do for you, Lady?"

"No, Lilah, you may go."

*   *   *

Kelev came limping into Camp Five and lay down panting at Rahab's feet. A shocked Rahab began to examine his fur for a wound. Only a back leg was torn and bruised. One of the Ephraimites picked him up and carried him into the compound. He gently laid him on clean straw and began to cleanse and bind the leg.

393

"You are quite skilled, soldier. Where did you learn this?" inquired Rahab greatly relieved that Kelev was alive.

"I was a herder and learned from a strange Egyptian wanderer how to save my animals when they were injured. Egyptians are advanced in knowledge of how the body works and how to help it heal itself."

The Ephraimite looked again at Rahab. "Have I not seen you somewhere before?"

"I am of Ephraim near Bethel. I have spent much time in the hills and in the marketplace."

"My cousin, Samuel, once sought your hand in marriage but then he learned you were a . . ."

"A whore? A loose woman? A fallen woman?"

The Ephraimite bowed his head in embarrassment. "I did not mean to shame you or judge you, lady. It caught me by surprise."

"The world would call me those things, but I have never been a whore. I am an independent woman, a life that is not honored by our people. For that reason I have lived apart."

"But how did you come to be here in this camp so far away?"

"I am a servant and friend of Deborah the prophetess and seer. The Lord has need of me to be with her."

The Ephraimite reached down and smoothed Kelev's furry head. "He will survive. Be well, Rahab, friend of Deborah. I will say nothing of our conversation." He turned, left the compound, and disappeared into the camp.

Rahab suddenly felt bereft and empty. Kelev was injured, Gideon was always in dangerous territory, and this man brought up her difficult past. Handsome Samuel had come to her father, recognized her as the one from the hills, turned and walked away without a word. She sat down beside Kelev and drew his head into her lap, her tears falling into his ruff.

Deborah sat down beside her and wrapped her arms around Rahab's shoulders. "All the sorrows of your life surface at this frightening time. They come to be healed. Weep for the moment and then rise in the strength you love. As you have wisely said to me, our greatest battles are within us, not on the battlefield of the war to come."

*   *   *

News of Omar's death came to Lapidoth and Joseph from a Danite spy commissioned by Manaoh to keep an eye on what transpired in Ashdod. "Word is he was murdered by Miriam and her guards. She has slain the servants of Omar and taken over his palace and fortunes. She now sits in the seat of Abdullah and Omar in the marketplace."

Joseph turned red with anger. "How did she go from dying in an asylum in Gaza to ruling Omar's estates? She is inhuman. She is evil itself! Lapidoth, you continue on here, sell the jewels and pay the Danites. Miriam is my responsibility and I will see that she does not remain in power."

Lapidoth was flabbergasted at the sudden turn of events. "But father, you cannot go alone! She will murder you as well. How can you stop her?"

"She will soon be after our lives, Deborah and Rahab included. No, my son, this has to stop here and I will stop her. I alone have the key to her power in the family, and it is time I used it to expose her."

"Does she know you have this?"

"No, she does not. Omar told me the last time we saw him. It was as if he had a premonition that something would happen to him."

"Will you also tell me what the key is? If something should happen to you, I will make sure your work is done."

Joseph wrote something on a piece of parchment and handed it to Lapidoth. "Do not use this unless you are certain I am dead, until you see my body. If you hear I am dead and take action, you may get in the way. I might find it necessary to spread the word of my death as a diversion. Only when you see my dead body will you take action."

Lapidoth was still regaining his equilibrium. "I understand. I will do as you have said. God keep you safe, my father."

They embraced and Joseph set off with a few of the Danites toward Ashdod.

*　　*　　*

Now that the Egyptians had set sail, Lapidoth booked passage to Sidon for himself and Manoah.

"Why go to Sidon? Why not stay in Acre now that the danger has passed?" asked Manoah.

"The danger is greater than ever," replied Lapidoth. "Miriam will send her vipers right up through the black market chain to Acre where she knows I do most of our business. We must leave at once. Remember to call me Marcus from now on. This is how I am known here. I have not mentioned that name south of Acre and, hopefully, Miriam will not know of it."

At mid day they boarded the ship owned by a captain of Lapidoth's acquaintance a few minutes before it sailed. To Lapidoth's relief, they were the only passengers on this trip, except for Akhmed who came aboard behind them. The craft carried only a few deck hands and a huge load of cargo. They were the same deck hands Lapidoth had seen on former trips, but he would still keep his eye on them.

The ship put in at Tyre's northern port for the night. Sidon was too far to make it in daylight and a storm was approaching from the sea. Lapidoth and Manaoh reluctantly disembarked and headed for an inn the captain recommended. Tyre was small, strange, and volatile. It was on an island near the main shore. The streets were dark and narrow. That night they took turns keeping watch. Lapidoth had never been there and prayed that the weather would not keep them marooned, as so often happened on the seacoast.

"What are all the military for?" asked Manoah shading his eyes toward the east. "They are encamped across the water on the far shore."

Lapidoth looked toward the shore as well. "They are here to guard the shipments of Tyrolean purple dyes. Only royalty can wear the color and the price is extremely high. Anyone else wearing it is killed immediately. A band of robbers would be delighted to get their hands on the dye or the murex shellfish it comes from, and make a fortune in the first sale."

"It is good to hear they are not looking for us," remarked Manoah.

"Yes, and it is one of the reasons I have passed up Tyre and continued on to Sidon. There is too much intrigue and tension here. Anyone selling high quality jewels here would be suspected of trying to buy the purple. It is a good place to stay away from. I will be glad when we are under way again."

"Do you know the other passenger who was on board with us?"

"Yes, I do. He is my bodyguard and keeps separate from us in order to keep watch. He works for my family from time to time."

"Then he is a mercenary."

"Yes, you could say that. I pay him well. That is where his loyalty lies, and he has done well by my family."

They boarded the ship in the morning and were soon heading for Sidon. Again Lapidoth looked over the crew for any strangers or signs of danger. Manoah was beginning to learn from Lapidoth the many dangers other than just Philistine marauders and kept his knife handy.

* * *

Gideon, Naham, and Jerib returned from scouting the movements of Sisera's army. Gideon was mystified. "We did not encounter them from here to the east. It is as if their whole army is moving west together toward Tyre and staying north of the mountains. I wonder if he has found out about our camps and wants to attack us from the west. But we are in rough terrain and his chariots would be useless."

Barak was puzzled as well. "There was an attack on us here at Camp Five. We managed to kill all the attackers, but I have been afraid one of them stayed behind to get away and report our location."

"Does that mean they know only of this location and not the others?" asked Naham.

"We have no reports of trouble from the other four camps," replied Barak. "Abel is bringing the troops from those camps here in the next few days and we will establish a perimeter from west to east instead of south to north. Whatever Sisera's movements, we will soon be in full force to meet them."

Deborah and Rahab listened from a corner of the tent. Deborah was especially intent on the news of the troop movements. Rahab was more focused on Gideon. She felt her earlier sadness lift at the sound of his voice.

Deborah stepped to the table where the maps were laid out. She traced with her finger the route Sisera would take from the west and where he would try to cross the Kishon River. The pass in the low mountains would lead him into the widest part of the valley that would be a muddy swamp. She made a mark on the high place where she would stand in the dazzling morning sun that would make her saffron and mica dusted robe look like fire.

Moving close beside her, Barak let his hand touch hers. She did not withdraw. He traced the way for his troops to move onto Mt. Tabor, staying to the south of the valley as they traveled east, then north.

"Perhaps we should travel these routes ourselves to be sure passage is possible," suggested Gideon.

"Yes, I think you are right. We will take some of the leaders to familiarize them with the area so no one gets lost," agreed Barak.

The next morning they rode out to find the best way through that would accommodate large numbers of troops. Deborah and Rahab were included. They would come close to Kadesh-Napthali and Deborah wanted to visit Rabbi Amri and Leah. She was sure her father would not be interested in seeing her, but Abinoam and Sarah would want to see Barak.

Deborah and Barak with a few guards slipped quietly into the town in the early morning when marketers would be setting up their stalls. In the busy market, they hoped not to draw attention.

Rabbi Amri and Leah were thrilled to see them and sent a servant to bring Abinoam and Sarah. "Our village has been peaceful these last several months," said Rabbi Amri. "I assume Sisera is no longer letting his soldiers entertain themselves by attacking villages, but has focused them on preparing for a battle. Do you agree, Barak?"

"Yes, I agree. Sisera is moving to the west. I cannot tell you more. We are still assessing the strategy, and Deborah is reassuring us that God knows the right time and circumstances."

The rabbi smiled and patted Deborah's hand. "We do miss you very much, Daughter. I pray you will return to us one day. Do you know the whereabouts of your husband?"

Barak flinched a little at the mention of Lapidoth. He had Deborah to himself for so long, he could not visualize her as someone else's wife. Indeed she had not been in a marriage since their ceremony. How odd it all was!

"I have no knowledge of him. I do not know if I am a wife or a widow. I sometimes wonder if I shall ever know. As you know Rahab and I did go to Acre to find him once, but he was not there. It seemed that no one ever heard of him. It makes me think he uses a different name and I do not know what it is."

"I have been to Acre to visit an ailing rebbe recently. There was one who sold jewels to the royal houses. They called him Marcus. Could that be the name he uses?"

"I do not know, but I will remember that name," said Deborah quietly. She was unaccustomed to speaking openly about Lapidoth. The words were ashes in her mouth. Did everyone assume they had a normal marriage? She felt like that part of her life was somehow a lie. The broken places in her life were many. How could she remember Ya'akov without pain, Lapidoth without anger, and now try to cover her feelings for Barak? It was all too much! She gratefully took the goblet of wine Rabbi Amri offered.

"You look pale, my dear. Are you all right?"

"Yes, I think so. Just tired," she lied. What else could she do? It was indeed all too much!

At that moment Abinoam and Sarah came in and threw themselves into Barak's arms. There was much weeping as Barak helped Sarah to a place to sit. Her hands shook and her legs were unsteady. Abinoam seemed to be faring well enough. Guilt always swept over Barak when he saw them, especially in their old age. A good son would have married and stayed in the village to care for them. But no, he ran off to join Israel's ragtag army! "How foolish we can be in our youth and eagerness for adventure," he thought trying to regain his own composure.

At dawn the next morning, Deborah and Rahab set off to see Hannah. "I feel like I am swimming in a fog," said Deborah. "I know she will help me regain my balance."

Hannah was at the door to greet them. "Come in my dears, I have been expecting you!"

Deborah threw her arms around her and burst into sobs.

Hannah led them into her kitchen and handed them hot tea. "You are carrying far too much alone in a most difficult time. Now, tell me everything, both of you."

Rahab and Deborah poured out their stories, including their feelings for Gideon and Barak.

"What was my marriage about, Hannah? It is not a marriage but two strangers who went through the ceremony and then parted, seemingly forever."

"I have tried not to question the Lord, but I have questioned myself. Surely if you had not married, you and Barak would have been too distracted to carry out the plan of God against Sisera."

"I do not know if I am a widow, or denounced and divorced!" wailed Deborah. "I used to think I knew who I was and what I wanted. But now I am confused and what I want now is denied me."

Rahab slipped her arm around Deborah and pulled her close. "Perhaps the plan was to make you an Ephraimite so they would come to assist Barak."

Deborah looked at Rahab in amazement. "This may be the truth! It makes more sense than anything else I have thought of."

"It is time for prayer before the day begins," said Hannah. They set down their tea and went into prayer together. A calm peace came over them and Deborah was home within herself. The feeling grew as Lapidoth faded from her mind, and Barak became clearer. Surely God was guiding her and filling her heart with love.

There was a tap on Hannah's door just as they were stirring out of the meditation. The deep voice of Barak was telling them it was time to bid farewell and continue on their way. "Do you want to stay here, Deborah? We will return for you."

"Thank you for your offer, but I will come with you."

They hugged Hannah. Gideon and the soldiers were waiting for them on the road. Deborah no longer felt torn or confused. She felt light and clear, and rode happily along side Barak knowing she was in her right place.

*   *   *

Miriam wasted no time in gathering servants, guards, and spies. The murder of Abdullah was fresh in the minds of the black market in Ashdod. The murder of Omar following soon after was another shock. The appearance of Miriam in his place terrified them. Her lopsided and haggard face, her half closed eye, and drooping shoulder terrified all who saw her. She limped, swung her cane at them, and screeched orders at everyone. The superstitious were sure an evil witch from Sheol had come among them.

Established as the queen of the black market, she set things moving at a quick pace. One focus was to find Lapidoth and Joseph and have them killed. She sent spies to the territory of Napthali to find Deborah and Rahab. Orders were sent to her suppliers for more and better jewels, plus gold and Tyrolean purple dyes. The dye was reserved for royalty and would have to come from Tyre.

Her merchants were worried. If they refused to go to Tyre, she would have them killed. If they did go to Tyre, the military guarding the coast and factory would kill them. They conspired together to go to Sidon instead and somehow disappear forever.

Joseph and the Danites made their way to Ashdod. At the gates to the city Joseph bid them leave him and go home. "This is my problem and I must solve it or die trying."

A young man stepped up to Joseph. "You will need someone to watch your back. I will do that."

"What is your name, young man?"

"Ham sir. My name is Ham."

"And where do you come from?"

"East of the Jordan. My betrothed and I fled the trouble there and we cannot go home. Barak of the Israelite army rescued us. We decided to settle in the territory of Dan and be herders like we were across the Jordan. But I have gained much experience moving from place to place. I have learned the languages of other people and I know how to move quietly and how to hide. I am good with the knife."

"Well, Ham, certainly no one will recognize you in Ashdod. Perhaps it is a good idea. I thank you. Come with me then."

Joseph and Ham disguised themselves and entered Ashdod just before the gates closed for the night. "Understand, Ham, I am not concerned for my life. If I am killed having killed Miriam, all is well. You are not to sacrifice yourself needlessly. Do you understand?"

"Yes, I understand," said Ham doubtfully. "I will try to see that does not happen to you. That is why I want to come with you. What will happen if you do not kill Miriam?"

"Then Sheol will reign upon the earth and fill it with darkness and evil. She will wreak vengeance on everyone who gets in her way. She is full of hate and it has made her insane."

"What do you plan to do? How do you get to her?"

"We will go into Ashdod through the back alleys into the cave where she sits. We will go when she leaves and I will leave her a gift. I will buy an Egyptian asp and put it in a gift basket."

Ham shuddered. "Those things are deadly!"

"Yes they are, so do not be curious and open any baskets or boxes, do you understand?"

They slipped into an alley near the waterfront and found a merchant ship that carried exotic animals. Joseph found exactly what he was looking for. He purchased the asp and the basket and wrapped it carefully so the lid would stay in place. In the night they went back through the caves to the place where Miriam would sit. A guard met them, recognized Joseph, and allowed them to pass. Joseph placed the basket beside her chair and left. Ham followed him. When they were well away Ham said, "That was so easy!"

"Far more dangerous than you might think. It was fortunate that Miriam kept the same guards and they knew me as one of them. She will not know where the gift came from because the same guard will not be there in the morning. Now we will go back to Danite territory and wait."

*   *   *

The port of Sidon came into view and the docks were nearly full. The captain moved the ship deftly into a slip and the crew jumped onto the dock to tie it securely. "We will go to the inn of Ammiel and see if we will be welcome there. Last time I stayed there someone tried to kill me in the night and I dispatched him. Ammiel was most distressed and saw to disposing of the body. He may decide I am a bad omen. Again, remember my name is Marcus."

Manaoh nodded and kept a wary eye as they walked through the port and into the markets. In the marketplace Lapidoth bought better robes and sandals for them, and set about seeking buyers in the upper class neighborhood.

They stopped at the inn and Ammiel greeted them with effusive assurances that they were welcome and safe in his inn. Akhmed was sitting in a dark corner of the bar. They took two rooms, stopped in the inns tavern for some food, and continued their search.

At a square near a well, a man approached them. "Are you Marcus the jewel merchant?"

Lapidoth was surprised at being approached. "I am he. What can I do for you, friend?"

"My master is a friend of Ammiel and asks that you come to his home."

Lapidoth and Manoah followed the man to a large palatial home high on a hill. Manoah was nervous in the unfamiliar surroundings. "I have not known anything but herding and fighting. This is all very strange."

"Strange, and no less dangerous. Stay silent and keep watch. I will transact the business and we will leave despite fervent invitations for us to stay. We must not place ourselves at the mercy of strangers."

"Am I your servant, Marcus?" Manoah nearly stuttered on the unfamiliar name.

"Bodyguard, Manoah. You are my bodyguard. This is common among the wealthy. You will be regarded with respect, the same as they respect me."

The master met them, briskly conducted the business of purchasing the jewels, and had them escorted to the gate of his residence. Just outside the gate Marcus cautioned, "That was too easy. Let us be wary and travel separately for a few blocks and meet at Ammiel's inn. If one person is following us, they cannot cover us both. If two, they will have to split up. Either way, we can spot them."

"If one follows me, he may not live long enough for me to discern his intention! Take no chances, Marcus."

They parted going down separate alleys and Marcus broke into a trot. After a few turns he discerned there was someone following him. He saw the follower begin to run as well. He cut back toward the alley Manoah took in case he was in trouble as well. They ran into each other at an intersection, Manoah just past the intersection. Lapidoth knocked down the man who was following him and turned to face his own follower with his knife drawn. Manoah killed his follower, but Lapidoth's disappeared among the buildings.

"We have to find him, Lapidoth. We cannot afford to let him get away and report to someone."

They backtracked Lapidoth's route and checked into some of the open buildings. "Let us go to the docks," advised Manoah. "I doubt that they were local thieves."

"There are only two reasons they would be after us. Either they knew we had money or Miriam sent them. If they were only after the money, they would have just robbed us, but if it was Miriam, they were here to kill us."

They scoured the docks and taverns, but found no one. Akhmed appeared in a doorway ahead of them. "There is no one following you any longer, but there may be more dangers. If Miriam sent one or two, she would send a dozen!"

They decided to book passage to Acre and leave as soon as possible. The only ship leaving immediately was not one Lapidoth knew, nor did he know the captain. They looked over the other three passengers carefully as they boarded. Akhmed stepped aboard first. Lapidoth and Manoah were the last to board, and kept watch at the railing to be sure no one else stole aboard.

They set sail into a rough sea. The wind came up and the cargo strained against the ropes as the ship rocked violently. A crewmember threw them a rope and they tied themselves to a mast to keep from being thrown overboard. Manoah kept a hand on the tail of the rope to pull them both free in case the ship capsized. Just when they thought they could stand no more, the storm passed and the waves calmed down. To Lapidoth's chagrin they again pulled into the port of Tyre to check for any damage and secure the cargo again.

"I can stand no more, Lapidoth. Let us buy two asses and stay on land the rest of the way."

"Have faith, my friend. Believe me the sea is much safer and quicker than over land right now. I have heard that Sisera's forces are mobilizing and may be coming this way."

"I shall be glad to return to Dan where I know the land behind me is secure and I have only to drive the rabble back into the sea where they came from."

The ship backed out into the harbor and prepared to sail. Again Lapidoth and Manoah kept careful watch for any trouble. The seas had calmed down to a glossy grayish white, and the port of Acre would come into sight soon.

*   *   *

Deborah could see the high place where she would stand by the swamp in clear sight of Sisera's army. The thought ran chills up her spine and down her arms. Rahab and Gideon were looking in another direction for the best way up onto Mt. Tabor.

"Are you all right, Deborah? You seem chilled," said Barak moving closer to her.

"I am chilled with excitement and the adventure of the unknown. I have very little experience of actually being in a battle as you know."

"That is good. You will be ready and on high alert. If we do not live through this, I am honored to die with you. It sounds better than being separated by life circumstances forever."

She smiled up at him. "I, too, am ready to die if I cannot be with you."

They walked to the high point together, her arm in his. The comfort of his body close to hers was almost more than she could bear. "If we are to die, Barak, there is a moment I want to live with you before that happens."

He stopped and looked at her, his body and mind running in opposite directions. "And if we do not die, and you carry my child? What shall we do then?"

"If it is in God's plan that I carry your child, so be it. The plan will not end there. I am already a woman who travels with an army far from her husband. What more could be said of me that is not already or going to be said?"

They were alone on the bluff. The others were down below. Barak picked Deborah up in his arms and carried her to a grassy place among the trees and bushes. He laid her down and kneeled beside her. He gently lifted her robe and she reached for his tunic pulling it up. He laid down on her kissing her passionately everywhere he could uncover. She raised her hips to his touch and he entered her, wild for the oneness they longed for. Too soon they lay spent in the freshness of the grass that mingled with the fragrance of their bodies.

Gideon called out for Barak. They rose up quickly and arranged their clothing none too soon. Rahab and Gideon came up the hill and marveled at the view of the valley. However, it wasn't the view of the valley Rahab marveled at. She faced Deborah with a knowing look and a sly smile.

"The way is open and the climb will be easy. There is a place from which to launch a surprise attack," said Gideon. Barak nodded almost unable to speak. Together the four returned to the soldiers down below who were coming back from scouting an approach to Mt. Tabor.

CHAPTER 28

Miriam gathered her robes around her frail body and moved closer to the fire in the palace kitchen. It was the only place she could feel warm. Her servants were busy building a fireplace in her rooms. Even though they lived in a hot climate, nights were cold and the worst for her when the night air crept in. Her shaking was uncontrollable. The kitchen servant brought her hot soup and wine.

"Take them to my room," she barked. Loathe to leave the heat of the kitchen, she was not going to look any weaker than she had to in front of servants.

The servant immediately took the food to Miriam's room without a backward glance. Miriam rose slowly to her feet, grabbed her cane, and shuffled toward the kitchen door. A guard offered her his arm but she brushed it away and continued on her own.

She knew she must rest, but she must also go to Ashdod early to inspect a shipment she was expecting. One supplier who tried to send her inferior merchandise now lay in his grave. She wanted news of Joseph and Lapidoth as well. Had those she sent to find them done their job? Truly this was not a time to be weak.

Morning came early and Miriam was on her way with her guards. The morning was cold and the cave would be as well. She had ordered the guards keep the braziers burning all night. With just her eyes visible above the edge of the thick robes, one guard mentioned she looked like an asp in a blanket.

Hobbling into the inner chamber to her seat where Omar and Abdullah once sat, she flopped down and heaved a sigh. The guard brought a warmed drink and lit more candles. "Who brought this basket? I have not seen it before!" she demanded. "Who was here?"

The guards had just come on duty a few hours before and looked at each other puzzled. "No one has been here on our watch, Lady. We will check with the night guards."

In an impatient gesture she snatched up the basket, the lid flew off, and the asp sprang out onto the floor. She shrieked, missed her footing, and fell onto the floor beside it. The asp was swift to defend itself with its deadly bite. It then slithered away in an attempt to escape, only to be stomped on by a guard's boot. The guard quickly cut her arm above the fang marks with his knife and squeezed out blood.

Her eyes were wide and wild. "Get a physician quickly!" she screamed at them. They ran out into the streets to a physician's house. Rajnish opened his door slowly.

"Come quickly," implored one of the guards. "Our Lady has been bitten!"

Rajnish grabbed a robe and followed them through the alleys, and into the cave where Miriam lay panting. The dead asp was still on the floor.

"Is that you Miriam?" He could hardly believe his eyes.

She looked up at him startled. "Well, we meet again dear physician. Snake bite! What do you have for snakebite? Where are your precious potions?"

He checked her pulse and the color of the whites of her eyes. "I am afraid, Miriam, it may be too late. The cut did not go deep enough and the poison has spread. I am *not* sorry to say you will be dead within the hour."

"You cannot mean that! I can pay! I can make you rich! You are a physician! Help me!"

"A physician, Miriam, not a magician. There is nothing I can do."

"You mean nothing you *will* do! Guards! Take him! At least I will not die alone!"

The guards turned their backs and Rajnish sat down in her seat to wait. Miriam suffered an agonizing death within the hour, and the guards then carried her body outside the city to the trash heaps.

Rajnish continued to sit in the seat of Abdullah, of Omar, of Miriam, and now it was his.

*   *   *

Sarah, Abinoam, Amri, and Leah awaited the return of Barak and Deborah. The day was waxing late when the soldiers made camp outside Kadesh-Napthali. Deborah, Barak, Rahab, and Gideon came through the gate of Rabbi Amri's home tired and hungry. Without delay they sat down to a meal together. Leah's servant prepared a banquet, and sent food to the small contingent of soldiers who were camped a distance away.

"My son, have you accomplished what you set out to do?" inquired the quavery voice of Abinoam. Abinoam long ago reconciled himself to the life his son had chosen. He and Sarah had looked forward to grandchildren, and a son who would sit with his father and the elders at the city gates. But it was not to be. God chose otherwise for him and for the good of Israel.

"Yes, Father. We are doing well. Thanks to Deborah, God is in our camp and the men and women rejoice in that."

"The women in your camp? Who are they? What do they do?" inquired Leah quite suddenly, a little embarrassed that the words tumbled off her tongue. "I must apologize. I did not mean . . ."

"It is good that you ask, Leah," responded Deborah quickly. "The women live in a walled compound on the edge of the campsites. They gather and prepare food for storage, tend the sick and wounded, and generally keep the morale high by being close to their male kin."

"How interesting an idea. However did you think of it?"

"Women were coming to see their male kin and some men were going home, missing valuable training. Gideon spied out the Canaanite camps and saw their compounds. We thought it would be good to build them as well, to give the women a place and keep them safe. The camps have been much more orderly since then," offered Rahab.

There was silence at the table and everyone attended to their food. Rahab looked nervously at Deborah. Deborah smiled reassuringly.

Rabbi Amri spoke up as the meal ended. "My friends, our world is about to change again. It changed when we left Egypt for a new land. It has changed with the need to defend our territories and our religion. It is changing again and who knows, is it for better or not? It is customary to doubt and even criticize those who bring the change, but they are also the very ones who carry us forward and strengthen our nation. Pray for success and peace." He sang some evening prayers and bid them all a restful night.

Deborah and Rahab went down stairs where they had hidden before. Barak and Gideon left the house and went out to the camp.

*   *   *

Joseph and Ham went to Omar's palace after they received the news of Miriam's death. Her frightened servants met them at the gate. "Go back to your homes," said Joseph. "Your mistress is dead. Someone has murdered her and taken her place. You will be next if you do not flee."

Within the hour, Omar's palace was deserted. Joseph went in and took coins, gold, and other riches owed to him and Lapidoth for the years Miriam and Abdullah cheated them. He packed a couple of donkeys and headed for home at last. "You are welcome to come with me, Ham. I will escort you back to Dan when I can."

"I will go with you and then I can find my way back to Dan. I am accustomed to traveling alone. We have only the Philistines to worry about here, and I can smell them a mile away."

Joseph laughed in a joyous way he could not remember ever doing.

Joab and Tamar rushed out to meet them. "Tell us what has happened. We thought we would never see you again!"

Joseph and Ham unloaded the donkeys and stowed everything in the house. Tamar brought cheese, lamb, bread, and wine. They sat together in the kitchen and Joseph told them the story, leaving out some details including the asp. Only Ham knew about the asp.

Joab frowned a bit. "So Miriam is dead, God be praised. Where are Lapidoth, Rahab, and Deborah?"

"I believe Deborah and Rahab are with the Israelite army. I sent Lapidoth north to dispose of the black market jewels. I know nothing else."

Ham left the next morning for Dan with a moneybag for the Danites. Joab was doubtful not knowing Ham, but Joseph assured him Ham was honorable and if anyone could get the money through to Dan, he could. The two of them set about digging out the herb cellar under the house to hide the rest. It would be enough for Joseph and Joab to take care of the family modestly, which was all Joseph ever wanted.

"The nightmare is over, Joab. It is the end of a terrible mistake I made in my youth, seeking the hand of the exotic and beautiful Miriam. I shall always regret that. Let us pray for Lapidoth's safety that he may return to us."

*   *   *

Abel brought the troops from the earlier camps and set up a perimeter of encampments east to west as they had planned. The winter rains had continued making the work difficult. Day after day the troops came in until they were all at the front with Barak. Abel created two lines, one to be a fall-back line if needed.

Barak, Abel, and Deborah spent days and nights planning and organizing soldiers, weaponry, food, spies, guards and maps. The details seemed endless. Deborah was amazed at what it took to mobilize an entire army. She looked at Barak with pride, trying not to let fears for his safety creep into her thoughts. The memory of their time together on the bluff was tucked safely away in her mind. "God let it always be so," she would whisper.

The compound was crowded with women from the other camps who refused to go home now that the battle was imminent. "Who will tend the wounded?" shouted one woman. "Who will feed them?" shouted another. Other compounds near the front camps were hastily erected and the women set about supplying them. There was rejoicing as if the battle were already won.

Naham came into Camp Five with news that Sisera was indeed mobilized and gathering west of them. "They are moving to the coast and then toward Megiddo! If we stay here our camps will be in their path!"

Barak was shocked. "We need to move further east near the foot of Mount Tabor quickly. The chain of temporary camps will not be safe. His chariots must stay in the valley along the Kishon River. He cannot take them into the mountains up to Megiddo or Mount Tabor. We will go up to Mt. Tabor now. The Ephraimites, Benjaminites, and Machir will go east toward Mt. Gilboa. Deborah, we will go to the place where you and some of the Ephraimites can be seen and lure them into the swamp. Rahab, please move the women back to Camp Three where they will be away from the battle but close enough to tend the wounded."

Barak and Abel gathered the captains and leaders of the troops into Barak's tent to redraw the plans. Deborah stood behind them listening, but also praying for God's guidance on the coming battle. She fought back tears when thoughts of them all being killed crept into her mind. If they did not defeat Sisera, he would surely wipe out defenseless towns full of innocent people. Her loved ones. "Oh God, if this happens to them do not let me live. Let me die with them!"

She went outside to breathe fresh air and clear her mind of the doubts and fears. She could hear Hannah's voice saying, "God's plan will not be thwarted! Be of good courage, Deborah."

Rahab came out to see where Deborah had gone. "All will be well, my sister. One way or another, all will be well."

They clung to each other for a moment and then rushed to the compound to begin carrying out Barak's orders. There were no women in the newest camp yet, so it would be a simple matter of gathering up the supplies, however much each could carry, and moving back to the south. It surprised Rahab that no one complained or opposed the plan. They seemed to know the time was here for serious preparation and not argument. Within the hour they left Camp Five for Camp Three with forty guards around them.

Abel began moving troops toward Mount Tabor. Soldiers packed all the maps and documents from Barak's tent and carried them. Others took down the tent and carried it and its contents.

"We want to leave no clues for the enemy!" shouted Abel. In a short time the camp was stripped of tents, food, and weapons. The rain was still coming down and they knew the Kishon would soon be a torrent flooding the valley. Deborah proudly rode beside Barak sensing the power of their partnership. Barak had never doubted her and never sought to diminish her role. Again her heart swelled with love and admiration for him.

Rahab went with the women, all the while thinking up excuses to return to Camp Five to be with Deborah and Gideon. But if she did that and the camp was deserted, she would be alone and endanger herself for nothing. It was a frightening turn of events. They all kept their silence and walked quickly over the crude roads the arriving soldiers had trod down and made smoother.

They passed Camp Four and found it deserted. Rahab took two guards and went in to search the camp for anything that might have been left behind. But there was nothing. It was stripped clean. Rahab walked into the women's compound and a soldier followed her. He moved close to her. Too close. Rahab pulled her curved blade from her robe and pretended to need it for something. He backed away and they moved on.

"Do not do that again, soldier, or you will not live to join Barak in the battle against Sisera," she whispered menacingly. "Do you want your troops to know you died at the hands of a woman?"

*   *   *

Lapidoth and Manoah gratefully disembarked at Acre. "I'll never be a sailor!" declared Manoah. "How do they manage to ride in those rocking vessels every day? They are worse than galloping camels!"

Two men approached them as they left the docks. "You are Lapidoth?"

"And who are you?" asked Lapidoth suspiciously, fingering his knife.

"We were sent by Miriam to Tyre to steal the Tyrolean purple. We would be killed if we tried and she will kill us if we did not. Do not go back there, sir. She is mad. She wishes to kill you also. We are fleeing for our lives."

"This is not news. What do you want of me?"

"Help us! Where can we go?"

"Manoah, I need to leave to go east. I need to find my wife and what might be left of my life. Take these men back to Dan and perhaps they can find their way home. Let us pray my Father was successful and we will all be free."

Lapidoth signaled Akhmed that he needed to talk to him. "I am going east to find Deborah. You can consider your contract completed. Here is your fee, my friend, with my deepest gratitude."

"I will shadow you for a while until you are on your way. God speed, Marcus."

Gispah's inn was the only place Lapidoth felt safe. He wished to avoid Galina, but there was no other way. Gispah was welcoming as usual. Galina was not present. "I have sent her away to her aunt's so she will not bother my customers. She is becoming unmanageable. She will be pregnant with God knows which customer's child or maybe someone at the market. I do not need trouble."

Lapidoth heaved a sigh of relief. He sat down to the meal being served and then went to a room to rest. He woke up in the night. Someone was stroking his body. He jumped but Galina whispered, "I knew you would come back. I love you Marcus. Please let me."

He moaned, "No Galina. Go away."

He tried to push her away but she avoided his hands and was on him naked and passionate. Even in the dark he could visualize the sway of her hips. He rolled over on her and found her small breasts. A rage suddenly burned within him and took over his reason. He placed his hand over her mouth and took her brutally over and over. All the anger at his mother for her cruelty came flooding over him, and he thrashed on until he was completely spent.

"Go away, Galina, before you are caught. Go!" he whispered harshly.

She whimpered, pulled on her tunic and left the way she had come in, through the window.

He fell asleep and nightmares assailed him of Miriam coming for him with a knife dripping blood. When the morning light dawned he was soaked with perspiration and blood. What had he done to poor Galina? Was it her blood? He reached for an urn of water, poured some into a basin, and washed himself. He left the inn very early, went to the livery, and bought an ass to take him east. He was shaken by the rage and violence that overcame him. He was faced with confusion, insanity, unsure of what his next move should be. His only thought was to see Deborah again and demand she come away with him.

"According to law she is my wife and must obey me. She should have stayed in Bethel instead of running off. She should have stayed with Joab and Tamar, and helped with the herds. She . . . what am I thinking? This is my mother's voice in my head! Oh, Joseph! Did you not see to her demise? Or is she dead and still pursues me in my mind? Was she the rage that engulfed me last night and nearly killed Galina?"

He urged the animal on south to the Kishon River where he could follow the valley eastward toward Kadesh-Napthali. "I must find her family. I must repair the wrongs I have done. I must have peace!" he shouted to no one but the wind.

*   *   *

Ashubaal was alone in her palace and feeling more alone than she had ever felt in her life.

She was accustomed to Sisera's absences, but this time was different. His bravado and bragging were loud, but Ashubaal heard only the warnings of the darkness. Their mantra was death, death, death.

Sisera began leading his army and chariots west through the valleys to meet the mouth of the Kishon. He would follow it east into the valley, and to victory in a war with Barak and Deborah. Then he would return to Harosheth and plan his next victory. Canaanite kings were joining him on the order of King Jabin, but Sisera laughed at their paltry troops. He had his chariots and iron weapons. They had spears. That was the argument that ensued between Jabin and Sisera before he returned from Hazor to begin the march.

"Deborah? That sounds like a woman!" he said to his captain. "Are we now fighting women?"

"It is a woman, Sisera. A woman said to possess great powers and has been sent by the Israelite god, Yahweh, to defeat us."

"Hah! We have been invading their tribes for twenty years and their god has not lifted a finger to stop us! Why should this time be any different?"

"I do not know, Sisera, but I think we should be on guard for anything."

"A woman! I will find her and rape her until she is dead. I will slaughter this Barak and his puny soldiers who carry only wooden spears and skins of bad wine. We will wipe their kind off the land and the memory of Joshua will be no more."

"The story is that her God has brought her to the head of the army and will insure her victory."

"And you believe this bopkis? Her god? Their god? How many gods do they have?"

"Think about it, Sisera. No woman would ever be allowed to lead an army. In their culture their women are nothing! And yet, here she is. How do we explain it?"

"They are all nothing and we are about to prove that. There will be no trace of them left because they are nothing. They build no castles, palaces, or monuments to their god. They are not a nation. Just a weak tribe that fancies itself important, and it is not. Enough of this. Where is my map? Get me some wine."

*   *   *

Ashubaal called for Lilah. "Yes, my Lady? How may I serve you?"

"I—I am afraid. The darkness grows in my mind. Sleep with me tonight. I do not want to be alone."

Lilah frowned. She had not seen the mother of Sisera so worried. "Of course. I will stay with you as long as you need me."

"Need you? Great Asherah! I thought I would never need anyone. But now that my son is in danger, danger he is not aware of, my need grows as his safety diminishes."

Ashubaal shivered as Lilah wrapped a warmed robe around her and ordered a servant to light a fire in the second brazier. Ashubaal went to her window and gazed out toward the west. Lilah sat with her for a while and then begged her to come to bed.

*   *   *

The valley was beginning to flood as Barak and his troops began crossing to Mt. Tabor. It seemed the valley was flooding more quickly than usual. He looked back over the long line of men, hoping they would hurry before the crossing became impassable. Deborah's Ephraimites followed closely and passed to the place on the north side of the river where they would be stationed.

Barak's campsite was erected on the north side of Mt. Tabor. It was a sparsely treed hill and offered no place to hide troops on the south side. But the barren places also offered an unobstructed path of attack for a mass of troops.

*   *   *

Sisera's troops arrived at the Kishon and started east down toward the valley. The chariots made a rumble that seemed to rattle the countryside. Wildlife scattered as the foliage was trampled. The rain continued and the stream became a rushing river.

The chariots stayed on the south side of the river ready to cross over toward Mt, Tabor. They could see some of Barak's troops moving at the top of the mountain. "Those fools are in plain sight with no cover!" shouted Sisera. He waved his troops forward and lashed the horses of his chariot to go faster.

Deborah and the Ephraimites moved down the southern side of Mt. Tabor and stopped high on a cliff. When the chariots arrived where the river passed the bottom of the mountain, Deborah stepped forth into a stream of sunlight that broke through the rain clouds. Her robe blazed in the light.

The Charioteers shouted and drove wildly toward her, but the chariots that made it across would not climb the steep slope. They tried to turn back. Sisera and his troops came down the south side of the river just as a torrent of rain descended upon them. The river rose up quickly. Charging chariots ran into retreating chariots and overturned as the horses reared in terror at the strain.

Taking advantage of the situation, Barak and his thousands rushed down the south side of Mount Tabor shouting and blowing horns. The charioteers turned in every direction but were forced deeper into the river by their own foot soldiers. The soft marshes caught the heavy iron chariot wheels. They sank deep into the mud and were useless. The foot soldiers of Sisera's army ran into the swamp to free the chariots and they sank as well.

Barak's archers fired volley after volley into the swamp slaughtering the Canaanite army. Small military guards of the other kings came from the southeast, but when they saw the trouble Sisera was in, they turned and fled with the Ephraimites close on their heels.

Sisera watched in horror as the rain pelted down, the swamp grew larger, and his army was helpless before the Israelites. He drove his chariot to the east as far as he could go until it, too, was stuck in the mire. Looking wildly around, he could find no one to help him. He leapt from his chariot and began to run for his life.

Barak wanted to send someone after him, but Deborah said, "Let him go. Remember I told you the victory would be in the hands of a woman?"

"Yes, but I thought you meant your hands."

"No, my love. Death awaits him at the end of his escape."

The Israelite soldiers began to carry their few wounded on liters toward Camp Three. Some watched at the edge of the swamp to be sure none of Sisera's men would come crawling out. Then they all made the soggy trek back to Camp Three exulting and celebrating their victory.

"Did any of the Canaanites survive?" asked Abel of his captains.

"There was one man among them who was not a Canaanite. He said his name was Lapidoth just before he died."

Abel hastened to find Barak.

"What? Lapidoth? Are you sure?"

"That is what he said. He was calling for Deborah. Do you know him?"

"I know who he is. He is an Ephraimite. Say nothing. I will find Deborah," ordered a shaken Barak.

Deborah was in the compound with Rahab supervising the women as they cleansed wounds and set broken limbs.

She was pleased to see Barak, but her smile faded when she saw the grim look on his face. "What has happened? Why are you so glum? Tell me!"

"I do not know how this came about, but it seems Lapidoth was among the Canaanites when they came through the valley. He was badly wounded and died before we could bring him here."

Deborah frowned. "How do you know it was Lapidoth?"

He told the men who picked him up, and he was calling your name in his pain just before he died."

Deborah sank down onto a cot. Rahab rushed to her side. "What has happened?"

"Your cousin, my husband, was among the Canaanites and was killed."

"Lapidoth? What was he doing with them?"

"Maybe he was trying to get to me and got caught in the battle."

Barak left the compound, knowing Deborah and Rahab would have to work this out together. He was no part of it. What could he say?

The soldiers were still celebrating far into the night, and Barak drank a sufficient amount of wine to keep his mind dulled. He appeared to celebrate for the sake of the soldiers, but his mind was on Deborah. What would happen now? He decided to take some men and pursue Sisera. He suddenly knew the identity of the woman who, according to Deborah, would kill Sisera. They rode with haste toward the tent of Heber the Kenite and the Priestess Jael.

*　　*　　*

Sisera was afraid to stop. He ran day and night through hills and valleys. At last there was a place he recognized, the tent of Heber the Kenite. "Ah, a friend of Jabin's at last! Heber will take me in and hide me."

He approached the tent and called for Heber. Jael came to the entrance. "Heber is not here."

"I am starving and nearly dead. Will you give me wine and a place to hide? Tell no one I am here."

Jael stepped aside so he could enter. She ordered sweet goat's milk to be brought to her and dismissed her servant. Sisera gulped the milk down and immediately fell asleep. Jael had prepared for this moment. When he was snoring raucously, the noise filling the whole tent, she picked up a sharpened tent stake and mallet. She moved to his head and turned his face aside. He smiled in his dreaming and she drove the stake through his temple with the mallet.

When the Israelites arrived Jael met them at the door of the tent. She invited Barak to come in and see Sisera lying bloodied on the floor of the tent to prove he was dead.

"I killed him lest my husband return home and think I have been disgraced by a man hiding in my tent."

Barak stifled a smile and ordered his men to remove the body and burn it. He turned to Jael and said, "You are an honorable woman and no one should say otherwise."

"I thank you. Is Deborah well?"

"Deborah is well, as our God has promised."

"Barak, she is with child. Your child."

"How . . . how could you know that?" stammered Barak.

"I am a seer, Barak. That gift brings me many things, including this blessed news."

Barak went down on one knee in shock. "Is it truly blessed, Jael?"

"Yes. It is meant to be."

*   *   *

On the way back to Camp Three, Barak's emotions soared up and sank down. Lapidoth was dead and Deborah could be his, but would she agree? A child is conceived but outside of marriage. What would it all come to? The great military genius, Barak, brought low by news of a child! This was a battle within himself he was not prepared for. He had no weapons and no battle plan. He felt alone and empty in a strange land.

He rode into camp tired and hungry. He avoided his tent and went to eat with the men.

"Did you find Sisera? Is he dead? How did he die?" The questions kept coming until all was told except what would dishonor Jael. There was another jubilant shout as they heard the news.

Barak decided he would not tell Deborah of his conversation with Jael. He would wait. When the time was right she would tell him, he was sure. Finally as the hour grew late, he went to his tent and lay down. Sleep came instantly.

He awoke late the next morning. Deborah was sitting beside his cot. "I would let no one wake you."

"Is it all true? We defeated Sisera? Or was I dreaming? I seem to have had a busy night of dreaming."

She smiled down at him, kissed his forehead and reassured him, "Yes it is all true. It was not a dream. I was worried when you went after Sisera. We were both safe here and then you left, to be in danger again. The captains told us about Sisera and Heber the Kenite this morning."

"But you knew it would be Jael."

"Yes, I knew. But I let them tell me all the gory details. Thank you for shielding Jael. You are a wise and compassionate man."

"And how are you since Lapidoth was killed?"

"Barak, he was someone I hardly knew. If you were paying attention when we joined in that moment of love and ecstasy, I was a virgin. Lapidoth and I never consummated the marriage. It was God's wise plan that everything kept getting in the way of our being together."

"Then let us go to Kadesh and arrange for our marriage within our families. I am sure the elders and Rabbi Amri will agree that we can be married."

Deborah wondered at the sudden urgency in his voice. They had never spoken of marriage. She was puzzled and pleased at the same time. Her last marriage had been so sudden, and now here it was again!

"I must have some time in prayer, Barak. I am sure this is good, but I went into the last marriage in haste. I want nothing to spoil our happiness."

Barak wanted to argue, but he could not without revealing what Jael had told him. She was right. He must be patient and let God's work be done without his stumbling interference. He smiled at her, hugged her tenderly, and said, "Of course. God is still God even though the battle is won."

CHAPTER 29

Ashubaal sat in her window day and night. The queen mother of Sisera looked out toward the west through the lattice and cried, "Why is his chariot so long in coming? Why do I not hear the wheels of his chariots and the hoof beats of his horses? Why are the troops not coming home celebrating, making a great noise? Why . . ." Her voice trailed off to a whisper.

"Perhaps they are dividing the spoils, my Lady. That takes much time, especially if there is not a woman for every man. They will argue, bargain, and fight."

"Yes, Lilah, Sisera will bring dyed cloth and embroidered pieces, two pieces of dyed work embroidered for my neck and one for yours!" She brightened for a moment and then went back to her vigil at the window.

Lilah's eyes were full of tears and she turned away to wipe them dry. Would Sisera return to her once more to share his bed with her? What if he did not return? Lilah went to the window as well and they watched together for hours until the sun sank in the western sky.

*　　*　　*

Rabbi Amri and Leah greeted them warmly. When he heard the whole story, except for what Jael had told Barak, the rabbi went into his study to think.

427

I must send a message to Joseph, father of Lapidoth, informing him of his son's death and asking if there are any kin willing to take Deborah to wife. Also I must ask the elders here if an unconsummated marriage obligates a widow to marry a kin of her dead husband.

Deborah caught her breath at the thought of being taken again into Lapidoth's family to be wife to a relative. She suddenly felt ill and Leah guided her to a bed to rest.

The next day Rahab and Gideon also arrived at the home of Rabbi Amri and Leah. They asked to be married as well.

"Then I will include a request for permission of Joseph for his cousin, Rahab, to be married. This is all very complicated at first, but it can be easily worked out if Joseph is willing to give his consent. You must have patience."

Deborah's praises were sung throughout the land. She was hailed as a Mother in Israel, one who keeps the laws of God in her heart for the good of the people. Time and again she was asked to tell the story of the battle. Amazement was on the faces of those who heard. No one condemned her for being in the company of soldiers without a husband, but only spoke of God's great plan for victory.

As weeks went by while waiting for word from Joseph, Deborah realized her woman's courses had stopped. Shaken and puzzled, she went immediately to see Hannah.

"Come in and sit down, my dear. The tea is hot." Hannah moved slowly. Her bones ached more as time passed and her hands shook a little more. She handed Deborah the tea and sat down beside her. "I see God has carried out his plan through you. What troubles you now?"

Deborah poured out the whole story to Hannah, including the affair with Barak and the death of Lapidoth. "And now my woman's courses have stopped. Does this mean I am with child?"

"Yes, Deborah, it does. Are you upset because of the child or because this is the second of your childhood nightmares coming true?"

Deborah looked at her wide-eyed. "My second nightmare?"

"Or maybe it was your first, that you would never have a child. Your Aunt Rachel died and your mother had a difficult delivery. Ah, now you remember," said Hannah smiling.

"I had not thought about that. I was concerned about . . . about . . ."

"Scandal. Who knows about you and Barak?"

"Only Rahab."

"And do you trust her?"

"Yes, with my life many times over!"

"Then let God work out the rest, Deborah. You have frightened yourself for nothing. God brought you through a battle with our worst enemy. You have freed Israel of this menace. Do you think God will let you down now, or discard you because you loved someone?"

Deborah took a deep sip of the tea and sat quietly thinking. "You always make so much sense, Hannah. Why could I not convince myself of that?"

"Because now it is not about Sisera, it is about you! That makes it very close to your heart. It is much harder to be valiant and to champion yourself."

"Yes, I suppose so."

"Do you want this child? Or do you want a draught that will end it now?"

"I want this child. It was conceived in the greatest of love and just before the greatest battle for the life of Israel. It must be special in the heart of God."

"Good. You know it is God's child, given as a gift of love to you and Barak."

"I have not told Barak."

"In good time, my dear. Choose a happy time and treasure your secret a little longer. Feel and commune with the life within you before the celebrations distract you."

Deborah ran her hands over her abdomen and smiled. "It is as if we already know each other."

"It is a good time now to properly mourn your mother, Judith. She passed on to sleep with the mothers just before the battle and you could not be here. Let us gather at Rabbi Amri and Leah's tomorrow morning. Leah and I will prepare the mourning and celebration meals."

"I wish she were here to know her grandchild," whispered Deborah, tears ready to spill over. "It would have been her dream come true."

"Nothing and no one ever passes beyond the reach of prayer," soothed Hannah. "Speak your heart to her in prayer. It is heard."

* * *

Ashubaal received the news of Sisera's defeat and death with the resignation that grew in her mind when Sisera did not return. She went to her throne to contemplate the next thing to do. She would gather what was left of Sisera's men and establish a guard. She would choose another general in case Jabin should try to depose her. That would mean death or exile. "Perhaps it is hopeless, but I must try," she whispered to herself.

Lilah was broken hearted. She stayed in her room for days unable to stem her grief. Ashubaal finally went to Lilah and took her hand. "Lilah, Sisera is gone. I am sure of it even though his body has not been found. We knew it might happen some day. I need you to be strong. We have work to do lest we die for not trying."

"Die?"

"Yes, Lilah. We are in danger. Come to my room and we will plan what to do. I cannot promise we will not be killed anyway, but let us not think of that right now."

"Is Barak coming after us?"

"No, but King Jabin might. He will surely want this throne to add to his power some day."

* * *

King Jabin did not come after Sisera's throne. He left Ashubaal and Lilah to languish in their grief, knowing there would be time to decide if he needed to add to his kingdom. He had much to do to pull his fractured empire together. The loss of Sisera and the whole army left him vulnerable as well. Soon it would be his for the taking, as a kindness to Ashubaal. She was still beautiful and King Jabin smiled to himself at the thought of her in his bed.

* * *

Barak and Gideon took a letter from Rabbi Amri and rode south to deliver it to Joseph. It was a condolence at the death of Lapidoth in Israel's battle with Sisera and a request to give his blessing for a marriage between Deborah and Barak. Also a blessing was requested for his cousin Rahab to be married.

The spring rains stopped and the hills were green. With the defeat of Sisera their travel was much faster because the main roads were again open to commerce. Only deserted roads were a danger. There was rejoicing wherever they went and prosperity began to flow in the land.

Joseph was in the fields with Joab. Tamar pointed out to Barak and Gideon the field where they were working. Joseph saw them coming and there was foreboding in his heart.

"I am Barak and this one of my soldiers, Gideon. We are sorry to bring you sad news." They all sat down together under a few trees while Barak told Joseph and Joab the whole story of the battle and of Lapidoth's death.

Tears flooded Joseph's eyes. "I brought this upon my son. The black market business has been a scourge on our family. I have lost my son and I fear I shall pay for my errors for the rest of my life."

They went back to Joseph's house for food and wine. Barak was not sure how to begin, so he showed Rabbi Amri's letter to Joseph who read it aloud. "You want my blessing to take Deborah as your wife? First I must consult you, Joab. You would be the one to marry her and have children in Lapidoth's name."

Joab thought for a while and finally took off his sandal and threw it down. Deborah has lived with an army of men without the permission or presence of her husband. I release her to marry Barak if you agree, Joseph."

"I want no more unhappiness in my family. I do not wish to force Deborah to live the life of a herder. She obviously has a greater calling from God and I will honor that. I will give my blessing to Rahab as well. Miriam is dead, as is Omar. Their evil has caused more than enough anguish and destruction to our family. Let us be done with the painful memories of our terrible past."

Barak embraced Joseph and Joab. "May God's loving goodness lift your burdens and give you peace, Joseph."

Barak and Gideon refrained from asking how Miriam and Omar died. They were happy to receive the blessings and be on their way back to Kadesh-Napthali.

Gideon embraced them both as well and they rode away, eager to return to Deborah and Rahab with the good news.

*   *   *

Kadesh was quiet in the early evening when they rode into the village. Deborah was sitting by the village well chatting with Rahab. Barak and Gideon left their mounts at the livery and joined them.

Nervously and fearing bad news Deborah said, "This is the well where we began, Barak. You were such a skinny little kid and I was a freckle-nose girl."

"Fear not, Deborah, as you always say to me. Joseph has released you to marry me if you will still have me. He has given his blessing to Rahab as well."

She flew into his arms, tears of joy splattering them both.

*   *   *

In the cool of the evening Deborah and Barak related stories of their childhood while Rahab and Gideon listened, held hands, and laughed with them.

Abinoam greeted them with tears in his eyes. Perhaps now his son would stay close by and sit with him in the council of elders at the city gate before he died.

"Yes, Father, I will sit with you in the council at the gate."

*   *   *

Deborah took Barak's hand and drew him a short distance away. "I have something to tell you."

Barak smiled and waited for her to tell him. He could feel Jael smiling on him. It was somehow exquisite that she shared this secret with him and trusted him to keep it. Yes, he was in God's plan. Not just for battle but for all time.

"We come full circle in life," mused Deborah. "Here we stand in the grove by the well where we started. I vowed never to marry, never to have children. Life brought me a long crazy way through a marriage, friendships, adventures, and battles to the place where I now want marriage, I want a child, and I want you my life-long friend to be my husband."

*   *   *

In the morning Hannah, Sarah, and Leah came to the well and drew some water.

"Why are you drawing water? Let me help you with that jug!" exclaimed Rahab. Gideon was beside her reaching to take the jug in his strong hands.

"We are drawing water to consecrate two marriages! There are plans to be made, banquets to be prepared and blessed! Wedding clothes to be made! We are your three mothers!" said Hannah triumphantly.

"Four mothers," came another voice. It was Jael sweeping up to them in her grand style. "I may be thought a prophet and seer, but I am also a woman and a Mother in Israel and not exactly useless with the cooking and the sewing. I would not miss this for the world!"

*   *   *

Deborah sat down on a bench by the well feeling a bit queasy. Hannah sat down with her and slipped a small bag of herbs into her hand. "To ease your distress. I have seen your child coming to you. Again I argued with God that you did not want a child, and again God became silent. Always a sign that I am wrong, or just a nosey old woman meddling in God's affairs. I hope to live to see the child come into the world."

"You will see it! You will be the child's grandmother since my mother is gone! You must stay with me! How could a loving god let it be any other way?"

There in the village of Kadesh-Napthali new life was beginning for a small group within the tribe of Napthali. God through Deborah and Barak had led them through the dangers of battle to victory. Love brought them all together, and for a while in their war torn lives, evil was defeated and they would know happiness, peace, and prosperity.